Whackadoodle Times Galore

Also by Kim Antieau

Novels

Broken Moon • Butch • Coyote Cowgirl • Deathmark
The Desert Siren • The Gaia Websters • Her Frozen Wild
Jewelweed Station • The Jigsaw Woman • Killing Beauty
Mercy, Unbound • The Monster's Daughter
Queendom: Feast of the Saints • The Rift
Ruby's Imagine • Swans in Winter
Whackadoodle Times • Whackadoodle Times Two
Whackadoodle Times Three

Nonfiction

Answering the Creative Call
Certified: Learning to Repair Myself and the World in the Emerald City
Counting on Wildflowers: An Entanglement
MommaEarth Goddess Runes
The Salmon Mysteries: a Reimagining of the Eleusinian Mysteries
Under the Tucson Moon

Old Mermaids Books

The Blue Tail
Church of the Old Mermaids
The First Book of Old Mermaids Tales
The Fish Wife
An Old Mermaid Journal
The Old Mermaids Book of Days and Nights
The Old Mermaids Book of Days and Nights: A Year and a Day Journal
The Old Mermaids Mystery School
The Old Mermaids Oracle

WHACKADOODLE TIMES GALORE

KIM ANTIEAU

CONTENTS

WHACKADOODLE TIMES

For
Guy Boss,
who laughed

ONE

I know exactly when things changed. Most people can't point to the time and place when life went whackadoodle. I can. I suppose if I were introspective I might be able to look back in time and say that life as we knew it started to dissolve when Henry Ford made the car. Or when God made man. Or Goddess made woman. Or when the first two haploid gametes fused to become a zygote.

Or when I got married. Had children. Became filled with ennui. Lived the dissipated life.

Only I wasn't filled with ennui—grief, maybe, but not ennui—and my life wasn't any more or less dissipated than anyone else's. At least anyone else on my block.

Which could have been part of the problem. I didn't exactly live on a block. More like an enclave. Or a bunch of big houses in an area that could be called a canyon, mountain, or hill. All of it slip-sliding into the ocean that was getting closer every day. But I digress. I babble. Thus my father's nickname for me:

Brook. I added the "e" for fun when I was in college. I thought that would stop my classmates from asking me if my brother's name was "Up a Creek" or "Down the River."

It wasn't a very good college.

Anyway, it began once upon a time, I suppose, the day Hayword and I were sitting out by the pool. It was a beautiful bluish kind of day. (We were close to la-la land at the time, so how blue could it be? It's what the locals call fog and the scientists call the Earth going to Hell in a hand basket—or in a designer handbag, given we were in Californ-eye-eh.)

Hayword was working on a script. Yes, I was married to a Hollywood writer—had been one myself for a while. And he was such a cliché, really. One day he was in great demand; the next day no one would return his calls. This made him slightly neurotic and a bit moody. Some might say he was manic-depressive, but he was not. (Can't a person drink to blackout some days and cry uncontrollably other days without being labeled?)

Not that Hayword ever drank to a blackout or cried uncontrollably.

Someone in our house did that, but I don't think it was Hayword.

On this particular day, Hayword was working on the rewrite of *Powerbreakers,* a script that had already sold. He had gotten the money, so he was on his way to the stage when he started to feel guilty over the massive amount of filthy lucre he received for writing down lies. That was how he characterized it. When he was talking to a stud head, he waxed on about story and drama and point of view. When he groused to me, Hayword said he was merely taking out a book from his library of lies—i.e., his brain—and transcribing it.

Hayword had more guilt about the good life than anyone I had ever met.

He was like that when we were kids, too. I'd known him

since we were in elementary school. He was a little kid—until he hit about thirteen. Then he sprouted up like a big old sunflower. (I'm spinning some corn now because I did grow up in the Midwest.)

Even when he was little he was always standing up for some cause or some kid, going toe to toe with the bullies that were twice his size. And then there was me, his best friend, motioning the head bully over to me to convince him it would be much more lucrative to let Hayword go. In return, I gave them the answers to some test or paid them a couple of bucks for a week. I'd try to convince Hayword to shut up, but he never would. At least back then. Felt it was his obligation.

Meanwhile, I was paying off his debts.

I was glad when he got tall.

We were sitting by the pool together and the doorbell rang. We both got up to answer it. Hayword may have wanted a break from the manuscript—or maybe he was trying to get away from me. I had been talking about our daughter Fern who was working on her master's degree in psychology up in Santa Barbara. (I named her Fern because I wanted to carry on the woodland fiction that began with my name. Was Fern grounded, rooted or feathery and wild like her name? No. She was mean. Hadn't liked me since I birthed her, as far as I could tell.)

Hayword and I, along with our twelve-year-old son David, lived in an exclusive neighborhood where we knew all our neighbors, and unfortunately, they knew us. We attended each other's birthday parties, our children's weddings, and any backyard barbecues, and we occasionally slept with each other's spouses. And by "we," I mean "they." Personally, I'd seen too many of them naked and heard their views on too many subjects to be interested in having sex with any of them.

What I'm saying is that we knew the people in our 'hood.

Still, Hayword should not have opened our front door without even looking through the peephole. We did have a gate; Hayword must have left it open. He wanted to pretend he was still that boy from the Midwest who knew and liked everyone. A boy from the Midwest who believed in the goodness of everyone. Every time he started dancing down this particular nostalgic yellow-brick road, I reminded him that he grew up fifty miles from Detroit, which was the murder capital of the world when we were kids.

"Not murder capital of the world," he'd say. "Just murder capital of the United States."

Hayword opened the front door. A startling-looking woman stood on our threshold. She wasn't dressed like a bag lady, but she was not dressed like anyone I had ever seen in la-la land or environs. She was Caucasian. (I hate that word. Sounds like something out of a police bulletin. That was how I looked at her just then. I wanted to memorize her features in case I had to describe her to a police sketch artist.) So she was white. Probably Irish. English. One of those pale tribes. Yet her skin was slightly brown, as though she'd been climbing a mountain or windsurfing. You know what I mean. She had that burnished look of someone who was outdoors a great deal. Her brown hair was pulled away from her head into those nasty Rasta braids. And she wore some kind of dress—truly nondescript—with pants on beneath it. She had a huge bag slung over her shoulder.

She did look like a bag lady. Or what I imagined a bag lady looked like. It had been a long while since I had been anywhere bag ladies roamed.

This woman looked at us with clear blue eyes and said, "You got a pool house?"

Conventional wisdom holds that women are sentimental suckers. Let me tell ya: It ain't so. It's men. They are such soft touches. Especially when it comes to women. Hayword was no exception. I don't mean he was leering at this woman. She was probably only a few years younger than I was. Men don't lust after women my age much, at least not in this town. She looked smart, like she had all her marbles. Hayword probably assumed she was down on her luck. I figured she was selling something.

Whatever it was, I wasn't buying.

Hayword was.

"Sure, we got a pool house," he said. "Why?"

I groaned. Whenever he was fully onto the path of the guilty rich guy, he wanted to do good deeds to assuage his conscience.

"It's not a pool house," I said. Hayword looked at me. "It's more of a garden house."

"Garden?" Hayword asked.

"I'm going to put in a garden," I said. Some freaking day I was going to put in a freaking garden.

"So you have a garden house?" the woman asked.

The wind shifted then, and let's just say that this woman standing on our threshold was a little earthy-smelling. Musky. Sweaty. Not sweat that has turned. But that rich sweaty smell you like on your lover but not on a stranger.

"Look, Eartha," I said, "whatever you're selling—"

"I'm not selling," she said. "And how did you know my name? My father nicknamed me Earth because I smelled like dirt. I added the 'a' so it wouldn't be so strange. But then people nicknamed me Eartha Kitten. I didn't really like that. Eartha Cat I can dig. Eartha Jaguar. Eartha Cougar." She was looking at me, but I could tell she was paying attention to my husband, too. "I would like to stay in your garden house for a while," she said. "I'm a traveller, and I need a rest."

"Just like that?" I asked.

"In exchange," she said, "I will do one great thing a day for you."

I looked at my husband. He was smiling. A sly smile. He loved these kinds of distractions.

"Oh yeah?" he said. "What one great thing would you do today?"

"Let me see the garden house, and then I'll decide."

"Okay," Hayword said.

"Hayword," I said. "Are you crazy?"

"Excuse us," he said. "My wife and I need to discuss this."

He shut the door gently, with Eartha on one side and us on the other. I stood looking at him with my hands on my hips, like some stereotypical woman in some bad movie who was always ruining the fun of her infantile husband.

"Brooke," he said. "This is gold, gold! We're locked up in this huge house where we never experience real life. Here's someone offering to do one great thing for us. Even if it's only for today, don't you want to see what it is? Just for fun?" He grinned. "Come on. In the old days, you'd walk a mile for a good time."

"And I'd walk ten miles away from a bad one," I said.

"Let's see where it goes," he said. "Might make a good movie."

"She could be a psychopath," I said. "A serial killer."

"I'll make sure she's not," he said.

He opened the door again. Eartha Kitten was still standing there.

"We'll let you do one great thing," he said, "and then we'll see. First, though, we need to know that you're not a psychopath, a serial killer, or on the FBI's most wanted list."

"Oh, good lord," I said. "Just stamp sucker on our foreheads."

Eartha held her bag out to Hayword. "You can check for weapons," she said.

Hayword didn't take the bag. Neither did I. If this were a

movie, millions of people in the audience would be screaming, "Don't, don't, don't let her in, you idiot!"

Well, maybe not *millions* of people.

She slung the bag over her shoulder again.

"My name is Eartha Jefferson."

I squinted. Her real name could not be Eartha. She was playing me.

She seemed to be waiting to hear who we were. I didn't say a word. Hayword moved out of the way so she could come inside.

"First, the one great thing," he said.

Eartha stepped into our house. I shook my head. Hayword was going to learn to lock that goddamn gate if I had to shoot him to get him to remember.

My daft husband led the way through the house and out the back to the pool. Eartha didn't look to her left or to her right. She wasn't obviously casing the joint. We walked along the pool and a bit away from the house to the garden house. Hayword opened the door and let Eartha go in first.

I stayed outside.

"Go sit by the pool," this strange woman said. "I'll be right out with the one great thing." She handed Hayword her bag. He took it this time. He looked at me and grinned. If I hadn't been so annoyed with him, I would have laughed.

We went back to the pool and sat in the lounge chairs. Hayword started looking at manuscript pages again. I lay back and wondered if I could really put a garden somewhere back near the pool house. I kept looking over my shoulder to see what Eartha was doing. Probably sticking our valuables under her baggy dress.

And then she came out of the pool house—garden house— carrying two filled martini glasses. She handed one to me and the other to Hayword. I looked at the drink. It was slightly darker than any martini I had ever had. And the glass was warm. Room-temperature.

"This is your one great thing?" I asked.

"How do you know we're not both recovering alcoholics?" Hayword asked, "and if I drank this it would end a decade-long dry spell?"

"If that's the case," she said, "you might want to do something about that garden house. If you named a place by what was inside it, you'd have to call it the liquor cabinet, not a garden house."

Hayword laughed.

"There is one caveat," Eartha said. "You have a choice. This will be the one great thing for the day. And there are only two glasses of this drink. One each. Once you drink it, it's done. It's over. I cannot make another. This one great thing will be gone forever. Do you understand?"

I frowned. I wasn't sure I understood.

Hayword said, "Sure."

He downed his martini. Just like that. I yelled his name to stop him, but it was too late. She could have poisoned it. She could have put drugs in it. She could have done anything to it. We had no idea.

"Oh, man," Hayword said. "What did you do, Eartha? Brooke, you've got to taste this."

I sighed.

"She's waiting to see if you'll go down," Eartha said.

"What?" Hayword asked. "Oh." He laughed and looked at me. "I don't think she poisoned it."

I smelled my drink. The scent of juniper went up my nostrils and seemed to tickle my brain a bit. I closed my eyes, carefully brought the glass up to my lips, and took a sip.

For a moment, I thought I was in a forest. I could smell the pine trees. I could feel the slight chill of the snow on the floor of the forest. And somewhere, someone was brewing hot chocolate.

The martini had a slight sweet taste of chocolate.

"Just the right amount of gin and vermouth," Hayword said. "And maybe lemon? I love lemon. Or orange. I wish I had savored it. That is a continual lesson for me to learn. Savor, savor, savor."

I took another sip.

It was the best drink I had ever tasted.

I held my glass out to Hayword.

"No," Eartha said. "One each. That's yours."

"Do you want the rest of it?" I asked.

"I don't drink," she said. "So do we have a deal?"

Hayword looked at me. I looked back at him.

"I want to see some ID," he said to Eartha. "And then we'll take it one day at a time. One great thing at a time."

"Good," she said.

Hayword stood and reached out his hand to her. "I'm Hayword," he said, "and this is Brooke."

"Nice to meet you," she said. "And now, I've been walking for a long while. I'd like to rest."

"I'll show you where everything is," Hayword said.

He picked up her bag, and together they went into the garden house.

I sat in my lounge chair looking at the martini. It was absolutely the best thing I had ever drank. I suddenly felt like that little boy in *The Lion, the Witch, and the Wardrobe* who wants more of the magical Turkish delight the White Witch feeds him. I wanted to keep drinking this liquid forever. I felt so relaxed after two sips. Happy. Contented. I wanted more. And more.

I stared at the gulp of drink left in the bottom of the glass.

Who did she think she was creating something like this and only making enough for two drinks?

I was no Edmund Peevish in Narnia. Or whatever his name was. And she wasn't the White Witch.

I tossed the rest of the drink in the straggly bush next to me.

I gasped. What had I done?

And then I licked my lips.

TWO

I didn't sleep very well that night. I kept getting up and looking out our window to see what I could see in the garden house. Didn't see anything. Which made me very suspicious. Maybe Eartha was sitting inside the house, in the dark, figuring out where to plant the listening devices so she could spy on us.

I even went into David's room and looked through his window. He sleeps through almost everything, including me tripping over whatever crap he has on his floor.

I still didn't see anything.

Except for David's electronic whatever flashing under his sheets. I took it out, turned it off, and put it on his desk. Shouldn't have those things so close to his body so much of the time. He was going to grow an extra appendage.

Or become as obnoxious as his sister.

I couldn't see Eartha or any of her kittens from David's window either.

I had tried to recreate her martini—even though I didn't ordinarily like martinis—so it was possible my psycho-detector was registering more than usual. I was a paranoid drunk.

I slept through breakfast and David and Hayword heading out for the day. Hayword took David to his private school. We'd sent Fern to public school—because we were idiots trying to remain "grounded in our Midwest values" or some such shit. But Fern could take care of herself. Someone picked on her, she'd punch them. Or outwit them with her words. She could be very cruel. In fact, for all we knew, she was one of the bullies going after poor defenseless kids like David.

David was nearly ten years younger than Fern, and we knew when he was an infant that he would have to go to school someplace special. Nurturing. He was a good kid with a soft heart. Sometimes I thought it was because his little brother Alberto died when David was two. He cried for about a year after his brother died.

We hardly ever talk about Alberto.

Or what happened afterward. I was a bit depressed and Hayword decided to fuck some woman in his office. She was a young blond actress who wanted him to write a movie for her. I imagine. I don't really know. He fucked her. I saw it all. Said I'd kill him if he ever did it again. He begged my forgiveness, swore it was his grief, and blah, blah, blah. I let him come home.

David still cried for a year.

After that, I told Hayword I needed a space of my own. You know, like Virginia Woolf. I even quoted Virginia Woolf when I was talking to him. Said if I didn't get a fucking room of my own, I was going to walk into the sea with bricks in my pockets.

Not that I was asking for Hayword's permission. We had come to California together as a collaborating couple. Got some points on our very first little film, *Love and Other Insanities,* so we made a mint right off the bat.

Hayword really got into the Hollywood thing. He liked to

schmooze and bullshit with all the other Hollywood people. Gawd. I hated it. They'd smile to your face and promise you the moon and the next day they'd sell you out or stab you in the back or whatever metaphor you want to use to indicate that on the whole they were a bunch of lying, thieving assholes. At least the ones with money.

Of course that is a gross generality. It's a gross generality based on my experiences. I'm not social in that way. And I didn't like trying to figure out everyone's motives all the time. So I stopped doing the circuit—as it were—and stopped going to meetings, concentrated on raising the one kid who couldn't stand me and on birthing a couple of others, one who died and another who was a bit more fragile than was good for—well, good for me. Hayword was already a handful. He wanted constant reassurance from me. Christ, I can't tell you how many times I wanted to tell him to grow a pair. I knew if his self-esteem went down, I'd be the one propping it back up, and I was tired of it.

Anyway, David went to a school he liked where the teachers nurtured him and the other students seemed to like him. Hayword took him to school some days; I took him other days. When I couldn't or didn't feel like it or I was late getting to my art studio, I sometimes asked Violeta to take him. Violeta was our housekeeper slash cook.

After I told Hayword I needed a room of my own, I found a house close to the village. It was a small old style ranch house from the 1930s. White with dark green shutters. White picket fence. Looked so California out under tall old sycamore trees, like a place Carol Lombard and Clark Gable would have lived. So I got it. I bought an easel and some paints, pencils, chalk. All the best material. My intentions were pure.

Thing was, I wasn't any kind of artist and never have been. I was a pretty good writer when Hayword and I started out. A commercial writer. I knew what kind of scripts to write to create a play or a movie that people would like. Not great art but something entertaining with a bit of heart.

But I was not an artist, not someone who used a brush and paints. It didn't matter: Hayword was so guilt-ridden about his affair he never questioned my artistic endeavors.

My Enclave neighbors, at least the female ones, called my art studio my love nest. I never confirmed or denied. Although sometimes I let on that I didn't love anyone who came there, but I was fond of all of them.

And today, one of the ones I was quite fond of was stopping by.

Hey, no judgement here. Remember my husband fucked a blond bimbo right after I buried my son, while my breasts were still swollen and sore from the milk my child would never drink.

I figured it was my right to fuck whomever I wanted to fuck until the end of time.

Anyway, that morning, the first morning of Eartha being in our house—or next to us in our garden house—I woke up with a headache. I stumbled into the bathroom, downed a painkiller, took a shower, then put on sweats. I looked out the window and saw the garden house. "Shit." I had nearly forgotten that some little hippy dudette was staying there. Last night I had made Hayword swear he would not leave me alone with her. But he was gone.

I texted him, "You better get your ass back here."

He texted right back, "I'm having my police source check her out. Chill. We've still got one great thing coming to us today."

"I'll 'chill' you, buddy," I said.

I went downstairs. Violeta was working in the kitchen, cleaning up Hayword's mess, no doubt. She looked up at me and nodded. Her eyes were red. She brought me a cup of coffee and a croissant.

"I told you that you don't have to wait on me," I said. Although I liked it. I liked someone bringing me things. I liked someone cooking for me. Loved it, actually. Violeta wasn't much of a cook, but she loved us—or faked it well. It used to matter to me whether she meant it or not. Now I didn't care. I took everything at face value.

It was much easier that way.

Okay, maybe not everything at face value. But Violeta, at least.

I drank the coffee—gulped it—and pulled flakes of dough off of the croissant and let them melt in my mouth.

I squinted and looked over at Violeta who was putting dishes into the dishwasher.

"How are you this morning, Violeta?"

She shrugged. "Do you want to know?"

I raised an eyebrow. Did I want to know? Hmmm. Well, hell, I had asked the question. I couldn't get out of it now.

"Yes, of course I want to know."

"*Mi madre* is dying," she said. "My sister said it'll be any time now."

Seemed like Violeta's mother had been dying for about ten years now. Or had she already died? I bit my tongue so that I didn't say that out loud. Violeta probably just wanted to go home early. Or take some time off. But she wouldn't lie about a thing like that, would she?

No. I would. I had. Once when I stood up one of my love nesters, I told him a relative had died and I had to go out of town unexpectedly. A place where they didn't have phones. I gave myself points that I picked a relative who was actually dead.

"Shouldn't you go home then?" I said to Violeta. See, this was why everyone who worked for us loved us. (Or pretended they did.) We always did right by them. "Be with your family. We'll be fine."

She shook her head. "She's in Mexico City," she said. "I can't afford to fly there."

She couldn't afford to fly to see her dying mother? That implied we were not paying her a decent living, didn't it?

"I'll buy you a ticket," I said. Hayword would love it. Helping the help always made him feel like we were one of the little people again.

"No," she said, shaking her head. "I couldn't leave you now."

"Why not now?" I had already gotten up and found my purse, had pulled out the checkbook.

"Mr. Lightman is so worried about this project," she said, "and David is having trouble at school. You've got the Benefit. The fires, the protests." She shook her head. "No. It is not a good time."

"Well, isn't it too bad your mother couldn't die on our schedule," I said. I wrote out a check for two thousand dollars. I ripped it out of the checkbook and held it out to her. "Is this enough?"

She came and looked at it but didn't take it.

"That is plenty," she said.

I set the check on the countertop.

"Mr. Lightman is always worried about some project," I said. "And David will survive." I had no idea what trouble he was having at school, but I wasn't going to ask her. Then she would know I didn't know what was going on with my own son. "I don't do much at the Benefit except stand around and still look cute. And the fires come every year and someone is always protesting something."

"The fires are bad this year," she said. "It feels like the end of the world some days."

"We live in California," I said. "Some days it is the end of the world. Please take this money as our gift. I'm so sorry about your mother. Go and stay as long as you like."

"Do you want me to find someone to help you out while I'm gone?" Violeta asked.

I shook my head. "Naw, we'll figure it out." I'd call the agency I used whenever Violeta went on vacation. "Go on."

"I'll finish cleaning up," she said. "Thank you." She looked like she wanted to hug me or something. But she didn't. I left the room. The kitchen felt more like her domain than mine.

I took my coffee and went outside to sit by the pool. I had two hours before I was meeting Mark P.—my former plumber—down at the art studio. I needed to do some yoga—or pretend to—and shower, put on my makeup so that it didn't look like I had any on, and make my hair look natural.

I didn't feel like doing any of that right then. I sat in the lounge chair and leaned back. I wished my coffee was a gin and tonic. Or one of the martinis Eartha had made. Oh Christ. I had nearly forgotten about her again. I glanced behind me. No activity that I could discern coming from the garden house. I sighed and leaned back again.

It would be so much easier if I could go to the art studio and fuck Mark P. looking like I did right now. What a relief that would be. I sighed. Who would have ever guessed that I would end up as a Hollywood wife, or an Enclave wife as we sometimes called ourselves?

Never. Never would have guessed in a million years. Hayword and I had come to California wet behind the ears, certain we were going to change the world and the movie business because we would be different from everyone else here. We didn't care about money. We didn't care what people looked like or where they came from.

We'd been in theater and we wrote this script that we

thought was a play, but then we realized it would work better as a movie. Someone knew someone who knew someone. And soon we got an offer on it. The studio loved it, loved every word, every scene. They handed us a contract and asked us how soon we could start on the rewrite.

Ah, Hollywood.

Yes, we love you, we really love you the individual you, now go get a face-lift, boob job, penile implant or whatever so you can fit in with everyone else.

Like I said, I'm not into that life much any more. Not that I don't look over the scripts Hayword writes. I do. He sends me the file and asks me to check the spelling and grammar. I agree and then I do whatever I can to make the script a bit better. I add the warmth. The humor. I make the characters real.

Although I would deny that to anyone. Even to Hayword. If he wants to believe the scripts are completely his work, let him. I could give a shit. Men's egos are so fucking fragile.

Nope. I didn't ask for this life but I got it. I'm not complaining. I let it happen, and now I've got everything.

So I am *not* complaining.

I supposed I should find out what was happening with David at school before Violeta left. Couldn't be anything too big. He loved his school. He was always texting or talking to one or more of his classmates on his phone or whatever.

I wasn't a fan of most of the new technology. I didn't even like telephones. But I used mine to make dates. Cancel dates. Never wrote anything sexually explicit or mushy on it. I wasn't an idiot.

"Wow, that was great."

I looked over my shoulder and into the sun. I put my hand up to shield my eyes. Eartha was standing there, half-dressed or half-naked, in a yoga outfit. She smiled at me.

"What was great?" I asked. Don't know why.

"Yoga," she said. "I did sun yoga out back of the garden house. Man, it is such a cool space. Do you ever do yoga back there?"

"No, we've got a yoga studio in the house," I said. I pretended to use it every morning. And every Thursday, or almost every Thursday, some of the women from the Enclave came over and we all did yoga together. Or our version of yoga: We drank, smoked some weed, lamented our lost youth and sagging breasts.

"Oh, it's so much better outside," she said. "You can really feel the energies of the Earth."

Eartha feeling the Earth. How quaint.

"Thank you for your hospitality," Eartha said. "I've got a good feeling about this place. Some good vibes. Some sadness, that's true, but good vibrations."

"So the Beach Boys would be happy here," I said.

"Yep," she said without hesitation.

Almost no one got my ironic sardonic hysterically funny sense of humor. Points for Eartha.

"How are you this morning?" she asked. She moved around to the front of me, so I wasn't staring into the sun.

"It's a little chaotic today," I said.

Not for me but for everyone else.

My phone vibrated. I looked at it. Hayword texted, "Philip checked out Eartha. She's clean as a whistle."

"Anything I can do?" Eartha asked.

I couldn't smell anything wafting off of her today. Perhaps she had had a shower.

"You can't cook, can you?" I asked.

"Yep," she said. "Cooked for a while in New Orleans. Then at a natural foods restaurant in Santa Cruz for a time. Then at a retreat center in Oregon."

I held up my hand. "I don't need your resume," I said. "Our

housekeeper has a family emergency and I have to run down to the village. I'm not sure I'll be back by dinner. I can get some takeout, but you could earn your room and board for the night by making us dinner."

"Oh," Eartha said. "I didn't know I'd get board. I like that. You need a cook, I'm it. Must be divine inspiration that I ended up on your doorstep."

"How *did* you end up on our doorstep?" I asked. "Is this some kind of real life *All About Eve?* You've been waiting in the wings to take over our lives?"

Eartha sat in the chair across from me—on the edge of it— and looked at me. She shook her head. "What's *All About Eve?*"

"The movie," I said. "You know, Ann Baxter is Eve and she is a fan of Betty Davis who is a famous theater actor. Eventually she takes over Betty Davis's life."

Eartha shrugged. "I don't watch movies."

"You don't watch movies? Well, you've had to be on this Earth a while. You've heard the line, 'fasten your seat belts; it's gonna be a bumpy ride.' That's from *All About Eve.*"

Eartha stared at me. Then she started laughing.

"I'm yanking your chain," she said. "Yes, I know that movie. I love movies. I loved that movie. But you're not an actor, right? And neither am I. What about your life would I want to take over?"

"Any part of it," I said. "I've got a pretty nice fucking life."

I kind of liked that she had tried to fool me. Didn't know why. Maybe because I figured it meant she was a little deeper than she appeared to be. Or a little meaner.

Just then Violeta came hurrying out of the house. "There's an emergency over at Mrs. Joan's place. Someone there called and asked for you to come right over."

"Me?" I said. I put my coffee cup on the table and got up. "If there's an emergency, they should call 911."

Violeta shook her head. "They said you should come right away."

"Oh Christ," I said. "All right, all right. Violeta, this is Eartha."

The two women nodded at each other.

"Eartha's gonna cook for us tonight," I said. "Could you show her around before you leave? And Eartha, if I'm not back right away, don't steal the silver. We've got your fingerprints and Hayword already had them and your name run through a database. Yeah, he's got a friend on the police force. Just like in the movies. Can't think of any particular movie."

"*Rear Window,*" Eartha said. "Jimmy Stewart's character had a friend on the police force."

"Yes, and look how well that turned out for the bad guy," I said.

Violeta stared at me. Eartha laughed.

I hurried past them and went through the house to our front door. I opened it.

Mark P. was standing on my front steps.

"What the?" I said. I quickly closed the door behind me.

"Hello, Mrs. Lightman," Mark said loudly. "Mrs. Donning sent me over to get you." He looked around. I grabbed his arm and pulled him over behind one of our bushes.

"What are you doing here?" I asked.

He was dressed in a T-shirt and jeans, a tool-belt hung from his hips, and his short black hair fell down across his forehead. I summed up the clues: He was working.

"I'm working for Mrs. Donning," he said. "I think she's crazy. She's got her toe stuck in the faucet and she's completely naked. I was downstairs working on the bathroom and she called me upstairs to help her. She is completely naked."

"You said that twice," I said.

He looked almost panicked, which was not Mark's style. He

was always cool and collected. Well, almost always. Sometimes when we were naked together, he was definitely hot.

"And she has her hands on herself in all sorts of places I don't want to see," he said.

I almost started laughing.

No need for us to hide in the bushes.

"Okay, well, I gotta see this," I said. "Take me to the spectacle."

We crossed the street and walked down the tree-lined road a bit, then went up a steep drive. I was surprised Mark P. hadn't driven over to get me. Everyone around here drove everywhere, even if it was only a block away.

"Why'd you call me?" I asked before I opened the front door to the Donning house.

"She told me to call you," he said. "She said you would understand. She didn't even want her housekeeper to know."

The door opened and Joan's housekeeper Beatriz was standing there. Mark and I hurried inside.

I smiled at Beatriz and said, "I'm going up to see the missus."

Beatriz gave Mark a dirty look and then walked away from us and went into the kitchen.

"I'll finish working on the bathroom," he said.

I looked at him. "You gonna be done in time?" I asked. "Unless this whole thing has turned you off women."

"I haven't decided yet," he said. He grinned and reached for me.

I moved away from him and hurried up the stairs. When I got to the top of them, I called out, "Joanie, I'm coming in."

I walked into the master bedroom and went to the partially closed bathroom door and pushed it open.

I had to laugh. So I did. Joan Donning was lying naked, smoking a cigarette, in her very large white recessed bathtub.

Her short black hair was slicked back, and she had on all of her makeup. Her breasts had not slipped to either side of her chest like mine would have if I were in her position. They were pointing at the ceiling, lined up together like two little soldiers waiting for orders.

"Why isn't there any water in the tub at least?" I asked.

Joan pointed to her feet. One of her toes was in the faucet.

"Have you tried turning on the water?" I asked. "Maybe the pressure would push your toe out?"

"It hurts when I do that."

I went to the window and opened it. "Gawd, Joanie. How can you stand all that smoke?"

"Can you bring me a towel at least?" she asked.

I grabbed a plush red towel from the pile near the towel heater. I unfolded it and draped it over her.

"You look even more strange now," I said.

"Do you want me to ring for coffee?" Joan asked. "Or some breakfast."

I laughed. "Joanie, why did you call me and what is going on?"

She stubbed the cigarette out on the side of the bathtub. The ashes fell into the tub with her. Then she looked around for an ashtray or something to put the stub in. Not seeing anything, she tossed it in the general direction of a small metal trash can in the corner. She missed.

"Ah, Beatriz will get it later," she said. "What do you think I was doing? I knew Mark was coming over today. I didn't really need any work, but I saw him when he came over to fix your plumbing. He looked so scrumptious. You've got your love nest. I figured I could have mine."

"I don't have a love nest," I said. "I have an art studio."

"Art studio?" she said. "Hah! We all call it the fuck studio. Like we call you Fucking Brooke. How do you do it?"

"But the plumber?" I said, ignoring her question. I was actually feeling her out—so to speak—to figure out if she knew Mark and I were lovers. Or fuckers. Whatever you call two people who occasionally copulate.

"When did you get so snobby?" she asked. "Didn't you fuck a preacher one year?"

"One summer," I said. "But that's beside the point. I'm not you. You're the one who told me you'd never even date someone who made less than a million dollars a year. And you're married to a billionaire. Mark doesn't make that much."

"I don't care about how much money he makes!" she said. "I want to fuck him, not spend him."

I looked at her.

"And Bernie is not a billionaire," she said. "And he's as flaccid as a ripe banana."

I groaned. "Thank you for that image."

"Come on," Joan said. "I'm a young woman. When I was younger, he came so quick he barely had time to insert his penis into my vagina. That wasn't much fun. And now he's too flaccid to get it into my vagina."

"I may never have sex again," I said.

"What about Hayword?" she asked. "Does he still have the wood, or is that why you go outside and play?"

"I'm not going to talk about my husband's sexual prowess," I said. "Or about my sex life at all."

"You should be careful with him," Joan said. "Katie Williams has been trying to fuck him for years. She's told me. She thinks he's a saint for putting up with you. Apparently Ken does not satisfy all of her needs despite the fact that they look like Ken and Barbie dolls together."

"Well, I wish her good luck," I said.

Joan sighed. "The only reason I volunteer to do these benefits is because I keep hoping I'll find someone to fuck," she said.

"But the waiters are all so young. They don't give me a second look."

I shrugged. "Flash some green," I said. "I'm sure they'd give you a second look."

"I'm not a prostitute," she said.

"No, that would make you the John. Or the Jill."

She actually had tears in her eyes. The last time I had seen her cry was. . . . Well, I had never seen her cry.

She obviously was not going to tell me why she had brought me here. Maybe on some level she considered us friends.

I went to the medicine cabinet and opened it, found a jar of petroleum jelly. I took it over to the tub, knelt on the floor, then took a gob out and began smearing it on her big toe as far up as I could.

"Mark said you were touching yourself," I said. "What was that all about?"

"Wow," she said. "That feels nice. Could you rub my whole body in that?"

"Don't be gross," I said.

"I had heard that men like to watch women doing it," she said. "You know, to ourselves. So that's what I was doing. Only I got a little carried away and that's when my toe got stuck and I kind of forgot about Mark."

I hung my head and laughed. "I thought I had a fucked up life."

"You? You have a perfect life. And what I experienced in this bathtub was the best sex I've had in years."

"If I cared," I said, "that would be incredibly sad. Now move your foot around and see if your toe will come out."

"I can't," she said. "I've been here so long I've got a cramp. You do it."

I sighed, took a hold of her heel, and gently moved her foot back and forth.

Still stuck.

"What if it's swelling?" she said. "What if they have to cut off my toe? I should get dressed so that no one sees me like this."

"Let me get some WD-40."

"What's that?"

"Oil. I'll be right back," I said. I got up and left the bathroom and hurried out of the master bedroom and down to the first floor bathroom where Mark was working. He stood up from the toilet.

"There's nothing wrong with this toilet or any other part of the bathroom." He looked disgusted. "I could have been on a really big job today."

I didn't have time for his plumber's angst.

"You got any WD-40?" I asked.

He pulled a can out of his big ass belt and held it out to me.

"You just happen to have it on you?"

"Um, yeah," he said. "Half my work involves WD-40. No, more than half. Eighty percent. Hell, if you count today, maybe ninety-eight percent of my on the job problems could be fixed with WD-40."

Oh my gawd. How much longer was he going to talk about WD-40?

I took the can from him.

"Do you know how to use it?" he asked.

"Yeah, don't I just pucker up and blow?"

He looked at me. "No. You put that little tube where you want the oil to go and then you hit this button."

Obviously not a movie connoisseur. At least not this morning. He usually got my sense of humor.

I didn't really care if he did or didn't get my humor. He fucked like he wasn't a movie star. Which was a good thing. Movie stars fucked like they were masturbating. Cared more about how they looked and how they were coming and going than anything else.

At least that had been my limited experience.

Movie execs were fast and furious.

Writers inventive and insecure.

Politicians? Please. Impotent.

Directors. Hmmm. Sometimes too instructive.

Regular actors were too varied to categorize.

Although, really, I tried to fuck outside the business. Felt too incestuous or something otherwise.

Plumbers, electricians, teachers, restaurant owners. Male, female. I didn't care. As long as they didn't care, except for the short time we were together.

Not that I was promiscuous. That sounded like I was fucking everyone in sight. Not at all. *Not at all.* I was fairly monogamous until it was over.

Oh Christ. I was staring at Mark and imagining him naked while Joan had her toe stuck up her . . . faucet.

I hurried away, went up the stairs, and back into the master bedroom.

"Where have you been?" Joan asked. "I think my foot is about to fall off."

"Good," I said. "Then this will be over."

I got on my knees. I raised the little tubing on the can of WD-40. Then I tried to put it up the faucet, near her toe. I was at the wrong angle. I went to the other side of the bathtub. Still wrong.

"Maybe if I do it upside down," I said. I tried that. Pushed the button. Heard something, but nothing came out of the can.

"I think you need to shake it," Joan said.

I shook it.

"Now try," she said. "You better hurry. I'm getting horny again. And you're looking good this morning. Although you don't have any makeup on. What's up with that?"

Oh crap. *I didn't have on any makeup.* I was dressed in

sweats. And Mark had seen me. That was it. I couldn't fuck him ever again.

"Don't look so distressed," Joan said. "You look good for someone who hasn't had any plastic surgery."

"Will you shut the fuck up," I said. "I'm trying to get you out of this mess. I can't find the right angle. I need to be closer to the faucet."

Shit. I was going to have to get into the bathtub with Joan.

"No one is allowed in my bathtub with their clothes on."

"Joanie, move your left leg over to the right. But keep the towel on. I don't want a view with a womb."

"All right, all right. Man, you're cranky in the morning."

She moved her leg up and over. I climbed into the bathtub. I tried to crouch between her legs and position the WD-40 so I could squirt it. The damn thing was supposed to work at any angle.

Finally I sat down, leaned over—with Joan's left leg practically pressed up against my cheek—and I squirted the oil up between her big toe and the faucet.

"That feels nice," Joan said.

I was about to give it another squirt when the door opened. Bernie Donning stood with his hand on the knob. His mouth fell open. He looked like a deer in headlights.

I could only imagine what we looked like.

Just then Joan's toe slipped out of the faucet and her foot fell down, knocking me back into her, so that she was kind of straddling me backwards.

"Much better." Joan.

"Good." Me.

"May I join you?" Bernie.

We both looked at him.

I didn't think he was joking.

We both started laughing.

Bernie closed the door, with him on the other side of it.

I pushed myself up off of Joan and got out of the tub. I held my hand out to her.

"I guess Bernie is a little lonely himself," I said.

Joan took my hand and I pulled her up. She got out of the tub, wrapped the towel around herself, and then looked down at her toe.

"It's a little sore," she said. "But I'll live."

I picked up the cigarette stub and put it in the trash. Not sure why I did that.

"You won't tell anyone, will you?" she asked. She put her arms around me and hugged me tightly. I could feel her hard breasts squishing up next to my . . . lower breasts. "You're the only one in this whole place I can trust. You understand life. You've had shit happen to you. The rest of these women are a bunch of bimbos."

Including you.

"We're all a bunch of bimbos," I said. "Amazon bimbos." She still held on to me.

"Sometimes I'm just so sad," she said.

I gently pulled away from her. Sadness is contagious, you know.

"Meaningless sex isn't going to make your sadness any better," I said.

Wasn't sure where that had come from. Meaningless sex was a way to pass the time.

"Then I'll make it meaningful by having a really good time."

She smiled. The tears were vanquished. She checked her makeup in the mirror. "All right. I've given you enough thrills for today. I better get dressed. I'm sure you have things to do."

I slapped her on her towel covered ass. Then I left the bathroom. Beatriz was standing in the bedroom.

I looked at her. "Where's Mr. Donning?" I asked.

"He went back downstairs," she whispered. "I told him there were cookies. She does this kind of thing for attention sometimes, you know."

We walked out of the bedroom and into the hall.

No, I didn't know and I didn't want to know.

"And her wanting attention from that boy," Beatriz said. She made a face. "She would look so foolish."

I glanced at her. Did she know about Mark and me?

"He's hardly a boy," I said. "And—"

She looked at me as we walked down the steps.

"Never mind," I said. "I'm glad everything worked out."

At the bottom of the steps, Beatriz went toward the kitchen while I went out the front door. I walked down the long curving drive. When I was almost at the end, I saw Mark's truck. He was leaning against it, his arms crossed over his tight white T-shirt. He shook his head when he saw me.

"You went running," I said.

"No, I finished my work," he said. "I always finish my work. Not that there was much to do. Some days it's tough. You have no idea how many of these old women come on to me."

I stopped about five feet from him. I had to stay at least this far away. Otherwise I'd want to touch him.

"I can imagine," I said.

"Don't give me that look," he said. "You're nothing like them. And I went after you."

"Makes me sound like I was prey and you were the predator," I said.

It didn't really sound that way. And it didn't feel that way. But I was so used to stroking men's egos that I did it without thinking.

He reached a hand out toward me. Apparently he didn't notice or care that I was dressed in sweats and hadn't put on any makeup. I guess I could fuck him again.

When I didn't move toward him, he dropped his arm to his side.

"You want to pick up lunch for us?" I asked.

"I could make you something," he said. "I make the best omelettes. I used to want to be a chef, you know, before I went into the family business."

I smiled. "I don't want you to cook for me, Mark; I want you to fuck me."

"I can do both."

I laughed.

"Isn't the way to a woman's heart through her stomach?" Mark asked.

I shook my head. "For one thing, I don't have a heart, so there's no sense searching for it. For another, I can cook, sort of. Violeta can cook, sort of. This new homeless person Hayword has brought into our house can cook. But none of them can fuck me like you can."

I walked toward the road and let my hand lightly touch his T-shirt near his belly as I walked past.

THREE

I hurried toward my house. In fact, I pretended I was jogging in case anyone saw me.

I jogged right through the open front door and into the house.

Eartha was in the kitchen, looking completely at home, chopping up vegetables at the counter. She looked up and smiled when I came in.

"You look refreshed," she said.

I really didn't want her remarking upon my appearance. Or anything else about me.

I was having second and third thoughts about her staying in our garden house and cooking for us. What had I been thinking?

"There's plenty of food in the house," she said. "I've got a great dinner planned for you."

"It doesn't have to be great," I said. "Fair to middling will work for us. I've got to go into the village."

"To your studio?" she asked.

I squinted at her. How did she know about my studio?

"Violeta was giving me the schedule for the day," Eartha said. "She told me you work at your art studio for part of the day. I'd love to see some of your work. I've dabbled in art some myself."

I leaned against the refrigerator and folded my arms across my chest.

"Where you from anyway?" I asked.

She looked back down at her vegetables. "Everywhere. Nowhere. Most of my family is gone now. So I wander the world and find community wherever I go."

"You do this all the time?" I asked. "Like with us? You find people and you stay with them?"

She nodded. "Sure. People are so bereft of real connection and community that they almost always welcome me."

"We're not bereft of anything," I said.

"Oh, not you," she said. She looked up. "You have everything. At least I would imagine you do. Although we don't ever know what's going on in another person's heart. Or in their home, do we? By the way, the house phone rang so I answered it. I hope that was all right. It was your husband. He wanted you to pick up David after school."

"Oh Christ," I said.

I hurried out back and got my phone from my chair by the pool. I found a text message and voice mail.

I didn't feel like talking to Hayword this morning.

I texted that I couldn't pick up David.

The phone rang, so I answered it.

"I've got a big meeting," he said. "It's at four. I'll never be able to pick David up and get back here in time."

"I've got an appointment," I said. "I can't break it. Can't David go home with a classmate or something?"

"It's about that movie," he said.

"*Powerbreakers?*" The movie he had been rewriting for who knew how long. Time to let it go. Let them hire someone else to fix it.

"No, no," he said. He sounded breathless, excited, the way he always did when he thought everything was going to change. "*Zombie Town.*"

I groaned.

"I don't give a shit about that stupid ass movie," I said.

I was going to be late. I had to shower. I had to dress. I had to imagine Mark and me together.

"Brooke, they are ready to shoot," Hayword said. "Another studio bought it when Jack Meredith agreed to direct. Jack Meredith, Brooke! It'll be a blockbuster. And they want some rewrites. They're going to pay me bonuses, give me points, and I'll be an executive producer."

Ahhh, Hayword's dream: to be a producer. What little boy or girl dreams of growing up to be a producer? They might dream of becoming a writer, maybe. A director. An actor. But a producer? I don't think so.

But Hayword wanted to be the one in charge. He still believed he could make things better. People and their talents would actually matter if he was the boss.

"This movie could change everything for us," he said.

I had heard this so many times.

"It's a fucking zombie movie," I said. "What could it change?"

"Jack Meredith mentioned you," he said. "In his e-mail to the studio head of AFT."

AFT? That was a decent studio. They did some artsy movies and some blockbusters.

"Me? Why?"

"They all remember *Love and Other Insanities,*" he said. "They liked the human touch you brought to the characters."

"That's because they were human," I said. "Zombies are not. Zombies are so stupid. Who could be interested in them? They aren't sexy. You can't fuck them. You can't have dinner with them for the same reason you can't fuck them: Parts of their bodies would be falling off into the soup or into you or else you would become dinner."

"See, there," Hayword said. "Nobody thinks like you do."

Oh no. Hayword was sucking up to me. That meant he really wanted this.

"I can't break this appointment," I said. "It's a doctor's appointment I booked months ago."

"A doctor's appointment?" His voice was suddenly different. No longer the weaselly Hollywood man. It was my husband's voice. "Is something wrong?"

"No, no, I'm sure not," I said. What a fucking manipulative liar I was. Like he didn't have enough to worry about.

"No," I said. "It's nothing at all. Just a woman thing. Don't want to talk to you about it or you may never want to have sex with me again."

"Brooke, you can talk to me about anything," he said. "I'll listen."

There were so many things wrong with those two sentences. But I didn't want to talk about any of that now

"Maybe you could pick David up early," I said, "and take him with you. He loves going to the office with you."

"I'll take care of it," he said.

"All right," I said. "I'll try to be home by dinner."

"Aren't you going to wish me luck?"

"Luck? For what?"

"For my meeting," he said.

"Uh, sure," I said. "But weren't you already paid? And aren't they going to shoot it anyway?"

"Yes, I was paid," he said, "and yes, they're scheduled to

start shooting soon. But if I get on as an executive producer and then they let me doctor my own script—or you doctor it—we could make a difference. This movie could change the lives of millions of people. It could change the world."

A zombie movie? Maybe I should read the script: I didn't remember any life-changing material in it when he'd told me the story. It was life-changing for the people who got eaten by the zombies. Or those people who became zombies. But those were merely characters in a movie. It wasn't going to change the *world.*

"Maybe you should change the title to *Zombie,*" I said.

"They do want to change the title," he said. "Why *Zombie?*"

"It could be like the movie *Gandhi,*" I said, "except we're following the life of an extraordinary zombie leader who changed the world by becoming vegetarian and learning to love the living and the dead."

"Man, I love the way your mind works," he said. "Gotta go, babe. I'll pick up David." He hung up.

I looked at the phone. "I was kidding," I said. "I was being a sarcastic bitch."

It was no fun when he didn't notice.

My hangover was beginning to dissipate, or I was beginning to dissipate. In any case, I was hungry. I needed to eat before I went down to the village. Damn. And Violeta was gone.

I went into the house and up the back stairs so I wouldn't have to see Eartha. I took a shower—man, that felt good—and then I put on my makeup and stood in my very large closet wondering what I should wear.

Mark had just seen me in sweats. He obviously didn't care what I wore. Or else he was too polite to say anything.

I put on a black camisole, a sheer blue blouse, and tight black jeans. No. Tight black jeans would leave creases. I pulled them off and put on a tight pair of black slacks made of something unnatural. No creases.

Then I stared at myself in the mirror. I was acting as though I cared what Mark P. thought about me. I didn't. He should care what I thought about him.

I looked at the clock. Another hour before I had to be there. I could pick up something to eat for us, or I could let Mark make me an omelette. No. That was too domestic. Didn't want set any precedent with that.

Oh crap. I would have to leave Eartha in the house alone. I couldn't do that. Okay. Wait. I could lock up the house so she would only be able to get into the garden house while I was gone. Wait. That wouldn't work. How could she make dinner if she was in the garden house? Perhaps that particular ship had sailed. We'd go out for dinner. Or I'd pick up a pizza.

I was not leaving her in this house. She could be waiting until we all left to call her accomplices. Burglars could come in and strip a house clean in a very short time.

I texted Hayword, "I have to leave, but I can't leave Eartha in the house."

He texted back almost immediately. "I told you that Philip thoroughly vetted her. She's fine. Besides Violeta is there."

"Violeta had to leave. Something about her mother. Maybe Eartha's such a good criminal that she never leaves any evidence behind during her crime sprees."

No answer from Hayword. I waited. Nothing. Was this his passive aggressive way of saying, "Shut the fuck up?"

I went downstairs. Eartha was still in the kitchen. I glanced over at the table. One place setting. With a bowl of something on the table.

"I made you a little salad," Eartha said. "Violeta said you'd only had a croissant for breakfast. And coffee."

"It's how the French eat," I said. "And they seem to do all right." I didn't like Violeta talking about me to strangers.

"You don't have to eat it," Eartha said. "You don't want it, I'll eat it."

I walked over to the table, pulled out the chair, and sat in it. I looked down at the bowl. It was filled with green leafy stuff. With specks of something salmon-colored throughout.

"What is that?" I asked.

Eartha came over and looked where I was pointing.

"Salmon," she said.

"Oh."

Some rice. Or else maggots. Wasn't sure. Bits of olive. Something red.

"What's that?" I asked, pointing.

"Radicchio," she said. "And that's spinach, dandelion greens. It was all in your refrigerator."

"I don't know why," I said. "I don't let Violeta make salads, except for David. He's gotten a little pudgy this year. But Hayword doesn't like anything green. He likes meat and potatoes. Reminds him of home."

"You're in California," Eartha said.

"So?"

"You can get anything fresh here," Eartha said. "Fresh salmon. Fresh greens. Fresh pasta. Fresh cheese. Fresh whatever."

"We're not a very fresh family," I said. "We're a little stale, and we like our food that way."

Eartha shrugged. "I'll eat it."

I held up my hand.

"I'll try it," I said. I dug the fork in, speared a bunch of stuff, put it into my mouth, and then chewed.

My eyes widened. How could rabbit food taste this good? I know, calling a salad rabbit food is a cliché. I actually would like to eat differently, but Violeta knows how to cook food with lard. Getting her not to use lard had been such an effort. As least as far as I was concerned. I couldn't teach her California cuisine. Or any kind of cuisine. I remembered how we had eaten when I was a kid. Meat, starch, and canned vegetables. Not that we had canned vegetables now, but vegetables weren't the highlight of our meals.

Okay. If I was really honest, I'd have to say I don't really pay much attention to what I eat, or what any of us eats. I make sure there's enough food in the house—I make sure Violeta makes sure there's enough food in the house. Beyond that, who cares? It's just . . . food.

"What kind of dressing is that?" I asked. "It makes everything melt in my mouth."

I suddenly felt starved. I kept eating the salad and talking.

"I added some avocado to a basic vinaigrette," Eartha said, "along with a few herbs and spices. Found a can of black beans and I added some to the salad. Be better if they were fresh beans, or at least dried beans freshly soaked and cooked."

The dish was almost as good as the martini she had made last night.

I finished every bit of it.

I wanted to lick the bowl.

"Is that your one great thing for today?" I asked, pushing the bowl away from me.

"I don't know," she said. "That's up to you."

I squinted as I looked at her. "This isn't like *The Cook* is it?"

"I don't know that movie," she said.

"It's a book," I said. "In it a cook comes to work for this very fucked up family. He makes the most amazing meals that satisfy each and every family member. They feel so obligated to him and so dependent upon him that soon they are all waiting on him and he's the boss of everything."

Eartha laughed. "I'm not sure I've ever met anyone as suspicious as you, although the suspicion seems to come and go."

"Look, I've got to leave now," I said. "I can drop you off in the village and then pick you up when I'm done."

I didn't know what else to do. I wasn't stupid enough to leave a complete stranger in my house all afternoon. I'd have to cut my time with Mark short, but that was the way it was.

"Sure," Eartha said. "Be nice to check out the village. Go to the library."

"Don't count on the library," I said. "It's barely open nowadays. None of them are. But you can buy liquor and semi-automatics 24/7. Gotta love California."

I brushed my teeth. By the time I came downstairs again, Eartha had tidied up the kitchen. She smiled at me and followed me outside. She seemed a bit subdued today. Yesterday I thought we had let a latter-day wild child into our midst. Today she seemed to have slipped easily into the role of a domestic.

What kind of game was she playing?

We got into my little maroon sports car. (I'm not telling you what kind of car. I don't intend to advertise for anyone or anything. This is my life. It ain't sponsored by nothing or nobody.) I put the top down, and we drove slowly down the winding road. Eartha stared up at the sky and the tall trees and bushes on either side of the road.

Today I smelled no smoke, and the winds seemed to have quieted down.

"You must love living here," Eartha said. "It's quite beautiful. You can feel like you're in nature out here even though you're in a community. Some beautiful trees and flowers."

I kept my eyes on the road. There was always some asshole driving these curves too fast. And half the people coming up this canyon road were all liquored up.

"I don't notice the fauna and flora," I said. "I don't leave my yard much, except to go to the studio. There are some trails down by my art studio, but I don't use them."

"Really?" Earth said. "I would imagine the three of you go out hiking all the time."

"Imagine all you want," I said, "but we don't get out much. Hayword is always working. David's always on the computer or some gadget and I'm always—"

Out of the corner of my eye, I could see her looking at me.

"You're always what?" she asked.

"Nothing," I said. "I'm always doing nothing." Drinking a little. Watching television. Making dates. Planning benefits. Only I didn't do that much planning. I did show up though. Always in the sexiest dress. I had that reputation. I liked having that reputation. Since I was from the Midwest, they thought I'd be all nice and full of cornball humor without any fashion taste. I liked to prove them all wrong.

Not that I had any fashion taste. I could give a shit. Really. I would wear my sweats all day long if I could. If I never had to see any people, that was probably what I would do. Although David and Hayword got a little concerned if I walked around in my pajamas for too many days in a row.

Not that I did that often. Probably once or twice a year. Went to a therapist for it once, when Hayword said he couldn't stand watching me drink and drug my life away (like I couldn't stand to watch him whore his life away as a Hollywood dickwad). The therapist concluded I got depressed twice a year on Alberto's birth date and death date. She said this to me as if it were a great revelation.

"No fucking shit, Sherlock," I told her. "You charge three hundred dollars an hour for that hunk of wisdom? For that kind of money, you better be going down on me."

Needless to say, I didn't go back to see her.

"I find time in Nature quite sustaining," Eartha said. "Do you want to go on a walk with me sometime? We could go on one of the trails near your studio."

I glanced at her. That sounded like she was going to stay for a while.

"I'll see if I can work it into my calendar," I said.

Eventually the road straightened, and we were headed for the village. At one vantage point, we were up above the ocean. I could see smoke billowing from some canyon or cliff side in the distance. More than one smoke column actually. I wondered if Hayword had encountered any trouble getting to Los Angeles.

Then the view disappeared and we were in the village. I drove slowly down the main road and passed by most of the touristy shops.

"The library is down there," I said, pointing. "How about I meet you on this corner in two hours."

"Sure," Eartha said. "Can I see your art studio first?"

"No," I said. "Nobody goes there. Hayword barely knows where it is. You got a phone?"

Eartha shook her head. "I believe in face to face communication. Who knows what all those waves are doing to our brains?"

"They're turning us all into zombies," I said. I leaned over and opened the glove compartment. I reached in, found something slick and hard, and pulled it out.

"Here's a throwaway," I said. I glanced at the number I'd taped to it. "Five." That was the speed dial number. "David is always losing his phone, so I've got extras. My number is on the speed dial." I showed her. "Right there. Number one. In case we can't find one another."

She nodded. "You want me to pick up anything for the house?"

Someone behind me honked. He was way too close to my car. He was so close to my bumper I could see the veins in his forehead popping out. Looked like he had eggs for breakfast, judging from his teeth. I motioned for him to go around. He inched closer.

"Hey!" I yelled. "I don't know you well enough for you to be that far up my ass!"

He couldn't hear me, but Eartha got an earful. "Fucking asshole. Like it's gonna ruin his day to wait two goddamned minutes. No, Eartha, I don't need anything."

Eartha got out of the car. She crossed the street and kept walking. I drove away quickly.

I took a circuitous route to the studio in case I was being followed. I wasn't paranoid, much, but I didn't want anyone I knew to know where the studio was. The only people who ever came there were people I fucked. Period.

Oh, and the cleaning lady.

I pressed the garage door opener and drove the car inside. Closed the door again. I nearly always used the garage so that no one would know if I was there or not. And my paramours always parked a few blocks over and then walked up.

I didn't know a single neighbor.

Hadn't a clue what they thought about me. But I kept the lawn mowed, and I was quiet, so they probably had no thought about me, which was fine by me.

I got out of the car, unlocked the side door, and went inside the house. It was cool and dark and felt empty, even though I'd been there a few days earlier. Sometimes I thought about getting a cat so that the house would feel lived in. But then I worried I might forget about the cat, and it would die, and I would never be able to get the stink out.

I went into the bedroom. The bed was made. The room had been aired out. Good. The cleaning lady had been here. Or was she the maid? What was the difference? I was never clear. All of my neighbors in the Enclave had maids and/or housekeepers.

I heard a tap on the window of my back door. I walked through the tiny kitchen and opened the door. Mark P. stood there, grinning, holding a bag of groceries.

"Hey, you," he said. He came in and kissed me on the mouth.

He quickly put away the groceries while I watched. Then he put his hands on my waist and pulled me toward him.

"I haven't been able to stop thinking about you," he said.

"I can feel that," I said.

"You looked so sexy," he said. "Straight out of bed. No makeup. Hardly any clothes. Oh man. Take it off."

"My clothes?" I said.

"No," he said. "Well, yes, but take off your makeup. I want to see you natural again. Take off your clothes. All of them. You always leave your bra on when we make love."

We walked toward the bedroom, holding onto one another.

"Mark, I don't like anyone telling me what to do."

"I'm not telling," he said. "I'm asking."

I shrugged. "Okay." I went into the bathroom and shut the door. I leaned close to the mirror and pulled off my fake eyelashes. I washed my face with soap, then looked in the mirror. I looked like a drag queen who had been crying. I turned on the shower and got in. I tried to keep the water away from my hair, but I scrubbed my face again.

Then I got out and rubbed myself dry with a towel. I glanced in the mirror. "Oh geez," I said. "Ah well. This is me."

Maybe seeing me like this would scare Mark off. Probably about time to end it anyway.

I let the towel drop, and I opened the door.

Mark was lying on top of the covers naked.

"Fuck," he said. "You are beautiful."

He was fucking blind.

He pulled down the covers, and I got into bed. I could see he was ready to rumble.

"I'm not ready yet," I whispered.

He smiled. Then he went down on me.

I was soon ready.

Very ready.

"It's gonna be fast and hard," he said.

I laughed. "Okay by me," I said.

He put on a condom and then he was fast and hard. We came almost in the same instant.

Geez fucking Louisc.

"Wow," I said when we moved apart. "That was fun. Let's do it again."

"Give a man a chance," he said, lying on his back.

I straddled him. I ran my fingers over his nipples and leaned over and kissed his ear. "I'm sure it won't take long," I said.

He grinned. I lay down next to him, and he turned on his side to face me.

"Now tell me that wasn't the best sex you've ever had," he said.

"It didn't last long enough for it to be the best sex I've ever had," I said. "But it was good."

"We should be together," he said. "We're so good together."

"We have good sex together," I said. "Besides that, we don't know if we'd be good or not."

I turned away from him. I didn't want to have this conversation again. It was usually at this point in my affairs that I'd break it off—when they got too needy—but I liked Mark. I was not finished with him or his body.

He curled up behind me and put his arms around me.

"We'd be great together," he said.

"The sex never stays this good," I said. "How long were you married?"

He'd told me, but I didn't remember.

"Four years," he said, "and the sex was never as good as this."

"Sex is the least of any long-term relationship," I said.

I could feel him getting hard up against me again.

"Although it is the most of our relationship," I said

He moved a little away from me, so I couldn't feel his hard-on. I turned around and smiled at him.

"I don't like it when you talk to me like I'm some fucking kid," he said. "We're only a few years apart in age. You're not some relationship sage. If you were, you wouldn't be down here fucking me."

"Right at this moment I'm not fucking anyone," I said.

I suddenly felt like a salesman: *What can I do for you today that'll put you into my vagina?*

"Do you still fuck Hayword?" he asked.

I flinched a bit. Didn't like him saying Hayword's name.

"Of course I do," I said. I felt naked. I wanted to put on my clothes. Some makeup. Have a fucking drink.

"Does he wear a condom?"

"Yes, he does," I said. I rolled over and got out of bed.

Mark reached for my hand. I tried to get away, but he was quicker than I was. He pulled me back onto the bed.

"He does?" Mark asked. "But you're married. Does he cheat on you?"

"He did," I said. "Once. At least as far as I know. I told him I'd kill him if he did it again."

"Was it a long time ago?"

"I don't want to talk about this." I lay back. Mark kissed my mouth.

"I want to know you," he said.

"You know me," I said. "I want to fuck or I want to leave. I don't have much time today."

I was trying to make him mad so that he'd stop talking.

Weren't men supposed to be so stifled in their emotions that they never wanted to talk?

Today Mark was a regular Chatty Cathy.

"I don't have sex with anyone else," he said. "Haven't since we started."

"I appreciate that," I said, "but you don't have to do that on my account."

"Why did he cheat on you?"

"What kind of question is that?" I said. "That sounds like you're blaming me."

"I'm not blaming you," he said. "I was wondering how anyone could cheat on you. You're smart, you're beautiful, I bet you're talented at more than just fucking."

"I never asked him why," I said. "My baby boy had just died, so I didn't care why. I was about to lose my mind and then I walked in on him fucking this blond bimbo. I mean I can still see it. They were standing up. He'd never fucked me standing up. And his pants were around his ankles. His shirt was still on. I could see his ass, could see him pushing himself up into this woman. And I'd just buried my child. *We* had just buried our child. Our baby boy. I couldn't be alone with the kids any more. David was two and he cried all the time, and Fern was becoming a teen and she hated me, blamed me for everything wrong in the whole fucking world. So I went to his office. I could see this woman's blond hair and huge bare breasts. Her huge bare *fake* breasts. And her mouth was slack. Couldn't see her eyes, but her mouth was slack. Like she was some kind of animal being fucked, like she didn't know we had just buried our child. But he knew. He knew. If I had had a gun that day, I would have killed them both."

I stopped. I couldn't believe I had said any of that out loud.

Fuck, fuck, fuck.

I sat up. I wanted my clothes. I was too fucking naked.

I didn't want to see Mark's face. Didn't want to see the pity.

Crap, crap, crap.

Now I was a human being to him. A human being with problems.

No, a human being with a past. That was all.

"Can I ask how he died?"

"Sudden infant death syndrome," I said. "He was eight months old."

"I'm sorry," he said. "I had no idea."

"Just forget I told you," I said. I grabbed his shirt that was still on the end of the bed and put it on. There, that felt better.

"I'm glad you told me," he said. "It makes me love you more."

Oh fuck.

"Mark," I said. "Don't say that. Don't feel that. We are ships passing in the night and occasionally bumping up against one another."

He laughed. "You know, Brooke, I can love you without wanting anything from you. I'm perfectly happy with the way things are." He shrugged. "Maybe not perfectly happy but happy. Now wipe that look of terror off your face—you remind me of me when I saw Mrs. Donning in the tub this morning. I'll make you something to eat or we can make love again."

"I don't want to make love again," I said. "But I would be obliged if you wanted to fuck my brains out again."

Afterward, we lay in bed together. Usually I was up and outta there, but something about telling him about Alberto had knocked the stuffing out of me. I lay in his arms, half asleep. I may have even fallen to sleep a couple of times.

"I'm surprised you never got divorced," he said. "That happened to a friend of mine and his marriage didn't survive. He told me that most marriages don't survive the loss of a child."

"I wanted a divorce," I said. "I was going to take David with me and move back to Michigan or up to Oregon. I told Hayword he could keep Fern. She was terror on wheels even back then. It was as though she came out of the womb loathing me. But Hayword begged me to stay. He promised it would get better. He swore he would never cheat again. I could have anything I wanted. I told him I wanted my son back and I wanted the image of him fucking the blond bimbo out of my brain. He couldn't accomplish cither of those miracles. Not that they would be equal miracles. He could have fucked anyone he wanted if that would have brought back my son. But life isn't like that."

Mark had to stop asking me questions because I kept answering them.

I wasn't going to tell him that I had never talked about this to anyone before. Not even Hayword. Certainly not Hayword.

"I told him I wanted a place of my own. This place. I saw it from the outside first. Seemed peaceful. Never went out back before I bought it—just saw the yard from the windows. Then after I got the keys and it was mine, I went out back. It's got a nice big yard. Used to be a garden there. And there was a swing set. An older metal swing set like the kind I had when I was a kid."

"In the olden days," Mark said, chuckling.

"Yep, like in the olden days," I said. "Something about that swing set broke my heart. I fell to my knees right then. Bawled my eyes out. I had someone come and take it away the next day. I've hardly been out back since."

And I had hardly cried since then either.

"I remember when I got divorced," Mark said. "I know it's not the same. Not even close. But it was so sad to me, and when I returned to the house, you know, months after I'd moved out, and I went in the backyard for something and saw a new swing set and plastic playhouse. I felt completely lost. It wasn't my life any more. I had always wanted a swing in the back for my son, Ian, but we'd never gotten one. And my ex had always wanted a little playhouse for him, but I couldn't stand the idea of him playing in plastic. I kept promising to build him a fort or tree house, but I never did. At least not there. I felt bad about it all for a long time, but then I bought my own house, and I built a tree house for him."

"Wow," I said. "You handle adversity better than I do. I'm still mad about all of it."

"Yeah," he said. "It was good, except Ian fell out of the tree house. Broke his arm. That was fairly traumatic. More for us than for him."

I got up on my elbow and looked at him. "Are you making that up? He really fell out of the tree house?"

Mark nodded.

I started to laugh. I lay back and laughed and laughed.

"You have a sick sense of humor," he said.

"Now that is the truth."

I heard the phone ring. An old-fashioned ring, like a rotary phone. That was the ring tone on my emergency phone. No one was supposed to call me on that phone unless it was a true emergency.

My heart started to race. I quickly got out of bed, found my purse, and dug around in it for the right phone. My other one was off.

"Please let Davey be all right," I whispered. "Let him be all right. Let Fern be all right."

I answered it.

"Brooke?"

Hayword.

"What's wrong?" I asked. "Is everyone okay?"

"Everyone is fine," he said. "I tried you on the other phone, but I couldn't get through."

"I told you I had an appointment," I said.

I went into the bathroom and closed the door. I began putting on my clothes.

"You scared the shit out of me," I said.

"I'm sorry, Brooke," he said, "but there's been a change in plans. The studio head really wants you to be at this meeting. If you were done with the doctor, I thought you could pick up David, bring him with you, and head into the city."

"I'll never get there by four," I said. "The traffic will be a nightmare."

"They'll wait," he said. "Look, they've really got a hard-on for this movie, but they need it doctored. They want you. They want to see your take on it."

"Did you tell them I don't give a shit about some goddamn zombie movie?" I asked.

"Yes," Hayword said. "But come on. Aren't you flattered? They want you!"

"For a fucking zombie movie," I said.

"I called David's school," he said. "I said we needed to pick him up early. You could even drop him at home. Let him stay with Eartha. I promise you she'll be great with him."

"Too late to send me a driver?" I asked.

"Yes," he said. "Come on, Brooke. You can do it. It'll be painless. These guys are the real deal."

"None of those guys are the real deal," I said. "Where are you meeting?"

"Juliet's, off Wilshire," he said. "You can call me when you're about twenty minutes out."

"Like I'll know," I said. "Okay. I'll try. But don't expect me to be charming."

"I expect you to be yourself," he said.

"Don't be nice to me, Hayword," I said. "I don't respond well to that."

He laughed. "But I'm always nice to you."

"Yeah, see."

I hung up. Turned the phone off. Whatever it was they called it now. I ended transmission.

I sighed. How the fuck was I going to do this? And why was I going to do this?

So I didn't have to spill any more of my guts to Mark P.

Christ with a camera.

I went into the bedroom.

Mark had his pants on.

Too bad.

I handed him his shirt.

"Everything all right?" he asked.

I nodded. "I have to go to a meeting in L.A. My husband thinks it's an emergency. Not sure why."

Mark put his arms around me. We hugged.

"Stay and eat the food," I said. "I don't want it to go to waste."

"It'll wait," he said. "When can I see you again?"

"I'll text you," I said. We let each other go. I started to leave.

"I don't have any work for the rest of the afternoon," he said. "You want me to drive you to Los Angeles?"

I hesitated at the bedroom door. I looked at him. He smiled. That was so fucking tempting.

No, I couldn't. I still had to pick up David and Eartha, take them home.

"I know a lot of shortcuts," he said.

"There are no fucking shortcuts from here to Wilshire Boulevard."

"You'd be surprised," he said. "Plus, wouldn't you be more relaxed for your meeting if I drive."

A minute ago I was trying to figure out how to never see him again because he knew too much about me.

I looked at him. His eyebrows were raised in expectation. He still smiled. His arms were loose at his side. I crossed my arms.

"I have to pick up my son and this homeless woman staying at our house," I said.

He nodded. "I could pick you up outside your house in twenty minutes. If anyone sees us, you could say I was working at the Donning place and I offered to take you downtown. Unless you don't think anyone would believe you would ride with the help."

"Ride the help, yes," I said. "Catch a ride with the help, no."

I did not relish driving in rush hour in L.A. Not that I couldn't do it. Twenty plus years of living out here had taught me a lot about driving in California. Mostly it went like this: If you are not going at least twenty miles over the speed limit, get the fuck out of my way so I can continue to hurtle down the drive/road/cow path/freeway past you at death-defying speeds while flipping you off and talking on the phone and eating all at the same time.

"Okay, let's do it," I said.

Mark looked speechless.

"What?" I asked. "You didn't think I'd do it?"

"Not in a million years," he said.

"Well, you can take it back," I said. "I can go by myself."

"No, I want to take you," he said. "It'll be the first time we'll be out in public."

"Public?" I said. "No, we'll be in your truck on the highway most of the time."

"What could be more public?"

"Oh Christ," I said. "I better get some sunglasses and a big floppy hat to disguise myself. Maybe wear a caftan and flip-flops. Will that do it?"

I made a face at him and then quickly left the house, got in the car in the garage, and pulled out into the driveway. I phoned Eartha and asked her where she was. Next I called the school and told them I'd be there in a few minutes to get David. I drove to where Eartha said she'd be, and I picked her up.

"Change of plans," I said when she got into the car. "I gotta go to L.A. Can you watch David for us and make dinner? That would be two additional great things you did today."

She closed the door, and I sped down the road, heading toward David's school. *"Two* additional great things?" she asked.

"Yeah, that breakfast lunch thing you made," I said. "It was really good."

"I'm glad you liked it," she said. "Cool. Yes, I'd love to meet David and hang out with him. Maybe he can help make dinner."

"David doesn't do much in real life," I said. "He spends an inordinate amount of time on his phone. I've checked. It isn't porn. No dirty pictures. I don't know what the hell he's doing."

Eartha didn't say anything.

"I'm not an overprotective mother," I said. "I was with Fern, maybe, and now she hates my guts. I figure I'll let David be his own little man and he'll still love me."

Saying that out loud sounded pathetic.

Or maybe I hadn't had enough to eat . . . or drink yet today.

"You don't have a flask or anything on you, do you?" I asked.

"A flask?" Eartha asked. "You mean something to drink? No, I'm sorry I don't. Had some weed, but I smoked the last of it last night."

"In my garden house?" I asked.

"Yes, I figured you wouldn't mind," she said.

"You figured wrong," I said.

"I sat by the window."

"What if David had smelled it?" I said. "Or the police came by." I was grasping at straws. I really didn't give a shit that she'd smoked it. I was annoyed she didn't have any left. Or any liquor.

"I don't drink anyway," Eartha said. "The fermenting process brings out the trickster spirits of whatever plant is being fermented. That can create problems. That's how people get addicted, I believe."

"Then how did you know how to make that martini?" I said. "You must have had to taste it."

"Sure, I had to taste it. I'm not religious about not drinking or anything."

I slowed the car as we neared the school. Tall eucalyptus trees circled the building. I had gone to school in a school built in a farmer's field. We didn't have any trees. Must be nice to go to a place like this.

"Besides," she said. "There wasn't any liquor in those martinis."

"What?" I slammed on the brakes a little too hard as a kid stepped in front of me. "That's impossible."

"Nope, not a drop. But it was really good, wasn't it?"

The broad had fucking tricked me.

I wasn't sure I liked that.

Wasn't sure I disliked it either.

I could see David up on the steps waiting for me. When he saw me, he smiled and hurried toward the car. I couldn't help but smile too. David always appeared to be glad to see me. Or anyone. He was a good-natured kid. Almost every time I saw him I thought of his sister, who was not good-natured. Maybe she was to other people but not around me. Or around her father as far as I could tell. She was working on her master's degree in psychology. I couldn't imagine anyone going to her for help. They'd have to be crazy.

"Hello, love," I said when David opened the door and got into the back seat. It wasn't much of a backseat, but it would do.

"I can't believe you got me out of school early," he said. "Thanks, Mom. What are we going to do? Do you have something planned?"

I looked back at him. "It's nice to see you, too, David. Actually, you're going home with Eartha. This is Eartha. She's staying with us for a while. Violeta had to visit her sick mother."

"Oh," he said. He sounded disappointed.

"How do you do, David?" Eartha said. "I'm really glad to meet you. Maybe you'd want to help me with dinner. Or we could go outside and I could teach you some yoga."

David nodded. "Sure. Whatever."

"David, what's that in your hair?" I asked.

"What?" He felt around and touched something pink in his hair. "Ewwww!" he said. "Get it out! Get it out!"

"Stay calm," I said. "It's probably gum. Were you chewing gum last night?" I turned to Eartha. "You got any scissors in your bag?"

Eartha dug around in her purse until she came up with a small sewing kit. She opened the top of it and took out a tiny pair of scissors and handed them to me.

"Get it out!" David said. He was nearly hysterical.

"David! Stop it! It's gum. If you hold still, I'll take care of it. Lean forward." I turned around in my seat. He put his head down. I grabbed his hair where the gum was and I cut it all off.

Now he had a hole in the top of his head.

"Much better," I said. I threw the hair and gum into the trash and didn't look at Eartha as I handed the scissors back to her.

"Can I look in the mirror?" David asked.

"Naw, you can get a better look at home."

I put the car into gear and started forward. I was careful not to hit any children or the strange man lurching across the road. He was wearing a raggedy suit and he looked like he was partially covered in dirt. He walked in a daze, right into the woods and disappeared.

"I don't like the homeless getting all the way up to David's school," I said.

"No, much better if they stay out of sight in the village," Eartha said.

"Do you know him, David?" I asked. He didn't answer. I glanced in the rearview mirror. He was doing something on his phone. "David?"

"Huh?" He didn't look up.

"I asked if you knew that man?"

"What man?"

"Never mind."

I drove us back to the house. Once inside, David went straight to his room. I looked at Eartha and shrugged.

"Okay, you've got the phone with my number," I said, "or you can use the house phone. I've got a list of the speed dial numbers next to it. I'm hoping the meeting won't be long. We might go out to eat or we might come home. Do you want me to call you and let you know?"

"How about I make David a snack now and then I'll make dinner around seven. If you're home, you're home. If not, we'll eat it."

"That sounds fair," I said. I needed to run upstairs and change and put on makeup. "You know, Eartha, I'm leaving you with my most valued possession." I put my hand up. "Now before you get on your high horse and point out that a child is not a possession, I think you should know I was talking about the Ming dynasty urn I have in our bedroom."

Eartha laughed.

"Don't let anyone in," I said. "Even if they promise to do one great thing a day."

FOUR

I changed clothes quickly. Then I heard David scream.

He must have looked in the mirror.

I hesitated, sighed, and then I went to his room. I knocked before I opened the door and went inside.

"Mom! What did you do? There's a hole in my head!"

"There's not a hole in your head. If there were, you'd be dead." I sat on the bed next to him.

"I wish I were dead," he said. "You know this means I walked around all day with gum in my hair and no one told me. I bet that's why Ariel Williams didn't talk to me all day."

Ariel Williams. Our neighbor's kid? I tried to remember her. Couldn't come up with a picture.

"Are you talking about Katie and Ken's daughter? From down the road?" Or up the road. Around the curve. Whatever.

"Mom," he said. "You know who she is. She's been my girl-friend forever."

"Forever is a long time," I said. "Does she know she's your

girlfriend? I mean, this isn't one of those things where you stare into her window at night while she's asleep and then you claim she's your girlfriend?"

"No!" he said. "And she'll be at the benefit party. I can't go like this." He got up and looked in the mirror again. Definitely a hole in his beautiful black hair.

"Well, maybe she won't be there," I said.

"It's at her house!" he said.

That's right. Katie was on the Benefit committee with me. She'd come up with this idea to host a mini-party for all the pre-teens and early teens in the neighborhood. They could go off and have their own ball while we were having ours. Her nanny and maid were going to chaperone. Parents could pay for the privilege of having their children babysat during the Benefit and any proceeds would go to our charity. (That's right: I'm not telling you which charity. Then my efforts to disguise myself, this place, and all of these people would be for nothing. If I told you what the Benefit was for, you could find out who organizes it, and then you could find out who I am. Nope. Ain't gonna do that. I'm not on facebreak, twatter, googleminus, or whatever newfangled social media is out there for a reason.)

"Look, the party isn't for two days," I said. "Your hair might grow out a little by then. Saturday morning we could take you to get your hair cut, before the party."

"I don't have an appointment with Henri for three weeks," David said. "I'll never be able to get in on Saturday."

"We'll go somewhere else."

David gasped. I rolled my eyes. How could a 12-year-old boy give a shit where he got his hair cut?

I sighed. "Can we figure this out later? I've got to go into the city."

"You always want to figure things out later," he said. "But we never do."

He sounded suspiciously like his sister.

He better not decide to go through his teen years being a jerk. I wasn't going to put up with it again. I'd send him to military school. I would.

I put my arm across his shoulders and hugged him. Then I kissed the top of his head.

"I think you're really cute," I said.

"You always think I'm cute," he said. He sounded a bit mollified.

"Yep, and I'm always right."

"No, you're not."

"Yes, I am."

"No, you're not."

I laughed. "Yes, I am!"

He giggled. I began to tickle him. "Yes, I am! At least about this I am."

I kissed him again. "Spy on this Eartha woman while we're gone. See if she's up to no good. Then report back to me."

"You're leaving me with someone you think is up to no good?"

I got up and went to the door. "No, no, she's perfectly fine," I said. "As far as I know, all of the other families she stayed with survived. At least all the ones they can find."

"Funny, Mom," he said.

"Anything else going on at school I need to know about?" I asked.

He looked at me. He suddenly reminded me of his father. Hayword had been shy and awkward at this age, like David was now. But he got over it.

"Why are you asking?"

"Can't a mother be interested in her son's school life?" I asked.

"A mother can be, but you're not," he said.

He said it without malice, but I flinched anyway.

We paid his school a great deal of money. I figured they knew what they were doing, so I didn't have to know every little detail.

"I thought you liked it there," I said.

"I did," he said. He picked up his phone and looked at it. "I do. But it's been different lately. A lot of kids have had to drop out because they can't afford it. And we keep having those end of the world drills. I don't like them." He was silent as he looked at his phone.

I sat next to him again. I gently took away the phone.

"What end of the world drills?" I asked.

"You know, earthquake, fire, tsunami, terrorist attack, epidemics. I feel like I'm learning more about how it will all end than anything else. Did you know the ocean is getting higher every day? Every day. Our village could be underwater soon. Or at least the beachfront property."

"I don't know why they're doing tsunami drills," I said. "You're too high up. We're too high up. And we're not near the beach so we'll be okay. And the rest of the stuff is just living in California."

"Some of the kids are acting weird, too," he said.

"Are they bullying you?" I asked. "Hurting you? Because I'll go kick their asses. Or you and me together, we'll kick their asses. You know we could do it."

"Mom."

He was trying to tell me something. I knew it. I wasn't quite sure what to say.

"Okay," I said. "Is there something I can do? Do you want to go to another school?"

He shook his head and tried to get the phone from me.

"No," he said. "I dunno. Seems like everything is getting bad."

"I understand it must seem scary," I said. I was going to have to call the school and find out why they were scaring the shit out of my kid. "But look at us. We're doing all right. No floods, famine, fires."

"I heard some of the fathers have killed themselves," he said. "And some people are homeless now."

I shook my head. "Every time there's an economic shake-up, you always hear stories about people jumping out of buildings. But in real life, that doesn't happen. Or it rarely happens."

"I see every day in the news where some father has gone out and killed his wife and kids because he lost his job," David said, "or he came back from the wars and he lost his job and he goes out and kills people."

Man.

"You need to stop reading the news," I said.

"But I need to stay informed," he said.

"You're twelve years old!" I said. "You don't need to stay informed about any supposed apocalypse or any psycho fathers. Or whatever. All of that stuff is designed to scare the shit out of you. It's designed so that you keep coming back to that website again and again to find out the progress of whatever horror is going on—or supposedly going on. You need to promise me you'll stop looking."

"But you and Dad don't pay attention," he said. "Someone has to protect us."

"I protect us," I said. "And Daddy protects us. We pay enough attention. I may act like I don't pay attention, but I do."

That was a lie. I didn't read the paper or check anything newsworthy online. It was all horseshit. Maybe not all of it, but it was too difficult to wade through it all to find the truth.

Cuz the truth ain't out there?

"Your father and I won't let anything bad happen to our family."

"Something bad already happened," he said. "And it could happen again."

I had no answer for that.

"And you and Dad are hardly ever together," he said. "Are you getting a divorce?"

"No," I said. "Come on. Actually I'm going to see your father right now. We have a meeting together with a studio head."

My lover was driving me to the meeting, but my kid didn't need to know that.

"Really?" He perked right up. Geez Louise.

"And I'm late," I said. "So I better get going."

"Can I come?" he asked.

I chewed my lip. I should let him come. Blow off Mark and drive the two of us to L.A.

I should. I should spend quality time with my son.

Quality time trying to navigate L.A. traffic.

"Mom, your lip is bleeding," he said.

"What?" I put my finger on my lip. Looked at my finger: Blood. Apparently I had chewed my lip a little too hard.

"How about this?" I said. "You stay here and spy for me. Then your dad and I will come and have dinner with you. Just the three of us."

I held out his phone.

Relieved, he took it from me.

"Sure, Mom." But he was no longer paying any attention to me.

I hurried out of the room and down the stairs.

"See you later, Eartha!" I called.

"Have fun," she said.

I ran out the front door. I didn't see Mark's truck. I hurried down the drive and went out onto the road. Mark's truck was down the street a bit. I hurried toward it. He pushed the passenger door open from inside. I got up into the truck and slammed the door shut. He started the engine, and we headed down the road.

We smiled nervously at one another.

"So this is what it is like to be in a truck," I said.

"So this is what it is like to be in a truck with you," he said.

I laughed.

"Have you really never been in a truck?" he asked.

"Sure," I said. "My dad had one all while I was growing up. And Hayword had one for a while."

I could see a silver Mercedes coming around the bend toward us.

"Is that Joan?" I asked. I ducked down so that my head was nearly in Mark's lap.

"No, it wasn't her," he said.

"Hm," I said. "While I'm down here, is there anything you'd like me to do?"

He laughed. "Get up! You wanna get us both killed?"

I put on my sunglasses. Then I looked around Mark's very clean truck. I opened the glove compartment. Ah. Just what I was looking for: a baseball cap. I took it out and looked at it.

"The Dodgers, Mark?" I said. "Really? Come on. That's a sucker's team."

I put the cap on. Now no one would know me.

"Put on your seat belt," he said.

"No," I said. "I don't wear a seat belt. Except when I'm in the car with my son, to set a good example."

"Put on the seat belt or else I'm going to have to take you back home," he said.

"Fascist," I said.

"Yep."

I put on the seat belt.

"So you don't like the Dodgers?"

"What kind of team is it?" I asked. "Are they from New York or are they from Los Angeles? And they never win anything."

"I've been going to Dodger games since I was a kid," he said. "My dad went to Dodger games when he was a kid. You don't know what you're talking about."

I made a noise.

"So who do you root for then?"

"I don't root for any of them," I said. "Like Seinfeld said, you're really only rooting for laundry now. And they're all so rich. Who gives a fuck any more?"

"You're talking about being rich?" he said.

"I'm not rich like baseball players are rich," I said. "We're writers. Or Hayword is. We're the lowest on the totem pole almost. Haven't you heard: No one in Hollywood can do a thing without writers, but no one in Hollywood has any respect for writers. We're all underpaid."

"I've been in your house," he said.

"Yeah, well, maybe we're overpaid, too," I said. "The whole fucking town is overpaid. Except the 99 percent who aren't. Or whatever the percentage is. I'm not complaining." Although it sounded like I was. "We started out in plays. The written word is more sacrosanct in the theater. But we got an offer on a script and we figured we'd take the money and run, start our own theater company. But you know, I didn't really like theater people. So many of them are so dramatic. I mean, they're fucking plays. Made up shit. Not brain surgery. There were so many divas. So we decided we'd come here for a while, to change things. Things got changed all right. Us things."

We drove out of the canyon and past the village. It was peaceful sitting in the truck quietly, watching the scenery. I couldn't remember the last time I had been a passenger in a car—or truck. Hayword and I always took separate cars wherever we went, in case one of us wanted to leave before the other, or in case I had a date—or a sudden burst of inspiration which would send me to the art studio. At least that was what I told Hayword.

It was strange Hayword never questioned me about the studio or what I did there. In the beginning he had asked if he could see some of the paintings. But then he stopped asking.

Didn't know what that meant. Figured he was respecting my space, man.

I smiled. "My space, man." Could be a title for a movie.

Mark took Highway 1 to 10. I leaned back, ready for the traffic. Or not ready for it. I had my left hand down on the seat. Mark put his hand over mine and squeezed it. I left my hand there for a minute. Let him have his domestic moment. Then he brought my hand up to his mouth and kissed the back of it.

"There," he said. "Now you can have it back."

The traffic wasn't bad. Although I didn't actually care.

"I don't know why I'm so talky today," I said. "Must be because I haven't had a drink all day."

"I don't mind it," he said. "I could listen to you rant about rich baseball players all day long. So there's no team you like?"

"When I was a kid, I liked the Tigers," I said. "Of course, we lived an hour from Detroit. My dad would take me to games at Tiger Stadium. Now that was a stadium. Loved it. Most of the time we listened to games on the radio. I loved that, too. Had to use my imagination."

"Your dad still around?"

"Sure," I said. "He and my mom live in Michigan half the year and go down to Florida the other half. He's been to some games at the new stadium—although I guess it's not that new any more—and he likes it. My dad's always been okay with what the world calls progress."

"Not you?"

"I like progress as much as the next gal, unless the next gal is a Luddite."

We slowed almost to a stop.

"Looks like there's an accident up ahead," Mark said. "Where am I taking you anyway?"

"Oh, yeah," I said. "It's called Juliet's and it's on Wilshire. Some of the studio execs like to go there, they say, because no one else goes there, but now everyone goes there."

"Do you know how to go there?"

I laughed. "Haven't a clue. I usually use my GPS which usually gets me lost and I drive around until I can find whatever place I'm looking for. Not that I go there very often. I don't come into the city much."

"Me, neither," he said.

"Where do you live?" I asked.

"Don't you remember?" he said. "You're the one who called me."

"No, I have no idea," I said. "I asked people at a party who they recommended. Katie Williams suggested you. She gave me your phone number. I never asked: Did you fuck her, too?"

Mark put both hands on the steering wheel.

He looked pissed.

"How long have we been seeing each other?" he asked.

"I don't know, Mark. What is going on up there?"

Seemed like someone was out of their car way up the freeway. Or someone was running down the highway.

Some lunatic, no doubt. L.A. County was rife with them.

All six lanes were now stopped.

The highway was a parking lot.

"Paved paradise and put up a parking lot," I sang quietly.

"You called me last February," he said. "It's been almost a year. Except for that month you were on vacation last summer, we've seen each other every week for months. How many times have I told you that I've never done anything like this before? I wish you wouldn't treat me like some goddamn gigolo."

"I wasn't on vacation for a month," I said.

"What the fuck?" Mark said. I followed his gaze.

Someone was running down the freeway. A man dressed in a dirty suit and tie.

He was yelling.

He was suddenly at the truck, almost on top of it, pounding on the hood.

His eyes were red, his hair filthy gray. His cheeks streaked with dirt and tears.

"Help me!" he yelled. "It's here. It's here. The end is here!"

Then he jumped off of the truck and kept running.

Mark laughed. We heard honking all around us. I looked at the drivers and passengers in the cars near us. People were laughing and talking.

"What the fuck was that?" Mark asked.

"Must be publicity for a movie," I said. "I wonder if they're doing another remake of *Invasion of the Body Snatchers.*"

A few moments later, the traffic started up again.

"Only in Hollywood," I said.

"Here we go," he said. "I think I might know where this restaurant is."

"Just put it in the GPS," I said.

"I'll find it," he said. "It'll be more of an adventure this way."

"An adventure where we get lost," I said. "You don't know some of these neighborhoods. They're dangerous."

"I do know all of these neighborhoods," Mark said. "I was raised here. Trust me. I'll get you there in one piece."

I really wanted to put the address into his GPS. I wanted to make him do what I wanted him to do.

But I took a deep breath. New experiences. I was supposed

to have new experiences. Was supposed to learn to go with the flow.

"What did you mean you weren't on vacation?" he said.

"What do you mean what did I mean?"

"What?" he said. He glanced at me. "You're trying to avoid the fucking question. You said it. Now what did you mean?"

"Oh crap," I said. "I wasn't on vacation in last summer. I was in rehab."

"What?"

"Mark, pay attention to the road."

"You're just telling me this now?" he said.

"I never intended to tell you at all," I said. "My family was worried. I had made some apparently incoherent phone calls. Hayword found a place and took me there. I denied I was an alcoholic. I'd been using some of Joan's sleeping pills. I didn't steal them. She gave them to me. It was around the anniversary of Alberto's death and I often have a hard time then. So I mixed the pills with the alcohol. I went into rehab to shut everyone up. I stopped drinking while I was there. Easy as pie. I left a little earlier than they thought I should, but I've been on my best behavior since."

Mark shook his head. "I can't believe this."

"It was court mandated," I said. "I ran into the ditch by my driveway. Since I didn't hurt anyone and there was no proof that I was drunk, I got to keep my license, but I had to go to detox and rehab for at least three weeks. That's what I did. I don't know why you're so upset. I'm not an alcoholic. I like how I feel when I drink."

Mark laughed.

"What?"

"I think that's what every alcoholic says about drinking," he said.

"Everyone who drinks drinks because they like how they feel when they drink!" I said. "And they can't all be alcoholics!"

I didn't want to have this conversation. I was having too many conversations today that I didn't want to have.

"You know I don't drink," he said.

"Yes, I know you don't drink anything when we're together."

"Didn't you wonder why?"

"No," I said.

"Your lack of curiosity about anything but yourself is astounding."

"Hey, let's not get insulting," I said. "I have a complete lack of curiosity about my own life, too."

"I'm a fucking alcoholic," he said. "That's why I don't drink."

"You never told me that," I said. "Every *fucking* alcoholic I've ever known always tells me they're an alcoholic or they're in the program or they're a friend of Billy Bob or something the minute I meet them. You've never said anything."

"How do you know every alcoholic you've known has told you?" he said. "Maybe just as many didn't say anything."

"Well, I can't argue with you if you're logical," I said. "Okay, so you're an alcoholic. Did you ever suspect I was an alcoholic? Alkies must have an alkie-dar. No, you never suspected. So I'm not an alcoholic."

Mark shook his head and chuckled. One thing about Mark was that he laughed a lot when he was around me. He didn't find me offensive or perplexing. He seemed to think I was funny.

"I don't have any goddamn alkie-dar," he said, trying not to laugh. "No, it didn't occur to me that you were an alcoholic. You were sometimes sad. Now I know why."

"You don't know nothing," I said. "Don't think you know

me because you've fucked me, or because I spilled my guts to you today. You don't."

"And don't think you can get mean with me because you're scared," he said. "I'm not your fucking enemy."

"Well, then who is? I'd like to find out so I'd have someone to blame and then I could shoot them, kill them, sue them, do something to make myself feel better."

I had said all of that out loud.

"Man," I said, "fuck me and the horse I rode in on."

Mark reached into his shirt pocket, pulled out his phone, and tossed it to me. I caught it.

"Can you read the text?" he asked.

"You read it," I said.

"I'm driving!"

"You are the biggest pussy in the world," I said. I read the text out loud to him. "'Giovanni tried to fix the sink. Water everywhere. Come quick!' There's an exclamation after 'quick.'"

"We've got to make a detour," he said. "Won't take long."

Mark got off at the next exit.

"Where are you going?" I asked. "I can't go down here. There's gangs. We'll get lost like Kevin Kline did in *Grand Canyon* and we'll be killed."

"He wasn't killed," Mark said. He headed away from the freeway, the gas stations, and fast food places. "Danny Glover saved him and they became lifelong pals. That could happen to us. But I gotta tell you, for living here for twenty years you don't know anything. We're nowhere near South Central. These are the 'burbs, man. You might see something you consider in bad taste, but that's about it. I don't live far from here."

"Oh Christ," I said. "You're kidnapping me, aren't you? I knew I should have never gotten into this truck."

Mark laughed. "Just shut the fuck up."

We were driving through a neighborhood. Reminded me of

Michigan, actually, some one story houses, a few two story. Looked working class and up, I supposed.

"You really should get out more," he said.

"Why?"

"It's called living, darlin'," he said.

He pulled the truck up into the driveway of a small yellow ranch house. He got out, then leaned into the window on the driver's side of the truck. "I'll be right back, but you're welcome to come in."

He got a tool box from the back of the truck, and then he went up the walk and inside the house.

I sat in the truck and looked around. Wondered if this was where Mark had grown up. If the house had been red instead of yellow, it could have been my parents' house. Only theirs was two story. Surrounded by oak trees and maples. A single oak tree shaded this house. Up and down the street, I could see cars parked in driveways. Many of the houses had basketball hoops on the garages. I looked at my phone. I still wasn't late for the meeting I didn't want to go to.

I closed my eyes.

I could practically hear the minutes of my life ticking away. Tick. Tock. Tick. Tock.

I vaguely wondered what would happen if I got out and walked away.

I opened the door and got out of the truck. I glanced down the street and then back at the house. I shrugged and walked to the front door. I knocked. No one answered. I could hear loud voices inside.

I opened the screen door.

"Hello?" I called.

Again no one answered. I stepped inside. The house smelled like freshly baked bread. I looked around. A living room. Knick-knacks here and there. A sofa, the TV on with no sound, a cat watching me from a chair next to a small table with a sewing machine on it.

"Hello!" I walked into the living room. I looked to my right and saw the kitchen. Inside several people were talking animatedly. A man dressed in a T-shirt and jeans was drenched in water. A woman about the man's age, with black hair, seemed to be trying to reassure him. An older woman was gesturing and looking down at the wet floor.

I couldn't see Mark, but I heard him saying, "Christ, Giovanni, you're a fucking lawyer. What were you doing here?"

"Hello," I said.

The three people stopped talking and looked at me.

"I'm sorry," I said. "I knocked, but no one answered. Mark said I could come in."

"Come in, come in," the older woman said, gesturing.

I crossed the living room and went into the kitchen.

Seemed like water was everywhere. On the ceiling. On the walls. On the floor.

"Oh dear," I said. Not my normal expression, but that's what came out.

Mark got up from the floor near the sink. "You're not a plumber," he said. "You're not an electrician. Stop trying to do this crap. You gotta always turn off the fucking water."

"Mark," the older woman said. She looked at me.

"Mom, this is my friend Brooke," he said. "Brooke, this is my mother, Margaret Pantano. This is my sister Jane and my brother-in-law Giovanni."

"I think we should all know how to do stuff around the house," Giovanni said. "I'm trying to learn to be more useful."

"Then ask me," Mark said. "I'll teach you."

"Do you want some tea?" Margaret asked me.

"No, thank you," I said.

"We've got to get downtown," Mark said. "I'm giving her a ride to a meeting. She had some car trouble."

"Can I help you clean up?" I asked. Again, I'm not sure why I asked. Seemed like the polite thing to do.

"No," Jane said. "This is our mess. Giovanni and I will clean it up. Come on, Gio. Nice to meet you."

"When the timer rings, take out the bread," Margaret said. She grabbed a paper bag off the kitchen table and handed it to me. "Just took it out of the oven."

"Thank you," I said. I looked inside. A loaf of bread. "Don't you want it?"

"What am I gonna do with that bread?" she said. "I've got a million loafs. You eat it, you and my son. You could use some meat on your bones."

She put her hand on my elbow and led me out of the kitchen.

"I'm happy to meet you, Brooke," Margaret said. "I'm glad to see Mark is meeting new people. He says he has a girlfriend, but he never brings her around. He never goes out on the weekends. I think she's married which would mean he was committing adultery which is a mortal sin."

We were standing in the living room. Mark came up behind us. His shirt was wet. He was wiping his hands on a towel.

"Mom," he said. "Don't bore Mrs. Lightman with my personal life."

"He wouldn't be committing adultery," I said, "because he isn't married. She would be committing adultery."

"I don't believe in any of that Catholic stuff any more anyway," she said, waving her hand. "I only care that my son is happy."

"Mom," Mark said.

"What?" she said. "You need to find a woman who will birth you more babies. Men. I don't know how they get along in the world when they can't make their own babies."

"Can't we have this conversation another time?" Mark said. "When it would be less embarrassing."

"No," she said. "I haven't seen you in a week and you live two blocks away. Since I can't talk to you, I'll talk to her. She looks like a good listener."

"Looks are deceiving," I said.

Margaret laughed. "She's a funny one. Don't you think he should have more babies?"

"I don't want any more children," Mark said. "Good grief. I've got to go." He kissed his mother on the cheek. Then he put his hand on my back to propel me out the door.

I gotta tell ya: I really wanted to find some back alley and have sex with him then and there.

We both left the house and hurried out to the truck.

"Thanks for saving us," his mother called as we left.

I got into the truck next to Mark. He started the truck and drove away. I waved to his mother.

When we were out of sight of the house, I started to laugh.

"It's not funny," he said. "I don't know what the fuck got into her."

"Aw, come on," I said. "It was sweet. The mother trying to get her son married with children. And the brother-in-law who can't do anything. It's very domestic. Better than TV."

"Hey, don't romanticize us," Mark said. "We're as dysfunctional as anyone."

"If you thought I was romanticizing what I just saw, then I said it wrong."

I reached into the paper bag and ripped off a couple pieces of bread. I gave Mark a piece and I ate the other one.

"Man, this is pretty damn good. If Eartha had made it, it would definitely be her one great thing today."

"What?" Mark asked.

"Long story," I said. "I'll tell you later."

Or I wouldn't.

"Giovanni has been out of work for a while," Mark said. "I think he's going stir crazy."

"Where are you taking us?" I asked. "Aren't we going back to the freeway?"

"No," he said. "Just sit back and relax."

"Do you know any place where we can stop and do it, quickly?" I asked. "Before my meeting."

"My house is a few blocks away," he said.

I thought about it. I did. But then that would seem too much like a date. And I would know where he lived. It was bad enough that I'd met his family.

"No," I said. "No. I better get to the meeting. So you've got another married woman you're seeing?"

He looked at me. I laughed.

"I'm so glad my parents pay little or no attention to my life," I said. "She knew I was your married lady. She's not stupid."

"No, she's not," he said. "But I don't think she knows."

"By the way, my name is not Mrs. Lightman," I said. "Don't call me that."

"But I've heard you on the phone," he said. "You always call yourself Brooke Lightman. When you first called me, you called yourself Brooke Lightman."

"Yeah, well, my name is Brooke McMurphy," I said. "That's how I signed the marriage license, so that's my legal name. I wrote under Brooke McMurphy. My friends called me Mac. I felt more like a Mac than a Brooke. But with the kids and everything, it just became easier to call myself Lightman. Everyone thought McMurphy was my husband's name anyway. But it sounded weird today, to hear you call me that."

"Okay," he said. "Duly noted. They called you Mac?" He glanced at me. "I don't see it. You're clearly a Brooke to me."

"A river maybe," I said. "A raging river. An ocean. But not a brook. That sounds like such a nothing and nobody name."

Mark shrugged. "I never thought about it before. When I hear the name now, I think of you. Strong, funny, beautiful, smart."

I moved across the seat until I was sitting next to him. He put his right arm around me and I put my head on his shoulder. We drove like that for a while. I felt strangely peaceful. He kissed the top of my head.

Then we were in traffic again and I moved away. Too many cars, too many people. Sometimes in these situations I felt a little overwhelmed. Completely overwhelmed, actually. This was when I really wanted a drink.

That did not make me an alcoholic. Come on. Modern society was fucking overstimulating. My nervous system had long ago fried itself out. Maybe everyone was completely burned out, too, and I couldn't tell. Sometimes it seemed as though everyone else was moving through life so easily. I tried to emulate those people who were doing it right.

Or seemed to be doing it right.

Maybe they were all pretending. Maybe we were all make-believe made-up people.

"That's it right up there," Mark said. "Do you want me to drop you off out front or a block away?"

I made a noise. "I don't want to go," I said.

But at least there I could get a drink.

"Then don't go," he said. "Come with me to the beach. Or back to my house. Or we could go to a movie. You love movies."

I looked at him. I couldn't remember the last time I had gone out to see a movie.

"What makes you think I love movies?"

"Because you're always quoting from movies," he said. "Or saying that this or that is like this or that movie."

"Really? I do that?"

"Sure," he said. "You talk about books, too. But more often it's movies."

"Huh," I said. I shook my head. I didn't have time to think about that or wonder why. I didn't love movies. I didn't like movies. They were so fucking fake. Everything turned out in movies even when it didn't, and if it didn't, I didn't want to see it. Or hear about it.

"Thanks, Mark," I said. "You can pull in here. I'll walk the rest of the way. I appreciate it. It's been an interesting day."

He pulled into a parking lot down the block from Juliet's. He parked the truck. I started to get out.

"Brooke," Mark said.

I turned around and looked at him.

"I'm going to see you again, aren't I?" He looked right into my eyes. He did that a lot. Wasn't sure I liked it.

"Um," I said.

He shook his head. "I knew it. You're thinking of ending this, aren't you? Because you told me all that stuff today. And now you know things about me. You've met my mother. You know I'm an alcoholic. Who hasn't had a drink in many years, by the way. So now it's time to say goodbye because if we didn't break up, then it would feel too much like a relationship."

I sighed. "Please don't try to psychoanalyze me."

"That's not what I'm doing," he said. "I'm speaking the truth, aren't I?"

"Yes," I said. "I guess. I've got to go. Yes, I would like to throw your ass to the curb now because you know a little tiny bit about me. Yes, I would like to throw your ass to the curb because I had no idea we had been doing this for a fucking year! Almost. But I happen to enjoy your ass and I'm not ready to make that decision or any decision right now. I've got to go to this fucking meeting."

"I've got another job up in the canyon Monday," he said. "How about I meet you at your place around lunch time."

"If I agree, will you stop talking and let me leave?"

"Hey, you've been free to go at any time," he said. "You'll always be free to go at any time. I've known and understood the rules."

I took off the baseball cap and ran my fingers through my hair.

"Your mom saw me in this dirty old baseball cap," I said. "What must she think?"

I kissed Mark on the mouth, then handed him the baseball cap.

"Later, gator."

FIVE

It was noisy outside Juliet's—and much too sunny. I stepped eagerly into the dimly lit restaurant. I looked around. The restaurant was noisy, too, and nearly full. On the other side of the room was the patio, surrounded by ferns and trees. I bet it was quieter out there.

Where was Hayword?

I had forgotten to call him and tell him I was twenty minutes out. Maybe they weren't here yet.

Then I saw Hayword stand up. He was outside on the patio. His long lanky figure seemed to unfold itself from his chair. He smiled when he saw me, like David had earlier, and he waved. I waved back and hurried across the restaurant floor and out onto the patio.

Hayword walked toward me and took my hand. He squeezed it. His way of reassuring me, I supposed. He held out a chair for me and I turned and saw the other two people at the table.

"Sally St. James!" I said.

"Brooke McMurphy," the woman said.

We leaned toward one another and kissed the air next to our cheeks. I sat down as Hayword pushed my chair in for me.

"Wow," I said. "Long time. Hayword didn't tell me."

"I had forgotten you two knew one another," he said. "And this is Irving Jackson. Irving is one of the creative execs and Sally is now studio head."

I shook Mr. Jackson's hand. He was probably in his forties, with dyed black hair, maybe a weave, dressed in khakis and a knit shirt with a jacket on over it all. He was trying to dress casually, but he was not casual or comfortable.

Sally looked like she always had looked: gorgeous. Her black hair was shoulder-length now, flipped up like Marlo Thomas used to wear on *That Girl* a long time ago. Decades ago. What had made me think of that? She wore a sleeveless red dress. She was slender and tanned. I remembered she hadn't a tan line on her whole body.

"Don't pay any attention to our titles," Sally said. "We're re-designing everything. Or re-inventing everything. What Irving is good at is getting things going. I saw the script for *Zombie Town,* and I was blown away. I think this can be a blockbuster. Jack Meredith is ready to go. But both of us want some changes. We know the kids will go see it. And that's good. But we're not sure the girls will go back to see it again. I like the idea of making this a zombie movie girls will flock to. And a zombie movie sophisticated enough for adults."

I looked at Hayword, and he smiled. He looked downright giddy.

"We've got the makeup figured out," Irving said. "And we're pretty much all set with the special effects. We want to shoot this picture quickly and get it in the theaters quickly. Make it seem like a home movie movie. You know what I mean. That's Meredith's idea. And he's a genius at this kind of thing. We've scouted locations in your area, actually. We can be ready to shoot before the month is out."

"What?" I said. "How's that possible if you don't have a completed script?"

The three of them laughed.

Sally said, "Brooke, you've been in this business a long time. You know we can do it. Hayword wrote a brilliant script. Having the zombies really be aliens from another planet: That was brilliant. But we need understory. We need some of your humor and brilliant dialogue."

This was one of the things I hated about Hollywood meetings. Everything was brilliant, perfect, awesome, a real money-maker.

Come on. A zombie movie could not be brilliant.

"I don't write much any more," I said.

"Bullshit," Sally said. "Everyone in Hollywood knows you doctor Hayword's scripts."

I looked at Hayword. He didn't say anything.

"That's not true," I said. "I check his spelling."

"The fucking computer can do that," Sally said. "You two together are brilliant."

I leaned my head back. I had planned on being as hospitable as possible. But all of this *brilliance* was getting on my nerves.

"Would you care for anything?" the waiter stopped and asked me.

"A gin and tonic," I said, "with more gin than tonic. And some bread."

"Even if I was doing any doctoring," I said, "I'm not interested in a zombie movie. I wouldn't know what to write."

"We want it a little more sexy," Sally said.

"A little more sexy?" I asked. "You mean it's sexy now?"

Sally laughed. She looked at me and smiled. I wondered if she was remembering us naked together, too.

"Actually it's not sexy at all," Sally said. "We want you to make zombies sexy the way vampires are sexy now. Or were-wolves."

"Well, Sally, as I told Hayword when he mentioned this all to me, zombies aren't sexy. Who would want to have sex with a zombie?"

"Anyone who is married to a banker is already having sex with a zombie whether they like it or not," Sally said.

Irving half-smiled. Hayword looked worried.

The waiter brought my gin and tonic.

I sucked it down dry.

I glanced at Hayword. He was drinking a beer.

I ordered another gin and tonic.

Someone brought me bread and butter.

Nothing better with gin and tonic than bread and butter.

I slathered the butter on the bread and took a bite.

Wasn't as good as Margaret's. Damn. I'd left the loaf in Mark's truck.

When the waiter put the second gin and tonic on the table, I said, "I don't think it's sexy when flesh is falling off of someone. It's disgusting. It's not sexy when the dead are eating one an-other."

"Have you read the script?" Sally asked.

I shook my head.

"She hasn't had a chance," Hayword said.

Sally looked at Irving.

He cleared his throat. "I'm going out for a smoke," he said. "You wanna come?" He said that last bit to Hayword.

"You don't mind?" Hayword asked.

I shook my head. The men excused themselves, then walked away.

Once they were gone, Sally leaned back in her chair.

"Hiya, Mac," she said. "I've missed you. Long time."

I nodded. "What's going on with this picture, anyway? Why the rush?"

"I'm trying to make my name," she said. "We need an influx of easy money. I think this will do it—if we're all still around by the time it comes out. Seems like everything is going to hell in a hand basket. Zombies are big now. Everything's a 'zombie.' They call those half-finished subdivisions 'zombie developments.' The kids talk about us all being corporate zombies, shilling for the man. There's some skin condition going around that some people are calling the zombie plague. Zombies, zombies, zombies. But the movies about them suck, so to speak. They're B movies, if that. They gross people out. Who wants to eat popcorn while watching people getting eaten? We want this movie to do for zombie movies what *Forbidden Planet* did for science fiction movies. MGM went all out on that movie. They took it very seriously. They wanted it to be a blockbuster."

"But it wasn't," I said. "It didn't do well."

"This one will be a blockbuster," she said. "It will do well."

"So you want it to be the same as *Forbidden Planet* but different," I said.

"See, you do understand Hollywood."

"I don't know what you think I can do to help," I said.

"Just read the script," she said. "See if you can humanize it. We'll pay you lots of money. Additional money. Don't forget to leave an opening for a sequel."

"A sequel? I don't want to think about a sequel."

"You should," Sally said. "Remember *Thelma and Louise.* They could have made a mint with *Thelma and Louise.* It could have been a very successful movie."

"They did make a mint," I said, "and it was a very successful movie."

"But think what could have been," she said, "if the final shot was of a hand coming up over the ledge. Sequels galore!"

I laughed. "I suppose you're envisioning Thelma and Louise dolls. T-shirt. Mugs. The whole shebang."

Sally St. James smiled. "Never underestimate the power of an iconic image."

"Them flying over the Grand Canyon was iconic enough for me."

"I'm just saying," Sally said. "Will you at least look at Hayword's script?"

"All right," I said. "I'll read it. I'm not sure when I'll get to it. I've got this benefit on Saturday. After that, though."

"Any chance you could read it sooner?" she said. "Like maybe take it down to your love nest and read it there. Shouldn't take more than a couple of hours. I could even meet you there and read it with you." She smiled. "You know I fuck all of my writers, so it's gonna either be you or Hayword, and I seem to remember you said you'd kill him if he ever cheated on you again. So—" She shrugged. "—you'd be saving his life."

I smiled. "You're so full of shit, Sally."

She laughed. "Yeah, you could always see through me."

"I can see your wedding ring," I said. "You always said if you got married you'd never fool around."

"I know," she said. "What an idiot I was. But I've been true to my word. I don't cheat on him. I don't fool around any more. Not since you broke my heart."

"You never had a heart," I said. "That's why we worked well together."

"And played well together."

We were silent for a few moments.

"How are you really?" she asked.

Like I was going to tell her.

Like I knew.

"I'm fine," I said. "When did you get married?"

"Don't you read the papers?" she asked. "Six years ago.

We've got a son and a daughter. I married someone who is not in the business, thank God. He's a normal guy with a normal life."

"Really?" A plumber? Electrician? Teacher? "What's he do?"

"He's the CEO at one of the biggest investment firms here in L.A.," she said.

I laughed. "That's a normal guy with a normal life?"

"Yes," she said. "I didn't say he was poor. He's normal because he's not in the business."

"He's not in trouble with all this economic stuff going on?" I asked.

She shrugged. "He says he's not. We seem to be doing okay. Plus I make a great deal of money." She smiled. "And I can make you a great deal money, too. I think writers are treated like shit and I'd like to help you out. Just like I did way back then. It was my idea to give you points on *Love and Other Insanities.* Did I ever tell you that?"

"Yes, every time we fucked each other you reminded me."

She grinned. "I wanted you to appreciate me. Gawd." She looked around. "I really need a smoke."

"I don't remember you smoking," I said.

"Why do you think I went out on the back porch all the time?" she asked.

I shrugged. "I don't know. I'm not very attentive. Go out with Irving and have a smoke."

"I can't," she said. She looked around again. "I quit smoking. And I signed a contract, a prenup, that if Jonathan ever found out I was smoking again, that would be grounds for divorce."

"Does he want a divorce?" I asked.

"I don't think so," she said, "but lately I've felt like someone is following me. And that made me nervous so I started smoking again."

I laughed.

"It's not funny," she said.

"I know," I said. "It's ridiculous. Why don't you just quit smoking?"

"I don't like anyone telling me what to do," she said.

I understood that.

"So you'll kill yourself to spite him?" I asked.

Like I should fucking talk.

"Come out with me," she said. "You can hold the cigarette and pretend it's yours and I'll smoke it."

"I'd rather go make out," I said. Although I didn't really. She had been a pain in the ass. One thing about having men as lovers, generally speaking, they didn't have troubling getting off. Sally had to have it in the right place at the right time.

And as I said, I was not really that attentive.

"Making out with someone is probably grounds for divorce, too," she said. "And I'm never getting divorced. They'll have to pry my cold dead fingers off his balls before I get a divorce."

"That's a pretty picture," I said. I motioned to the waiter. "We'll be right back."

Sally got her purse, and she and I walked through the now nearly deserted restaurant and out the door. The street was lined with customers having a smoke, including Irving. Hayword stood next to Irving, his hands in his pockets.

We went back inside. I followed Sally through the kitchen and out back. No one tried to stop us. No one said a word. We went by the overturned milk cartons where two of the kitchen workers sat having a smoke. Sally walked to the alley and leaned against the wooden fence.

She looked around. "Seeing if they've got cameras," she said. Then she took out a cigarette and lit it. She handed it to me.

I put it between my forefinger and middle finger. I had never smoked. I didn't know what to do with it.

"Hold it like you enjoy it," she said. "Hold it like you'd like to fuck it."

"Sally, that's disgusting," I said. "And this is ridiculous."

She leaned over and took a drag. She held the smoke in her lungs for a moment. Then she turned to the fence and let the smoke out through the slats.

"Much better," she said. "Much better." She sighed. "So how's the love nest these days?"

"I'd rather not talk about it," I said.

"The kids okay?" she asked.

She was acting as if we were old friends. Intimate friends. We had been intimate, but we were never friends. At least I didn't think so. Just like Mark and I were not friends. No one I had ever brought to the art studio was a personal friend of mine.

"The kids are fine," I said. "Everyone is fine."

"Speaking of fine," Sally said. She looked over by the kitchen door. Mark was standing there with a waiter next to him who was pointing to us.

"I bet he works out," she said.

I started to say, "He doesn't work out; he works for living." But I had been living this double life for so long that I was used to keeping my mouth shut until I knew the lay of the land.

Mark stepped down out of the restaurant and walked toward us.

What was he doing here?

Before I could say or do anything, he held out my pocketbook and the bag of bread Margaret had given me.

"You left these in the cab," he said.

He wasn't lying. I had left them in the cab of the truck.

"I thought you might need them," he said.

I took the bread and pocketbook from him.

"Thank you," I said.

Mark glanced at the cigarette in my hand. Then he nodded to both of us. He turned around and walked down the alley toward the street.

"He was your cab driver?" Sally asked. "I would have done him in a second." She took another drag on the cigarette.

Then I dropped the cigarette on the ground and rubbed it out with my foot. I picked it up and threw it in the trash.

"It's been a long day," I said, "and I've got a script to read."

We went back into the restaurant. Irving and Hayword were waiting for us at the table. We all talked for a bit, and then Hayword and I said our goodbyes and left. Hayword was more than a little surprised that I was going home with him.

We got into the car together.

"I feel like we're on a date," Hayword said as he pulled out of the parking lot and onto the street. "It's been so long since we've been in the car together."

The day was starting to wear on me and I was less and less talky. Maybe if we had stopped by a bar on the way home, but David was waiting for us at home. We'd be in traffic for a while.

"Was it nice to see Sally again?" Hayword asked. He was trying to make small talk. We'd known each other over thirty years and he was trying to make small talk with me.

"She's looking good," I said. "She's got two kids now. And a husband who will divorce her if he catches her smoking."

"Really?" He glanced over at me.

"Yep," I said. "It's in her prenup."

"What was in our prenup?" he asked.

I didn't say anything. He was trying to joke with me.

I wasn't in the mood.

Why was it always easier to be nicer to strangers or people who were not family?

"How'd you get to L.A. today?" he asked.

When telling a lie, it was always better to tell as much truth as possible. Meant I didn't have to remember as much.

"Joanie had some trouble at her house today," I said. I wouldn't tell him the gory details. No need. "I went over to help her out. The plumber was there, you know, the guy we used."

"Mark Pantano," he said. "I remember him. Seemed like a nice guy."

I glanced at him. Why would he remember Mark Pantano, our plumber?

"I mentioned I was going into Los Angeles and he was on his way there, so he offered to give me a lift."

"I'm surprised you said yes," Hayword said.

He drove us out onto the freeway. Everyone was driving too fast, and it was too crowded.

"I wish you'd put on your seat belt," he said.

I didn't argue with him. I put on the belt.

"I'm glad you got a ride," he said. "It's good for you to get out and see people."

"Don't talk about me like I'm sick," I said. "I'm not sick."

"Wasn't saying you were," he said.

"I don't know how you do this drive almost every day," I said. "I would go crazy."

"Gets me away from the house," he said.

He said it too quickly. I could tell he was sorry he had said the truth.

"If this trip is hard on you," I said, "you should start using your office in the house again. We won't bother you. It'll be nice and quiet."

I had my left hand on my leg. Hayword put his hand over my hand and squeezed it.

"Won't it be nice to work together again?" he said. "I always loved our collaborations. You the brains, me the brawn. You the lover, me the—" He stopped. "What does follow that?"

"I don't know," I said.

He took my hand and started to raise it to his lips.

No.

That was too weird.

I pulled my hand away.

"David had a tough time at school," I said. "Had gum in his hair all day and no one told him. Then I told him about it and he went a little hysterical, you know the way he gets. So I cut it out for him and that made it worse. Well, maybe not worse but not better. Don't know what we're going to do about it. And he said they've been doing all these drills in school to teach them about emergencies. It's scaring him a little. I told him he had to stop watching the news for a while. So if you see him watching, please encourage him not to."

"Maybe we could tell him the news is really like a movie," he said. "It's all make-believe."

"I wonder how far from the truth that actually is," I said.

"I can't wait for you to read the script," he said.

I shrugged. "I was going to fuck you tonight. But if you'd rather I read the script, I will."

"Can't you do both?" he asked.

"At the same time? Sure. Why not? But in the future I may associate having sex with you with zombies. Your call."

I was ready to be home when we finally got there. I wanted a bath, a shower, or a highball. Maybe all three.

But I had promised dinner with my kid, and I was not going to break that particular promise.

When Hayword and I walked through the door together—that hadn't happened in a while—David came running out of the kitchen toward us.

His hair was short. And spiky. No more hole in his head.

He looked good. And he was smiling.

"Wow, kiddo!" I said. "Turn around. You are the dude!"

"Hey, buddy," Hayword said. "Lookin' good."

"It's Eartha," David said excitedly. "Eartha did it." We all walked into the kitchen where Eartha sat at the table. She smiled.

"You can do hair?" I asked.

"Sure," she said. "We looked online for some styles he liked and then we did it. I told him he was taking a chance letting me cut his hair, but he was willing to take that chance."

David beamed.

"And we made dinner," David said. "I helped. It was so much fun. We're ready to eat. Can Eartha eat with us?"

I laughed. "Sure," I said.

"Go wash your hands, David," Eartha said.

He ran from the room.

I looked at her. "So this isn't *Hand That Rocked the Cradle* or anything, is it? Cuz I don't have asthma. I'll whip your butt if you try to steal my kids or my husband."

Hayword laughed. "I'm gonna wash up, too."

"No," Eartha said. "If you'll remember, the Rebecca De Mornay character didn't fare well in that movie. And I've never lost a child."

Oh man. I had forgotten that part of the movie.

Who cared? It was a stupid demented movie anyway.

"In any case," I said, "thank you for that. He looks great. More importantly, he's happy. I'd say that's your one great thing today."

"And you haven't even eaten dinner yet," she said.

We had a nice dinner, the four of us. I can't remember what we talked about. Maybe we listened to David talk about his day. Afterward, David went to his room, Eartha went to the garden house, and Hayword and I went to our room. He gave me a printed copy of *Zombie Town*.

"First thing we've got to do is change the title," I said.

We got naked together. He tried to go down on me, but I wouldn't let him. Seemed too personal. But he did his best to rock my world. And he succeeded. Then he wanted to cuddle. I was so tired I actually did it. I put my head on his shoulder and let him hold me.

"Remember when we were kids planning our lives together?" he whispered.

I nodded.

"Did you ever imagine we'd be where we are?" he said. "We are so fortunate."

I didn't say anything. I wanted to scream. I wanted to cry. I wanted to feel something besides this vast emptiness that seemed to grower wider by the day.

I wanted to hit Hayword. Instead, I turned away and pretended to sleep.

When I heard Hayword sleep breathing, I got out of bed, got my phone, and went into the bathroom. I texted Mark, "It wasn't my cigarette."

Why on Earth had I texted that? I wanted to take it back, but I got an immediate answer. "Really? Phew, I thought maybe my smoke-dar was off. Thinking of you. Love."

I shook my head, turned off the phone, and went back to bed.

I heard Hayword and David laughing when I woke up. I lay under the sheet listening. Sounded like they were in David's room. Must be about time to leave for school. Or maybe time to go down for breakfast.

I turned my head and looked at the clock.

Why was I awake so early?

Didn't even have a hangover.

What were they saying to one another? How easy they seemed together. Like friends, buddies. Or father and son.

Would Alberto and Hayword have been buddies? Would he have been like me? Or like David? Like Fern? Hopefully not like Fern. I didn't hate my daughter, no matter what it sounds like. I didn't. I didn't like her. It was hard to like someone who had been so consistently unkind for so many years.

Perhaps that was the way Hayword felt about me. Did he think I was consistently unkind to him? Or maybe inconsistently unkind.

Who cared?

The laughter had stopped. I could hear them going downstairs. I thought about going down and joining them for breakfast. We could have another family meal. Like normal people.

Did normal people eat together? When I was a kid, we had eaten together as a family. Sometimes it had been torture. My little brother didn't like to eat anything. My sister ate everything. And I was always mouthing off to my parents. At least in my teen years. So, often, dinner consisted of me saying something and then my father slapping me across the face.

Words. Smack. Words. Smack.

I must have been a terror when I was a teen.

Maybe Fern had gotten it from me.

Only I had grown out of it. Fern hadn't.

My father didn't remember hitting me. Swore he didn't do it, would never have hit his own dear child.

Once he got mad at me and took a hold of my arms and shook me, hard. The house was full of relatives. I was wearing jeans and a pajama top and the top came unbuttoned as he shook me. I wasn't wearing anything underneath the top. My father kept shaking me, and there I was with my beautiful teen breasts exposed to everyone.

It was a deeply humiliating experience.

Not that it scarred me for life. I didn't believe in that psychological bullshit.

What was past was past.

"Goddamn it, goddamn it," I said.

I did not want to think about any of this.

Today I was having lunch with some of the other Enclave women who were organizing the Benefit. We were meeting at a restaurant in the hotel where the Benefit would be. (Let's call it the Shilton Hotel and leave it at that.) I didn't know why I was going to the lunch or to the Benefit. I hadn't done much this year.

We'd donated some money; I'd called some donors. I'd gotten the hotel to give us a deal. Beyond that, I was along for the ride. I guess I was going because I had been taking part in the Benefit for years, even before.

Before Alberto died.

I wondered if my life would always be before and after?

Or would it change when someone else in my life died? If I died, would my children talk about their lives as before and after Mom died?

I got out of bed and took a quick shower. Then I got dressed and went downstairs. Hayword and David sat at the kitchen table eating. Eartha was at the stove. She looked up and smiled at me. How domestic she looked standing there in her apron.

"I thought I heard you moving around up there," she said. "I found this bag of stale bread and wondered if you would like some French toast made from it, with strawberries and powdered sugar on top?"

"Shouldn't my son have something more substantial for breakfast?" I asked.

"I fed him oatmeal with fresh fruit and a scrambled egg," she said.

"It was good, Mom," David said. "Better than cereal."

"You like oatmeal?" I asked. I couldn't imagine anyone liking oatmeal.

"Sure," David said. He seemed so animated. And his hair still looked good.

"Yep, I liked it, too," Hayword said. "It'll stick to my ribs."

"The French toast was for you," Eartha said. "I didn't want your homemade bread to go to waste."

French toast for breakfast. Wasn't that kind of like having dessert for breakfast? I could definitely go for that.

"Hey, if you wanna make it," I said, "then I wanna eat it."

I went over to the kitchen table. Hayword put his arm around my waist and drew me near as I stood between him and David. I put my arm across his shoulders.

"We need groceries," Hayword said. "You care if Eartha uses your car?"

"You can drive?" I asked Eartha. "I thought you were a little hippie girl who was against the combustion engine and everything."

Eartha laughed. She was slicing Margaret's bread. "I'm too young to be a hippy," she said. "I do believe we have to get off oil, but I blame big business more than I blame the average person. Most people do what's easiest and what everyone else is doing—which is just walking around pretty senseless, following the crowd."

Wasn't sure what that had to do with anything.

"Like the zombies in your movie," David said. He put his arms out straight in front of him and rocked back and forth. "Take me to your oil or I'll eat you."

Hayword laughed. "It's *our* movie," he said. "Your mom is working on it, too."

I groaned. Did he really have to tell anyone I was working on a zombie movie?

"Cool," David said.

"Whether we are zombies or not begs the questions," I said. "Eartha, can you drive?"

"Sure," Eartha said. "Unless you want to take me. We could go grocery shopping together. That would be fun."

I looked at her. Who was this woman? I thought she'd be a huge disruption in our house—I mean, she wore Rasta braids for chrissakes. Yet now she seemed almost like a cipher. She went along, got along, did whatever we needed her to do.

She hadn't done something to Violeta's mother in order to weasel her way into our family, had she?

I wasn't sure what movie that had come from.

But it seemed plausible.

I stared at her.

Actually, it didn't seem plausible. She didn't seem particularly nefarious.

Those were the people to watch out for: the non-nefarious ones.

Oh lord. I was tiring myself out, and it wasn't even eight a.m. yet.

"I won't be going grocery shopping," I said. Unless hell froze over. "I've got a meeting in the city today. We're tying down the details for the Benefit. Or nailing them down. Whatever someone does with details."

I sat next to David while he finished eating. Hayword looked at me and winked. The morning after we had sex, he was always happy, hopeful. I was certain he was certain that now everything would go back to the way it had been before.

"I put the script in your office," he said.

My office?

Oh yes. That room I never went into. Next to his office.

I nodded. "Thank you."

He was waiting for more.

"What are you doing today?" I asked.

"The director wants more changes on *Powerbreakers*," he said. "I don't know if I can change one more word."

Hayword always said that, but he kept rewriting, any time anyone asked. He was easygoing, easy to work with, a pleasant guy who would do anything to make everyone else's lives easier, even if it pained him.

I had read the *Powerbreakers* script. It was about lawyers working in a big corporation who discover their bosses are working with politicians to assassinate the president and take over the government. He originally had three main characters, three lawyers, all young dewy-eyed men. Nobody takes them seriously or listens to their findings. One of them gets killed pretty early on and then the other two have to run for their lives and expose the conspiracy.

After I read it, I suggested this to Hayword, "Make the two surviving lawyers women. And make the woman at the farmhouse—the one who cooks for the men and sleeps with one of them—change her to a man. Don't change any of the dialogue of the characters."

"None of it?" he said.

"Nope," I said. "Remember that's what Alan Ladd, Jr. did when he got the script for *Alien*. He said make the main character a woman, put another woman in it, and don't change the dialogue. See how that turned out."

I had heard that story for decades and didn't knew if it was apocryphal or not, but I told it to Hayword then. He rewrote the script as I suggested and the studio loved it, thought it was perfect, great, brilliant. When could he start the rewrite?

The studio kept trying to tart up the women. Hayword fought them on that. Fortunately the director was on his side.

I kept telling him I was tired of hearing about it. He should tell them he was finished with it. Let someone else do it if they wanted any more rewrites. But I was glad he had stuck with it. Some other asshole would have come in and rewritten it so that one of the women got raped or tortured or at least fucked in the ass. Those were often the kind of changes the studio wanted.

"I'm proud of you for sticking with it," I said.

He looked at me, surprised.

"Really?"

"Sure," I said. "It would have been a lot easier to give in to them, to let it go."

"I keep thinking of Fern," he said. "These women aren't much older than Fern. I want to keep them safe, safe even in an unreal world."

"I forgot to tell you," David said. "Fern texted me she was coming to Los Angeles this weekend."

"Really?" I said. "To see us?"

"I don't know," David said.

I did not want to deal with my daughter right then.

Eartha brought over a pile of French toast and set it next to me, along with maple syrup.

"Have you eaten?" I asked Eartha.

"Yep," she said. "Bright and early after my yoga. I'll clean up and go shopping, if that's okay."

"Sure, there's an extra house key and car key over by the house phone," I said, pointing. Yesterday I couldn't and wouldn't leave her in the house alone. Now I was giving her the keys to my house and my very expensive car.

"And I'll make certain I'm home by the time David gets out of school," Eartha said. "Mr. Lightman said Mrs. Williams was driving him home."

I glanced at David. He grinned at me. He was going to get to ride home with his girlfriend.

"Okay," I said. "But you don't have to call him Mr. Lightman. His name is Hayword. I'm Brooke. You don't work for us."

Eartha smiled, but she didn't say anything.

I put several pieces of French toast on my plate. I scooped up some strawberries from a bowl already on the table. Then I poured maple syrup over all of it. If only I had a screwdriver to drink with it: orange juice and vodka. Oh man. Perfect.

I cut into the toast, stabbed if with a fork, then brought it up and into my mouth.

I chewed.

Oh. My. God.

How did she do it?

"I want to have sex with this French toast," I said.

David giggled.

"I think I need a bite of that," Hayword said. He picked off a piece of it from my plate with his fork and ate it. "That is good."

David picked up his fork.

"No," I said, "you're too young for this."

He laughed and quickly speared a piece of toast and put it on his plate. Then he ate some.

"Such a child," I said.

"I don't know if I want to have sex with it," David said, "but I might want to dance with it."

"I don't want to hear this kind of talk from my son," I said.

I kept eating.

"I'm glad you like it," Eartha said.

"Is this your one great thing?" I asked. "Because it is pretty damn good."

"We'll see," she said.

I was soon alone in the house.

I did not want to go to Los Angeles again today. Maybe I could get out of it.

I called Joan. "I don't want to go to the city," I said. "We all live here. Let's have the meeting here. We can meet outside by my pool."

"Come on," Joan said. "Katie is having her chauffeur drive us. We can drink all the way in. And gossip."

"I don't gossip," I said.

"But you do drink," Joan said. "And Melissa Peake is coming."

"She never has anything nice to say about anyone," I said.

"I know!" Joan said. "That's why it'll be so much fun."

"I don't like any of you," I said.

"And we don't like you," Joan said. "Another reason it'll be so much fun. Come on. You can tell them about rescuing me from the tub."

"You made me swear never to tell anyone," I said. "I keep my promises."

Well, I kept those kinds of promises.

"Okay," Joan said. "Please come for me. Those women scare me. You never let them get away with anything."

"All right," I said. "But I'm wearing something slutty. And if I see anyone fuckable, I'm gonna fuck them."

"I love it when you talk dirty," she said.

I went upstairs and found something to wear. Something a little bit see-through. Low cut. I liked dressing like a cougar. I liked trying to look ridiculous and then taking it back, a little, so no one could be sure if I was completely tasteless or actually stylish.

We did drink in the back of the limousine: Katie Williams, Joan Donning, Melissa Peake, and me, myself, and moi. Since it was Katie's car, we only had champagne. Then we could pretend we were actually upstanding people on our way to an upstanding luncheon where we would figure out how to save the world.

Melissa was some kind of broker or investment banker who only worked part-time. She always had something in her ear, and half the time, I couldn't tell if she was talking to us or to the thing in her ear. Katie was independently wealthy from some internet company she'd started when she was in her twenties, and Joan, well, Joan was in real estate. The market had tanked some time ago, however, so she hadn't been doing much.

I was the only one in the group who didn't actually work.

"How's Hayword's latest script?" Katie asked.

I glanced at Joan. She raised her eyebrows knowingly.

"All of his scripts are fine," I said. "He's doing great. Had a little run-in with the clap. Got it from me. You know from all the guys I fuck. I think he's about over it now, but it put him off sex for a little while. He was afraid I'd accuse him of screwing around on me because he knows I would kill him if he cheated on me."

"Really?" Melissa asked, leaning forward. "I had no idea. You two seem so . . . vanilla."

I grinned. "I'm kidding. Hayword has never had the clap. Neither have I. We are very . . . vanilla. I was trying to throw a little Neapolitan in there."

"Or mocha fudge," Joan said. "That would be good. With strawberries on top."

"Well, Ariel is looking forward to spending time with David this weekend," Katie said. "He's a good boy."

"Yes, he definitely doesn't take after his mother," I said.

"Hey, did you hear Dorothy and Peter Pritcher lost a child?" Melissa said. "Died in its sleep." She snapped her fingers. "Just like that. The police were going to investigate, but they figured out it was SIDS. So glad my kids are over that age."

Joan and Katie glanced at me. I didn't say anything.

Katie finally cleared her throat and said, "No, I hadn't heard. I should send them a condolence card."

I took a sip of champagne.

"What's wrong?" Melissa said. "What did I say?"

I didn't feel like explaining anything to this woman. I barely knew her. She'd been my neighbor for five or six years and we'd been to countless parties together, but that didn't mean anything. All I knew about her was that she liked to gossip and she was always on the phone.

"Someone said Dorothy had the baby blues psychosis," Melissa said, "so she could have smothered the kid. The police were being careful."

"Let's not talk about it," Joan said.

Melissa shrugged. "Yeah, it is sad."

I wanted to punch her.

Instead I drank more champagne.

Joan took my hand and held it, discreetly, between our legs. I let her. Her way of supporting me.

I stared out the window and drank.

By the time we got to the Shilton, I was three sheets to the wind. I didn't think anyone noticed.

We ordered appetizers first.

They brought us crackers with cheese on them. Or bruschetta. I never knew the difference. Melissa and Katie oohed and aahed over the little crackers. I looked down at them and something black fell onto my plate.

Melissa screamed. Or maybe it was Joan.

I leaned closer to the plate.

It was a fake eyelash. I looked up and around. Nobody here but us chickens. I felt my eye. Yep. One of mine was missing.

"Brooke!" Katie said.

"I know," I said. I pulled off the other one. "Phew. Now that feels much better."

The waitress was there now. She must have heard the scream.

"Here," I said.

She held out her palm and I dropped the false eyelashes on them. "Could you dispose of them properly, Miss? We wouldn't want them to end up in a land mine."

"Landfill," Katie said. She smiled at the waitress.

"What's that on your arm?" Melissa asked the waitress.

I tried to focus and see what she was seeing.

The waitress quickly pulled her sleeve down.

"I burned it," she said. "It's almost all healed. I'll take these now. Lunch will be here soon." The waitress left us.

Melissa leaned forward. "That's no burn. I bet she's got it."

"Got what?" Joan asked.

"You know," Melissa said. "You've heard about it. A lot of

the help, a lot of illegals, have this disease or rash or something. It's very contagious. Their skin gets really scaly or something. Someone told me she was at a restaurant and a piece of skin fell off into her food."

"I don't believe that," Joan said.

"That is complete horseshit," I said. "Only a complete asshole would believe that."

"Shhh," Katie said. "Brooke, you're talking very loudly."

"Okay, okay," I whispered. Or maybe I shouted.

"I thought you said she went to rehab." Melissa or Katie whispered that to Joan. Or to each other.

"That's what I heard," one of them said. "It doesn't always take."

"And a child is a he or a she," I said. "Not an 'it.' Do you know how devastated that mother must feel to have her baby die and then some little bitch like you talks about her smothering her baby? It's sick. Babies are not 'its'. You're an it. You're a shit."

Then I laughed.

Katie whispered something to Melissa. Or the other way around.

I kept smiling.

Joan asked me if I was all right.

I think I ate a lobster. I told the waitress I wanted to donate the empty lobster body to the poor. Melissa and Katie tried to figure out the seating chart for the Benefit. Then they all got up to go look at the ballroom.

I stayed seated.

"I'll wait for you here," I said.

I ordered another drink.

Then I called David's school and asked why they were scaring the shit out of my son with all the emergency drills.

"Are you drunk, Mrs. Lightman?" the principal asked.

"No, it's my allergy medicine," I said. "Hello? I can't hear you. Must be going through a tunnel." I turned the phone off.

I felt sick to my stomach.

I motioned to the waitress. "I'm not feeling well," I said. I'm sure she recognized the illness. "Could you please get me a room?" I handed her my credit card. "I want to go lie down for a bit."

A few minutes later, she came back with a keycard and my credit card.

"Do you want me to take you?" she asked.

I waved her away. "I'm fine, fine. Tell my friends they're a bunch of insensitive assholes, and I can't stand to be here with them any more."

"Do you really want me to tell them that?" she asked.

I wished I could see her face clearly. She was being quite kind to me.

"Naw," I said. "Tell them I wasn't feeling well, so I went home."

I stood up. I should not have worn high heels. Why the fuck did I ever wear them? Bad for the back and if I had to run for my life . . . well, I wouldn't be able to.

"Fourth floor," she said.

The waitress walked with me to the elevator.

"My little boy died," I said.

I could hear myself and I couldn't seem to stop myself.

"I'm so sorry," she said. She put her arm around my shoulders.

"No, it's okay," I said. "It's been almost ten years. He'd be ten this month if he'd lived."

"Still," she said. "It hurts. My brother has been gone for twelve years and I still miss him."

"Did he get to grow up?" I asked.

She shook her head.

"Ah, so you understand," I said. "They never got to grow up. They never got to figure out if they were sinners or saints. Carpenters or preachers. Bellmen or bell-weathermen."

The elevator door opened. The waitress leaned in and pushed the "four" button. Then she stepped out. I think she had tears in her eyes. The doors shut.

"Fourth, fourth, fourth," I said. I looked at the keycard. It was difficult to read. Lucky this hotel wrote the room number on the little envelope they put the keycard in.

The elevator doors opened. I felt like I was going to throw up. I could barely walk.

"I need a fucking drink," I said.

I walked down the hallway.

It was a long hallway.

I thought I saw a rabbit running down it.

Or was that a man coming toward me?

Oh fuck. He was going to rob me.

No. He had white hair. And a beard and mustache. How many white-haired robbers were there?

"Brooke? Is that you?"

I recognized the voice. Could barely see his face.

"Greg," I said. I slapped his chest with my hand. "Greg Douglas as I live and burn. How are you? I am not fine. My lunch, liquid as it was, did not agree with me. I had lobster, too, or some kind of thing that is not happy in my stomach." I laughed. "But I can't find my room. What are you doing here?"

"Your room is right down here," he said.

He put his arm around my waist and walked with me down the hall. Then he took the keycard and opened the door. At least that was what I thought happened. I didn't really know. I went into the bathroom and threw up. That felt better. Somehow I got into bed, got all the way under the covers, and I fell to sleep.

Either that or I blacked out.

SEVEN

I woke up with a throbbing headache. The blinds were closed, but I could tell it was still daylight. I threw off the covers and sat up.

I heard someone talking in the other room.

I got out of bed, straightened my dress, ran my fingers through my hair, and then walked into the other room.

Greg Douglas was standing in the middle of the room talking on the phone. He waved at me and smiled. He was still as beautiful as he had been when I had last seen him—nine years ago? He and his wife Lizzie had attended the same grief counseling group for parents that Hayword and I attended for a while. Greg and I often pretended to go out for a smoke, and then we'd sit in the courtyard talking. Sometimes we shared a drink from a flask one of us had. We hadn't seen each other often, but I had always thought he was a good guy, a strong guy. He could sift through bullshit and see the truth, something Hayword was not very good at, as far as I was concerned.

Lizzie and Greg had always seemed like normal people even though they were in the business. She did editing, and he was a cameraman. They never talked about work. The four of us had gone out for coffee a couple times after the group. I don't remember what we talked about, but it wasn't about the biz.

Maybe we talked about our children, dead and alive.

Lizzie had the saddest smile.

I had never taken Greg to the love nest.

Of course, back then, I didn't have the love nest.

Too bad.

But then again, he was married.

I did not dabble in married men.

I went back into the bedroom. I got my purse and went into the bathroom. I brushed my hair, dabbed my eyes. Looked in the mirror.

I wasn't drunk any more, but I was still a bit high.

What a scene I must have made.

I hoped Hayword never found out.

I went into the other room.

Greg hung up the hotel phone.

"I ordered some seltzer," he said. "And soup. Crackers."

I sat in one of the chairs. He sat opposite of me.

"My hero," I said. "I always suspected you were a knight in shining armor."

He laughed.

"It's good to see you," he said.

"Yeah, well, I'm sorry you had to see me this way," I said. "It was stupid. I was in the car with a bunch of women and one of them was talking about someone whose baby had died and she was so stupid and ignorant and I wanted to punch her or kill her or crash the car. Something. Instead, I sat there and drank."

He nodded. "I know. Sometimes something little sends me into a tailspin. I still miss him so much."

I pulled my feet up underneath me. "There's no one I can talk to about it. I went to rehab for a while and they said I had trouble because of Alberto's death and I thought that was so stupid. They didn't understand. I'm not having *trouble* because he died. I am a completely different person because he died. And I won't be the person I was before because I stop drinking. Because he'll still be dead."

Greg nodded. "I hear ya."

"How's Lizzie doing?" I asked.

He shook his head. "I don't know. We don't talk any more. We divorced about eight years ago."

"I'm sorry," I said.

"No, it was good. She remarried and had a couple more kids. I've got Suzanne, you know, from my first marriage. But Leonard was Lizzie's only child. She wasn't going to get any more from me. So it worked out. How's Hayword and the kids?"

"Hayword's still Hayword," I said. "No different. David will be a teen soon. I dread that. Fern is grown and in college, getting her master's degree in psychology. She still is not very fond of me."

Greg laughed. "Mothers and daughters," he said. "That's always a tricky thing. I bet David adores you."

"David is a good kid," I said. "He's older than his years in some ways and younger in other ways."

Greg nodded. "Yep. Suzanne still likes her dad, but we don't see each other often. She's living in Chicago now."

"Is that where you moved after you left here?" I asked.

"No, we went to New York for a while," he said. "Then we divorced and Lizzie came back here. I can get more work out here so I came back, too. It's only been a couple of years." He shrugged. "I'm getting used to it again. Kind of isolating. I don't always notice."

I laughed. Maybe I giggled.

I had an instant crush on this man.

Maybe I had had a crush all of those years ago. Most of the time I didn't like people to know about Alberto. Well, I didn't want them to know he was dead. They looked at me differently after they knew. Treated me differently. But Greg had always known. And I had always known about his loss. And how he took it. It wasn't good what had happened to his son, but he wasn't going to let it ruin his life. It didn't make him better or more saintly if it ruined his life.

Shit happens and you move on.

That was my motto, too.

I was sure it was my motto.

I rubbed my face.

At least I wanted that to be my motto.

I had moved on. My life was completely different from before Alberto died.

Completely.

Almost completely different.

"Gawd, I want a drink," I said.

Someone knocked on the door. Greg got up and answered it. I didn't even watch him go. I let him take care of it. How refreshing. Hayword was always asking me what he should do. Always asking me what I wanted.

Don't ask me! Just fucking do it!

Only make certain it's what I want you to do.

I heard the door shut. Greg came back into the living room. He set a tray on the table in front of me. On it was a plate of crackers, butter, grapes. A bowl of soup. And a glass of bubbly.

Bubbly seltzer.

Greg sat across from me again.

I took a sip of the seltzer. Then I got a cracker and chewed on it.

"Dig in," I said.

"I'm good," he said.

I laughed. I wasn't even sure why it was funny.

"Man, it's great to see you," I said. "I feel like I've been in a cage, and now I see you and the cage feels open. I'm not even sure why."

"We come from the same clan," he said. "We bear the same scars. So we know each other. We don't need words."

I felt like I was going to cry.

But I didn't.

"How long was I asleep?" I asked.

"A few hours," he said. "I went downstairs and had lunch and came back up and you were still sleeping. I decided to stay and make sure you're all right."

"You don't have to stay now," I said. "I'm okay."

He smiled. "You don't seem okay. You got an anniversary coming up?"

I nodded. "Alberto's birthday. I don't know why every year it's such a surprise to me." I sighed. "I better call home. They're going to be worried about me."

"He nodded and stood up.

"Don't go," I said. "I'll call in the other room. I'll be right back."

"All right," he said.

I got up and went into the bedroom. I pulled my phone from my purse.

Damn. About twenty messages and texts. I didn't listen to or read them. I called Hayword.

"Where are you?" he answered. "I've been worried sick."

"I'm sorry," I said. "I wasn't feeling well so I got a hotel room here."

"Joan and Katie said you disappeared," he said.

"Yeah, well, I'm fine," I said. "Are you still in the city? I need a ride home."

"No," he said. "I came home early. Thought I'd take you all out for pizza."

"You go ahead," I said. "Take Eartha, too."

"She's already started dinner," he said. "She's amazing. Hardly spent any money and she's making this feast for us. You want me to call a car for you?"

"No," I said. "I'll call in a bit." I started to tell him that I'd run into Greg Douglas. It was on the tip of my tongue. But then I didn't. Not sure why.

Not sure why I wanted to tell him in the first place.

"You really all right?" Hayword asked. "They said you were a little . . . tipsy."

Goddamn women. Bet it was Katie. Laying the groundwork to fuck my husband.

"I'm fine," I said. "I'll be home in a while."

"You're not spending the night there are you?"

He knew I wouldn't do that. David got a little upset if I didn't come home every night. We thought my stint at rehab would have cured him of it, but it hadn't. We'd taken him to therapists. They hadn't been sure what was going on. David didn't care if Hayword was gone. But I had to spend the night at home.

"No," I said. "I'll be home. Have a good dinner."

I went back into the living room. Greg looked up as I came into the room. He smiled.

I couldn't get over how beautiful he was.

I couldn't see any scars.

I sat across from him again. We talked for a while. He told me about the first baseball game Leonard had played. Talked about all the hours they had spent together practicing because Leonard was so nervous about playing in front of people.

For some reason, it wasn't painful listening to him. Even when he talked about the day Leonard died. And then I was talking about Alberto. About how different he had been from both of my other children. Fern had growled coming out of my womb. David was colicky and he cried a lot.

Alberto cooed. Seemed so happy. Blissful. I liked sitting in the room with him. Being in the room with him.

He was such a happy baby that I never felt guilty when I left him. Like when Hayword and I went out for dinner. David had always cried when we went away, and babysitters hated that.

Alberto was happy when we left and happy when we came home. Fern was twelve years old, so we let her babysit him and David. She insisted she was old enough. We were certain she was right.

When we came home that night, Alberto was fine. In the morning, he was no longer alive.

Fern screamed so long and so loud that her father slapped her. He was afraid she was going to pass out.

David was too young to understand. He was less than two years older than his brother. But he cried.

I didn't remember what I did or said. Did I cry? Did I curl up into a ball?

We tried to resuscitate Alberto. Hayword called 911, and they told him how to do CPR on an infant.

Greg listened to all of this and nodded.

At the grief group, they had wanted us to talk. But it was excruciating. I didn't want to relive the most horrible thing that had ever happened to us. Some of the people kept telling the stories of their children's deaths over and over.

At least it seemed that way.

It didn't help me to hear what they said. It seemed like every week I learned new, surprising, and horrible ways that children could die. I'd hurry home and examine my children for signs of anything untoward.

I didn't go to the grief group very often. Hayword went for a while.

We sent Fern to a therapist for a time. She blamed herself because she had been babysitting him.

I told her, "He was fine when we got home. You didn't have anything to do with it. He just died."

She screamed, "It's all your fault! You should have known I couldn't handle it!"

I nodded. Of course it was my fault. In Fern's mind, everything was my fault.

Where had I gone wrong?

I said all of this out loud to Greg.

"Lizzie thought it was my fault," he said. "She even said it was my fault a couple of times when we were fighting. She is pretty religious. She thought God punished us when we didn't behave. I said if God killed children because their parents did something wrong, then he was an asshole."

"Exactly!" I said. "I remember hearing something on talk radio soon after Alberto died. This man's son had died, and the talk show host told the man he should consider what sins he had committed and he should repent so god would forgive him. I started swearing at the radio. 'Fuck you, god! Fuck you, god!' I thought if I'm being punished for some supposed sin to get me to change my ways, it wasn't going to work. I was going to do whatever I wanted to do. No invisible being in the sky was going to force me to live a certain way."

"That's right."

"Of course I heard this radio thing a few months after the house had burned down. So I had been starting to wonder what the hell was going on. First my son dies and then my house burns down. The house burning down didn't compare. In fact, I hardly noticed it. It was a good excuse to move. But my family was traumatized. Fern asked me what we were being punished for. I don't know where she got that. We never took them to church, so guilt must be in the air."

"That's tough," he said. "When did that happen?"

"A few months after you left," I said. "It was all the talk of Brentwood. The house could have been salvaged. In fact the insurance company wanted to rebuild. Our lawyers worked some magic so that we could leave. It was amazingly freeing to leave the house and almost everything we owned and move away from the city. I really thought my life was going to change."

"And did it?" he asked.

"Sure," I said. "In some ways."

I looked at him. I wanted to tell him everything.

And nothing.

He knew my son had died, but that was not a stain on me. That wasn't anything horrible I had done. It was something awful that had happened to my son and to my family.

All the other stuff, well, that was all on me.

I looked at this man and I wanted to be in his arms. I knew he could comfort me. I was absolutely certain of it. He knew. He understood.

He was separate from me. I looked at him and didn't feel like I had to take care of him.

I didn't feel as though I had to take care of any of the people I brought to the love nest either. Oh crap. Now *I* was thinking of it as the love nest. If I started to feel responsible for my lovers or how they felt, then I ended it. I imagined I would never have to worry about Greg Douglas, yet he would take care of me.

Not that I needed anyone to take care of me.

But wouldn't that be nice? For an instant. A day. A week.

I had been responsible for the care and feeding of Hayword

and my family since I was . . . a child, really. And I had failed so miserably. I had failed in the worst way possible: One of my children had died.

But Greg Douglas knew.

He knew it wasn't my fault.

I sighed and leaned back in the chair.

What was wrong with me?

I wanted to keep this man. I wanted to walk into the bedroom and be in his arms. Have him tell me it was going to be all right.

Suddenly I felt dizzy. The room seemed to be trembling.

I glanced at the curtains. They were moving. That meant it wasn't me: It was an earthquake.

I heard rattling. Things falling.

Greg and I both stood. That didn't help. The hotel was swaying. I tried to remember what I was supposed to do in case of an earthquake. I'd been through enough of them in the twenty years or so I'd lived in California. I should remember.

I bet David remembered.

Greg grabbed my arm and took me to the table behind the couch, near the bar. We got underneath it.

"I'm not sure this is sturdy enough," Greg said. "But it'll have to do."

We were so close to each other that I could smell him.

Funny, I didn't want to fuck him. I wanted to smell him. I liked being this close and smelling his smell.

Hadn't there been a time when I had felt that way about Hayword?

Goddamn it. I was tired of Hayword popping into my brain.

The swaying stopped. We slowly got up from underneath the table.

The lights were off.

I looked around the room.

Didn't look like much damage.

"5.4 I'd guess," Greg said.

"That was a 6.0 I bet."

I picked up the phone. No dial tone.

We went to the window, Greg opened the blinds, and we looked down at the street. Cars were stopped out front. I saw broken glass on the sidewalk. The street looked like it had buckled a bit. I had never seen that before. I heard car horns blaring. In the distance, I heard sirens.

"I better call home," I said.

I got my cell phone. No service.

I felt a little panicky. I needed to know everyone was all right. I couldn't be off someplace drunk, with a strange man, and find out someone in my family was hurt. I didn't think even I could come back from that.

"Greg, I want to go downstairs to see if I can get service," I said.

Greg took out his phone. "Mine's working," he said. He handed it to me.

I couldn't remember anyone's phone number. Except the house phone.

I tried that. The phone rang.

Eartha answered.

"Is everyone all right?" I asked. "Did you feel it there?"

"Yes, we're all fine," she said. "I think. Hayword slipped coming down the stairs."

"I'm fine!" I heard Hayword's voice in the background.

"Here's David," Eartha said.

"Mom!" David. "It was so cool. I knew exactly what to do. The wind was really howling. Did you notice? Just before."

The Santa Ana winds no doubt. They'd been off and on for weeks. Driving some people crazy. I had hardly noticed them.

"And then the ground was shaking," he said. "I thought a

tree had fallen on the house. I told everyone to get under the kitchen table."

"Everyone as in Dad and Eartha?"

"Yep," he said. "Dad slipped on the bottom step, but he's okay. You gonna be here soon?"

"It'll probably be late," I said. "I don't know if I can get a car."

"Okay," David said. He didn't even sound afraid. "Love you!"

He must have handed the phone to his father.

"Hi, Brooke," Hayword said. "You all right."

"Yep," I said. "You hurt your foot?"

"I twisted my ankle a bit coming down the stairs. It's starting to swell. It's my right leg. I don't think I can drive to come get you. Should I ask Eartha?"

"No," I said. "I wouldn't send a newbie to downtown Los Angeles after an earthquake. I'll try to get a limo."

"I don't know if they'll come out this far," he said.

"I'll figure out something," I said. "Keep in touch."

I handed the phone back to Greg.

"I wonder if the electricity is out all over town," Greg said. "I've got to be on the job in about an hour. Maybe I'll have the night off. Well, maybe not." He looked down at his phone. "Nope. Studio is fine." He looked up at me. "I guess I better get going. You all right? You have a way home?"

"Sure," I said. "I'm fine."

"What were you doing here anyway?" he asked. "Not that it's any of my business."

I smiled. "We're organizing the Benefit here on Saturday," I said. "Tying up loose ends while tying one on."

He smiled. "You always were very funny." He said it, but he was not laughing.

"I've got a ticket to that benefit," he said.

"Oh good," I said. "So I'll see you on Saturday?"

"I wasn't actually going to come," he said. "But maybe I will now."

I felt a nice little tickle in my stomach over this news.

"Good," I said.

I got my purse and the two of us went into the hallway—dark except for the emergency lights. We walked down the stairs together until we got to the lobby. People were milling around, inside and outside of the hotel.

Greg and I embraced. I wanted to keep a hold of him, but I let him go. I watched him walk away.

I felt like I had finally met the man of my dreams.

Or gotten reacquainted with the man of my dreams.

I went to the desk and asked if they could call me a limo to take me home, or a taxi, anything with wheels. The man at the desk said he doubted he could get anything, but he'd try.

It was almost dark outside.

I heard a click as the electricity came back on. People cheered.

I wished I could go back upstairs to bed.

They tried to get a car for me. I called Hayword, and he tried to get a car for me. I tried to get a car for me.

Nobody could come.

"This is Los Angeles, for chrissakes," I said. "We know earthquakes."

"David's getting a little nervous," Hayword said. "He doesn't think you'll be able to get home. The winds have whipped up one of the fires, by the way. He's worried it's going to get all the way here."

"Will it?" I asked.

"I doubt it," Hayword said. "The closest one is two canyons away, I think."

"Let me try to figure something out," I said. "I'll call later."

Crap, crap, crap.

I paced the lobby. How was I going to get home?

Got a text. "You okay?" Mark.

"Stuck at the Shilton," I texted back. "No car." This was the last time I went anywhere without my own damn car.

"Be there in thirty."

"No. I'll be fine."

"What about David?"

Shit. Had I told Mark about having to be home for David? I thought I never told him anything. Yesterday being the exception, of course.

"On my way," he texted.

I went to the restaurant and asked for a sandwich. The electricity hadn't been out long enough to put my life in jeopardy by eating any of their food, plus I thought it was a good idea. I'd thrown up everything I'd eaten for lunch. Time to fill up again.

I took the sandwich up to my room. Ate it. Then washed up. Tried to make myself look like I wasn't the whore of Babylon.

I looked at myself in the mirror.

"Well, maybe the older sister of the whore of Babylon."

Oh, who was I kidding? I looked like a two-dollar hooker.

If there was such a thing.

Or I would be if I were any place besides Los Angeles or New York.

Or Mexico City.

Or . . . shut up!

I went downstairs to the lobby. I felt too tarted up.

What the fuck was wrong with me? I was seldom embarrassed about anything.

That was my fucking charm.

People in the lobby were talking about the earthquake. I could still hear sirens outside. Wondered if anyone was hurt.

They had the news on in the bar. A dozen or more people stood watching.

I went outside.

It was now night.

A few minutes later a blue electric or hybrid car drove up to the hotel. I heard a honk. I looked around. Then looked down.

It was Mark.

I walked over to the blue car, opened the door, and got in.

"Did you have any trouble?" I asked.

He quickly pulled away from the curb.

"Traffic is a nightmare," he said. "But I can get us through it."

"Thanks, Mark," I said. "You're a lifesaver."

I glanced at him. He looked good, as usual. Dressed in jeans and a shirt.

"Were you out?" I asked. "You look nice."

"Went over to a friend's house," he said. "For dinner."

"Did you already eat?" I asked. "It's barely six."

He didn't say anything.

"Did you blow off dinner on my account?" I asked. "Christ, Mark. Why would you do that?"

"It was a set-up," he said. "They had some women they wanted me to meet. Or woman. Supposed to be a dinner party, but it was mostly my two friends and a bunch of women and myself. I was glad to get out of there."

I laughed. "Oh shit, Mark. Your friends are going to be pissed."

"I have the earthquake as an excuse," he said. "Everyone needs a plumber after an earthquake. How was your day?"

I laughed. "You have no idea." I started to tell him about Greg. And then I realized he wasn't my goddamn girlfriend. He was my fucking partner. My lover. I shouldn't be telling him about my knight in shining armor. Or whatever Greg Douglas was.

"Did you like any of the women?" I asked.

I didn't pay attention to where he was going or what he was doing. I only knew we weren't stopping, which was good. If he saw a flashing light or a traffic slow-up, he made a U-turn or went down another street.

I enjoyed competent men.

"Sure," he said. "They all seemed nice. I've never had trouble finding women, Brooke. I'm not looking for anyone else. I'm happy with you."

I made a noise. "How is that even possible?" Oops. There I was. Speaking my thoughts out loud again. "Oh, wait, I know. You're not really interested in a long term relationship either."

"No, that's not it," he said.

"You knew I wasn't available from the very start," I said. "We talked about it. You said that was fine with you."

"I know," he said. "I'm still fine with it. *You* keep bringing it up."

"I do?" I looked out the window. Really? "Why did you call me, you know, last February? I mean, you said you've never gone after a married woman before. But you called me. You asked me if we could see each other. Why?"

Usually I was forward with the men or women I wanted. But I hadn't said anything to Mark. I hadn't thought about him that way. I mean, he had worked in my house. It seemed tacky to lust after the handyman.

Although I did love handy men.

Oh gawd.

"It was the way you looked at me when we talked," he said. "You listened to me. You seemed to respect my opinion. You didn't treat me like the help or like someone you wanted to fuck. That's usually what I encounter: People who don't really see me, or people who want to get something from me, either a deal—money wise—or sex. You didn't do any of that. You seemed so real. And then I saw you with your husband and something changed in you. You were a completely different person. I didn't want that person. I wanted the person you were when you were with me."

"And which person did you get?"

He didn't say anything for a moment. Then he said, "A little of both. Except some days I get a lot of you. Like yesterday."

"Too much blathering on yesterday," I said.

"So did you have a good day?" he asked. "At your meeting for the Benefit?"

He knew my schedule?

"What, are you my stalker? How'd you know about that?"

He laughed. "You told me," he said. "You tell me things. I pay attention."

"Well, stop it," I said. "The meeting was horrible. And things have started to bother me." I shook my head. "Must be the Santa Anas, or the fires, or the earthquake. Or the stupid zombie movie. They've conned me into rewriting a zombie movie. A fucking zombie movie. Can you imagine? They want me to make it sexy."

Mark laughed. "A zombie movie? Never saw a zombie anyone would want to have sex with."

"That's what I said! For some reason I agreed to do it. Hayword seems to have his heart set on it. Thinks it'll change the world."

Mark glanced at me.

"Yes, he's fucking delusional," I said.

"Maybe you could make it fun," he said. "Or funny."

"I never wanted this life," I said.

"What?"

We were on the freeway now. It was pretty jammed up.

"You never wanted to write scripts?" he asked.

"I never wanted the Hollywood life," I said. "I don't know how it happened. I guess I let it. Everybody says they want to be rich and famous: I never did. I don't mind the writing part. Just all the other stuff. I mean, who the fuck is real here? What is real here? I can't tell. Sometimes I feel like I'm living a really bad movie. Or a really good one. I'm not sure."

"What kind of life did you want to live?" he asked.

I shrugged. "I don't know," I said. "I wanted Hayword and me to be happy. Maybe run a regional theater. I wanted us raise our children. Have nothing bad happen. I've never been extraordinary, and you have to be extraordinary out here or else you disappear. I feel like I've disappeared." I closed my eyes and leaned back against the car seat. "Maybe have a little bar or restaurant or something, by the beach. People I love coming and going. People I'm comfortable with. I'm never comfortable, Mark. Everyone and everything makes me nervous. What about you? You wanted to be a chef?"

"I wanted a family," he said. "I figured we'd each have our jobs—my wife and I—but the primary focus would be our family. I knew pretty early on I wasn't going to be a chef. A cook maybe, but not a chef. But even that would have been difficult. I'm good at what I do now. People need my services. I can pay my bills. That feels nice. Worrying about a restaurant? Naw, I don't think so. Not unless it was really easygoing."

I glanced over at him. "Maybe I should let you cook for me. I don't give a shit about food, you know. Although lately Eartha has been making some really good dishes."

"Who is this Eartha, anyway?"

"She's the homeless person Hayword let move into our garden house," I said. "So far it's been going all right. Why'd you and your wife break up anyway?"

"It doesn't matter," he said. "We didn't work out."

"Come on," I said. "I've spilled my guts to you."

"She was cheating on me," he said. "And she fell in love with the guy."

"Did you ever cheat on her?" I asked.

"No, never," he said. "I've always been a monogamous guy."

"You shouldn't waste your monogamy on me," I said. "If you knew who I really was, if you knew all the things I'd done, you wouldn't want to have anything to do with me."

"I know who you really are," he said.

I shook my head and looked out the window. Then I closed my eyes and leaned back again.

I opened my eyes when Mark stopped the car. I looked around. I was home. I must have fallen asleep.

"Thank you," I said to him. "Do you want the key to the studio? You could sleep there. I could come by tomorrow."

"No, thanks," he said. "I've got a job in the morning. I'll see you Monday."

"You okay?" I asked. I felt like I should say something. "Was your mom's place okay in the earthquake? Your son's?"

He nodded. "Everyone's fine. Go on in and be with your family."

I looked at the house. The car rocked a little from the wind. I leaned toward him to kiss him. He put his hand on my arm.

"No," he said. "You better not."

I looked at him. What had happened? Something had changed.

"What's wrong?" I asked.

He shook his head. "Nothing," he said. "We'll talk about it later. Go on."

"Fuck 'em and leave 'em," I said. "That's your MO. I understand. I'll see you later."

He smiled. But he was not laughing.

I got out of the car and went into the house. Eartha, David, and Hayword sat at the kitchen table playing Scrabble. David looked relieved when he saw me: His whole body relaxed.

"Hi, Mom. You wanna play Scrabble?"

I wanted to say no. I wanted to go to sleep. Hide under the covers. Run away. Go away. Do away.

But I went to the table and sat next to Eartha. She smiled. Then she put her arm across my shoulder, as a way to welcome me, I supposed. It was gentle, it was quick, but not too quick. I leaned into it, although I doubted she noticed. It was exactly what I needed at that moment. A human touch. A human touch from someone I hadn't fucked, disappointed, screwed over, or otherwise harmed.

Now that was her one great thing for the day.

EIGHT

We felt a couple of aftershocks during the night but nothing major.

In the morning, Hayword's ankle wasn't any better. I suggested he go in for an X-ray.

"I'll drive you," I said. Once again I was up at the crack of dawn.

"No," he said. "I want you to read the script."

"I can read it in the doctor's office."

"Go to your studio," he said. "Or stay here. I don't care. Get takeout. Make a day of it. I want you to be able to concentrate. Eartha can take me. Then she can drive me to work. I won't stay long and she'll get to tool around town. She said she wanted to check out some places."

I shrugged. "Hey, trying to do my wifely duty. I really have no desire to sit in a doctor's office with you."

"I knew that," he said. "You didn't need to say that out loud."

"Didn't know I did."

After the three of them left and the house was empty, except for me, I went upstairs into my office. I stood and looked around. It seemed cold, unused, stuffy. I opened the window. It was too chilly out. I closed it again. Then I picked up the manuscript.

"*Zombie Town,*" I said out loud as I looked down at the first page. I shook my head.

I tucked the script under my arm, went out to the car, and drove to my bungalow.

The house seemed different today. Felt lived in. I could still smell Mark. Or the two of us. I went into the bedroom. The bed was still unmade. Guess the cleaning lady hadn't been in yet.

I straightened the sheets and covers. Then I went to the kitchen and opened the patio door a bit. I sat at the table and started to read *Zombie Town.*

It went quicker than I thought it would. I groaned but not as much as I thought I would. The zombies were actually aliens from another planet. They had destroyed their own environment which had let loose a plague that caused the people of that planet to become the living dead with an insatiable desire to feast on human blood. Well, first they wanted to feast on each other's blood, but they soon ran out of candidates, so before someone was the last person on that planet, they decided to invade another planet: Earth.

A band of heroes—made up of men and women of different ethnicities—tried to save Earth from the zombies. In the end they succeeded in blowing up the zombie ship, but more ships were on their way.

Boys would like this movie. Lots of shit blowing up. Lots of aliens eating people. Good times.

How was I going to make this movie sexy?

I put the script down. I looked at my phone. Maybe if I had some sex, I could make it sexy.

I started to text Mark. Then I threw the phone across the room because I knew I would be too lazy to get up and get it.

I was not calling him. I should be thinking of ways to break up with him, not get him to come over. I had every intention of hooking up with Greg Douglas at the Benefit tomorrow. I rarely kept two lovers (and a husband) at the same time. That was too much juggling even for me, so I would have to get rid of Mark. Or never start with Greg.

And he seemed too perfect to resist.

I thought about calling Sally St. James. Not to have sex with her but to ask what her ideas were for sexing up the script.

No. I wouldn't do that either. She'd have me smoking her cigarettes for her again.

I opened my laptop and got the "Zombie Town" file Hayword had e-mailed me. I stared at the screen.

How could I get people to care about zombies?

Someone in the movie would have to care about zombies.

Someone cute would have to care about a cute zombie.

There were no cute zombies.

Beauty was in the eye of the beholder.

Remember *Beauty and the Beast.*

I selected "Zombie Town" on the title page and began typing over it: "Beauty and the Zombie."

I leaned back in the chair.

Maybe the aliens who come to Earth have a plague which distorts their looks so they look like the undead to humans. Humans are afraid of them—they are afraid of catching the zombie plague. But the zombies also look like humans, except they have the plague, so they are probably some kind of human cousin.

The zombies could come in teeth blazing to eat everyone or

they could do it the American way: Hire (or acquire) a good PR person. Or have an attractive zombie leader.

I looked around the room. What could his name be? I glanced at an old newspaper on the coffee table. The lead story was written by a Dennis Thomas.

Thomas. That was a good normal name for an alien. He's got the plague, but he's a good-looking *normal* guy.

How could a character be undead and still be good-looking?

I remembered Melissa mentioning yesterday at lunch that there was some kind of skin disease plaguing the migrant workers.

"That can't be real," I said. "Just more anti-immigrant bullshit."

I googled "skin disease migrants." Scanned the list of articles popping up. Clicked on one.

"You're kidding," I said. Melissa hadn't been completely wrong. There was some kind of peculiar skin disease that was considered contagious and a bit disfiguring. The CDC hadn't figured out what was causing it yet or how to stop it. It was more prevalent in the migrant populations and amongst the poor.

I shook my head. Truth was always stranger than fiction.

"The zombies have a mysterious skin disease," I said. "That'll work."

I got up and opened the living room curtains. I rarely did that. It was such a beautiful day, though. I wanted the light. The sky was blue. I saw no signs of the fires. I could see the trees outside moving to the wind, but it didn't seem too wicked. A nice breeze came through the partially open patio door.

I almost felt peaceful. Again. Third time in so many days.

I typed up my ideas so far.

What next?

What would Thomas, the alien leader, do? He's a smart good-looking alien. He decides to find a scientist sympathetic to his cause. Instead of saying "take me to your leader," he says, "take me to your leading exobiologist." They take him to a group of scientists and he notices a female scientist who seems a little shy, a little out of place.

I smiled. Okay. Now I had a love story.

What could her name be?

I knew immediately. Colleen. I liked the name. It was a good Irish name. It would go with McMurphy. I remembered Colleen McMurphy from the TV show *China Beach.* She'd been a nurse in Vietnam. She was always falling in love with the wrong guy. She was strong and fucked up. Always admired her.

I thought about typing in Colleen McMurphy.

I shook my head. No, then I'd keep seeing my Colleen as the *China Beach* Colleen—Dana Delany. My Colleen had light brown hair. She might even be blond. Wears glasses. Doesn't care about makeup or clothes. She cares about saving the world and protecting it from Menace with a capital "M."

I laughed.

Wouldn't it be great to actually be able to protect the world—or anyone—from Menace with a capital "M."

Colleen Kelly. That was her name. She didn't drink. She didn't go out with bad men. She was sensible and smart.

I started typing as I was thinking. "Colleen and Thomas hit it off right away. She's suspicious of him, but he assures her the zombie aliens have come to Earth in peace. After a while, the audience won't notice his skin disease—his zombie disease. He's so kind to Colleen. He encourages her to take blood and tissue samples from him and any of his fellow aliens. She'll discover they are not contagious.

"'There are some bad aliens,' Thomas tells Colleen. Those are the ones where the plague has gone to their brains and they can't help themselves. 'I thought Earthlings were compassionate,' he says. 'But your people keep killing us. It is a sickness we have. We've come to this planet for your wisdom, so that we can learn to take care of our planet better, to follow your lead.'"

I laughed and shook my head. "Poor girl. She doesn't have a chance."

I continued typing.

"Colleen and Thomas spend a great deal of time together. All of her tests indicate that the zombie plague is not transferable from the aliens to the humans. Colleen falls in love with Thomas. They make passionate love. She defends the zombie aliens to anyone who will listen. She cites scientific proof that they are harmless. She kisses Thomas on camera.

"Soon zombies are popular all over the planet. Celebrities are seen with their favorite zombie alien. They're all the rage.

"Then one morning Colleen wakes up and her skin has started to change. Soon there is no denying it: She has the plague and so do many others. She is a pariah amongst her colleagues— and all around the world. She's called the zombie traitor. She realizes Thomas duped her. She should have never trusted him. She asks him why he did this to her. He says he knew that with her help they could spread the plague all over the planet. Unlike the aliens, humans could pass on the plague by touch or through the air, and the plague was terminal for them. He laughs and says she was so easy and so stupid.

"Colleen is devastated. She has to hide from everyone. She works tirelessly to find a cure for the human zombies. Colleen becomes a zombie in looks, but she has no desire to eat human flesh. Only the humans who get it from humans eat other humans. Since she got the plague from Thomas, she has no thirst for human blood or appetite for human brains."

I laughed. It was almost fun to be so ridiculous.

"Human brains. Hah!"

I glanced out the window. Some guy in a dirty business suit

was walking by. If he'd held his arms out straight, he'd have the zombie look down.

I stared at my screen and started typing again.

"While the human zombies devour one another, the zombie aliens begin taking over planet Earth. They are using up the planet's resources faster than humans have been. The weather changes drastically. The air and water are choked with pollution. Colleen finds another scientist and they go on the run."

I looked around the room. What would the other scientist's name be? I could name her after Melissa who told me about the zombie skin condition. No. I wouldn't want her to think I was honoring her. Marissa. She'd have the zombie plague, too, but she got it from an alien so she doesn't want to eat people either. Or maybe she does. Probably the studio will want to change her to a man so the man and Colleen can have heterosexual sex. And then he can try to eat her. Her brains, that is. And Colleen would have to kill him. I shrugged. If they asked us to do that, maybe I would.

Although in the end, the studio would have the final say anyway.

I typed, "Colleen and Marissa run from the aliens and the human zombies. Eventually they stop trying to find an antidote. They're too ill. They're not willing to be captured or eaten, so they decide they'll drive over the Grand Canyon, homage *Thelma and Louise*. Just before they go over the cliff, they stop the car. Colleen wants to watch the sun come up one more time."

I stopped. I suddenly remembered when I was a kid I used to like getting up at sunrise. I'd go outside and watch the world change from gray to gold, watch the sun light sparkle on the dew on the grass. It was so quiet, except for the bird songs and my own breathing. Me breathing with the world. And I'd walk on the damp grass, barefoot, let the dew and the grass tickle my feet while the sun warmed my face. It was utterly peaceful.

I continued typing. "Colleen wants to feel the earth beneath her bare feet like she used to do when she was a kid, one more time. Both women take off their shoes and feel the dirt under their soles. They watch the sun come up, even though the light hurts their eyes. This connection with the earth and the light of the sun at the same time causes a chemical reaction in their bodies which instantly kills the plague."

I laughed. It was a little deus ex machina, but the simple and easy solutions were often the best solutions. In *The Day of the Triffids,* water killed the human-devouring plants. In *War of the Worlds,* it was a human virus. In *The Blob,* it was the cold.

"Colleen and Marissa are cured," I wrote. "They send out messages via short wave radio to people all over the world. Soon all the humans are cured. And because the zombie aliens can't stand the light, the humans have an advantage. The aliens are soon all killed or incarcerated. Colleen gets to watch Thomas hauled off to indefinite detention in chains. She shouts after him, 'I never loved you.' When he's out of earshot, he whispers, 'I wish I never loved you.' The last shot of the movie is of Colleen watching another sunrise. We see her back, first, and then the camera pans around to her front, where the audience sees that she is very pregnant—and she looks very afraid. The End."

I smiled. Sally St. James would love the last shot of *Beauty and the Zombie.*

"Always leave an opening for a sequel," I said.

I saved the document, wrote a quick e-mail to Hayword and Sally, and then I sent it off. If they liked it, I'd write the dialogue. Or maybe Hayword and I would write the dialogue. Just like old times.

I suddenly felt chilled. I got up and closed and locked the patio door. Then I pulled the living room drapes together.

I wished I had gotten Greg Douglas's number yesterday. I wanted to talk to him again.

Excitement was a red flag, I reminded myself. This had happened before and it wasn't good.

I looked at my phone. Joan had texted me. "You okay? Didn't you say Violeta was visiting her mom in Mex? Saw her yesterday in L.A. as we were leaving."

I texted back, "I'm fine. Couldn't be V. She's in Mex."

Unless she lied to me for some reason.

I called her house.

It rang and rang. No answer. Of course she could be screening her calls.

I tried her cell phone. It went straight to voice mail.

Joan had probably been drunk.

My phone vibrated. I looked at it. Joan again. "Melissa P is such an asshole, BTW. Wanna get dressed together tomorrow? I've got a room at the Shilton."

I laughed. I texted her back. "As long as MP isn't invited. Don't want to see her naked talking on the bluetooth. Horrors."

"You drive. 5ish."

"You bet your ass I'm driving," I texted.

Hayword texted me his ankle was slightly sprained, and he was supposed to keep it elevated for a day. No dancing allowed.

I knew what that meant: I was going to the Benefit alone.

That was absolutely all right with me.

I got takeout at some fast food hovel, ate it quickly in the car, then threw the wrapping out so David wouldn't see any evidence of it. I figured I should set a better example for him, especially now that Eartha was feeding us such healthy and delicious food.

French toast not withstanding.

I picked up David from school. He seemed happy and excited. He told me about his day as I drove him home.

"And Jimmy Kenan is going to the party, too," he said. "He asked if I could spend the night at his house after the party, along with a couple other boys. You're supposed to call his mom. Or Dad can do it."

"I can do it," I said. "Do you want to spend the night?"

"Are you going to be home?" he asked.

"Um, yes," I said, "but you wouldn't be."

"That's all right," he said. "As long as you are."

"David, I wish you'd tell me why I have to be at home every night," I said. "Sometimes it cramps my style."

He shrugged. "I get nervous if you're not."

I sighed. "Well, if you want to spend the night at Jimmy's after the party, it's all right with me. And I'll be home here, too."

"Where would you go if you could spend the night some place else," he said, "without me? Rehab again?"

"No! No rehab. Sometimes when I'm at the art studio, I want to work late and if I'm tired I don't want to drive. Or like tomorrow at the Benefit, we'll be there late, and Joanie has a suite. It might be nice to stay there with her. Have a girl's night out."

He nodded. "Maybe you could try it," he said. "Tomorrow, when I'm gone. We could see how it goes."

"We'll see," I said. "Thanks for the offer."

I pulled into the driveway. Hayword's car was there. David got out of the car and ran into the house. I followed. I wondered if Hayword had read my quick and dirty *Beauty and the Zombie* treatment yet.

"Hayword?" I called as I came into the house.

"In here."

I followed David into the kitchen. Hayword sat at the table with his right leg propped up on a pillow on another chair. Eartha was cutting up something at the counter. The counter seemed to be her sweet spot.

"Thanks for taking Hayword to the doc, Eartha," I said. "That was certainly your one great thing today."

She shook her head. "You always say that before the day is over!"

I heard someone coming down the stairs.

I turned toward the sound as Fern came into the room.

She was frowning. The frown deepened when she saw me.

"Hello, baby," I said.

"Hello, Mom."

I leaned over to kiss her. She moved away. I glanced at Hayword.

"How's your ankle?" I asked Hayword.

"It's fine," Hayword said. "It's great, actually. For one thing it got me out of going to the Benefit tomorrow."

"Maybe I should fall down the stairs, too," I said. "So I can get out of it."

I didn't really want to get out of it. Not if Greg Douglas was going to be there.

"Don't they have free booze there, Mom?" Fern said. She didn't look up from her texting. "I figured you'd be all over that."

My daughter was not actually very clever. Her insults usually lacked wit.

Maybe that was why she pissed me off so much.

"I've got free booze here," I said. "No reason to leave home for that. Plus the Village Boozery delivers."

Eartha smiled as she chopped. Then she said, "There's a snack in the fridge for you, David. Some veggies and hummus. Maybe your mom wants some, too. I've already fed Fern and Hayword."

David went to the fridge and took out the plate. He brought it over to me. We sat on stools at the counter together and shared the food. He leaned up against me a little.

"What brings you to our fair village?" I asked Fern.

"It's my home, isn't it?" Fern asked. "Do I need to call and ask permission ahead of time?"

David glanced at me and rolled his eyes.

"You're welcome here any time," Hayword said. "Fern is attending a demonstration in Los Angeles tomorrow. She thought she'd come hang out with us for the evening and then we could take her into the city when we go to the Benefit. Her car wasn't working. We picked her up at the train station."

"Well," I said, as I chewed on a carrot, *"we* are not going to the benefit tomorrow. *I* am. And I'm going with Joanie. You can catch a ride with us to the hotel. You can take a cab from there."

"What are you demonstrating?" David asked. "Is that like a protest?"

"Yes," Fern said. "We're protesting the unfairness of everything. The rich keep getting richer, and the poor keep getting poorer. There's no equity in this country. Eartha, do you want to come? I bet you've been to lots of protests."

I could hear the underlying message in her words: "You've been to lots of protests, unlike my own parents who never did anything."

I smiled and ate the vegetables.

"I think I'll stick around here tomorrow," Eartha said. "But thank you for the invite."

"Eartha, you need a day off," I said. "Or days off." I realized we had never talked about any of that. We needed to pay her, too.

She shook her head. "No, I'm fine. I've been having so much fun. I want to keep doing what I've been doing, at least for a few more days."

"I don't know why they need you anyway," Fern said. "My mom doesn't do anything except sit around on her ass all day."

The kitchen got very still for a moment.

I glanced at Hayword. He looked furious, but he didn't move or say anything. David looked like he was going to cry.

Eartha put down her knife. "Don't talk so disrespectfully about your mother," she said.

"Well, at least she didn't say I sat on my *fat* ass all day," I said. "Thank you for that, daughter."

I kissed David on the top of his head. Then I picked up my purse and keys, and I walked out of my house.

I wasn't sure if I was ever coming back.

NINE

I drove around for a while. I wished I had a girlfriend I could talk to. Not that I actually wanted to talk. I could go to Joan's and get drunk.

That sounded like fun.

Christ. I hadn't even found out if Hayword liked *Beauty and the Zombie.*

David texted me right away. "Fern is a bitch."

"Don't call your sister that. Don't call any girl or woman that."

"What about boys?"

"Knock yourself out. I might not get home until after you're asleep."

"Knock yourself out."

I laughed. I texted, "Eye love u sew much."

"Sew much," he texted back.

When David was younger and learning to spell, he often got confused by the soundalikes. One year he gave me a Valentine's

Day card that read, "Eye love u sew much, Mom." So we'd been loving each other "sew much" for years.

Soon, no doubt, I wouldn't be able to tell him I loved him at all. I did dread the teen years.

Sometimes it seemed as though children got some kind of plague when they became teens. One day they were normal loving kids, and then suddenly they were monsters.

Maybe monsters was too harsh a word. And then suddenly they were zombie aliens?

Yep, that worked. Because the zombie aliens had agendas, too. Fern always had an agenda. Of course, Fern was no longer a teenager, so there went that theory.

I laughed at myself and drove to the bungalow.

I went inside the house.

It was Friday night and I was going to hide out in this house alone because my daughter was a brat?

Nope.

I pulled out my phone and stared at it.

I needed to break it off with Mark.

I knew I had to. Had to.

He was too serious.

Or maybe I was beginning to see him as part of my life.

I had to break it off.

I went to the fridge and opened it.

Mark's fixings for omelettes were still there.

I sighed. Then I texted him, "I'm at the bungalow. Could use some company. Might break all the eggs if someone doesn't stop me."

I went and sat at the kitchen table.

I got a text.

"I read the treatment." Sally. "Fucking rocks. Sequel potential. So glad I only ever fucked you and never fucked you over. Thanks, kid."

I laughed.

Another text. Hayword.

Shit. I hoped I hadn't sent him Mark's text by mistake.

"Thought the treatment was great," he wrote. "You want to start rewrites tonight?"

I didn't answer him.

I stared at the phone.

Mark wasn't answering me.

I wasn't answering Hayword.

Was this passive aggressive behavior or a pretense that we were civilized?

Another text. Hayword. "She doesn't know how she sounds."

I answered this one. "Someone should tell her." Besides Eartha. "Tell Eartha I said thanks. Be home late."

"Don't drink and drive."

Shut the fuck up.

"Shut the fuck up," I texted.

"Like daughter, like mother."

I made a noise and flung the phone across the room.

"I hate you, you motherfucker!" I screamed.

I sat on the floor and put my head in my hands. I wished I could cry. I wanted to cry. It would be a release, wouldn't it? A fucking release.

I heard a tap on my back door.

I got up and walked toward it.

Mark was standing there.

I smiled and opened the door.

"What took you so long?"

He put his arms around me, and we kissed.

Just like in the movies.

I closed the door.

"What's going on?" he asked.

I shrugged. "How'd you get here so quickly? Please tell me you aren't stalking me."

"I'm not stalking you," he said. "I told you I had a job. I finished. I changed my clothes and I was going to get an early dinner somewhere. You hungry?"

I shook my head.

I was sad. I was fucking sad.

I was mad.

I was hurt.

Shit. I was feeling all those things, and I didn't like it.

"Could you please just fuck me?" I asked.

It was that or I was going to drink myself into a stupor.

He sighed. "All right," he said, taking my hand. "But just this one time."

"Baby, fasten your seat belt," I said. "It's gonna be a long and bumpy ride."

For a few minutes, while we were making love, I felt better.

After, Mark made me an omelette. He told me what he was doing the whole time. Each step. His voice was deep and quiet. Soothing. As though he were telling me a bedtime story.

We sat on the couch together to eat the omelettes. He fed me a piece of his and I fed him pieces of mine. He started talking about farmer's markets he liked to go to, about his garden, about how he liked to dig his fingers into the ground because it felt cool and quiet and necessary. Tears began to stream down my face. I didn't notice them at first. Then Mark wiped them away with the palm of his hand. Then he kissed them. We went to bed and I curled into a ball. He curled up around me. Was I the seashell and he the ocean? Or was I the empty air that sounded like the ocean and he was the shell?

I didn't like either of those images.

I waited until Mark fell to sleep. Then I slowly extricated

myself from his arms. I went to the kitchen and found a bottle of wine. I sat down on the couch and drank it.

I awakened to the sound of someone pounding on the front door. At first I couldn't tell what it was. The room spun a bit when I sat up. It was dark.

"Brooke! I know you're in there!"

Oh fuck. Hayword.

Well, I supposed he was bound to turn up eventually.

I got up from the couch and staggered to the door.

"Go away!" I shouted.

"Brooke, David is hysterical."

"I told him I'd be home," I said.

"Open the fucking door," Hayword said. "It's three a.m. Someone's gonna call the police."

I opened the door but left the light off.

He limped over the threshold. I didn't move. I didn't want him coming any further into the house.

"I'll come home now," I said. "I thought your ankle was too hurt to dance. But you can drive down the hill?"

"Eartha drove me," he said. "I had to go and wake her up."

"Thank god you didn't bring Fern."

Oh shit. I had said that out loud.

"I didn't want her to see this."

"See what?" I said. "It's a fucking house."

I was still drunk.

"Brooke," he said. "You've got to stop doing this. Stop punishing yourself and me. Alberto didn't die because of anything you did or anything I did or didn't do."

"But did you ever wonder," I said, "what would have happened if he'd never been born? If all of that had never happened? I mean, then maybe everything wouldn't have fallen apart. Sometimes I feel so stupid. I was so gullible."

Hayword tried to put his arms around me. I pushed him away.

"Come home with us now," he said. "We'll get your car in the morning."

"David's a good boy," I said. "A good boy. Alberto was too. But maybe . . . Fern is not a nice person. I think there must have been a mix-up at the hospital."

Hayword laughed. He had always found me amusing, too, just like Mark.

"Come home," he said.

I shook my head. Then I nodded. "I will."

"You can't drive," he said. "Have whoever is with you drive you home. But David's pretty bad off. Have some coffee and a shower. Then come home."

"Okay," I said. "Okay. Now go away. You're invading my space, man." I giggled. "My spaceman."

I pushed Hayword out of the house. He limped down the walk.

I shut the door.

Fuck. Fuck. Fuck.

I turned around. I could see Mark's outline inside the dark bedroom.

"Did you hear all that?" I asked.

"Yep," he said. "I'll make you coffee."

"I'll shower," I said.

First I threw up.

I had been doing too much of that lately.

How come suddenly I couldn't hold my liquor?

Wine wasn't liquor. It was fermented fruit. Of course it was going to make me sick.

I took a shower.

I felt better. Mark gave me a cup of coffee when I came out of the bathroom. He sat on the edge of the bed next to me.

"Brooke, in the last two days, you've gotten drunk twice and passed out at least once. That's a lot of brain cells you're killing. You asked me if my alkie-dar was on. Well, it wasn't. Now it is. I've known you for nearly a year and I've never seen you drunk before today."

"That you know of," I said.

"That I know of," he said. He reached for my hand and held it between both of his. He glanced away for a moment, and then he looked directly at me. "I can't be around you if you're drinking like this. It's not good for my sobriety. It's not good for you."

"Are you leaving me?" I asked.

"I'll take you home," he said. "I'll drive you to rehab. I'll take you to a therapist. I'll sit with you when you want a drink. I'll go with you to AA meetings. But I can't be with you when you're drinking."

I pulled my hand away from him.

"I've been to rehab," I said. "I've talked to a therapist. I can go without a drink. That's not the problem."

"Whatever's eating you isn't getting better," he said. "You might want to face it, whatever it is."

I wasn't going to argue with him. Or defend myself.

"I love you, Brooke," he said.

"I don't love you," I said quickly. "This is me. This is the real fucking me. Love me or leave me. Oh wait. You've decided. You're going to leave me."

He rubbed his face. I could see dampness on his fingers.

I stood. "Well, good," I said. "I was going to end it anyway. I met someone. Someone who understands me. You and I are at the end of our run."

Mark stood. "Don't say anything that you'll be sorry for later."

I looked down at him.

Please don't leave me.

"Already said and done," I said.

We left the house together, walked down the block to Mark's truck. He drove me to my house. We sat together in the truck for a minute.

"Do I smell like I've been drinking?" I asked. "I don't want David to know."

Mark didn't say anything.

"It's better this way," I said. I didn't want to get out of the truck. "If you really knew me, you'd be sorry. I mean, you'd probably stay for a while, but then you'd go."

"What more could I possibly know about you?" he said. "I know you've been cheating on your husband for what, eight years? My wife cheated on me. Thought it ruined my life. But then I try to take you away from your family. I don't think very highly of myself, but I do admire you. I've always known you're more than some lonely woman I fucked."

"I'm not lonely," I said. "And it's been eleven years."

"What do you mean?" he said. "You told me you got the house eight years ago. And Alberto died ten years ago. That's when you caught Hayword with another woman."

I felt completely sober. And completely unable to get out of the truck.

"He died almost ten years ago," I said. "I met this man. He worked with Hayword on a picture. He was nice. He paid attention to me. I wasn't just the wife, I was somebody. I had just had a baby so I felt frumpy and ugly, like some kind of breeding cow. And he was beautiful. Ryan Nichols. I was so in love with him. I was like a teenager. Like when I first was in love with Hayword. I had never cheated on Hayword before. But I was unhappy. This deep unhappiness. I thought Hayword was living this beautiful life and I was nothing. I was invisible. When Ryan and I had sex, it was like I was alive again. I was fucking besotted. I wanted to leave my family. I think I would have. Then I got pregnant, and Ryan was gone. Just disappeared. Changed his phone number. It was awful. I thought I would die."

I stared at my house.

"Hayword took care of me," I said. "He forgave me. Even that made me angry. Why should he forgive me? Because I'd been happy for a brief moment in time? I hurt all the time. I wanted to forget what had happened. But I had this baby. He was so beautiful. He reminded me of Ryan. Something about his eyes."

I breathed deeply. "And then he died. Everyone thought I was so unhappy because he died. And I was. I loved him. But I had been unhappy before. I was unhappy during his life. Then I was unhappy after. I didn't really change, Mark. I was still the same unhappy person. I wasn't more unhappy. I wasn't less unhappy. Isn't that the definition of a sociopath?"

The door to the house opened. Hayword stood on the top step looking out.

"Then I found Hayword with someone else," I said, "after he had promised to make everything better, right after we buried Alberto and I knew then that he had never loved Alberto like he loved the other kids, like he promised me he would. And now I could blame him. Blame him for everything. I told everyone he had cheated on me. He never told anyone that I had cheated on him. Never told anyone that Alberto was not his son. He waits. Waits for me to get better. For it to be the same as it was before Alberto died. But the thing is, Mark—" I turned to look at him. "—the thing is that everything is the same as before Alberto died."

"Brooke," Mark said.

I turned away, opened the truck door, and got out. I went up the walk. Hayword held out his hand for me. I slipped my hand into his, and we went back into the house.

David was asleep when I went into his room. I lay down on

the bed next to him. I watched him sleep and breathe, sleep and breathe. He opened his eyes once and whispered, "Momma." Then he went back to sleep. But for those few moments he had his eyes open, he looked just like his brother.

TEN

I woke up in David's bed. He was up and gone. I could hear him downstairs somewhere, laughing and talking with his father.

I got up and went into our room.

I felt strangely refreshed. I could hear the wind blowing outside, could see the trees rocking in the wind. To the southeast, the sky looked a little smoky or ruddy.

I didn't hear Eartha or Fern.

Maybe Eartha had adopted Fern. That would certainly be her one great thing for today as far as I was concerned.

I laughed, grabbed my phone, and lay back on the bed. I was feeling downright . . . okay.

I checked my messages. I was to pick up Joan no later than five. Unless we wanted to go earlier and drink our lunch somewhere.

No.

A text from Mark. "I'll see you on Monday as planned. We'll talk. Call any time."

"Thanks." I texted. "Lv."

He knew the truth, and he still wanted me. I didn't understand it. Hayword was the same way.

Did I surround myself with men with incredibly bad taste and poor judgment?

I went downstairs to the TV room. We were supposed to call this room something else. When we bought the house, the real estate agents had some name for it, but that's where we put the TV and that's where we watched it. So it was the TV room. Hayword had his foot up on a stool. David sat next to him. They were watching a hockey game.

I went over to the couch and kissed the top of Hayword's head. Then I went and sat next to David.

"Good morning, you two," I said.

"Mom, it's way past noon," David said. "This would be the afternoon."

"Good *afternoon,* you two," I said.

"Quite the slackard today," Hayword said.

"I know," I said. "David, I'm sorry I scared you last night. I went to the art studio and I stayed too late. I got tired and fell to sleep on the couch."

"Fern said you were drunk," David said.

I glanced at Hayword.

"Your sister is actually right," I said. "For once. Where is she anyway?"

"Eartha took her into town for her demonstration," Hayword said. "They're going to make a day of it. Protesting and shopping. The best of both worlds, I guess."

"Wow, that woman does more great things in a day than I do in a year," I said. "We should give her a raise. Anyway, David, I did drink too much. I'm going to stop that."

"You're going to stop drinking?" David asked. He seemed overly pleased by this prospect.

"I'm going to stop drinking to excess," I said.

"Can't you stop altogether?" David asked. "It makes me nervous."

Oh fuck. What kind of mother was I if I couldn't say yes to that.

"Okay, David," I said. "I won't promise you that I'll never drink, but I won't drink today. How's that?"

"But tonight's the Benefit," Hayword said.

David looked at me.

"I don't have to drink at the Benefit," I said. "Please. It'll be a good time without a drop to drink." I smiled. Hayword looked skeptical. "Okay. I've got to get ready. You have a good day."

"Are you coming home tonight?" David asked.

"Do I have your permission to run away from home?" I asked.

He shook his head.

"Okay, then. I guess I'll be home tonight," I said.

Joan and I decided to leave early for the Benefit. I carried my specially made low-cut red dress to the car, and then I drove across the street to Joan's house. It was the first time I had seen Bernie since the bathtub incident, and he wouldn't look me in the eyes.

When I mentioned this to Joan once we were in my car, she said, "I've gotten a couple really good fucks out of it. I think he's imagining you and me in bed together. We should get naked together and take pictures, so I can show them to him and that'll get him really hard."

The road out of the village and onto the freeway was blocked by fire trucks. Smoke billowed from trees in the distance, but I didn't see any flames.

"We could run the fire line," Joan said. "I bet we could make it."

"No, we couldn't," I said. "You just want to be rescued by some cute fire fighter."

"Yes, take me to your leader," she said.

We left the village in a roundabout way. People and cars kept coming out of and going into the smoke. I tried to find a way around it all.

We ended up far out of our way, on the 401, headed to the city. We soon left the smoke behind as we tooled down the expressway. Hardly anyone was on the freeway. The sun was out. Palm trees moved slightly with the wind, as though they were hula dancers. We put the windows down and turned up the radio.

"Ventura highway, baby!" I said.

Joan and I laughed and sang off key to whatever rock 'n' roll song was on the radio.

I couldn't remember the last time I had felt this good.

Maybe the truth did set us free.

I looked at Joan and she was smiling, too.

It was a glorious moment in time.

Ahead I could see traffic.

We put our windows up again.

"Joanie, I'm fucking the plumber," I said, apropos of nothing.

"What? You mean the guy who saw me—who saw me naked in the bathtub?" she asked.

"Yep."

"Oh, I'm mortified," she said.

"Why? He doesn't care," I said. "He's a nice guy."

"Are you going to leave Hayword?" she asked.

"For Mark?" I said. "No. I've had lovers on the side for years. I don't leave Hayword."

"Why not?"

I laughed. "What do you mean why not? He's my husband. He's the father of my children." At least some of them. "He's a good man, kind, good-looking, works hard."

"But you hate him," she said.

We caught up to traffic.

"I don't hate him," I said. "What makes you think that?"

"Brooke, you hate everyone."

"What? I do not," I said. "I don't hate you. I don't hate David. What are you talking about?"

"Hey, don't shoot the messenger," she said. "I thought you hated Hayword. I've never seen you be nice to him. Or anyone else for that matter."

"Aren't I nice to you?"

She shrugged.

"Nice is overrated," I said.

"Yeah, but sometimes it's . . . nice," she said. "You are quick with the quips. Sometimes people deserve them. But sometimes they don't. Like yesterday you told the three of us that we reminded you of the balls on a ball-less terrier."

"That doesn't make any sense," I said.

"Still, it was insulting," she said.

"Essentially I was saying that you reminded me of something that doesn't exist," I said.

"Exactly," she said. "No one likes to be told they're nothing."

"Okay, noted," I said. "I'll try not to be such an asshole."

"An asshole on a shitless terrier," she said.

"That would mean I was completely useless," I said.

"Now you're getting it," she said.

I looked over at her. "You're smarter than I give you credit for."

"See," she said. "Was that a compliment or an insult?"

"Uh, neither. Just a statement of . . . my opinion."

"Oh, take this exit," she said. "There's a guy at that gas station on the corner who is too beautiful for words."

I laughed. Then I drove us off the freeway.

We got a suite at the Shilton Hotel. We had them bring up lunch. Joan got champagne and some kind of mixed drink. I asked for coffee and water. Joan didn't ask me why I wasn't drinking. Maybe after Thursday she figured it was a good idea.

After lunch, we took turns taking a shower, and then we helped each other get dressed, put on our makeup, and do our hair.

"Do you love him, this plumber?" she asked.

"His name is Mark," I said. "You know that. Do I love him? I don't even know what that means. I've been seeing him for nearly a year. I have a lot of affection for him."

"A year?" Joan said. "That's more than a fuck. That's an affair. That's longer than one of my marriages."

"Really?"

Joan laughed. "No! I've only been married twice. I divorced the first guy after five years."

"Did you feel like you were a failure," I said, "because you divorced? I mean, did you feel like you had wasted those five years?"

"No! We were happy together," she said. "And then we weren't. So we divorced."

"You're not happy with Bernie," I said. "Why don't you divorce?"

"I don't know," she said. "Same reasons you gave. I love him. He's the father of my kids, worthless bastards that they are. He's got money, and I don't have to work too hard. It's easier to stay with him. Divorce is not easy or fun even when it's amicable."

"Can you imagine if we said these kinds of things to our younger selves?" I said. "What would they say? 'You stayed with someone because it was easier? What about passion? What about happiness?'"

Joan made a noise. "I think if my younger self knew how her older self was going to turn out, she would have blown her brains out."

"Good thing she didn't know then," I said.

Finally it was time to go down to the Benefit. We weren't walking the red carpet. We didn't have to greet anyone at the door. We had no responsibilities tonight except to have a good time.

Joan and I rode the elevator together, both of us dressed in red dresses, our arms linked. The doors opened, and we stepped off the elevator and walked to the ballroom. We stood on the threshold and looked inside. The room was dimly lit but bright enough for us to see all the sparkling jewels and tanned bosoms. Men in black and women in red, blue, purple, cream, yellow. Bernie turned and saw us. He smiled. He looked smitten. I looked at Joan. She was smiling, too.

"See you later, love," she said.

The two of them went off together.

I walked around, talking to people I knew, introducing my-self to people I didn't know. Sally St. James was there with her husband. He was a good looking man. He didn't smile much, except when Sally said something. He, too, seemed clearly in love.

And then this gorgeous white-haired man walked into the ballroom. He stood so straight and tall, as though he was a Marine dressed in a tuxedo.

"Wow." I had almost forgotten about him, but now here he was: Greg Douglas.

Greg saw me, smiled, and walked over to me.

We quickly embraced.

Man, he smelled good.

"I'm so glad you came," I said.

"Wouldn't have missed it," he said. "Would you care to dance?"

"I'd love to," I said.

We danced through several songs. I introduced him as a friend of Hayword's and mine whenever someone stopped to say hello. Then we sat at a table away from the others and talked. We didn't sit close together. I was a married woman. I had to be discreet.

We got up and danced to the next slow dance. He held me close. I could feel his hard-on. I looked at him.

I guessed this meant he liked me, he really liked me.

"I feel like I've been waiting for you for years," I whispered.

He pushed himself up against me. "I've always been attracted to you," he said. "But I couldn't do anything about it. Now we meet again like this, at this difficult time in your life. I think it's a sign."

Yes, a sign. That was it.

Maybe it was meant to be.

Not that I believed in any of that shit.

"I want to feel your cunt around my cock," he said.

He whispered it, but I glanced around. Had anyone else heard?

I would not have guessed that Greg Douglas was a dirty talker.

That was all right.

A little dirty talk never hurt.

And my cunt responded appropriately.

"I want to feel your creamy cunt around my cock," he said.

It ain't that creamy any more, I thought. I ain't no spring chicken.

I wanted to laugh.

And I wanted to take off my clothes and do the wild thing with him.

"I won't ever hurt you," he said. "You must know that I'll always protect you. You will come so hard. I promise you. I've never wanted anyone so much. I wanted to fuck you the other day. Wanted my cock in your cunt. Would have happened, too, if it wasn't for that earthquake. Mother Nature responding to our passion. Never wanted anyone the way I want you."

Someone was bound to hear. We had to get away.

And even though his dirty talk sounded silly, I was very wet. I was ready to be fucked and fucked hard, as he said.

"Meet me in room 405," I said. I slipped the keycard in his pocket. "I'll be up in five minutes."

The song ended. I thanked him, and we walked away from each other. I found someone I knew and didn't care about— pretty much everyone there—and I had a quick chat.

Then I went to the bathroom. I went into a stall and closed the door. Oh my god. My vagina was pulsating. I was going to come before I got upstairs to Greg. Maybe I should masturbate before I went up to the suite, so I wouldn't come too soon. So it would last longer.

No. I wasn't having sex in a hotel bathroom, even if it was only with myself.

I would have sex upstairs in a hotel room with an almost complete stranger.

At least I hadn't had anything to drink.

I got in the elevator and went up to the fourth floor. When I got to 405, I realized I had given my keycard to Greg, so I wouldn't be able to get in.

I knocked softly. The door opened, but I didn't see anyone.

I went inside. The door closed behind me.

Greg was right there. He pressed me up against the wall.

"Do you want it?" he asked.

We kissed. He pushed himself up against me, and he began dry humping me against the wall. It was working. I was about to come. Then he pulled up my dress and put his finger between my panties and my skin. His fingers found the wet place and slid up easily inside. He finger fucked me until I almost came, was about to come, *please don't stop, please don't stop, please don't stop,* and then he pulled his fingers out. He began kissing me again and leading me into the bedroom. He quickly took off his clothes. I could see his erect penis. Knew it would be inside me any second and then I would come. Then I would have an orgasm that would rock my world. *Now, now, now.*

"Take off your clothes," he said.

I got quickly naked.

His penis was pulsing.

My vagina was pulsing.

Now we had to put the two together.

"Get on the floor on the your hands and knees," he said.

"What?"

"On the floor on your hands and knees," he said. "You want it, don't you? You want my hard cock up inside your cunt. Now get on your hands and knees like the little bitch you are."

"Pardon me?" I said.

"Don't you want it?" he said. "Don't you want to be punished for all the wrong you've done?"

I suddenly felt very naked.

But I was also still aroused.

For an instant—only an instant—I considered it. Maybe I did need some humiliation to get my mind right.

Fuck. That. Shit.

"This is the way I like it," he said, in a stage whisper. "Don't you? I thought we were on the same page here."

"I'm not a Catholic," I said. "I'm not really carrying around any deep-seated guilt about anything I've done."

"Really?" His voice was no longer seductive. Just perplexed. "After all the secrets you told me the other day."

"I don't remember telling you any secrets," I said.

"When I put you to bed," he said, "you told me all about your secret affairs, about your baby not being your husband's son. You said you felt like you should be punished. I knew then we were simpatico."

His erection was beginning to fall.

Mine certainly was.

"No!" I said. I grabbed the sheet and covered myself up. "I'll have sex with you but not like a dog. I don't need to be punished or humiliated."

His erection was completely gone. I couldn't even tell he had a penis or balls.

"Are you telling me you can't do it unless . . . ?"

"'fraid so, darlin'," he said.

Don't call me darlin'.

He picked up his tighty whities and put them on. Then his T-shirt, his shirt, pants, cummerbund, his slacks. He sat on the bed and pulled on his socks and shoes.

He looked at me. "Different strokes for different folks," he said. "I'll see you in the funny papers."

He tossed the keycard on the bed.

And then he left.

As soon as the door closed behind him, I started to laugh.

"Oh my god," I said. I shuddered. I couldn't believe his fingers had touched me. "Bleck!"

I didn't know if I ever wanted to have sex again.

I wanted to call Mark and tell him all about it.

Or maybe Hayword.

No! Sheesh.

Joan.

I would go tell Joan. She would laugh her ass off.

I got dressed again and went downstairs. I found Joan and pulled herself aside and told her what had happened. She laughed so hard she nearly pissed her pants. She laughed so loudly that half the people in the ballroom looked over at us. Bernie came over to see if she was all right.

Just about then I got a phone call from Eartha.

I went outside to talk to her.

"Everything all right?" I asked.

Outside the winds were strong and hot. It felt hot even though it was evening in January.

I went back into the hotel and sat at a table in the lobby.

"Fern is in jail," Eartha said. "And I don't have any money to bail her out. She told me not to call you, but she'll have to stay the night if someone doesn't come. She doesn't have any money either. They put her away from the other protestors because they got full. She's with the derelicts. At least that's what she said."

"I'll be right there," I said. "Which precinct? Do you have the address?"

I went back to the Benefit and told Joan that I had to leave. Then I had the parking valet get my car. As I slid into the seat, I realized I should have gone upstairs and taken off the dress and put on my jeans. Ah well. Fern would have to deal with it. I put the address into the GPS, and then I followed directions to the police station.

I felt a little silly walking from the parking lot to the police station in my evening gown. It was a busy Saturday night at the cop shop. Of course I'd never been at a police station on a Saturday night, so maybe it was slower than usual. What did I know? Despite the activity, it was quieter than I would have thought. In all the movies and TV shows, every cop shop was noisy.

I got a couple of wolf whistles. Wasn't sure who did the whistling, but Eartha saw me and came over.

"Sorry, Brooke," she said. "I don't know what happened. We got separated and then suddenly the police were pepper spraying and arresting people."

"It's not your fault, I'm sure," I said. "Where do I pay?"

She took me to the window where I paid Fern's bail money. Fern had already been arraigned with a group of other protestors. Eartha and I sat on a wooden bench and waited for her.

Finally the door buzzed open and Fern came out to us. She looked a little pale.

"Do you need to wash up or anything?" I asked.

"Mom, what are you doing here?" she said. "You look like the whore of Babylon."

"This whore of Babylon can leave you here," I said, "or I can give you a ride home. Your choice."

Fern walked ahead of us. Eartha put her arm through mine as we followed.

"You want her?" I asked. "Cuz you can have her. She's yours."

We got into the car, with Fern sitting in the back. I drove us away from the police station and headed in the direction of home. I glanced back at my daughter every once in a while. She looked like she was going to be sick.

"Do you want me to pull over?" I asked. "Or take you to the hospital? Were you pepper sprayed?"

"Yes," she said. "I was standing up for what is right while you fat cats sat around eating caviar on crackers and drinking champagne."

"There was caviar?" I asked. "Damn it. I missed it. We can go back and get some."

"Did you have a good day?" I asked Eartha.

"Yes, we had fun," she said. "Some really good people out there."

"Maybe next time I'll join you," I said. "I'm proud of you for standing up for what you believe in, Fern."

"Don't be sarcastic," she said. "I don't feel very well."

"I'm not being sarcastic," I said. "I meant it."

"Oh. I don't know if we'll do any good."

"How's school?"

"I don't want to talk, Mom. My stomach is upset."

We traveled the rest of the way in near silence. At least Fern wasn't screaming at me. So a little pepper spray slapped the bite out of her. I should remember that and stock up.

Bad mother.

I smiled.

"Sorry about last night," I told Eartha. "Those days are over. I'm on the straight and narrow."

I frowned: I didn't really want to be on the straight and narrow.

"How about on the windy and the broad," Eartha said. She must have noticed my frown. "You could come up with something. You're the writer."

"I wrote up a treatment for the zombie movie," I said.

"Hayword told me," she said. "He was very happy. Did you have fun?"

I shrugged. "It was all right."

We got off the expressway, but we weren't able to go very far. Fire trucks blocked the way. I turned the car and took us a back way, up and around and down again.

"Mom, these roads are making me sick," she said. "Stop the car, stop the car!"

I stopped the car. Fern got out. I heard her throwing up. I got out and went over to her.

"You want me to hold your hair?"

"I'm done," she said. "I don't want to go on that windy road home. It's making me feel worse."

"Okay," I said.

I drove us to the bungalow.

I parked the car in the driveway.

Eartha didn't say anything. She knew where we were.

Fern didn't say anything either. She trudged to the front door, got the extra key from under the rock, and went inside. I followed. She went straight into the bathroom and threw up.

I got her water.

She came out of the bathroom and stumbled to the couch.

"How did you know where that key was?" I asked.

"Come on, Mom," she said. "Anyone could figure it out. I come here sometimes on the weekends, and during that month you were gone. Or the almost month. It's been my home away from home."

"I never saw any sign of you," I said.

"I'm good at being invisible," she said. She looked at Eartha. "This is where Mom brings all her boyfriends. Slut Central."

"Fern," Eartha said. "I thought you wanted to talk to your mother. Remember what we talked about. About you being kind and respectful."

I got a cloth from the bathroom. I ran cool water over it. Then I squeezed it and brought it back to the living room and put it across Fern's forehead. She let me be near her. She closed her eyes.

"It's my fault," Fern said.

"What's your fault?" I asked.

"When we were kids, I told David that Alberto died because you weren't home. Little boys died when their mothers went away, I said. I was mad at him about something. It was a mean thing to say. I tried to take it back, but he believed it."

"But I was home when Alberto died," I said. "That doesn't make any sense."

Fern opened her eyes. She sat up a little so that she wasn't close to me. I got up and sat in one of the chairs. Eartha sat in another one.

"I've asked him why he gets so scared," I said. "He doesn't remember. I'm sure he doesn't remember you telling him that."

"If you're so sure then it must be true," Fern said.

I shook my head.

"What did I ever do to you that makes you hate me so much?" I asked. "I birthed you. I took care of you. I took you to every dance class, music lesson, doctor's appointment. I was always there for you and with you, and you always hated me."

"I didn't hate you," Fern said. "And you weren't always there. You were never there. Maybe when I was very young. But then you were gone! It made me so angry. I wanted you to come back. You were so sad all that time. And it got worse after Alberto died."

She started to cry.

"Everything got worse after that," she said. "And that was my fault. I must have done something wrong. I must have fed him something wrong. Or put him to bed wrong. He was a perfectly healthy boy and then he was dead!"

"We've told you again and again that you didn't do anything wrong," I said. "He just died. No one was to blame."

"David thinks he's to blame," Fern said. "He thinks Alberto died because he—David—cried too much. You and Dad always talk about how much David cried those first two years, so he's convinced he cried Alberto to death."

I laughed.

It wasn't funny, but the laugh just came out.

Fern wiped her tears.

"It's not funny," Fern said.

"I know it's not," I said.

She started to sob.

"What is wrong, Fern?"

"There's more, Mom," she said. "You have no idea what I've done."

Besides treat me like shit all of your life. You mean there's more?

"I burned down the house," she said.

"What?"

I felt instantly sick to my stomach. It couldn't be true.

"You did not burn down the house," I said.

"I did." She was crying so hard that she could barely breathe. She started hiccupping as she tried to catch her breath. I went and sat next to her. She moved away.

"I was so tired of you being sad," she said. "Dad was all right. He moved on. He made certain we were okay. You just sat in Alberto's room. You cried and cried. It was worse when you didn't cry. And you and Dad didn't even seem to like each other. I thought if we had to move, if we left Alberto's stuff behind, we could leave it all behind. I thought we could be happy again. So I waited until everyone was gone and I started the fire."

"They said it was an electrical fire," I said. "You couldn't have done this. You weren't even thirteen years old."

"I did it!" she screamed. "I put a lit match near the dryer and I left it there and the house burned. I did it, I did it! And nothing got better. Nothing. We all kind of disappeared. And sometimes I wish so much that Alberto was never born because then he wouldn't have died!" She was yelling. I reached for her. She tried to pull away from me, but I wouldn't let her. I put my arms around her and held her as she sobbed.

"I've thought the same things," I said. "It's normal and natural." Although I hadn't realized it until that moment. "Only Alberto didn't cause it, not his birth or death. I was sad. I was sad before he was born. I was unhappy with my life. He wasn't to blame and you aren't to blame. Well, maybe you're to blame for burning down the house; I don't really know about that."

She laughed a little. "Why couldn't you be happy?"

"I don't know," I said. "Somehow I got off track. I followed your father. Not that I'm blaming him. I followed him when I didn't want to. I settled for things I didn't want. And then I began to disappear. I don't know."

"I've been worried for ten years that someone is going to find out," Fern said. "And they'll send me to jail and they'll make you give the insurance money back because they'll figure it was an inside job."

I looked at her. "I don't think that's going to happen," I said. "In fact, it's not possible. They've built another house on top of our old one. They couldn't reconstruct anything. Besides, no one has doubted the findings. You're safe. You're in the clear. I'm not glad you burned the house down, but I was glad to leave it." I let her go and looked at her. "Have you burned down any other houses?"

"No!"

"You didn't go into psychology because you're an arsonist or anything? I mean, there are a lot of fires out there right now."

"No, Mom, no!"

Fern sighed, shuddering a little as she breathed out.

"Why did you come here when I wasn't here?" I asked.

Fern looked around. "I wanted to be closer to you," she said.

"But I wasn't here," I said.

She nodded. "I know."

ELEVEN

Fern slept in the guest bedroom. The guest bedroom that had never been used before. I got a blanket and pillow for Eartha to sleep on the couch. I called Hayword and told him where we were. We decided we wouldn't tell David, since he had a sleepover. If he called me in the middle of the night and asked where I was, I would decide then what to tell him.

I took a long hot shower. I wanted a drink, I gotta tell ya, but I knew there wasn't anything in the house. I had downed what was left the night before.

I crawled under the covers and thought about my day. Greg Douglas turned out to be a pervert. Who would have thought? Although I suppose pervert was too strong a word. If consensual adults wanted to humiliate one another—or pretend to—who was I to object? My own daughter called my little home Slut Central.

Perhaps beauty was not the only thing in the eye of the beholder.

I could still see Greg Douglas standing in front of me naked, strong and proud as his erection withered.

So glad I had not laughed out loud.

I closed my eyes and fell to sleep.

I dreamed I was at a zombie ball and we were all dressed to the nines.

I heard someone whispering my name.

I opened my eyes.

It was still dark out.

I saw a shadow next to my bed.

"Brooke." Eartha's voice.

"What's wrong?" I quickly sat up.

"I have to talk to you about something."

"Now? What time is it? Is Fern all right?"

"It's something after six, I think," she said. "Fern is fine. I checked on her."

"Can't this wait until morning?" I asked.

"It is morning."

"I mean real morning," I said. "Your one great thing today would be to let me sleep."

"It's important," she said. "I made coffee."

"All right." I got out of bed. Felt chilly, so I found a pair of slacks and a shirt and pulled them on. Then I went into the living room. Fern's door was closed. The house creaked a bit from the winds. One dim light was on in the corner of the living room. I sat in one of the chairs. Eartha brought me a cup of coffee. I held it in my hands to warm up. She sat on the couch across from me. She had already folded up the blanket and put it on the pillow at the end of the couch.

I felt strangely awake.

"I have to tell you something," Eartha said.

"Never a good way to start a conversation," I said. I took a sip of coffee. Damn. This woman could do almost anything. This was a great cup of coffee. How had she done it? I didn't even think I had coffee in the house, besides instant, and this was not instant coffee.

Eartha cleared her throat. "I want you to know that I have really enjoyed spending time with you and your family. It has been amazing. One of the most amazing weeks of my life, actually."

I didn't know what to say. This had been the week everything had fallen apart. Or so it seemed to me.

"I'm glad you enjoyed yourself," I said.

And?

"I've been here under false pretenses," she said. "I should have been honest with you from the start. I want you to know that everything was done with the absolute best intentions for you."

"What the fuck are you talking about?" I asked.

"I'm an interventionist," she said. "I often work with VIPs and famous people who don't want to go to rehab or a clinic."

I stared at her.

"What?"

"Hayword called me," she said. "He had gotten my name from a friend of a friend of his. I can't reveal that person's name, of course. He said you'd been to rehab and it hadn't worked, but you wouldn't get help, and he was afraid something bad was going to happen."

"What?"

"I said I'd be glad to come and talk with you," she said. "He thought you'd never agree to it. He begged me to come stay with the family for a few days and see if he was overreacting or not. I said I couldn't deceive you. But I let myself be convinced it was for your own good. I loved *Love and Other Insanities.* It was so big-hearted and beautiful and funny. I couldn't let the person who wrote that disappear into addiction. Or so I told myself. I was wrong. I should have been straight with you all along."

I wanted to say "what" again, but I realized that was getting repetitious.

Plus, what she was telling me was beginning to sink in.

"So you're saying you coming to the house was a complete set up?" I said. "You weren't some homeless gal wandering the streets?"

"I have done some wandering," Eartha said, "and most everything I ever told you was the absolute truth."

"Hayword told you all about our lives?" I said.

"He did," she said. "About the affairs, the baby, his death, the art studio."

I didn't know what to say.

I was actually speechless.

"I thought we were becoming friends," I said. "I was beginning to trust you."

"I know," she said. "I felt that, too. So I had to tell you."

I took a sip of coffee.

I wondered if I should hurl the coffee at her.

Or beat the shit out of her.

Or should I ask her questions?

I got up and went into the bedroom and got my phone. I called Hayword.

"Hello?"

Sounded like I woke him up.

Good.

"Get your ass down here," I said. "I know who Eartha is. I'm holding her hostage until you get here."

He coughed. "All right," he said. "I'll be there soon."

I went back into the living room and sat down.

"I guess this explains why Joan saw Violeta in Los Angeles," I said. "Violeta never left home."

"She didn't want to do it," Eartha said.

"But it's difficult to turn down a paid vacation," I said. "How about you? Why did you agree to the deception? Did Hayword offer you lots of money?"

Eartha shook her head. "I'm getting paid my standard fee."

"So if you had been honest with me," I said, "how would this have worked?"

"I would have come in and talked to you," she said, "and then we would have worked the program together. I would have taken you to private AA meetings. Things like that."

"And you think I need all that?" I asked.

"What do you think?"

Now that made me want to scream.

I kept my voice down.

I didn't want to wake Fern.

"Tell me what *you* think," I said. "My husband obviously thinks I'm a raging drunk. What's your opinion?"

"I think anyone who drinks to near blackout two days in a row has a problem."

"Who knows about this?" I asked. "Do the kids? The women in the Enclave?"

"As far as I know, only Hayword and me."

"All this time I wasn't the only one with a dirty little secret," I said. "You were so good at so many different things. How'd you do that? I was completely fooled by you. Completely."

"I can do lots of different things," Eartha said. "I wasn't trying to fool you. I was trying to be with you to figure out how I can help you."

"Can you bring my son back? No. Can you prevent me from having an affair eleven years ago? No. Can you tell me how my life got so off track? No. And who gives a fuck how? I'm here.

I know I'm more fortunate than 99 percent of the world, even with a dead child, and I feel—"

What? What did I feel?

I sat there for a moment.

Maybe it was for many moments.

What did I feel? What did I feel?

"I feel so goddamn angry," I said. "And if I'm not angry, I'm sad. I much prefer the anger." I sighed. "Is Eartha even your real name?"

"Does it matter?"

"That means it isn't your real name," I said.

Suddenly the door opened and Hayword and David walked in. Hayword was no longer limping, and David looked sleepy.

"When I left I noticed smoke from the fire," Hayword said, "so I went and got David. I feel better if he's with us."

I nodded. David came over to me, and I hugged him.

The door to Fern's room opened. She came out, rubbing her eyes. For a moment, I could see the little girl she had once been.

I smiled. Couldn't help myself. There had been a time when she wasn't spitting venom at me, even though it was difficult to remember.

"Eartha, could you take the kids to the donut shop?" I said. "It's only a few blocks down." I got my keys and tossed them to her. "Hayword and I need to talk."

I thought Fern might offer up resistance. She didn't.

"There's some clean clothes in my closet you can wear," I said. "If you don't want to put on yours."

"Dad said you were in jail yesterday," David said. "Was that fun? Did anyone try to kill you?"

"Yeah," Fern said, "the cops."

A few minutes later, Eartha, Fern, and David left the house. It wasn't quite night any longer. Black was turning gray.

"How could you bring Eartha into our home like that?" I

asked. "I thought part of recovery was being completely hon-est."

"You're supposed to be honest," he said. "I'm not in recovery. I was trying to save my wife. My life."

We both stood in the living room, several feet away from one another.

"But why now?" I asked. "What's changed? Haven't we been living like this for years?"

"I've been waiting," he said. "I've been patient. I thought you needed time to grieve. But it hasn't gotten any better. The drinking was worse. And you'd been seeing this new guy for almost a year. I felt like I should do something."

I laughed. "So because I was fucking the same guy for almost a year, you thought I needed help? Or did you think I was going to run off with him?"

"Both," he said. He sat on the couch, leaned forward, and ran his fingers through his hair. "I want our life back, Brooke. I'm sorry I had sex with that woman. I'm so, so sorry. If I could take it back, I would. But it's done and over with. There's nothing I can do about it. I want our life back!"

I sat across from him. "What life do you want back?"

"The one we had before Alberto died," he said.

"But I wasn't happy in that life either," I said. "I hadn't been happy for a long time."

"Why? We were successful," he said. "You had the family you always wanted. We were living this dream."

"This was never my dream," I said. "I wanted *us*. I wanted us and our kids. I wanted us to work together. I liked that. I didn't like the way you were here. I'm not trying to blame you."

"That's new," he said.

He was right. That was new.

I didn't want to blame him any more.

"You love it here," I said. "You love your work. I think that's great. I don't love it here. I don't like the weather. I don't like the people I meet. I don't like the company I keep. I don't like who I am here. We wanted to write great plays. We wanted to do great work. Now you're writing zombie pictures."

"So what?" he said. "We're entertainers, Brooke. That's what we've always been. You always thought we should do something different. I didn't. I wanted to write stories, so that's what I did. Whether they're zombies or young lovers, I don't care. I want people to see my stories. I love watching actors bring my stories to life."

"But that isn't life," I said. "It's pretend."

He laughed. "Of course it is," he said. "We get to make shit up for a living. How cool is that? And we get to hang out with the rich and famous."

"I don't care about the rich and famous," I said. "I don't. I don't want their approval. I don't want to know them."

"But Brooke, we are the rich and famous now," he said.

I laughed. "Maybe rich but no one in the real world could name a single screenwriter."

"That's right," he said. "Our stories become part of the communal zeitgeist. Like public art."

I looked at him. He seemed so animated. I had thought less of him because he cared about his work: I had thought his work was trivial.

"We're storytellers," he said. "I thought we were living our dream."

He was right. I was the one who was unhappy. I was the one whose son had died. I was the one who had the first affair. I was the one who had had countless affairs.

Maybe not countless.

But a bushel full at least.

I rubbed my face.

Hayword said, "The problem is that you don't love me any more. And you don't know how to let go."

My chest felt tight.

I sighed.

I looked at Hayword. He was right. I had thought he was oblivious, obtuse, kiss-ass. But he was kind, loving, and a little obtuse. He was happy with himself and his life. He had waited for me for a long time.

"I always thought that you had chosen this life over me," I said. "I blamed you. But the truth is, I walked away. I was unhappy and I didn't try to fix it. I walked away."

Oh man.

"You always came first, Brooke," he said. "I had to do what I had to do to keep the family afloat. I'm sorry if I failed."

I got up and sat next to him. I put my arm across his shoulders.

"You didn't fail, Hayword," I said. "You didn't fail."

I did.

I failed.

Now what could I do about it?

Suddenly the door flew open and my children came running in, followed by Eartha and a bit of daylight and cool air.

I could smell smoke.

The wind slammed the door shut again.

"Mom, Dad!" David said. "There's a tsunami coming!"

"What?" I said.

"I heard on the way down here about an earthquake somewhere in the Pacific," Hayword said. "They didn't mention a tsunami."

"It was on the news at the donut place," Eartha said, "and David got it on his phone."

"I have a disaster alert app," he said.

"Of course you do," I said.

"We should get up the hill to our house," Hayword said.

Eartha said, "We can't. Didn't you feel the wind? There are trees down everywhere. We could see fire, too."

"There's a huge tree down on this road," Fern said. "We couldn't even get all the way back here. We left the car and climbed over the tree."

"Shit," I said. "Armageddon is coming to a village near us."

I felt a little bit of panic.

What to do? What to do?

"David, you've had all those drills," I said. "What did you learn?"

"For smoke you should cover your mouth with wet cloth and get down low. For fire, I think you can get into a swimming pool. And for a tsunami, you need to get to high ground."

"Okay," I said. "We don't have a swimming pool, but we can get wet towels. Kids, go into the bathroom and wet towels down for us. And I think I can get us to high ground."

"When's the tsunami supposed to get here?" Hayword asked.

Eartha looked at her watch. "In about fifteen minutes."

"Let's move it," Hayword said.

Fern and David came out of the bathroom with a wet towel for each of us. We put the towels around our necks so that it would be easy to put them over our mouths.

We hurried outside. The sun was coming up, so the sky was beginning to lighten.

"Where to?" Hayword said.

"Your car."

We piled into the car, and then I told Hayword where to go. He drove us to a spot about a block and a half away. We parked on the side of the street. I pointed to the sign: Trailhead 405.

"You lead," Hayword said. "I'll be last to make sure every-one gets up."

"Can you walk up with your ankle?" I asked.

"I'm fine," he said. "Thanks for asking."

I nodded. I'd never been up this trail before. I started running as fast as I could, considering we were going up a steep incline. I glanced back to make certain the kids were right there behind me. Eartha. Then Hayword.

Trees swayed all around us. I could smell the smoke, but it wasn't thick. I put the towel near my mouth.

I couldn't run for very long. I was soon out of breath.

"Fern, you and your brother keep going up the trail, put the towel over your nose and mouth if you smell the smoke."

I didn't know if that was the right thing to do, but that's what I told them.

"But make certain you can breathe!"

Then I hurried behind them.

Eartha passed me.

The wind didn't howl, but it was noisy. The trees seemed to be swaying too much. I hoped one of them didn't fall on us. I remembered Joan telling me once that she didn't like nature because she was certain it was going to kill her one of these days. "Something is always waiting to git ya!" she said.

Something *was* always out there to git ya no matter where you were.

Hayword put his hand on my back, letting me know that he was there, spurring me on.

The trees thinned out.

The sun was turning the sky blue. The smoke seemed to be clearing.

We walked and ran.

And then we were at the top of the hill. Mountain?

We could see the village below us and the ocean beyond that.

I turned around to see the trees and mountain below and behind us.

I could see the whole world.

"Wow," Fern said. "I've never been up here. It's beautiful."

The sun coming up over the mountain was turning everything gold.

Suddenly I thought of *Beauty and the Zombie.* I began taking off my shoes. I glanced at Hayword. He smiled. He knew what I was doing.

"Dad, Mom," Fern said.

"Come on," I said. "Take off your shoes and socks, stand on the dirt, and face the sun."

My son sat on the dirt and took off his shoes and socks. Fern did the same, standing up. Eartha kicked off her shoes. She was barefooted beneath.

The five of us stood next to each other, on the cool dirt. We turned from the ocean and faced the sun. I raised my hands up to the sky.

The sun warmed my face and cooled my feet.

All was still for a moment.

I stretched as tall as I could, and I said, "Happy birthday, Alberto! I'll never forget you, darlin'! I love you. I'm so glad you were born."

"Happy birthday, son." Hayword.

"Happy birthday, brother." Fern.

"Happy birthday, Al." David.

"Happy birthday, baby boy." Eartha.

I heard footsteps on the gravel dirt and I turned around. One of the disheveled young men in business suits I had seen wandering the 'hood was standing behind us. He was taking off his shoes and socks.

"Did you hear about the tsunami, too?" he asked.

He came to stand by us, shoeless. He stared at the bay. We all turned and looked toward the ocean.

"There it is," he said.

I could see a slight rise in the water as the wave came ashore. Saw some boats lift up and bump each other.

Didn't look like the water went too far in. From up here, it seemed almost peaceful.

Ah, perspective.

David was filming it all with his camera phone. "This is great," he said. "It'll look dramatic close-up."

Another disaster diverted.

Or averted?

"Are you all right?" I asked the young man. "I've seen you walking around the neighborhood the last few days."

The young man nodded. "Sure. I'm all right. They're going to film a zombie movie in this area. At least that's what I heard. I'm getting into character for the audition. Figured zombies wouldn't be afraid of the dark, so I came out early this morning when it was still dark. Kind of spooky."

Hayword and I laughed.

"But this was the first time I've been out here," he said. "I don't know who else you've been seeing. Hey, before I got here I thought I heard someone call my name."

"What's your name?" Fern asked.

"Alberto," he said.

"Your name is Alberto?" I asked.

He nodded.

I went up to him and put my hands on his cheeks. I looked into his eyes.

Would Alberto have grown up to look something like this young man?

Where was Alberto now? Was his beautiful little spirit in some other body?

I put my arms around this young man named Alberto, and I held him against my body, held him close, like I would never get to hold my son.

He didn't try to get free. He put his arms around me and held me for as long as I held him.

When I let him go, he said, "Thanks. I have been missing my mom lately." He smiled. "I think it's safe now. I guess I'm ready to get back to the land of the living."

He slipped his shoes back on and started down the trail.

My children came up to me and put their arms around me. I began to weep. Hayword and Eartha embraced the three of us.

We all wept.

After a while, we let each other go.

I said, "I guess I'm ready to get back to the land of the living, too."

We walked down the mountain together.

TWELVE

I went into rehab again. This time to a different place, away from the city.

When I came home, Hayword and I decided to live apart, at least for the time being. They encouraged us not to make any life-changing decisions right after we got out of rehab, but Hayword and I decided it was for the best.

I repainted the bungalow, inside and out. Fern, David, and Hayword helped. Got rid of the old furniture and bought new. Let Fern and David help me choose pictures for the walls. We changed it from a love nest into a home.

I rewrote *Zombie Town* into *Beauty and the Zombie,* and everyone loved, loved it. (When can you start the rewrites?) I began script doctoring for other people besides Hayword. And I started a couple scripts of my own.

David stayed with me half the time and with Hayword the other half.

Eartha taught Hayword and me how to cook and make non-alcoholic margaritas. Hayword and I helped Violeta find another job. Not that she needed our help, but we didn't want to leave her in the lurch.

Production started on *Beauty and the Zombie.* We made sure Alberto got a part in it. Some days I took David to the set. It was a lot of fun watching people say my words.

Some months later, Joan called me to tell me she was having trouble with the plumbing in her kitchen. She had called Mark Pantano and told him she would be out of the house when he arrived. Beatriz would let him in.

He was going to be there between ten and noon on Wednesday, in case I cared.

I waited until eleven before I drove up to the house.

Mark's white truck was parked in the drive, and he was standing next to it, looking for something in the side toolboxes.

I pulled my car up behind the truck, parked it, and got out.

He turned to see who it was. I couldn't tell if he was relieved or alarmed when he saw who it was.

He set down whatever was in his hand and looked at me.

I smiled.

"Hello," I said. "My name is Brooke McMurphy. I used to live in this neighborhood. I'm a friend of Joan's. My husband lives across the street. I live in the village. I haven't had a drink in almost nine months. I write zombie movies."

He chuckled and shook my outstretched hand.

And then he quickly let go of it.

"Your turn," I said.

He rolled his eyes. "I see some things haven't changed," he said. "Still telling me what to do. Okay, my name is Mark Pantano. I don't live anywhere near here. I have a son and an ex-wife. And . . . I have a significant other."

I felt a flutter in my stomach.

Oh.

It should have occurred to me that Mark hadn't been sitting around waiting for me.

I hadn't wanted that or expected it.

I mean, Hayword and I weren't divorced. We didn't know if we would divorce.

Although we had agreed to see other people.

I looked at Mark.

"I'm pleased to meet you," I said. "And I wish you all the best. I'm so glad that you're happy."

Time for a graceful exit.

I was glad I'd gotten to see him one more time. He was still beautiful, body and soul.

I went to hug him goodbye. He embraced me, too. We held onto one another.

Then he let me go.

"Hell, I was lying," he said. "There's no one else. I've been waiting for you to get your shit together to see if we had a shot."

I slugged him in the arm. "That's mean," I said. "And for your information my shit is far from together, but I'm working on it."

We put our arms around each other again, and then we kissed.

I hadn't realized how much I had missed him.

Did this mean I loved him, really loved him?

"Joanie's been helping me look at real estate, by the way," I said. "She found this building on the coast, in a small town north of here. There's a place for a small restaurant on the first floor, already equipped and ready to go, and there's an apartment on the second floor, complete with a deck that looks out at the ocean. I've been envisioning myself on that deck, sitting by the dock of the bay. I'd need someone to open a restaurant there, in the space below the apartment—just in case you know anyone who might be interested."

"Aren't you a little ahead of the game?" he asked.

I shrugged. "I always am."

So where does this story end? With a list of what happened to the players? I always like that.

So here goes:

David doesn't mind if I spend the night away from home now, after Fern told him that it had been her suggestion that had so terrified him.

Fern finished her master's degree and then got a job as an assistant to Sally St. James. She wants to work within the system to change things. I told her that was a fool's errand. She accused me of never supporting her. So I said, "You go for it, dear."

Hayword is now executive producing. He's writing, too, and we cowrite some scripts together. He is dating. I think he had a crush on Eartha, but he never told her.

Eartha closed her business and began riding the rails. She promised us she'd get in touch when she returns to the area.

Katie Williams came out as a lesbian and left her husband. Melissa Pearce and Katie now live together.

Mark's mother Margaret seems to still like me. Giovanni, Mark's brother-in-law, now has a job as a lawyer at AFT, Sally's studio.

Sally St. James and her husband are still together. She has stopped smoking, as far as I know.

The mysterious skin disease plaguing the area has not yet gone into remission. The PR department at AFT is using it as best they can to promote *Beauty and the Zombie.*

Mark Pantano is seriously considering opening a restaurant in my new building.

And me? How does this end for me?

In the last scene of the movie of this part of my life, I am watching another sunrise.

The audience sees my back first and then the camera pans around to my front. I am holding the script of *Beauty and the Zombie: Part Two: Escape from Alcatraz*—and I look very afraid.

And then I laugh my ass off.

The End.

WHACKADOODLE TIMES TWO

For Mario

ONE

I can pinpoint exactly when things began to go whackadoodle again. Later, everyone else said it had something to do with a peculiar full moon. It was green, blue, or so close to the earth you could French kiss the man in the moon. For me, it began and ended with my daughter dearest who was trying to blackmail me as we sat in Juliet's eating breakfast together.

It was already shaping up to be one of those weeks, and it was only Wednesday. They were supposed to start shooting *Beauty and the Zombie Part Two: Escape from Alcatraz* soon, and I hadn't finished the script yet. All the studio and the director had seen was my treatment—which wasn't as detailed as it should be. Sally St. James, the studio head, called me every fifteen minutes to ask about it. My fourteen-year-old son, David, kept nagging his father, Hayword, and me about his science project presentation coming up in school Friday. He seemed almost desperate to have us there. I secretly hoped he wasn't planning on blowing up his school. Not that he would do something like that on purpose. Plus my man Mark Pantano's restaurant was opening this weekend. In our house.

Now Fern was trying to blackmail or coerce or guilt me into attending some AFT function that I couldn't care less about. I hated those phony baloney Hollywood parties where everyone pretended to love everyone else when in truth they were all fucking each other's spouses and/or stabbing each other in the back over some new or old development deal. It was one of the reasons Hayword and I ended our marriage—even though we were still not technically divorced. He enjoyed all the schmoozing. I did not.

In the last two years, I had been to more Hollywood functions than I'd been to in the previous twenty years—I was now on the A-list because *Beauty and the Zombie* had been such a big hit. I was invited everywhere and sometimes I said yes.

So now Fern wanted me to go to this party and talk to some new up-and-coming writers. I didn't have anything to say to them except: run for the hills. I could warn them against trying to fuck their way to the top. A writer could stumble to the top, but she could stumble right back down, too. Besides, Hollywood hated writers. The general culture here loathed us. The power-brokers knew they needed us—kind of like a junkie needs their drug dealer—but they still hated us.

Writers weren't as pretty, we weren't as rich, and we were smarter than all of them put together, and we knew it. At least, that's what the studio heads and producers thought we thought. They believed they could get anyone to do anything by either fucking them or bribing them (or both), and most of the EPs thought writers were too ugly to fuck.

Truly.

God's honest truth. I'd had more than one EP—executive producer—tell me that. First they'd say something along these lines: "This doesn't apply to you, of course, because Jesus, you are more than fuckable. But most writers . . ." You get the gist. And then I'd say something like, "You, on the other hand, are just too *stupid* to fuck. So let's call the whole thing off."

I really hated producers. As a rule. Except Hayword, who longed to be a producer and was finally one for *Powerbreakers* and *Beauty and the Zombie*. He did a good job. Sally St. James was an okay producer, too. I guess. For me, producers do a good job if they leave me alone.

Hayword and I had just separated when they began filming *Beauty and the Zombie*. Now we've been apart for two years. We still work together, but we don't have sex. I don't have to pretend I want to have sex with him anymore. Gawd. What a fucking relief. I don't have to wipe his tears or prop up his fragile writer's ego. And and and I don't have to pretend I don't miss our son Alberto who died when he was an infant. He wasn't actually Hayword's son by blood, but I'm not going to go through that story all over again. If you want to know more, go read my first foray into memoir, *Whackadoodle Times*, and then come back here. Enough to know Alberto's death haunted our entire family for many years. I became a drunk and a fucker. David got neurotic. Fern . . . well, Fern burned down our house so we'd have to move, but she was a kid so you can't blame her.

I'm still hoping no one will or can charge her with anything should it ever come to light that she was a bit of an arsonist when she was a child.

Fern worked for AFT now, against my wishes, for Sally St. James, who was as talented as a studio head can get. Sally wanted to do good work, she wanted to treat people well, she wanted to have a life separate from her job—at least she said she did. She said she didn't want to work so much, but she made excuses to stay at the office too many nights. She said she wanted to be monogamous, but over the last couple of years, she had tried to seduce me more than once, usually when she was drunk. And I'd tell her I didn't do women anymore.

In fact, I didn't do men anymore either, except for Mark Pantano, my plumber turned restaurateur. Or about to be restaurateur. He had studied to be a chef before he settled for the plumbing life, and I was helping him achieve his dream of having his own restaurant.

Did I mention the restaurant was slated to open in about four days (Sunday), two days before David's science project (Friday), one day before my script deadline (Saturday), and three days after the party (Thursday) Fern was blackmailing me to attend?

Perhaps "blackmailing" was too strong a word. Guilting?

We were sitting in Juliet's when Fern started asking me all sorts of stupid questions. You remember Juliet's. It's the restaurant where movie people go who are pretending they don't want to be seen. So they go to Juliet's to be seen by other people who pretend they don't want to be seen. I went there because I'd been going there for a long time. It was where Sally St. James talked me into script-doctoring Hayword's zombie movie. I told her I thought zombies were stupid. She said she wanted a sexy zombie movie: She wanted me to sex up zombies the way other writers had sexed up werewolves and vampires.

Gotta tell you I didn't see any way to make zombies sexy.

Until I did.

I made it into a love story. *Beauty and the Zombie.*

Yep.

AFT made the movie. Jonny Black played Thomas, the alien zombie who supposedly betrayed the heroine of the piece, Colleen Kelly (who was played by Kate Becker). Colleen is who we see pregnant in the last frame of the movie.

Sequel heaven.

Both Kate Becker and Jonny Black were on board and ready for filming the sequel.

If I could just write the damn thing.

Now at Juliet's, Fern was drinking Bloody Marys at eleven a.m.

"Don't do the 'like mother like daughter' thing," I told her after the waiter took our food order. He was a cutey patootie, and we both watched him walk away.

"What are you talking about?" Fern asked as she stirred her drink with a celery stick. Organic celery stick, mind you. We might get fucked up at eleven a.m. here in la-la land, but we do it organically.

"This is fucking health food," she said.

Oh gawd. She was trying to be a tough guy. It just didn't suit her. She wasn't really tough. She was angry. She was smart as hell. But I had damaged her clear to the marrow, and that had let all the true toughness leak out. Sometimes, like right this moment, I wanted to take her in my arms and squeeze all the shit out of her. Make it better. Make her all better. When her brother Alberto died, I was depressed for a long time. In Fern's addled pre-teen brain, she thought the family would be better off if we could leave the house where her brother had died. So she set the house on fire. We didn't know it at the time. Didn't know until about two years ago when she confessed to me and her father. Since then we'd offered to go to therapy with her. Offered to do whatever she needed to feel better.

She said a job made her feel better. Making something of her life made her feel better.

Didn't quite sound right, but my brain had been pickled from years on alcohol and drugs. Might just be getting right about now, I supposed, so I wasn't positive sure about anything.

"Darlin'," I said to Fern as she sipped her Bloody Mary. "Please don't try to be like me. Live your life opposite to mine.

Do everything differently from what I did and you should be fine."

She put down her glass and rolled her eyes. "Mother, how you do or don't live your life doesn't come into my mind at all, ever."

"Maybe it should," I said, "so you can avoid my mistakes. I drank because I'd lost a son. I drank because I was monumentally unhappy living this Hollywood life. Why are you drinking?"

"I'm not drinking, Mother," she said. "I am having *a* drink. Because it tastes good. Especially with scrambled eggs. Would you like a sip?" She held the glass out to me.

For a moment, I wanted to smash the glass out of her hand. Man, she could piss me off more than any other human being alive.

For another moment, I wanted to take a sip.

I didn't like that feeling. Much better to feel angry than . . . to want to drink. I didn't like seeing my daughter try to tempt an alkie back to the bottle.

"Really, Fern?" I said.

Her eyes widened for a moment, as though she hadn't realized what she was doing. She set the glass down again and then pushed it away from her. Then, as if realizing she had pushed it toward me, she grabbed it and slid it toward her again.

"I'm just tired, Mom," she said. "Work has been rough lately."

"I accept your apology," I said.

She started to say something else—I could tell it was a mean smart-ass remark—but she stopped herself. She wanted something from me, and she wanted it badly. She was even wearing the blue and green swan pin I had given her after Alberto died. He had loved that pin—or loved the way it sparkled in the light because he always reached for it when I wore it. Always tried to pull it from my shirt or sweater, whatever I had pinned it to. We could never figure out how the swan had gotten green and blue. When my mother had given it to me when I was a teen, it had been white. Then one day it was blue and green. Figured I must have washed it with something that ran, but who knew?

"You're wearing the swan," I said.

"What?" Fern said. "Oh, the pin. Yes, I was thinking of Alberto this morning, so I wore it."

I didn't believe her. She wore the pin to try to manipulate me.

She smiled. "I miss him."

We were silent for a moment.

"So did you always want to be a writer?" she asked.

Okay. Now we were back to her asking me bizarrely stupid questions.

I could play along.

"As long as I can remember," I said. On some days, I couldn't remember a whole lot. That ole pickling of the brain. Some experts said my brain would eventually return to normal, whatever that was. Other specialists said it wouldn't. If it wouldn't return to normal, why the fuck had I bothered to quit drinking in the first place? No. I couldn't think like that. I kept telling myself my brain *was* healing. It was learning to produce its own opiates. Or whatever it was missing. Sometimes I imagined my brain as a black hole that was slowly filling up with good times. Or chocolate. Or love. Sometimes I had to think good thoughts—even though that was antithetical to who I was now.

Sometimes I just had to *not* think good thoughts.

Reality was reality, man, and we had to face it.

"And Dad, too?" she asked. "He always wanted to be a writer?"

"And Toto, too," I said.

She looked at me and made a face.

"Did you hear about this weird full moon tomorrow?" Fern asked. "Or late tonight."

"Just something about it being very close to Earth," I said, "and some people are afraid its pull will awaken the undead."

She smiled grimly.

"And Mercury is in retrograde," she said. "A shit storm of misunderstandings, miscommunication, and crazies coming up. At least that's what I've been hearing."

"Some of the more New Age radio stations have been telling people to pay attention," I said, "because something really good or really bad is going to happen." I laughed. "You could pretty much say that any time, couldn't you? What the hell is Mercury retrograde, anyway? I've never understood it. The planet goes backward but doesn't really. It just looks like it. What does that mean? It does a moon walk?"

Fern shrugged. "I don't know. I wish I'd paid attention earlier though. I would have changed my plans."

"You mean this breakfast?"

"No! I've been looking forward to this breakfast."

"Darlin', just ask me what you have to ask me," I said. "You don't have to butter me up. For one thing, you really suck at it. If you're going to stay in this business, you'll probably have to work on your sucking up skills."

She bit the inside of her lip.

"Look, Mother."

Oh, so we were back to Mother instead of Mom.

"I know you've really been trying these last couple of years," she said, "and I appreciate it. I know it's been tough. You've had to change everything about your life. Tough work."

She didn't mean it. She didn't really think it was tough.

"I've changed, too," she said. "I'm no longer protesting corporations, I'm working for one. I'm trying to keep it a good business."

Christ on a bender. She was falling into the same trap her father and I had fallen into when we first came to Hollywood: We thought we could change it, make it kinder, gentler.

"Good god, daughter," I said. "Learn from our mistakes. This business will suck the motherfucking life out of you. Unless you're careful. It's like any relationship. It's best to see it truthfully and not try to change it—because it will not go gently into that good night."

"Hollywood isn't a person," she said. "It's just a place. It's a company town, and I happen to work for that company."

"It's actually a two-company town," I said. "If you count rehab."

"Mom, could you just shut up and let me finish," she said. "Please."

The cute waiter brought our meals: Fern got scrambled eggs, potatoes, and sausage, and I got a mushroom omelette. I suddenly craved a glass of champagne, but I bit my tongue before I asked for one. What was with me? I go two years without a single craving, and now in the space of five minutes, I had two?

If I were prone, I would have broken out into a sweat just then.

We watched the waiter walk away again.

"Sally is feeling a bit vulnerable," Fern said quietly. "I'm not sure why. She's the damn studio head. But Irving Jackson seems to be causing trouble. Not sure how. He's nice to me, but Sally doesn't trust him. They're really counting on your movie and Daddy's new movie. With me there, it's like our family is the heart and soul of AFT. Sally is counting on us. I think we need to nurture some new talent. We can't rely solely on you and Dad."

"Because we're old and feeble and likely to die soon?"

I began eating the omelette. Lovely. So nice to have my sense of taste back.

"Yes, that," she said, "and you keep saying you're not going to work in Hollywood anymore. We can't rely on you to continue to produce work."

I made a noise. "I've been saying that for years," I said. "Now that I'm sober and in a happy relationship, I'm having fun writing."

Oh crap. I had said that out loud. Never, *ever* say publicly that you're in a good relationship or you're with the love of your life. Or whatever. Not in Hollywood. Within minutes, hours, days, you'll be eating your words. Trust me on this. The evil eye was now going to come snatch away my sobriety and/or my relationship.

"Not that I'm really that sober and my relationship with Mark pretty much sucks."

"What?"

"Nothing," I said. "I was just taking it all back."

"But you're *not* writing," she said. "I bet you a year's salary you haven't even started on the new *Beauty and the Zombie* script. You did the treatment and that's it."

"Let's move on," I said. "What is it you want from me?"

"Just come to this party," she said. "It's on Thursday, tomorrow, so you won't even need to think about it ahead of time. Talk with these writers. They're young. They've got ideas. I think they could work for us and with us. But they need convincing."

"Convincing? Write them a check. That will be all the convincing they need."

"Mom, please just come," she said. "If you don't, I'm going to tell Dad that you and Sally had an affair."

I glanced around the restaurant. She had said that last bit a little louder than I liked. It wasn't that I had suddenly become discreet. That ship had long ago sailed—and foundered, and sank with all aboard. But Fern was just starting out. She didn't want to get a reputation for . . . anything . . . but most of all, she didn't want a reputation as a gossip.

"So that's how you're going to get me to do something for you," I said. "You're going to try blackmail? Lordy, sister, I've done so many things worse than that. Not that that was especially bad, or anything. I'm sure your father knew, and if he didn't, he wouldn't care now. I tried making amends to him, but he didn't want a whole list or anything. It was enough that I apologized and meant it. Why would you want to open his wounds to get me to come to a party? None of this conversation is making me want to come. Why the desperation? Are you dating one of these writers?"

"Mother, that's insulting."

"Why? I assume you wouldn't try to blackmail your old mother over just any schlub."

"No one is a schlub," she said. She took a couple of bites of her scrambled eggs. She blushed, put down her fork, then picked up her Bloody Mary and drained the glass.

"All right," I said. "I'll go to this party. Is your dad coming? Maybe we can go together." Mark didn't like industry parties.

"Yes, I think he's coming," she said. "You'll talk nice to the writers? You'll encourage them to work for us?"

"Sure," I said. "On one condition."

She rolled her eyes. She really needed to stop doing that. It was a teenager's gesture, not something an adult did on a regular basis.

"You don't have anything to drink from now until the party is over," I said.

"So now *you're* resorting to blackmail," she said.

"I wouldn't call this blackmail," I said. "Just honest deal brokering."

She pressed her lips together. Then she shrugged and said,

"Okay, sure. Why not? Not all of us are lushes like you, Mom. I can stop any time."

"You have such a charming way with words, my daughter," I said.

"I learned from the best," she said.

Her version of a compliment.

Just then, two gunmen burst into the restaurant.

Seriously.

They were both dressed all in black, with Ninja masks covering their faces.

The dozen or so patrons in the restaurant gasped. I did, too. But I wasn't afraid. Not sure why.

One of the gunmen locked the restaurant door. Turned the deadbolt.

The maitre d' just stood there, dumbstruck.

"What the—?" Fern said.

"Everyone stay still and no one will get hurt!" the taller gunman shouted. He held his gun high.

His yellow gun.

What?

"Don't anyone look at us!" the other one shouted. He had a black gun.

They were moving all over the small restaurant, quickly, restlessly, as though searching for something or someone. Fern looked over at me.

"Don't worry," I whispered. "It's not real."

"What?" she whispered loudly.

"No talking!" The shorter one was at our table.

He had the bluest eyes. And the slightest of accents.

He had the bluest familiar eyes.

He looked at me and squinted.

"Enrique?" I whispered to the gunman. Enrique deChamp had been the leading man in our first movie, *Love and Other In-*

sanities. He had been a rising star then and had taken a chance on our indie movie. He had taken a chance on two new writers and a movie few people thought would go anywhere. It had paid off for all of us. At least it had then. I hadn't seen much of Enrique in quite a few years. Had heard rumors of drug and/or alcohol abuse.

A fellow lost soul on this rocky sober road?

"Brooke?" he whispered, leaning down to get a better look at me. "God damn!"

"No talking!" the other man screamed. "Everyone under the tables!"

"Mom!" Fern said. She ducked under our table.

"It's fine, Fern," I said.

"It's not fine! We're being held hostage!"

"I know this man," I said.

"Now he'll have to kill us!"

"Sense the room, Fern," I said. "He's holding a fucking squirt gun."

"Which could be filled with poison!" she said.

"Enrique," I said, "what the fuck are you doing?"

I got under the table, too, and Enrique squatted next to us. I glanced up and saw a phone number scratched into the underneath of the table. "Julia. Will work for oranges. Call xxx xxx-xxxx."

Really? Who did she think would see her number there? Why had *she* been under the table?

"The police are going to be here in two seconds," I said to Enrique. "You've got to get out of here."

"It's not a real robbery," Enrique said. "It's an audition. No one has called the cops."

"An audition!" I said. "Christ! Every single person in here has a cellphone. The cops *are* coming!"

"John Maloney was supposed to be here," Enrique said.

"John Maloney, the director?" I whispered. "He's not here!"

I glanced around the room, although it was difficult to see everyone who was underneath a table at this point.

"He's casting for that new thriller," Enrique said. "*Ten Most Wanted*. About a serial killer who kills people on the FBI's top ten wanted list. I want to be that killer. So I thought this would be a good way to show him my range. Since *Love and Other Insanities*, I've been typecast. Everyone thinks I'm gay."

"You weren't gay in that movie," I said.

"No, I was hetero sensitive," he said. "Same thing."

"But aren't you gay in real life?" Fern asked.

"No," he said. "I've got a family to feed, and I haven't had an acting job in a couple of years."

"Gay people have families to feed, too," Fern said.

"Oh my god," I said. "Can we have this conversation later? John Maloney isn't here and you're about to be arrested for kidnapping or whatever and grand larceny." I glanced over at the other guy. He was taking jewelry from the restaurant customers. "Is he an actor, too?"

"Sure," Enrique said.

"Don't tell me his name," I said. "Come on. Let me get you out of here."

"Mom!" Fern said. "What are you doing? They're criminals. You can't *help* them!"

"They're not criminals," I said. "Those aren't even prop guns. I told you. They're fucking squirt guns. I promise." I shook my head. "Christ, Enrique, how stupid can someone be?"

I heard sirens.

Enrique's baby blues suddenly looked terrified.

I got up from underneath the table.

"Hey, you!" the other gunman shouted at me.

"Hey, you!" I shouted back.

Enrique stood, too, and motioned to his partner. I leaned

down and said to Fern, "Stay here. I won't be long." I hurried to the rear of the restaurant and through the doors into the kitchen with Enrique and his friend following close behind me. For some reason, the kitchen was completely empty. Maybe everyone had run away?

"My god," I said, when the doors swung closed behind us. "How could you think this was a good idea in this day and age when crazy people are running around everywhere shooting people in malls and restaurants and schools? That's just fucking stupid. And it's not very nice."

Enrique pulled off his mask and shook his head. "No one would have been hurt. It was all planned! Maloney was supposed to be here with a big group. Our friend Manny arranged it for us. We'd pretend to be bad guys, and then we'd give the director our cards and say it was an audition."

"Worst idea ever," I said. "You know directors. Biggest control freaks on the fucking planet. You think anyone likes to have the shit scared out of them?"

"But Maloney is supposed to be a man's man," Enrique said. "He'd understand. I know he'd understand."

"Couldn't your agent get you an audition?"

"She dropped me."

"I didn't see Manny," the other man said. He reached up to take off his hood.

"Leave it on," I said. "I don't want to know who you are."

But it was too late. The hood was off. The other burglar was a nondescript twenty-something man.

I put my hand up. "Don't tell me your name. I'll just call you John Doe. You both have got to get out of here now. You could go to prison for a long time if they catch you."

John Doe started pulling out jewelry and watches from his pockets. He held them out to me.

"Jesus," I said as I took the jewelry from him.

"It worked," he said. "They believed me. They fucking believed me as a thief. I've never stolen anything in my life. I *am* a fucking good actor."

He raised his gloved hand in anticipation of a high five from Enrique.

Enrique gave him one.

At least they had worn gloves.

"You've got to go," I said. "Out the back, near the overturned milk crates, there's a gate. Go through that and then get out of fucking Dodge. And don't ever do anything like this again."

"What about the guns?" Enrique said. "Should we leave them here? It's proof we weren't really robbing the place."

They handed me their guns, and then they were out the door, after Enrique shouted, "Call me!"

I looked down at the guns and jewels in my hands. I set the jewels on the island counter. Then I grabbed a towel and wiped down the plastic guns, just in case. I picked up everything again and walked back through the swinging doors and into the dining room.

"It's okay," I said. "You can get up now. They're gone. Here are your jewels and watches." I held them up. "Someone should let the police in before they batter down the doors."

The diners emerged from under their protective tables.

"You saved us," one of them said.

Someone else said, "It's Brooke McMurphy. The writer. She saved the day."

Someone knew what a writer looked like? Someone knew what *I* looked like?

People began to clap. Several uniformed cops came through the door. Fern was watching me, shaking her head.

"No," I said. "I didn't save anyone. They weren't real robbers. It was an audition gone bad. You know actors. Kind of stupid sometimes."

"What?" someone said. "What did she say?"

Two of the policemen pulled out their guns and pointed them at me. They were shouting. Goddamn it, they were shouting so loudly that I could barely understand.

"No, no, you assholes," I heard someone say. "She's not the criminal. She fucking saved all these people." Then the someone stepped between me and the boys in blue.

My daughter, Fern.

Several other people did the same thing.

"No, she's one of *us*," one of them said. "The robbers went out the back."

I said, "They aren't robbers. See, I've got all the stuff."

The cops ran past me. I was tempted to trip them, but I realized in time that would be wrong. Customers came up to me and took back their jewelry. I had no idea if everyone got back their right jewels. Another cop tried to stop them, saying something about evidence. But my hands were soon empty. Even the squirt guns were gone. I think I accidentally on purpose dropped them into the garbage.

More than one person came by to say thank you. I saw admiration in their eyes, and that made me uncomfortable. I straightened my little red dress—why had I worn a dress?—and said, "It was nothing. They were actors. It was an audition."

I felt a lot of goodwill in that room.

I should have known it would not last.

TWO

The cops talked to all of us for far too long. They interviewed me longer than anyone else. I kept saying, "They were actors. It was an audition. They didn't mean to scare anyone."

"How do you know?"

"They told me."

"Why did they tell *you*? Did you know them?"

"No! I saw they had fucking squirt guns," I said. "I figured they were out of their depth. I just wanted them gone so I could finish my breakfast, which is cold now, thank you very much."

In fact, it was way into the lunch hour.

Donna, the owner of Juliet's—she always wanted to be a Juliet—had her crew make us another breakfast, after she found them. They had all run off when they'd heard the gunmen come into the restaurant.

The media showed up. The paps and legit apparently. (They all look alike these days.) The maitre d' kept them out, but Donna asked if I would go talk to them.

"Me?" I said. "Why would they want to talk to me? No! I don't want to talk to them."

"Mom," Fern said, "this could be good publicity for the movie. You know the old saying, all publicity is good publicity."

"That is complete and utter bullshit," I said. "Whoever told you that is full of shit." I held up my hand. "If you're going to tell me I said that, I plead drunkenness."

She shook her head. "Sally said it."

"Sally is full of shit."

Donna was still standing next to our table, waiting. Apparently my "no" hadn't been adamant enough for her. She must be one of these people who believed everyone secretly wanted to be famous.

Let me tell you: I did not secretly or openly want to be famous. I wanted people to know my writing—people who could hire me for a job. But that was about it.

"No, Donna, I do not want to talk to the press," I said.

Donna shrugged and walked away. I continued noshing on my now fresh mushroom omelette.

"Mom, you could mention the movie," Fern said. "You could say this has given you ideas for the movie."

"The movie that I've supposedly already written?" I said. "The script the actors are waiting for? I can't go out and admit I haven't written a word of it."

"Are you kidding me?" Fern said. "Not a word?"

I shook my head.

"Don't worry," I said. "I've done this before."

"That's not reassuring," she said. "A lot of people are counting on you."

"I understand that completely," I said.

Donna came back to the table and cleared her throat. We looked at her.

"There's a Ruby Shirley out there," she said. "She says she knows you."

I sighed. Yes, Ruby was a friend from way back. She'd been kind to me during some tough times in my life: She never wrote about my . . . lifestyle. Neither did anyone else, but she knew the life I was leading.

I glanced at Fern. She mouthed, "Please." I shrugged.

"Okay," I said. "She can come join us. But no cameras."

"Of course," Donna said. "No cameras are ever allowed in here."

"Except for the hundreds of cell phones with cameras," I murmured as she walked away.

Soon Ruby Shirley was walking toward us. I smiled, got up, and embraced the woman. She was a little older than I was, small, curly graying hair, wide grin.

"You look good," she said to me. "Sobriety becomes you."

"You look like a Jewish grandma," I said. "Trolling for gossip becomes you."

She smiled.

"Sit," I said. "Ruby, this is my daughter, Fern Lightman."

The waiter brought Ruby a coffee, and then she asked us what happened. We told her. I left out the part about knowing the "actor" who pulled the stunt. Fern didn't say anything either.

"See," I said. "It's not newsworthy. Just a stupid kid who believed he could get a director's attention. No harm, no foul."

"Except no directors were here," Ruby said. "In fact, I got the list of people who were here and you two are the only movie people. The police told me you'd mentioned John Maloney, so I called his office. He's never even heard of Juliet's."

"I heard the man say John Maloney," Fern said.

"Look, Ruby," I said, "There's no story here. Now, tell me what you've been up to."

She put down her long reporter's pad. (Yep, she still used one.)

"You keep saying there's no story," she said. "That must mean there's a story."

We looked at each other for some long seconds. Then I smiled and said, "No, I'm just trying to extricate myself from this thing. I've got a deadline to finish up the sequel to *Beauty and the Zombie*, and I can't get hooked into anything else. Although this gives me ideas. Perhaps I'll have to add a scene in a place like Juliet's."

"I thought you were finished with *Escape from Alcatraz*," she said.

A fan then?

"You know, a writer's work is never done," I said.

Ruby looked over at Fern. She seemed to be about to ask Fern something and then decided against it.

"I'd love to get a backstage pass to the filming," Ruby said. "Jack Meredith directing this one too?"

I smiled. She knew the answer to that.

"Of course," I said.

"Bet that was tricky," she said.

"Why?" I asked. I glanced at Fern.

Ruby shrugged. "Heard you two had history."

"If my mother wasn't able to work with people she had 'history' with," Fern said, "she wouldn't be able to work. In the end, everyone loves my mother. Including Jack Meredith."

I looked at my daughter and then over at Ruby. Ruby smiled.

"She knows whereof she speaks," I said. "But no, we didn't have any trouble getting Meredith back. He loved the first script. He made a lot of money on the first one—we all did—and he'll make a lot on this one."

Although Jack Meredith was pissed that he hadn't seen a script yet. I had several unanswered texts from him.

"I can get you a pass," I said. "Sure." I wasn't sure, but I didn't want to talk about the robbery anymore. I wasn't a very good liar. Wasn't particularly good at secrets either. I didn't want to blurt out Enrique's name.

"Okay," Ruby said. "Doesn't look like there's anything to see here. Maybe we should have a bunch of directors do a PSA warning actors not to do stupid things like this." She picked up her notebook and then stood. She held out her hand. "It's nice seeing you again, Brooke. I'm glad you're doing so well. You deserve it."

We shook hands, she said goodbye to Fern, and then she left. Fern motioned the waiter over and ordered another Bloody Mary. When he was gone, she said, "Why was she so nice to you?"

"When Alberto died, she was one of the reporters they sent out to dog us. The others were assholes. She was kind. We became friends of a sort. I gave her a couple of exclusives and nudged others in her direction when she was having a difficult time a few years ago. She still tries to do journalism even though she's covering Hollywood."

"We don't want any real journalism, Mom," Fern said. "We don't want them to know the truth."

The waiter brought her drink, and she took a gulp. Then she looked at me.

"No, I'm not giving up drinking," she said. "I don't have to. But you have to come to my party. You owe me after entangling me in your little lie. Why the hell didn't you just keep quiet and let the police come and take them away?"

"Because I know what it's like to feel desperate," I said. "Enrique is making decisions from that desperate part of his brain. I've been lucky, Fern. You've been lucky. Your dad has been lucky. We're working. We can pay our bills. Enrique did a stupid thing, but he didn't deserve to go to jail. I wish he had called me. I would have put him in the film. Or talked Jack Meredith or your dad into giving him a part. He could be the alien leader."

"You mean Jonny Black's part?" she asked.

"No! Jonny's boss, if you will," I said. "The real alien leader. I could make him very bad."

"Are you seriously thinking of writing a part for him?" she asked.

"I might," I said.

Fern looked nervous. "I don't like the police involved," she said.

"Who does?" I said. "But Enrique and his accomplice were stupid not to figure the cops would come."

She nodded. She looked like there was something else she wanted to say.

"I didn't think they'd question *me*," she said. "I'm worried. I'm worried they might go back to the arson."

"There was no arson," I said quietly. "There was just a kid who didn't know any better. You're safe, Fern. There's no evidence, and no one is looking into it. They've built another house where the old one was. You're okay, darlin'. I wouldn't let any harm come to you."

She looked at me. We both knew I had let harm come to Alberto, her baby brother. I hadn't been able to stop SIDS. But I could stop an arson investigation should one begin. Couldn't I? Maybe not, but I was confident no one was going to go digging into the truth about a house fire that happened over ten years ago.

"This will all blow over," I said. "Betcha."

"But you're coming to the damn party?" Fern said.

"Yes, I'm coming to the damn party."

We finished breakfast, talked a bit about her brother who was now a teenaged boy without an ounce of obnoxiousness in his soul. Seemed Fern had gotten the whole kit and kaboodle when it came to teenage rebellion. Only she was no longer a teenager—although when she was around me, she certainly acted like one.

I hadn't been much of a mother when Fern was going through her tweens and teens. I barely remembered her childhood, but I couldn't admit that to her. She'd never let me live it down.

"Hey, Mom," Fern said as we got ready to leave, "I saw Mark the other day at Surfas. Did he mention it?"

"No," I said.

"Yeah," she said. "He was with some woman and a kid. A boy."

"You mean Ian?" I asked. "Was it his son Ian? You've met him. He's about 10 years old."

"I don't know," she said. "The woman was pretty."

I kept eating my omelette.

"I've met his ex," I said. "She is quite attractive. A nice woman. A little blond for my taste, but you know."

"She wasn't blond," Fern said.

I glanced at my daughter. What was she trying to do? I thought she had come to terms with her father and me being apart. In fact, I figured she thought it was better if we were apart since clearly, I didn't deserve the love of a good man like Hayword Lightman.

"She had dark brown hair," she said. "They were laughing and having a good ole time."

"Good," I said. "I wouldn't want him to be having a bad ole time. It was probably his sister."

"Really? They didn't seem like brother and sister."

My eyes narrowed. If Fern had been a friend, I would have

said, "What the fuck are you trying to do? I'm not the jealous type, remember. I fucked half of Hollywood and never cared if they all were fucking the other half of Hollywood."

"Wait," I said. "Surfas? That's a little chichi for Mark."

She shrugged. "I wonder why he didn't tell you he'd seen me. You think there was something going on?"

"Fern," I said, "why are you trying to stir up trouble? I thought you liked Mark."

"I do like Mark," she said.

"Oh, so the implication is that you don't like me," I said.

"I just thought you'd want to know," she said. "The woman looked more like she was his age."

I started to laugh. "Fern, you are about as subtle as a Mack truck. Yes, I am older than Mark. But, we only fuck in the dark, so he can't really tell how old I am and vice versa."

"Mom, someone is going to hear you."

"You started it," I said. "Don't try to bust my balls, cuz honey, I don't have anything that easily crushed."

She put up a hand. "Just trying to help out."

"No, you weren't," I said. "You were being passive aggressive. If you're pissed at me, be pissed at me. If you have something to say to me, say it. This constant poking me, trying to get a reaction, is just fucking tiresome."

"I am not passive aggressive," she said. "I would never be passive aggressive. That would be following in your footsteps."

"What are you talking about?" I asked. "I've never been passive aggressive in my life."

"What do you call drinking?" she asked. "What do you call having sex with every other person you meet? Weren't you trying to get back at Dad? Weren't you trying to get back at us?"

"What?" I said. "Trying to get back at *you*? You mean you and David? No! Why would I want to get back at you? For what?"

"For surviving," she said. "For not being Alberto."

"Good grief," I said. "No. I wasn't trying to get back at your dad. Not really. I was trying to get back at myself. Trying to drown the pain. Or myself. I don't know. Fern, addiction is so complicated."

"And yet so simply destructive," she said.

"Yes," I said. "I am so sorry for the damage I did to you and your brother. But you know, honey, it's a disease. A brain disease. In many ways, I didn't have any control."

She rolled her eyes. I hated when she did that.

"Fern," I said. "I'm trying to talk to you about something important. You can be angry at me all you want. But I'm trying to tell you that addiction isn't much different from diabetes or asthma. Cancer. It's a disease. I can send you the studies. I blamed myself—I still blame myself—but one thing I learned in rehab is that it's not about willpower. It's about brain chemistry."

"I don't understand that," Fern said. "If it's a disease, why don't they just give you a pill? Why then does the addict have to decide to stop in order to get better?"

"That's confusing to me, too," I said. "I think it's because they don't really have a pill to make you stop. But every day, I have to decide not to follow the destructive messages from my brain. I have to decide not to drink. That's not always easy."

"You make it look easy," she said. "You never talk about it. I never see you go to AA. Most alkies I know talk about it all the time."

"I know," I said. I shrugged. "I figured you're not interested in my life. Why should I burden you with my struggles?"

"I wouldn't mind," Fern said. "I mean, you always look like things are so easy for you."

I laughed. "That is the art of an addict," I said. "We thrive on making everything look easy. Easy does it."

"I don't think that's what addicts say," Fern said. "Isn't that what they say in AA?"

"Um, everyone in AA is an addict, darlin'," I said. "So tomato, tomahto."

"I thought we were having an honest conversation."

"Sorry," I said. "Just habit. Trying to get out before I get speared by you."

Fern made a face. She used to make the same face when she was a kid, when I had caught her doing something wrong.

"So tell me how work has been," I said. Perfect parental dodge. It was either that or ask her how her car was running.

Fern looked at me. For an instant, I thought she was going to launch a stream of invectives at me. Instead, she said, "Except for Sally stressing out about being toppled from power, it's been going all right. We've got some new projects I'm excited about."

As she talked, I tried to figure out who Fern had seen Mark with. Didn't like that I was even wondering about it. A dark-haired woman his age or younger. Could be Sherry. She was the general manager at Mark's new restaurant. Marco's End of the Road Cafe. Yep. The café—and my house—was on a street called End of the Road. Someone had a stupid sense of humor when they named it. Or else, they had just run out of . . . imagination. Mark's childhood nickname was Marco. His mom and sister sometimes still called him that. So, there you go.

Anyway, Sherry Burns was his general manager. Not sure he really needed a GM for a place that pretty much only served breakfast, but I didn't know nothing about running no restaurant, so I kept my mouth shut. Sherry was nice enough. Used to be an actor until she gave up the life to have a kid and live the quiet life.

Like me.

Only I hadn't really lived the quiet life. I sometimes wondered if she had either. If I were truthful—and I tried to be nowadays—I'd have to admit I didn't really like her. She smiled too much. She seemed too upbeat. She was never sarcastic.

I didn't really understand her at all. Didn't trust her as far as I could see her. But I never suspected anything was going on between her and Mark.

I was sure it wasn't. They were probably just getting supplies.

"Sherry Burns," I said, interrupting Fern's description of an upcoming project at AFT.

"What?" she said.

"I bet he was with Sherry Burns," I said. "His general manager. She has dark hair, and she's got a kid. Of the boy variety, I think. Yep. Bet they were shopping for restaurant things."

Fern raised an eyebrow. "I thought you didn't care who it was?"

"I didn't," I said. "It just got stuck in my head."

She smiled. A triumphant smile.

"What?" I said.

"It's good to see you're human," she said.

"What else would I be?" I asked. "A zombie from one of my movies? Of course I'm human."

She shrugged. "Just saying."

"Sometimes you're a mean kid," I said.

"Like I said, I learned from the best."

After we finished our meal and I paid the tab, we walked out to the parking lot, kissed the air next to our cheeks, and then started toward our separate vehicles. But then I stopped and turned in her direction. "Hey, kiddo," I called.

"What?" She stopped and looked at me.

I smiled and held out my arms to her. She rolled her eyes, but she came over to me. I wrapped her up and held her close. I rocked her and buried my face in her neck and breathed deeply. "I love you, baby girl."

She sighed and did not put her arms around me.

"I'm not a baby girl," she said.

I kissed her on the cheek, she flinched, and I let her go. She hurried toward her car, as though it was 30 below zero and she had to get to some warm protected place before she froze to death. When she got to her car, she shouted, "I love you, too, old woman."

I flipped her off.

"Nice, Mom."

I smiled and got in my car.

It was good we were finally establishing a solid mother-daughter relationship. I knew my mother had wanted to flip me off most of my life and never had.

It was early enough that I could either go to my writing studio (the former love nest) or to the ocean house without encountering much traffic.

I should go to the studio and write the damn script.

But I wasn't in the mood.

I drove home.

Hardly any traffic and soon enough I could feel the difference in the air, in the world. And then there was the Pacific Ocean. I breathed deeply.

Just then someone on the radio said, "Don't breathe too deeply, friends. The radiation is hitting the coast just about now. Get out those Geiger counters. Check your fish. Your greens. Stay out of the rain. Or just ignore all of this and pretend we are not living in the end times. It's all whackadoodle, my lovelies."

I glanced at my radio. "Who are you?" I asked.

Must be talking about the plume of radiation leaking from the nuclear power plant in Japan. I thought that had come and gone. I shook my head. I should really get my children away from this place.

"Ain't nowhere else to go," the radio said. "We're going to hell in a handbasket. Bet you wish you hadn't quit drinking after all. We're all zombies, baby."

"What the fuck?" I said. I pushed the button on the radio and changed the station to some old time rock 'n' roll. Led Zeppelin. No DJ.

I parked the car behind my house and then walked up the drive to the café, which was on the bottom floor. Mark's pickup was at the front of the house, so I knew he was there.

I opened the front door—and smiled. The place smelled of fresh bread and basil. Or butter. Even from here, at the front door, I could see the ocean stretching out beyond us.

"Mark?"

I heard music coming from the kitchen. I glanced around the dining room—tasteful and small—and walked to the kitchen. The cooler door was open and Mark was bending over to retrieve something inside. I came up behind him and grabbed his ass.

"Hey there, superman," I said.

And then I knew something was off. Mark's ass had suddenly gotten flabby.

The man at the fridge jumped and turned around.

I laughed.

It wasn't Mark.

It was his brother-in-law, Giovanni, holding a cooked chicken leg in his right hand.

"Sorry about that," I said. "You and Mark have very similar asses."

"Uh, thank you, I think," Giovanni said. He was clearly embarrassed. I was amused.

"I was just—" he started.

"Sampling the food?" I asked. "He's a great cook, isn't he?"

Giovanni had worked at AFT for almost two years, but then he got fired or laid off. Or maybe he quit. I couldn't be sure. He was a lawyer, had passed the bar and everything, but he couldn't seem to hold on to a job to save his life.

"Yeah, sure," he said. "Great cook. He's around here somewhere. Said I could raid the fridge."

Giovanni always acted like he had just gotten caught with his hand in the cookie jar. He never seemed comfortable around me. Wasn't quite sure why. Maybe he sensed I thought he was a loser. People knew when someone wasn't on their side. I was actually. I rooted for him. I wanted him to succeed because he was part of Mark's family. But he made one bad choice after another.

Of course, right this second I couldn't think of what other bad choices he had made, besides blowing a gig at AFT. Sally tended to surround herself with people she liked and trusted—people who did good work and were loyal. All Giovanni needed to do was be good at his job. But something had gone wrong, and he no longer worked at AFT. I didn't ask him why. Wasn't my business.

Mark came into the kitchen. He put his arm around my waist, and we kissed.

"I just grabbed your bro-in-law's ass," I said. "Mistook it."

"Mistook it for mine?" He leaned around as if trying to look at Giovanni's ass. "I have a much better ass than that."

"Fer sure," I said.

"All right," Giovanni said. "Can we move on?"

"Gee is helping me tie up some loose ends here," Mark said.

I didn't remember Giovanni being particularly handy. In fact, he was kind of a klutz at home repair. The first time I met him, he was working on the kitchen sink at Mark's mother's house, and he practically flooded her out of home and house.

"Don't you have a contractor for that?" I asked.

Mark shrugged and looked away from me. Ah, something else was going on here. I'd ask him later. I put my arm around Mark's waist, and we walked into the small dining room.

"You wouldn't believe the morning I had," I said.

"You were with Fern," he said. "So I'd pretty much believe anything."

I laughed. "Actually didn't have anything to do with her," I said. "Two actors pretended to rob Juliet's as an audition for a movie role. And on the way home, some guy on the radio seemed to be talking to me."

"How does someone pretend to rob a restaurant? And what was the radio guy talking to you about?"

"They had squirt guns," I said. "And once I figured that out, I asked them what was going on and one of them told me it was an audition."

"Crazy ass actors," he said.

"No shit," I said. "And Mark, I knew—"

Just then Sherry came into the restaurant, hurrying through the front door.

"You're on the news, Brooke," Sherry said. "They say you're some kind of hero." She came over to us and showed us her big screen phone. I didn't really understand why these phones kept getting bigger. Pretty soon people were going to be walking around with big screen phones in their overly large purses. Until the trend changed and everyone had a tiny phone again.

Couldn't keep up.

On the screen, I saw some blow-dried Botoxed woman with breasts out to there looking at some blow-dried Botoxed man with no soul in his eyes as he said, "Yes, Jenna, that old saying that writers will save the world came true today, didn't it?" Then they laughed. Jenna said, "Maybe Brooke McMurphy will once again save us from the zombies in her upcoming movie *Beauty and the Zombies Part Two: Escape from Alcatraz*. I for one can't wait. I toured Alcatraz once. Just fabulous."

"And there you have it, folks," the man said. "We have our own escapee from Alcatraz in this studio. Maybe she'll get a part in *Beauty and the Zombie Part Two*. Me, I'm holding out for Part Three."

Then they laughed.

Sherry tapped the screen, and it went dark.

"You wrestled guns from robbers?" Sherry asked. Her eyes were wide.

"No!" I said. "They were actors."

"They didn't mention that," Sherry said. "Just said the bad guys escaped but not before you got all the stolen goods back."

Mark looked at me. I dropped my arm from his waist.

"That's not what happened," I said. "This is why I hate the media. They get everything wrong."

"Aren't you part of the media?" Sherry asked.

"No," I said, "I am part of the *entertainment* industry. Completely different. We just make stuff up."

"Sounds like that's what they did, too," Mark said.

"Yep," I said.

"How exciting!" Sherry said. "Were you scared?"

"No," I said. "I was annoyed."

Sherry was smiling at me. She wanted to hear more. I'd already told the tale to the police. I didn't feel like telling it again, at least not to her. To Mark, Hayword, David. Maybe. Might stress out David. He was always worrying about the end of the world.

"Hey, Sherry and I have a meeting," Mark said. "Big opening coming up soon."

"Yes, I know," I said. I smiled. "You kids go have fun. I'll see you for dinner?" Mark nodded and kissed me.

"I want to hear all about your adventure later," Sherry said.

I gave her the thumbs up sign. "Can't wait to tell you."

Mark gave me a look. I shrugged, almost imperceptibly. I got my keys and went to the locked door that opened on the stairs leading up to my apartment. I could get into my apartment this way or go around to the back.

Now I unlocked the door, started up the steps, then closed the door behind me. I hurried up the rest of the stairs to our place. Truth to tell, I wasn't sure I really wanted a restaurant in my home. When I'd bought this place, I thought it would be perfect for Mark and me. He'd have his restaurant; I'd have my peace and quiet. But how much peace and quiet would I have with a restaurant below me? It was only going to be open four hours a day, five days a week. So that wouldn't be too bad. At least, that was what I told myself. It had been my idea, so I couldn't back out now.

My phone was buzzing in my purse. The house phone was ringing. (Yes, I still had a landline. I liked it better than the cell phone. Cell phones were turning us into zombies.)

I pulled out my cell phone. David.

As I answered it, I walked over to the landline to see who was calling.

The police.

The police?

"David, hang on," I said. Then I picked up the other phone. "Hang on," I said. "I've got my son on the other phone." Back to the cell phone. "Everything okay, David?"

"You were robbed?"

"No!" I said. "I thought the school confiscated cell phones at the beginning of the day."

"We were in the computer lab," he said.

They still had computer labs?

"No, I wasn't robbed, honey," I said. I could hear the panic in his voice.

"And the radiation is coming," he said. "They found a two-headed whale."

"I bet that didn't have anything to do with the radiation," I said. "Darlin', I've got another call, but I promise you everything is okay. I can come pick you up from school today, if you want. I'll text your dad."

"Okay," he said.

He ended the call. I put the other phone to my ear.

"This is Brooke McMurphy," I said.

"This is Detective Alex Baxter," he said. "I have some questions for you about today's robbery at Juliet's. Can you come down to the station?"

"I was just in the city," I said. "I answered questions already. Don't you have the notes? It wasn't a robbery. It was a job audition. A screwed-up job audition."

"But there was no one to audition for," he said, "except for you and your daughter."

"My daughter?" I felt a knot in my stomach. "My daughter is an assistant to a studio head. She doesn't have any power. And I'm a freaking writer. No one listens to us. I don't hire actors. This was *not* for my benefit!"

"But you figured out it was an audition," he said. "You helped them escape."

"I figured out it was something besides a robbery when I saw the squirt guns," I said.

"No one else figured that out?"

"It happened so quickly," I said. "One of the guys told me it was an audition, and then I took them to the back room. They gave me the jewelry and stuff and left. End of story. Don't you have real crimes to investigate?"

How to win friends and influence people.

"This is a crime, Mrs. McMurphy," Baxter said.

"I don't have time for this," I said.

"You better make time," he said. "And you might want to bring along your lawyer."

"My lawyer?" I said. "What for? I didn't do anything wrong."

"You helped two felons escape from the scene of a crime," Baxter said.

"No," I said, "I did no such thing. I encouraged two actors to stop being stupid and to leave the premises."

"The truth of all of that is yet to be determined," he said. "Maybe a jury will have to sort it out."

"Are you calling me a liar?" I asked.

He didn't say anything.

I made a noise. "Look, do you know Philip Case? He works in Major Crimes. Or major case. I don't know what they call it. He knows me. He'll vouch for me."

"It doesn't really work that way, ma'am," Baxter said.

"Can't you just call him?" I asked. "He'd tell you I'm the last person who would go out of my way to help someone, especially a criminal. I'm law-abiding. Keep my nose clean. Etc."

"I do know Phil," he said. "I'll call him. But just because he *knows* you, it doesn't mean he knows you. Everyone has their dark side."

"I know," I said. "That is my dark side. I don't go out of my way to help anyone. And I don't think we're supposed to say dark side. That's equating darkness with evil, and that's racist. Maybe we should say anti-social? Or our criminal side?"

"The media is calling you a hero," he said. "We hate heroes."

"I hate the media," I said.

"I thought all you movie types loved the media."

"I'm not a movie type," I said. "I'm a writer. I don't like the glitz and glory. I don't even know how the media got this story."

"You did that zombie movie," he said.

"Yes." I hesitated. Did he love it or hate it?

"I don't really understand zombies," Baxter said.

"Me neither," I said. "That's why I made them into aliens."

"Yeah, that makes a little more sense."

"I wrote *Love and Other Insanities*," I said. "Many lifetimes ago."

"I saw that," he said. "Really liked it. Took my wife to it early on, when we were dating. Seemed like an honest film."

One thing I loved about Los Angeles—and sometimes hated about it—was that you could go anywhere and talk about movies to anyone. Everyone had an opinion. It was such a company town.

"Thanks," I said.

"Being in love is a little bit like insanity," Baxter said.

"Yes."

How could I get out of this?

"But zombies?" he said.

"My husband asked me to help him out with the script," I said. "I didn't want to do it, but I wanted to make him happy. Love and other insanities, you know."

"It was kind of . . . cute," he said. "My wife is really looking forward to the next one."

I wanted to offer to get him opening night tickets, but I had enough sense to keep my mouth shut. I didn't want to sound like I was trying to bribe him.

"I'll call Phil and then get back with you," he said.

"Thank you, Detective Baxter," I said. "I appreciate it."

Since I had stopped drinking my head was so much clearer: I could actually remember names, places, times.

People seemed to appreciate being remembered.

"Thank you, Mrs. McMurphy," the cop said. I didn't correct him. I wasn't Mrs. anyone. Never had been.

I was glad the call was over. Two other people had called my cell phone while I was on the phone with the cop. Media outlets.

Man. The longer I was in the media spotlight, I knew, the worse it was going to be. I hadn't done anything wrong. Not really. But I knew that in the media one could go from hero to whore in about 60 seconds flat. My 60 seconds were just about over.

THREE

I didn't want to interrupt Mark's meeting—or deal with Sherry's cheerfulness—so I texted Mark I was leaving, texted Hayword I was picking up David, and then I went out the back way to my car.

I hadn't even been home ten minutes.

Fern called me before I was out the driveway. I sat still and listened to her yell at me.

"Mother! What have you done? The police want to talk to me. They think we had something to do with this. Why did you lie?"

"Fern," I said, "I did not lie. Can we talk in person or on one of my burner phones." Was that what they called them? "Just in case someone is listening. You don't have to talk to the police. You didn't do anything wrong. Just tell them you're too busy to talk to them."

"I am too busy!"

"There you go," I said. "I just talked to the detective on the case. I told him you had nothing to do with it. I told him I had nothing to do with it. That's the truth, Fern."

"Okay, okay," she said. "Sally is ecstatic."

"Did you say *ecstatic*?"

"Yes! It was all over the news, and most of the reports mentioned the movie. Great free publicity. They're calling you a hero."

I didn't mention that the detective was not calling me a hero. In fact, he seemed to be calling me an accomplice. I was going to kill Enrique.

"I gotta get David," I said. "He heard about it and is a bit scared. Heard about the radiation coming, too."

"Little freak," Fern said. "We're all going to fucking die anyway, what's his problem?"

"His problem is he's 14 years old and he shouldn't have to worry about radiation or maniacs coming into restaurants threatening to kill everyone."

"They didn't actually threaten to kill anyone," she said.

"What?"

"They didn't threaten to kill anyone," she said.

What was going on here? Suddenly she was defending the faux robbers?

"So you don't think I need to go talk to the cops again?" Fern asked.

"No," I said, "but ask Sally, and ask for the company lawyer if you do go. Remember, you didn't know the so-called gunmen. You'd never seen them before."

"I don't know them!" she said.

"Good," I said. "I was just reminding you."

Christ. Why was every conversation with my daughter so fraught with . . . peril, nuance, atomic war, end of life as we knew it?

Soon enough, we ended the phone call, and I headed back to my own 'hood, sort of, to pick up David at his school. My phone kept vibrating, but I didn't answer. I had promised David years ago that I wouldn't talk and drive. I also promised him I wouldn't drink and drive. I didn't do that either. Anymore.

I was a few minutes early, so I parked the car under the tall eucalyptus trees near the school and sat back in my seat and closed my eyes. When I lived at the big house with Hayword and the children, I had gotten more down time than I did now. We had a huge back yard—beautiful back yard—and a garden house. Even though I was drunk for most of the time I lived there, I still appreciated the solitude and quietude. Plus it was across the street from Joan Donning, who was the closest thing I had to a best friend. She was completely fucked up—as most of us are—but she was fun to be around, even now that I wasn't drinking. And now that I wasn't drinking, she didn't seem as stupid. Or more to the point, I tried not to categorize people as stupid or not stupid. Perhaps I was just a wee bit more compassionate than I had been in the past.

Maybe not.

The phone buzzed and would not stop.

I finally answered it.

"What the fuck?" Hayword's voice.

"Hello to you, husband o' mine," I said.

"You were robbed?"

"I wasn't robbed," I said. Gawd. How often was I going to have to tell this story? "They were actors trying to audition for a role, only the director they were auditioning for wasn't there. I sent them on their way and all was well."

"Not *that* well," he said. "Philip just called and said some detective Baxter called him and wanted Phil to vouch for you, vouch for you that you wouldn't be involved in helping criminals escape the long arm of the law. Philip didn't know what to say."

"What do you mean he didn't know what to say?" I sat up in my seat. The kids were beginning to stream out of the school. "He better have said all good things. You've gotten him more consulting jobs on more shows than I can shake a stick at."

Granted not a great metaphor, but I was rattled.

"In other words, we've made him rich," I said.

"Not quite," Hayword said. "He did say nice things about you to this Baxter, but he wants to talk to you later. You're not mixed up with anything, are you?"

"Hayword," I said. "That's a stupid question."

"Doesn't it all seem strange to you?"

"Actors always seem strange to me," I said. "Maybe they were high or on drugs. I don't know. I just know they didn't really have guns, and everyone got back their jewelry and whatnots."

I saw David coming out of the school building. I stuck my hand out the window and waved. It was February, but it was warm out for a Midwestern gal like me, so I had driven up the hill with my windows down.

"I see David," I said. "You at the house? I'll be up in a bit."

Hayword was saying something, but it was too late. I had already pushed end call.

"Hiya, sugar," I called to David. He grinned and waved. He always looked glad to see me. I loved that about him. I did him a favor, though. I didn't get out of the car and hug and kiss him in front of all of his friends. He did have friends now. He had his own group of fellow geeks—if that was even what they called smart technologically capable people these days. Maybe they were just called teens. In any case, some of David's anxieties had lifted once he had more friends. And then he got a girlfriend and then later another girlfriend. Although now he had a different set of anxieties.

He was so gorgeous. Looked a lot like his father with some of my softening features to make him drop-dead gorgeous. My guess was that once he reached sixteen, the girls (and some of the boys) would be swooning over him.

He got in the passenger seat next to me.

"Hey, Mom," he said.

"Hey, kiddo," I said. I started up the car and drove us carefully around the other kids looking for their rides. David's school didn't have any buses. Buses were for the poor or for parents who didn't care enough about their kids to pick them up. Yep. That was the attitude.

"So what happened?" David asked. "Why were you in the news?"

"I was in the news because there are hardly any true journalists left in the world," I said, "and certainly none in Hollywood." Maybe Ruby. "There were two actors who were trying out for a role, so they were pretending to be criminals."

"How'd you figure it out?" he asked. "Were you afraid?"

"I wasn't afraid," I said.

I didn't get afraid like that. The worst thing had happened— one of my children had died—so I didn't sweat the small or big stuff. Of course, I had been afraid something might happen to my other kids, afraid something might happen to Hayword, and afraid of feeling my grief and despair over Alberto's death for a long while. But that was different. I didn't have the free-floating anxiety that haunted David.

If I had it at one time, I didn't remember anymore. Now I was more afraid of taking a drink than I was of radiation, climate change, or creeps with guns. Didn't know what to do about any of it, anyway, so why be afraid?

I did feel some responsibility in fixing these things so that my kids didn't have to live their lives in fear and misery. So I gave money here and there, and I tried to live the simple life. As simple as a Hollywood mogul can live.

Not that I was a mogul.

With David, we had tried to change his diet, had sent him to a therapist, had put him on medication. He was better, but he still had these attacks of anxiety, and we weren't sure why.

Maybe because he was the only one in the family who was actually paying attention.

I had had some anxiety attacks after Alberto died, but I had buried those with medication. After a time, they stopped. Maybe because I drank them away.

"Did you hear about the moon?" David asked. "It's so close to the Earth they think the tides might be really high and low. We should go to the ocean and see. Could be so low some ancient civilization might be uncovered."

"I thought the full moon meant the undead would roam the planet," I said.

"Who told you that?" David asked.

I laughed. "I heard it through the grapevine. Or maybe I'm just trying to get in the mood to write my script."

"Maybe that's why you were robbed today," he said.

"I wasn't actually robbed," I said, "but, hell, let's blame the full moon and Mercury retrograde on people being stupid."

"Can we do that every month?" David asked.

"Done!" I said.

"I did find a place online that said there was an ancient prophecy about this time of year and this moon and some other astrological things," David said. "Mountains will fall and the earth will open. And that which was dead will come alive."

"See," I said. "I told you I heard it through the grapevine."

"I don't believe it," David said. "They were vague about

who the prophets were. One place said it was a Vedic prophecy, and another place said it was Navajo. I've decided it is bullshit."

"Good decision," I said. "One less thing to worry about."

Joanie was walking up our drive when I pulled in. She waved with the hand that was holding the martini.

David started talking before he was out of the car. "Aunt Joanie, Mom got robbed by two actors. It's all over the news. They're calling her a hero."

"Hi, David," Joanie said. "She's not a hero anymore."

I got out of the car. "What are you talking about?"

David pulled out his pad and looked at it. The three of us walked toward the house as the front door opened and Hayword stepped out.

"She's right, Mom," David said. "It's trending away from hero. Now they're saying the police suspect it was a publicity stunt—and you're part of it."

"What?"

"I just heard," Hayword said. "Come in. All of you."

For an instant I wanted to snap at him, "It's my goddam house, too," but then I remembered I was the one who had left the house and the marriage. I was the one who was living at the seaside with the man I had been fucking for a year, more or less, before I finally left Hayword. Before I finally stopped drinking—and then left Hayword.

Hayword wasn't a bad man. He was a good man, actually. Even though I had caught him fucking some blonde bimbo right after Alberto died. That image was seared into my brain. Granted, I had already cheated on him—that's how we got Alberto in the first place—but it didn't matter. He screwed some woman with fake breasts, and I had wanted to kill them both.

Instead, I stayed with Hayword and cheated on him nearly every day of the next ten years, more or less. Publicly. I mean, I didn't hide it from him or anyone else, really.

To this day, I couldn't forgive him for the image in my brain of him fucking that woman up against the wall, or up against the copy machine, or wherever it had been. It seemed so crass and brutal and animal-like.

So I started drinking. Not that I blamed him for my drinking. Not anymore. Maybe I started drinking before that. When Alberto died.

It didn't matter. None of that mattered.

I went into the house with Hayword, Joanie, and David. Violeta—who had been our housekeeper before I left—wasn't there. Someone still came in to clean and cook occasionally, but we—or they—didn't have full-time help any longer. We figured we all needed to learn to take care of ourselves. Violeta had her own housekeeping company now, so she still worked for us, sort of, even though we seldom saw her anymore.

"Brooke," Hayword said, touching my elbow. "Phil wants you to call him ASAP." He handed me his phone. Phil's number was right there. I walked away from the chatter in the kitchen.

"Phil," I said when he answered. "This is Brooke."

"I heard you had an adventure today," Philip said.

"I wouldn't call it that," I said. "It's turning into a big pain in the ass. Can you get the police off my case?"

"I talked to Baxter," he said. "He's an okay guy."

"They're saying in the news that police think I had something to do with it," I said. "Phil, you've known me forever. When have I tried to get publicity for anything?"

"You might want to get your publicist on this," Phil said. "An hour ago, the media was singing your praises. Now they're talking about your imminent arrest."

"Arrest?" I must have yelled this because everyone else stopped talking. I glanced toward the kitchen. They were all looking at me. I waved them away and then walked into Hayword's office and closed the door behind me. "What could they arrest me for? I don't have a fucking publicist! Phil, I don't want publicity!"

"Then the studio you work for," he said. "Something. You need to get on top of this."

"This is crazy," I said. "I didn't do anything except tell two actors to quit being assholes. I stopped what was happening! I got all the jewelry back from the fake robbery. No one was hurt. What did I do wrong?"

"They could charge you with aiding and abetting," he said.

"But I didn't do that," I said.

"That's what we have a court system for," he said.

"Oh my god," I said. "Can't you do something? David is already a wreck about it." Okay, so I exaggerated. But I wasn't afraid of using my children in this small way if it meant it could help me avoid jail.

"I wish I could," he said. "I spoke up for you. The problem is that all the jewelry wasn't returned. One woman says she is missing a bracelet worth ten thousand dollars."

Oh Christ.

"Maybe she's lying," I said. "Maybe it's insurance fraud."

"Maybe," he said. "It's not my case. But when I suggested the woman might be lying to Baxter, he suggested *you* might be lying."

"Fuck, fuck, fuck," I said.

Philip didn't have an answer to that.

"Do you have any suggestions?" I asked.

"Get a lawyer," he said, "and talk to your studio. Maybe they can spin this back in your favor. It is Hollywood, you know."

Christ on a stick.

"Okay," I said. "I appreciate all you did, Phil. Thank you."

I stared at the phone. Now what was I going to do? Had Enrique or his friend actually pocketed someone's bracelet? This was why I should never get involved in anyone else's life. I should have just let the police storm the restaurant and arrest them.

Clare Boothe Luce was right: "No good deed goes unpunished."

Now I'd have to find Enrique and get the damn bracelet, and I'd have to talk to Sally St. James about all of this. But I couldn't. I couldn't let her know I had actually helped these people because I knew one of them.

Stupid. I had thought Enrique was stupid. Lord love a duck. *I* had not acted very intelligently either.

First, I needed to reassure my son, and then I needed to do some major damage control.

I went into the kitchen. Hayword opened his arms to give me a hug. Normally, I didn't want to get that close to Hayword. It was just too familiar. Too strange. Right this minute, I felt a wee bit vulnerable—which in the past would have caused me to act nastiest to the person who was being nicest to me. But I went into Hayword's arms. It did feel familiar, and it did feel nice.

"Okay," Joanie said after a bit, "get a room. Or tell me what's going on."

David said, "Yeah."

I laughed and pulled away from my husband.

"It'll be fine," I said. "I was a witness to an audition, but the cops believe it was an attempted robbery." I didn't say they believed this because a ten thousand dollar bracelet was missing. "It'll all get straightened out. I probably need to talk to Sally, though. David, you want me to make you a snack?"

David rolled his eyes, and Hayword laughed.

"Hey, I can put peanut butter and jelly on a piece of bread as well as the next person."

"Darling," Joanie said, "that's what we have maids for."

"We don't have a maid," I said.

"Mom, I don't eat peanut butter," David said. "It can have a fungus that causes liver cancer."

"David, you have got to stop reading that shit," I said. "We buy only organic peanut butter."

He shook his head. "Nope. Doesn't matter. Peanuts—"

Hayword held up his hand. He and I both knew this listing of toxins in the environment meant David was stressed. Probably worried about me going to jail.

"I will make us all a snack," Hayword said. "Joanie, you want to stay? Brooke, go make your phone calls."

Hayword went to the fridge. Joanie sat on one of the kitchen stools and sipped her martini.

I put my arm around David's waist. "How's your science project coming?"

He nodded. "It's good," he said.

"You want to tell us about it?" I asked.

"Not yet," he said.

"You're not going to make zombies of us all, are you?" I asked.

"Too late," David said.

He was smiling. I squeezed him and then let him go.

"I'm actually looking for a cure for zombies," he said, "so you can use it in the movie."

"Cool," I said. "I'll steal any good idea. I might even steal some bad ideas. Just pitch them to me."

"I think you should have her alien zombie baby burst out of her belly like in *Alien*," Joanie said. "At the very beginning of the movie."

"That would mean she'd die," I said, "at the very beginning of the movie. She's a big star. We want her for the third movie."

Oh good grief. I was talking like Sally St. James—like a studio head. I was talent. I was the writer. I couldn't think like an exec.

"She *can't* die!" David said. "Why'd you make her pregnant anyway, Mom? You always said it was lazy writing when writers could only think of two things to do to a woman: rape her or get her pregnant. Wouldn't she have used protection, especially in a world where people were dying of a mysterious contagious illness?"

I leaned against the counter and glanced at Hayword. He smiled and shrugged as he peeled carrots.

"I didn't say it was *always* bad writing. But often. I just loved the shot, though. I loved how the camera came around and then you saw she was pregnant. Chilling."

David and Joanie nodded.

"Yes, I'm sure she used protection, David, my son. But such things are not always 100 percent."

"Besides," Joanie said, "we don't know about alien sperm. They could have eaten right through any condoms."

"Alien zombie sperm," I said.

"Okay, I give," David said. "No more talking about sperm, sex, or condoms."

I laughed. David was beginning to relax, so now I could, too.

"I'll make these calls and be right back," I said.

I went up the stairs to my old office. I hadn't used it when I lived here, and it was still unused. Hayword hadn't changed a thing. It was a shrine to . . . me. To me not using it. I sat at the desk and called Sally St. James.

"What the fuck, Brooke?" Sally said. "You go to lunch and now there's an international scandal. You know, you were a lot more discreet when you were drinking."

"Fuck you," I said. "First my daughter tries to get me to drink and now you."

"Really? Geez. I was just kidding. We've got our lawyer, Stanley Takata, standing by to go with you to the police station. You remember Stan, don't you? Good guy."

"I don't want to go," I said.

"Why? If you didn't do anything wrong—"

"I can't believe you just said that. Lots of people who 'don't do anything wrong' end up in jail. I gave the police a statement at the time. If they want to charge me with something, show me the evidence and charge me. Otherwise, I don't want to go down there."

Sally made a noise. "Brooke, can't you ever do anything the easy way?"

I thought for a moment, and then I said, "I do lots of things the easy way. That's how I often get in trouble."

"Okay, I'll have Stan talk to the police on your behalf," Sally said. "On the behalf of AFT. He'll tell them that this wasn't a publicity stunt. You'd never be involved in anything like this, and we'd never be involved in anything like this." She paused. "You weren't involved in this, were you?"

"Of course not!" I said. "Like I want any publicity."

"You've got it," Sally said. "The publicity, I mean. First there was this nice photo of you and Hayword. You look so much like middle America. They talked about *Love and Other Insanities*. Then an hour later, the photo they showed was one taken right before rehab. I don't know where they got it. You look like hell. They noted your stint in rehab. Noted the monstrous success of *Beauty and the Zombie*. But they said you had a reputation for living *la vida loca*."

"Oh Christ on a freaking cross," I said.

I was mortified.

"Maybe it's only on the local news," I said. "I mean, who the hell cares about this kind of stuff?"

"Wish I could reassure you," Sally said. "But the media smells a scandal. *TMSleez* and *ET* are both running with it. They called AFT and asked us for a comment. Don't worry, we didn't have one—beyond saying we had complete confidence in you.

I'm surprised they haven't called you. But I know how protective you are about who gets your phone number."

"This is really stressing David out," I said. "I'm going to go home for a while to be with him, let him see all is well."

"At the beach?"

"No," I said, "at the house. Ah, at Hayword's place." *Our* place? We owned the damn house together still. But it wasn't *our* place. It was strange how I felt possessive over it even though I had never liked it. Thought it was ostentatious.

"Stan Takata will help," Sally said, "and if you could get this all to calm down, that would be great."

She sounded a little off. I remembered what Fern had said: Sally's position was tenuous at AFT. Or Sally was worried her position was tenuous. Everyone in Hollywood was paranoid, and everyone thought they were about to become obscure and unimportant—if they actually were important—and they were right. I mean, come on, we were all about to become dust in the wind.

Especially with this drought.

And since the radiation from Japan was coming our way, we'd become radioactive dust in the wind.

"Sally, this has gone from me being great to me being scum in about two hours. Maybe it'll go back to me being a hero in the same amount of time. Or better, they'll forget about me."

"Hero is better," Sally said. "I didn't want to mention this to you, but the suits are iffy about *Beauty and the Zombie Part Two*."

"The suits?" I said. "I thought you were the suits."

She made a noise.

"I'm serious," I said. "And beyond that, *Beauty and the Zombie* was the highest grossing—"

"Yeah, yeah," Sally said, "I know all that. But they're not sure they want to be associated with the franchise any longer."

254

"Fine," I said. "Any studio in town would snatch it up."

"I think they'd tie it up for years," Sally said, "until it was dead, dead, dead. Just for spite."

I shrugged. "So what? I'd be okay. Hayword would be okay. You'd be okay." But I did feel butterflies in my stomach. Did this physical response mean I actually wanted to write the script? I had fun with the last one. I wanted to have fun with this one. In fact, *Beauty and the Zombie* had been the best work experience of my life, from beginning to end.

"Damn it," I said. "What can I do?"

"Turn this around," she said. "Get it out of the news or change the story so you're the good guy again."

"You always said all publicity was good publicity," I said. "I don't understand."

"The entertainment media is so different now," Sally said. "I don't think you understand."

I rolled my eyes. I wasn't an ignorant child.

Although I did tend to ignore the rest of the world.

"If the media decides to go after you," Sally said, "it won't be pretty. They'll dredge up everything, Brooke. *Everything*."

I groaned. My past wasn't pretty, but it also wasn't public. How could they find out anything unless people talked? Most of the people involved in my past wouldn't want to discuss our relationship. It wasn't like Sally was going to blab about our love affair. Our sex affair. But there were all the others. Someone at rehab could talk. They weren't supposed to but they might.

No. Couldn't jump to the future.

It was all about now, babies. All about now. I closed my eyes. Had to get this under control.

"You have a morals clause," Sally said.

"No, I don't," I said. "I wouldn't have signed such a thing."

"You've got it," she said. "We all have it."

"For stuff I did before I was under contract?" I said. "I doubt it. What the fuck, Sally. AFT is supposed to be all about the artist. It was created for us. The talent, man."

"I'm just saying there are some forces at work who aren't happy with me," Sally said. "It's sexist bullshit. Or some kind of bullshit. I don't know what's happening yet. But they could use this to get rid of you and then get rid of me."

And then where would Fern be? Working at AFT was the only thing that had ever made her even vaguely happy.

Fuck, fuck, fuck.

"They might even look at the fire, you know," Sally said.

That woke me up.

Why was she mentioning the fire?

"What do you mean?" I asked. I could hear how much higher my voice had gotten. "What about the fire? My fucking house burned down not long after my baby died of SIDS. Why would they look at that?"

"Jesus, Brooke," Sally said. "Calm down. I just mean they might go back to that time. You know, Alberto. Might even dredge up your affair with Alberto's father."

What?

"You knew about that?" I said.

It had been a fucking state secret.

"Yeah," she said. "You told me. One of the times, you know, one of the times we were naked together."

"Christ, Sally," I said. "When did you get demure? Are you saying I told you Ryan Nichols was Alberto's blood daddy when you and I were fucking?"

"Drunk and fucking," she said.

I closed my eyes. Ryan Nichols. I hadn't thought about him in a long time. I didn't know where he was. He'd been an assistant director on one of Hayword's movie. I didn't know if he'd actually gone on to be a director or a producer. Maybe he got out of movies. I only knew I fell for him hard, got knocked up, and then he deserted me. Left me broken. Open. Never had been in love like that before or after. Maybe not even during. Hayword didn't care about me cheating on him or even about being pregnant. He cared about us staying together, no matter what. So we did.

Which was why I was so shocked the day I saw him fucking the blonde. The day of the funeral. Couldn't have been that exact day. Could it? In my memory it feels like the day of the funeral.

Every time I think I've let go of that memory, it pops up again.

Hated that.

Now, I had to concentrate.

Had to go to a meeting. AA. Work the program, man.

No, wait. First I had to find Enrique and get the fucking diamond bracelet back. Somehow get the bracelet back to Juliet's. Get someone to find it. Then the police couldn't say anything had been stolen.

"Okay, Sally," I said, "I'll do the best I can."

"You're magic, baby," Sally said. "Always have been."

I ended the call by setting the phone face down.

Wished I could end the whole day.

I went back into the kitchen.

"Okay, here's the buzz, peeps," I said. "Don't anyone panic." I looked at David. "It's not a tragedy. As an old friend of mine used to say, 'no one is bleeding.' But I need to go back to the city. Gotta put the kibosh on this, whatever it is. If anyone calls you or comes up to you on the street and asks you anything about anything, don't talk to them. You have no comment." I looked directly at Joanie.

"What?" she said. "I don't talk to anyone. And what street? You think some reporter is going to come down this road? I don't think so."

"Just in case," I said. "Don't talk to anyone about me or the family. Not the guy who reads the meter. Not Maria." (Joanie's maid.) "Not anyone."

"Not anyone?" David asked. He thought about it. "Okay, okay, I can talk to my friends about regular things but not about you. If someone asks me if you're a hero or not, I don't say anything."

I laughed. "That's right. Although if you slip and say I'm always your hero, that would be all right."

"But that would be a lie, Mom," he said.

The kitchen got very quiet. I stared at my son. He looked dead serious. Except for the glint in his eyes.

I laughed. David laughed, too, and Hayword and Joanie breathed.

"For yo momma," I said, "a little fiction might be a good idea."

Hayword had put out a plate of veggies and hummus.

"Stay for a snack," Hayword said. "Or stay for dinner. You leave now and you're gonna be in traffic for hours."

He was smiling. How happy he was when we were all together. If Fern showed up, and we were all nice to each other, he would be in heaven. Until he got restless, and then he'd have to call one of his Hollywood friends and talk about his latest project. Get reassurances now from someone besides me.

I wondered why he was so mellow.

Maybe he was seeing someone. Sex always calmed him.

"No," I said, "as tempting as that is. I better git."

"Mom," David said, "at least go to a meeting."

"Or call Mark," Hayword said.

Joanie emptied her martini glass, crossed her pajama-draped legs, and nodded.

I laughed. "Um, don't be telling me what I need to do. What's wrong with you guys?"

"It's got to be a bit strange," Hayword said. "All this. I mean, I kind of shivered listening to it."

"I haven't heard any of it," I said. "Are they saying I have horns? That I'm a zombie? That I beat my children?"

"No, nothing like that," Joanie said. "Just that you might be a thief."

I made a noise. "That is not going to cause me to drink," I said. "Geez Louise."

"You were shouting when you were on the phone," Joanie said. "Reminded me of the bad old days." She shrugged. "Or the good old days. We did have some times."

Hayword gave her a look. They did all handle me with kid gloves, still, sometimes. As though I was a bomb just about to go off, but if they talked quietly, sweetly, that would disarm me.

I didn't feel like a bomb. Didn't feel like I was going to blow up.

I just needed to take care of some things.

Like find Enrique and wring his freaking neck.

"Mom, do you think those two-headed whales are because of the radiation?" David asked. He was looking down at his phone. Should never have let him have a phone.

"There aren't any two-headed whales," I said.

He glanced up at me. "But if there are," he said. "Should we move? Go live with Grandma and Grandpa?"

My parents. In Michigan.

No.

"It'll get in the rain, won't it?" he said. "It'll be everywhere. Nowhere will be safe."

"Honey," Joanie said, "nowhere is safe."

"And this is nowhere," I said, "so it is safe." I gave Joanie the nastiest look I could manage. "David, your dad and I will protect you. I wish you'd stop worrying about that stuff. It's good to know what's going on in the world, but concentrate on the stuff you can actually change or fix. Try to look for inspiring things. That will help your body chemistry. Then your stress level will go down. And then you can eventually come up with solutions to all this stuff. When you're older."

The room was very quiet again, and the three of them were watching me.

"What?" I said. "I learn stuff. How do you think I've stayed sober for two years? This constant overload of news and media crap isn't good for us. You pick a problem and then you work on it. Right?"

Hayword put his arm across my shoulders and squeezed me. "Right."

I squinted at him. Why was he being so tender with me? I wasn't a melon they could bruise. I shook my head. Who cared? He could be nice to me if he wanted to.

"Okay, I'll stay and snack," I said, "but David has to put away his phone and each of us has to tell a funny and inspiring story. No tragedies. No end of the world scenarios. Deal?"

"Deal," David said. Hayword and Joanie nodded.

"Okay," I said. "David, you start."

"Can I look something up first?" he asked, staring down at his phone. I snatched it away from him.

"No," I said. "Just start. Once upon a time. Or there are seven continents. This story comes from the eighth continent."

David nodded. "All right. There are seven continents," he said. "This story comes from the thirteenth continent."

I grinned. "That's my boy."

FOUR

After I left my family and Joanie, I sat in my car for a moment and breathed—and listened to the sound of my breathing. Normally if something like this had happened, I would be sitting in my car drinking and making a date.

Normally in the *past*. But this wasn't the past. It was here and now. What did I need to do *now*?

First up, I had to get the diamond bracelet from Enrique. I shouldn't call him on my phone just in case the police one day got a hold of my phone records. I had disposable phones down at my writing studio—old ones that I had when I was drinking and screwing. In my former life as a double-lifer.

I drove down the hill to the writing studio, parked the car, and went inside. I hadn't been for a couple weeks so the air was stale. I felt anxious. Even though I had redone the place since it was my love nest, even though I'd been here many times in the last two years, I had mixed feelings about it. Sometimes—not certain why—I walked in the door and recalled all the lovers who had come through that door. I remembered—or didn't—all the nights and days that I had drunk my weight in booze. Or close to it. I remembered bringing Mark here. For a year or more, this place had been our place. Our love nest. It was here that I first decided maybe I did have a drinking problem. It was here that my daughter admitted setting fire to our house after her brother died, when she was a pre-teen.

Sometimes I felt sad here. Sometimes I felt peaceful. Sometimes I felt incredibly happy.

I suppose that was just life, eh?

At the ocean house, I still felt like a stranger. I did worry about the radioactive sea water, although I'd never tell my kids that. The radiation was from the plant in Japan that had been leaking for . . . years? Decades? Some scientists said it was going to be the end of the world as we knew it. Others said the leaking radiation meant nothing; we'd be fine.

I figured it was somewhere in the middle. We were living in a fucking cesspool, and we couldn't do anything about it now.

I couldn't focus on that or else I'd want to drink.

So when I looked out at the ocean, I tried not to think about Japan. Or radiation. Or the sea of plastic. Or the level of toxicity in the great mammals that lived in the ocean.

When I was a kid, I had worried about living in a science fiction future of a polluted toxic world. Now here I was, living in a polluted toxic world.

Fucking whackadoodle times.

I dropped my keys on the counter and shook my head.

Nope. Wasn't gonna go there. Everything was not bad. Everything was not lost.

I got one of the burner phones from the junk drawer and plugged it in to charge it up. Then I went on the computer and tracked down Enrique's number. Didn't take much. I cleared all evidence of my search—I hoped. I also searched my own name under news.

I was not happy with what I found.

Several short articles had been posted on how I had thwarted a robbery at Juliet's. Each article mentioned I was coauthor of *Love and Other Insanities* and *Beauty and the Zombie*, and that was about it. Some sites had that same article with an update above the original article: "Police sources now say they suspect Brooke McMurphy may have been involved in the attempted robbery at Juliet's restaurant off Sunset Blvd. McMurphy is the cowriter with her estranged husband of *Love and Other Insanities*. She is also the scriptwriter of *Beauty and the Zombie*, which came out after McMurphy's stint in rehab."

Crap.

How the hell did they know I'd been in rehab?

Not that I was surprised they knew it. But how did this all blow up so quickly? It wasn't overnight. It was over a freaking hour!

I shouldn't exaggerate. It hadn't blown up. Just a few . . . *dozen* articles.

Ugh.

I started to turn on the TV but decided against it.

I got the burner phone and called Enrique.

"Hello?" He sounded so cheerful. Didn't he understand the shit storm he had generated for me?

It suddenly occurred to me that Enrique's phone records might be examined should the police come to suspect him. This phone couldn't be traced to me. Could it? Crap. I couldn't remember if I had bought it with cash or a credit card. At the time I wasn't worried about the police; I was just trying to keep my sexual escapades private.

"Hello?" he said again.

"Enrique," I said. "You have ruined my life."

Ah, the drama queen was never far beneath the surface, was she?

"Brooke? What's going on? It was great seeing you today."

"Ricky!" I said. "We didn't just run into each other. You tried to rob the restaurant where I was having breakfast."

"No, no," he said. "It was an audition. An audition!"

"Please tell me you haven't told anyone about what you and your friend did."

"Besides Manny?"

"Manny?"

"He was our inside man at Juliet's," Enrique said, "even though he wasn't there. Remember? I told you."

"I wish I could forget this entire thing," I said. "Listen to me. They're calling it a robbery. They're saying I was in on it. They're talking about me on the news. The studio head believes they're going to dig up everything they can on my private life."

"No worries there," he said brightly. "You've had a blessed life."

Blessed?

I had never heard that word in relation to me before.

"Blessed? What the hell, Ricky. You found god or something since I last saw you?"

He laughed. "Naw. Just AA. I'm straight as an arrow now. You're a friend of Bill, too, I hear."

"Who'd you hear that from?" I hadn't seen the man for fifteen years, give or take. How could he know anything about me?

"I don't remember," he said. "Just heard it. Am I wrong?"

"Look, Ricky," I said, "you've got to make this right. The police told me there's a ten thousand dollar diamond bracelet missing."

"What?" He actually sounded surprised. "We didn't steal anything. We gave everything back to you."

"No, you didn't," I said. "Or your *friend* didn't."

"Maybe the woman is lying," he said. "I didn't take any bracelets from anyone."

"Okay, so I'll go to the police and say, 'I'm sure the woman is lying because the robbers said they didn't steal any bracelet.' Ricky, they might charge me with aiding and abetting!"

"What? You didn't have anything to do with it. I mean, you helped us get away, so I guess they could argue you were aiding us."

I groaned. "No, I did not *help* you get away! I got the loot from you and pointed you to the door. I was trying to end the whole thing. If this ever becomes public, you can't say I helped you!"

"What does abetting mean?" he said.

That stopped me. I had to think about it.

"I think it means aid or help," I said.

"That's pretty redundant then isn't it?"

I'd never realized how irritating he was. Maybe he hadn't been back then. Twenty years of pickling his brain with alcohol might have changed him.

"I have to have that bracelet back," I said. "Now. Today."

"I can talk to—to my friend," he said. "I can't believe he'd do that, but I'll see. Are you going to take it to the police and turn us in?"

"No," I said. "I'll take it back to Juliet's and leave it someplace and hope someone finds it."

Or something. I'd figure it out once I got there.

"Do you know this guy well?" I asked.

"Well enough," he said. "We've been to a lot of auditions together. For different parts, of course. He's—"

"Naw, remember, don't want to know him. Just get the bracelet back, Ricky. If you don't have it, he does. If he doesn't, we might all be in a lot of trouble. Right now, I might be able to make it right. Call me back on this phone."

I ended the call. I wasn't sure where to go or what to do. I was not made for the life of a criminal. I wanted to fix this now, get it taken care of now, get it off my plate *now*.

The AA people talk about being in the now. I was in the now *now* and I wanted this shit done.

But I had no control over what was going to happen next. My day wasn't even half over and I was ready for a nap.

I stayed in my studio for a couple of hours waiting for a call from Enrique and looking over the original treatment for *Beauty and the Zombie: Part Two*. The movie opens with Colleen Kelly giving birth to her alien baby. The alien father is still in prison, but he feels some kind of shift in the world. In the first *Beauty and the Zombie*, Thomas had been a good guy and then a bad guy who tricked Colleen Kelly into having sex with him—and into vouching for the aliens, telling everyone they would cause no harm. Only they were causing harm. Colleen woke up one morning to discover she had the deadly alien plague that turned humans into zombies. Thomas and the other alien zombies had spread the plague on purpose, to kill off the human race.

Only in the end of the movie, as Thomas is going off to jail, he says that he loves Colleen. She doesn't hear him—or at least the viewer doesn't think she hears him.

So now I was supposed to continue the love story between a mass murderer and Colleen Kelly, the scientist who was duped by the mass murderer and who actually ended up pregnant by him.

I should have never done that. The pregnancy made her weak. No way of getting around that. I was pregnant three times. I birthed three children. Although it was the most powerful thing a human being could do—create life—on the screen, pregnant women were not often the heroes of the piece.

Maybe I should change all that. Maybe she shouldn't deliver

until later in the movie. Make her like Ripley in *Alien*. Kicking some ass and taking names.

Except Colleen was a scientist. She was a peaceful person. She had figured out how to save humans from the plague (a combination of dirt and sunlight). She had literally saved the world. All without any gunfire on her part.

No. I'd stick with the treatment. She would give birth to the child immediately. Then all hell would break loose. I wasn't sure how yet. In the treatment, the alien zombies attack the earth again, but I wasn't sure I cared for that plot line anymore. Lots of shit blowing up would make it popular. What about the human element?

I laughed at myself and pushed the laptop away from me. The movie was supposed to be loud and funny and fast-moving. I could sandwich some human element in-between all that.

I took a break and checked online to see if the media was still discussing me. Apparently they were. I was "trending." I made the mistake of going to some of the sites. Most had added this line, "Two years ago, McMurphy went to rehab for alcohol and drug abuse and sexual addiction."

"I did not go to rehab for sexual addiction, you assholes," I said. "Or drug abuse. Unless you count alcohol as a drug, which I suppose I do."

The comments were wild and rude. All about how nasty Hollywood people are. We're all a bunch of drinkers, druggers, and whores, according to the commenters. Several posts were about how "fucking ugly" I was, so they couldn't understand how I had gotten any partners for my sex addiction.

The only photograph on any of these sites was the one of me going into rehab. Or leaving? In any case, I wasn't ugly. I just looked like a normal woman. One or two commenters said, "I'd do her." Which was more upsetting than the comments about how ugly I was.

Not that I was seriously upset.

Just kind of pissed me off.

I wanted to call Mark, but I was annoyed he hadn't called me to see how I was doing now that my name was mud. Guess he was too wrapped up in his meeting with what's her face.

I rubbed my forehead. I couldn't believe Fern had put that idea in my head and now I couldn't get it out: about Mark all cozied up to Sherry at some store.

Wasn't like me to be jealous. Sure, I'd punished Hayword a good ten years for fucking some bimbo on the day we buried my son, but that wasn't jealousy. That was fury. I knew Mark loved me, and he wasn't the cheating kind.

End of story.

Of course, Hayword hadn't been the cheating kind either.

No! Wasn't the same thing. Mark and I were committed to one another. We lived together. Most of the time. He still had his house. He usually stayed there when he had his son, Ian. Ian liked my house, but it was away from all of his sports and his friends. He came over now more often, now that the restaurant was almost open.

Sunday was opening day. That's when everything would change. Again. The restaurant had been turning our lives a bit upside down for the last year. Sometimes I thought Mark was doing it all just to please me.

"It's okay to have a plumber as a lover," Mark had said to me more than once, "but not as a permanent boyfriend or husband."

"What the hell are you talking about?" I'd say. "I don't care what you do for a living—as long as you can dedicate nearly every waking hour to me."

That would usually end the conversation or we'd continue it in the bedroom.

The docs and therapists at rehab had warned me not to ruminate. Rumination was a trigger for depressives. And that's what

I was. Or had been. Suffering from depression. Rumination just made everything worse. But ruminating about Mark and me having sex was kind of fun.

I heard the key in the back door. In another moment I heard the door open.

"Anyone home?" Mark.

I got up and went into the kitchen. Mark was carrying a bag of groceries. I grinned.

"Hey, baby," I said, "I was just thinking about you."

"Was I naked or clothed?" he asked as he put the bag on the counter.

I went to him, and we kissed and then embraced.

"You started out clothed," I said, "but you ended up naked. Just like now."

He laughed. I took his hand, and we went into the bedroom.

Where we tripped the light fantastic.

You don't need the details. Suffice to say, everyone was very happy at the end of it all.

After I stopped drinking, sex wasn't that much fun for a time. Actually, I didn't have any sex for a while, but once I got back on the horse—so to speak—or back on Mark, or vice versa, sex seemed muted or something. I was incredibly self-conscious. I'd been drinking so long that I couldn't remember if I had been self-conscious before I started drinking. Probably not. Except for Alberto's biological father, Ryan Nichols. I'd been sober then and the sex had been amazing. Quick, but amazing. We weren't together long enough for it to get routine. Weren't together long enough for the milk in the refrigerator to go bad.

In other words, we lusted, we had sex a few times, I fell in love—it was like being drunk, that feeling just before you go over the edge and you know you've had too much to drink and you're gonna be sick soon. I doubt we would have stayed together if I hadn't gotten preggers. But once I told him I was pregnant, he left town. Or the country. I didn't try to track him down—not after I called his phone and discovered it was no longer in service. Hayword could have found him, if I had asked. But I didn't ask. I just threw up a lot, told Hayword about the baby—and the fact that he was not the baby daddy—and we went on with our lives.

Sort of. Then baby Alberto died and the house burned down and we moved into the canyon, into one of those obscenely ostentatious mansions, and I became a drunk who slept with everyone and anyone I could. At least, it felt like that sometimes. The sex always seemed great. Now I understood that was my alcohol besotted brain changing reality for me, but sometimes I missed how alcohol relaxed me. Got rid of my inhibitions. I didn't do anything freaky or kinky—I liked face-to-face sex—but I had sex often and in a variety of places until I settled on the love nest, aka my studio.

I was thinking about all of this while Mark made us omelettes. Ordinarily I didn't like thinking about the past so much. It was done and over. It couldn't hurt me anymore. I had dealt with it. But now, thinking of the past was making me nostalgic for my drinking days. Thinking that sex while drunk was better than sex while sober was a lie the alcohol was telling me—or a lie the part of me who wanted the alcohol was telling: Sex had *not* been better then.

Right?

Right.

Now, sex was just sex. It was fun. But I pretty much did it to get off. The intimate part where you hugged and talked about your deepest feelings—you know that part?—that was not what I longed for or even wanted after sex. I wanted to do the deed and then move on.

Remember that scene in *Network* when the filmmakers were trying to demonstrate how bad—evil really—Faye Dunaway's character was because when she had sex she wanted to get on, get off, and then get off? I remember seeing that at some film festival at college with a group of friends. Afterward, everyone was talking about how disgusting the Faye Dunaway character was. How she was the bane of civilization. I didn't particularly like her, but when my friends kept bringing up how she used men to have sex, I didn't understand: I didn't think she was bad or evil because of that, and I didn't understand the outrage. She was efficient. She did what she had to do, and then she moved on.

Point being, sex was still fun sober, but it wasn't one of the central pillars of my life as it had been before. Mark understood that I wasn't prone to spilling my guts after we had sex. Or any other time, actually. I did try to be more honest and open about my feelings these days—even though I still didn't often recognize when I was actually having feelings.

So after sex—or after we made love—we'd hug for a few minutes while our heartbeats went back to normal, and then we'd get up and carry on. I liked it best when we carried on in the kitchen.

This time Mark made us omelettes filled with mushrooms and spinach and who knows what else. It melted in my mouth. No one could make breakfast quite like Mark. Which was probably why his restaurant was going to be a breakfast place, mostly.

We sat next to one another at the counter. We could see the backyard from our perches. Wasn't much going on there, but it was green and wild-looking.

"So why didn't you let me know what was happening?" Mark asked. "My mother called and told me they were accusing you of being part of some robbery."

"I bet she loved that," I said. "Good excuse for you to dump me."

"Where the hell did that come from? My mother loves you."

I looked at him. "She thinks I'm the whore of Babylon."

Mark laughed. "She certainly does not. She was worried about you. She asked me to tell you to call her later if you need someone to talk to."

I nodded. "Sorry. I am feeling a bit raw. I'm not sure what happened. The studio is telling me I have to take care of this or they might dump Sally and the movie. And the police want to interrogate me."

"Okay," Mark said, "how much of all that is just a horror story you're telling yourself? My guess is that Sally encouraged you to do something to stop the bad press, and the police just want to talk to you."

"I wish it was all exaggeration," I said. "I talked to the police—some detective named Baxter—and I tried to explain that the so-called robbers were just actors. They weren't actually robbing anyone, but he told me one of the customers at Juliet's claims she is missing a ten thousand dollar bracelet."

Mark shook his head and made a noise.

"I know what you're thinking," I said.

He raised an eyebrow. "I bet you don't."

I leaned into him and laughed. "Bet I do. Hundred bucks?"

He shrugged. "Bet."

"You're thinking what the fuck is someone doing with a ten thousand dollar bracelet."

He laughed. "Dead on. You're a scary woman, reading my mind. Guess that means I should take back the diamond bracelet I got you to celebrate my grand opening."

"You know how I love the bling," I said.

Mark smiled and pushed away his empty plate.

"I wonder if it is just someone trying to hit up the insurance companies," I said.

"The police will investigate to see whether she actually owned a bracelet like that, right?"

"I assume so," I said, "but I better call someone and make sure."

I went to the couch, retrieved my phone, and texted the lawyer via Sally's number. I saw there were several texts I hadn't read. Must have turned the sound down again.

I scanned the texts quickly. Four from Fern. One from Irving Jackson. What the hell could he want? One from David. I checked the kids' messages. David was reminding me again about coming to his school on Friday. He was being a little weirder than usual about this. And Fern: "WTF, Mom. What's going on?" "They're going to dig up dirt." "Brooke! Where the fuck are you?"

I sighed.

"Mark, I've got to call my daughter," I said. I went into the bedroom and shut the door. Fern answered on the first ring. She sounded panicked.

"Mom," she said. "They're saying terrible things about you."

"No, they're not," I said, trying to calm her. "They just say the police suspect I had something to do with it. And that's not true."

"But you talked to the robbers! You know them! What am I going to say if the police ask me?"

She sounded . . . hysterical.

"Honey, tell them the truth," I said. "I *didn't* have anything to do with it."

"What would they do to you if they thought you did have something to do with it?" she asked.

"I don't know," I said. "I can't imagine it would ever go to trial." Actually I *could* imagine it. Wouldn't be fun. But would they really send me to jail for showing those two idiots the door?

"If they don't drop it, they'd probably try to make a deal with me if I'd tell them who the robbers were."

"Actors," she said. "You said they were *actors*."

"Yes," I said, "and if I have to choose between going to jail or giving up—" I started to say Enrique's name. But I stopped. Maybe Fern had never heard me say it when we were under the table together. Or maybe she'd forgotten. She had been under stress. "I'd give up the person I knew," I said. "That's the truth of it, honey. I know it's not courageous. But it was an asshole thing for them to have done."

"People do stupid things," she said.

"You have sympathy for them?" I asked. "I figured eventually you'd get around to blaming me for the whole thing."

"Why?" she asked. "You didn't do anything."

She was still sucking up to me. Probably wanted to make sure I'd show up to the party tomorrow.

"You still having the party?" I asked.

"Of course," she said. "Sure." She sounded uncertain, or far away. "Mom, one of the media outlets—I forget which one—mentioned Alberto's death."

"What?" I sat on the bed. I felt rage rising. I stood again.

"In what fucking context?" I asked.

"They mentioned you had gone to rehab," she said, "and that ten years earlier your son had died from SIDS. They didn't mention the house burning. Mom, what happens if they start looking into the house?"

"So what if they mention the house?" I said. "It was just a family tragedy." Hmmm, did a burning house constitute a tragedy? A baby dying was definitely a tragedy. But a house? "A family hardship." Hardship? Really? We went out and bought a more expensive house. Fortunately most of our photographs and important papers had been conveniently stored in the garage.

Amazing how a kid her age had the presence of mind to put that stuff in the garage—before she set the house on fire.

"Besides," I said, "I don't think they can do anything about someone burning down their own house."

Well, except for insurance fraud.

"It wasn't *my* house," she said.

"Sure it was," I said. "It was our house."

"So when you and Dad finally divorce," she said, "and you sell this house, will I get a quarter of the money?" She was slurring her words.

"Fern, are you okay?" I asked. I knew if I asked her if she was drunk, she'd deny it. She'd say she was just tired; that's why she was slurring her words.

At least that's what I had always told people when I was drunk.

"Just worried," she said.

"You're slurring your words." I couldn't resist.

"I'm fucking tired," she said. "Sally works my ass off. What if the police didn't offer you a deal? What if it went to trial? What if they found you guilty?"

She sounded frightened. Did that mean in her heart of hearts she actually loved me and wished the best for me? I knew she did, really, but sometimes it was difficult to tell.

"Darlin', I am not going to jail."

"You are not listening to me, Mother," she said.

Now I was "mother" again. She was back to being pissed at me.

She continued, "What kind of sentence would you get for aiding and abetting?"

"How the fuck should I know! Do I look like a lawyer?" Fern was an adult. Couldn't she clue into the fact that I might be a little worried myself about going to jail?

"Mother, do you remember the time when we were kids and

David said the word *butt*, and I said to him, 'It's not *butt*, it's *bottom*.' Do you remember what you said?"

I sighed. "No, but I can tell this is going to be a bad parent story."

"You said, 'It's not *butt* or *bottom*. The proper word is *ass*.'"

I laughed. "And your point is?"

She *was* drunk. She didn't have a point.

"My point is you are being a butt, bottom, and ass. I'm giving you the same look I gave you back then."

"You better not be driving anywhere," I said. "It's a little early in the day to be drunk on your bottom, isn't it?"

"Hah! The black cat calling the kettle a cauldron. Or something like that." She laughed. "I'll see you at the party tomorrow. I'll text you the address. Love you, ass mom."

I stared at the phone. Now that had been a weird ass conversation. What was going on with my daughter? I needed to talk to Hayword about her. Or Sally.

I looked at the text from Irving Jackson. He was creative director or something at AFT. Their titles always confused me. His in particular since he didn't seem very creative. He acted like a suit, even though he rarely wore one.

"Need to speak with you ASAP," his text read.

Probably just wanted to rag on me about the media coverage of the robbery.

Crap. Now *I* was calling it a robbery.

I went back into the other room.

"Your omelette is cold," Mark said. "You want me to heat it up?"

I shook my head and sat next to him. "Your food is delish cold or hot." I stuck my fork into the omelette and then brought a piece to my mouth. Wasn't actually very good cold. Mark got up, went around the counter and into the kitchen, and leaned over and grabbed my plate.

"No," I whined. "I hate microwaved food. Eggs get so rubbery."

He gave me a look, and then he slid the omelette back into the pan. Like he would ever microwave something he had made for me.

He stayed at the stove, not looking at me, and said, "Honey, something else is going on here. The police may not know it, but I can tell." He turned to look at me.

I shook my head. "There's nothing. Nothing I can tell you." He made a noise and turned back to the stove. "Look, Mark, if this goes to trial, they could call you as a witness, and then you'd have to tell them what I said."

He flipped over the half eaten omelette and then looked at me again. "I'd lie," he said.

"You wouldn't really," I said.

"To protect you? Sure."

"Mark, how would our justice system ever work if people went around lying all the time?"

He laughed. "Lordy, woman, you can surprise me."

He brought the pan over to me and slipped the omelette back onto my plate. Man, some champagne and orange juice would be good right about now.

"Okay, if you won't let me lie—"

"You continue to surprise me, Mr. Upstanding citizen."

"If you won't let me lie," he said, "then marry me. They couldn't force me to testify against you then."

I laughed, my mouth full.

"Then I'd be a bigamist," I said.

"Yeah, what's up with that?" he asked.

"You want to have this conversation now?"

"I'm just saying," he said. "We never talk about it. Why are you still married?"

"Because the split would be horrible," I said. "The money thing. The house the kids grew up in."

"People do it all the time," he said. "I did it. If you don't want the family to lose the house, just let Hayword have it. You've got enough money."

I ate in silence. I didn't like anyone nosing around my business, even Mark. If I'd been a cat, my hair would have stood on end.

"Unless we're not making a life together," he said. "Unless we're just playing. Then that's a different story."

"Do you want to get married?" I asked.

He sat next to me. He was silent for a moment, and then he said, "Yes, I do. I love you."

"But why should that mean marriage? It's a lousy institution."

He put up a hand. "Okay. You're right. We can talk about this another time. We can expound on our philosophies of marriage later."

"You saw how I treated Hayword," I said. "I wouldn't want to do that to you."

"Then don't," he said. He looked at me and shrugged. "Then don't. It's your choice."

I nodded.

"So what can't you tell me about the robbery?"

"I know one of the robbers," I said. "It was Enrique deChamp. He was one of the leads in *Love and Other Insanities*. He played Daniel."

"You're kidding!"

I shook my head. "No. He said it was an audition gone wrong and I believe him. I don't know the other guy. Thank god, I don't know two people who are *that* idiotic. I took them in the back and showed them the door. I wanted them gone so that things wouldn't go bad. One of the patrons could have had a real gun. The cops could have stormed the place. So I helped them leave. It didn't dawn on me that that was a crime. I got all the jewelry back. Or I thought I did. The police told me a $10,000 bracelet is missing. I called Enrique and told him he better get the bracelet back come hell or high water."

"Oh crap."

"Understatement of the century," I said. "But I concur."

"What are you going to do with the bracelet if Enrique does give it to you? Then you'll be in possession of stolen merchandise."

"Oh crap."

"There's only one thing we can do," Mark said.

"Leave the country? Confess? Throw myself on the mercy of the court?"

"AA meeting."

"Good idea," I said, "but I don't want to go around here. Too many rich people."

He laughed. "And that's bad because you hate rich alcoholics?"

"No, I'm always afraid I'll meet someone I slept with and don't remember."

"Don't know what to say to that," he said.

"Why do you think I picked you?" I asked. "I had run through most of the rich people around here."

"Ah, the romance never ends with you."

FIVE

I started to relax as I sat in the truck next to Mark, heading somewhere in the dark. I didn't care where. Mark still had his truck—his plumber's truck—because he continued to work as a plumber, part-time. He said he liked it. And he needed the money for the restaurant, although I told him I would finance it. I mean, I owned the building. The rest was gravy, right? Not right. Renovating and opening a restaurant was a lot more expensive than I ever thought it would be.

Not that I had ever thought about that. I encouraged Mark to follow his dream. If his dream was to open a restaurant, I was right there with him. What else was I going to do with the money from *Beauty and the Zombie*? I had points, man, and AFT actually did honest accounting, so Hayword and I were rich all over again and again.

We all got rich from that movie. That was why I wasn't convinced AFT would dump Sally and me just because of some silly misunderstanding about a robbery. A non-robbery.

Anyway, I didn't mind riding around in Mark's truck anymore, even though he did have a car—an electric one—which I wished he would get in the habit of driving.

"You wanna go out to eat?" he asked. "Or we could get takeout and hang out at my place for a while, after AA."

"Is that where we're going?"

Mark laughed. I knew why. I didn't always know where I was. Even though I'd been to Mark's house many times over the last two years, I couldn't find it on my own, not without GPS. I could get to my house at the beach and in the canyon, could get to any of the studios or downtown Los Angeles, could get around Brentwood where we used to live, but that was about it. The valley, the 401, or any of the burbs—yes, Mark still called them that—were a complete mystery to me. It was like asking me to drive to *The Twilight Zone*. How could you drive to *The Twilight Zone*? It wasn't a fucking destination. Same with Mark's house.

"You should be fucking ashamed of yourself," Mark said, laughing. "You should know the land beneath your feet."

I shrugged. "I do. I know my place, baby. I know my pl*aces*. This ain't my place."

"It's my place," he said. He sounded vaguely hurt. I looked over at him.

"Really?" I said. "Dude, you know who I am. These kinds of neighborhoods creep me out." I looked out the window, but it was dark and I couldn't see anything.

"What are you talking about?"

"You know," I said, "places with basketball hoops on the garage. Cars up on blocks. Women exchanging casseroles. Creepy, creepy, creepy."

"Um, that's pretty much how I grew up," he said.

"So did I," I said. "I never wanted any of it. That kind of lower middle-class suburbia nightmare. Gawd."

"I like how I grew up," he said.

I shivered. "No roots. No culture. No tradition. Just . . . zombies."

"Seriously?"

I looked at him. "Seriously. Hey, I'm glad you had a great childhood. So did I, I guess. But it had no depth. No ritual, no ceremony. Don't you ever wonder about that? Big fucking surprise that I became an alcoholic. Something terrible happened in my life and I had absolutely no backbone—if that was the right word—nothing to fall back on. Nothing to hold me up. Nothing to hang on to. No traditions, no community. When I finally called my mother to tell her about Alberto, she said, 'That happened to Aunt Jane, too. Never got over it.' Really, Mom? Fucking really?"

"We had Christmas," Mark said. "Easter. Halloween."

"All consumer holidays," I said. "Presents on Christmas. Eating jelly beans and chocolate eggs pooped out by some Easter bunny to celebrate the Jewish zombie. Bunnies don't lay eggs, you know. So those eggs were pure shit. Maybe even literally. And Halloween: more candy. Although the undercurrent of Halloween is very cool. Honoring and celebrating the dead."

Mark glanced over at me. He was frowning. Then he looked back at the road.

"What's going on, Brooke?" he asked.

I looked out into the darkness. What *was* going on? I was suddenly sounding bitter and angry. Too much thinking about the past today. My conversation with Fern had been weird. My mother and I never talked to one another like Fern and I did. We never talked period.

I could feel myself wanting to pull away from everything and everyone. I didn't want to fight this battle—or whatever it was—about the robbery. It would have been so much simpler if I'd kept my nose out of the whole fucking thing.

"I feel like I'm starting to fall away," I said.

Fuck. I hoped that old bugaboo depression wasn't about to raise its ugly fucking devouring head again.

"I don't want to deal with this," I said. "There's too much going on. I feel overloaded."

"You're not still hungry?" he asked.

I laughed. "No, I'm not hungry. I am a little angry." Maybe a lot angry. "I'm not lonely." Well, maybe a bit. I was always a little lonely. "I am tired. I've been tired since 1980, I think."

That was an AA thing: H.A.L.T. If you were feeling hungry, angry, lonely, or tired, you could be, would be, might be . . . you were vulnerable for relapse.

Fuck, fuck, fuck.

"This will help, baby," he said. "You can't focus on the negative."

That was unlike Mark. He didn't usually give me advice. Must be seeing signs that scared him. And *that* scared me.

"You thought I'd already been drinking," I said. "Didn't you?" I could hear how pissed I sounded and I didn't know where it was coming from.

"No," he said. "But you know, you never mentioned Alberto's birthday this year. That was just a week ago, right?"

"Oh fuck," I said. "Oh my god. I completely forgot. How could I have forgotten?"

I had never forgotten Alberto's birthday.

"That means they all forgot," I said. "The entire fucking family."

"Or maybe they just didn't mention it because in the past you've had such a difficult time."

Mark stopped the truck in some parking lot next to what looked like a church. I hated AA meetings in churches. Always felt there was something a little judgmental about AA meetings in churches, as though someone was listening just outside the door to discover what our sins were.

I felt a wave of panic. Was there something wrong with my brain that I'd forgotten Alberto's birthday? Or was there something morally bereft about me that I could forget my own son's birthday? My *dead* son's birthday.

The jury had long ago come back on the morally bereft question.

"It's okay," Mark said. "It doesn't mean anything except that you've had a lot going on."

"But I haven't," I said. "You've had a lot going on. You and Sherry. And Fern and Sally are busy at AFT. David and Hayword are busy with their lives. I have not been busy. I know I'm supposed to be working on the screenplay, but it hasn't happened. I've been busy avoiding my work. That's no excuse for forgetting my son's birthday. No kid likes to be forgotten."

"I'm sure if he were alive, you wouldn't have forgotten."

"But that's kind of the point, isn't it? He's dead."

Gawd. I felt like I was going to throw up. Either that or take a drink. I didn't want to go to this meeting.

"Brooke," Mark said.

I looked over at him. "What?"

"Are we going in? Do you need to talk?"

"Nothing to talk about," I said. "The past is past. Live in the now, baby. Isn't that what we're supposed to do?"

I didn't feel as sanguine as I tried to sound.

I got out of the truck and closed the door. I felt like I was in a bit of a fog. Mark came around the truck to me. He reached for my hand and I let him have it. I even leaned on him as we went up the walk and into the church and then down the steps to the basement. Lovely. I hated being in basements more than I hated being in churches. What a banner day.

I was being too negative. Too critical. I was thinking too much about what I didn't want. What I didn't like. I had to change my thought patterns.

Think about what I did want. Living children, for one. Except for the dead one, I could check that off: I had two living children. A sober life. Check. Satisfying work. Check. Safe and beautiful home. Check. Good health. Check. Except for this panic and depression. Hated that these feelings—or whatever they were—could descend almost without warning.

But there had been warning. I should have been paying attention. When the media accused me of being a criminal and then brought up my dead son's name, I should have realized that might trigger a reaction in me.

Or maybe it didn't have anything to do with that. Perhaps it was seeing what Enrique had been reduced to because he couldn't get a job.

I'd always liked Enrique. But we hadn't kept in touch, probably because he had been friends with Ryan Nichols. I never knew if Enrique had been aware of our affair or not.

Things had seemed so normal this morning at breakfast as I parried with my daughter. How easily they could go askew.

The entire basement of the church was filled. Lots of people I didn't know milling around. I felt a jolt of panic.

"I'm gonna make a call," I said. "I'll be right back."

Mark kept a hold of my fingers for a moment, as if trying to tug me back to the meeting. I didn't look at him. I didn't acknowledge that I was having a difficult time. I didn't even snatch my fingers away. I just squeezed his hand, let go of him, and then hurried up the steps again to the foyer of the church. Only they don't call it that, do they? What was it? The lobby. Vestibule. That word came into my brain, and I was grateful for it. Perhaps I could stave off this panic attack after all.

So I stood in the vestibule with people streaming in around

me to get to the AA meeting. Like fish to slaughter. . . . No, like fish to their freedom. *Come on, Brooke.*

This must be a popular group. I didn't actually like big AA meetings.

Didn't much like little ones either.

Right now I couldn't think of anything I liked.

Except a drink. I would like a drink.

I called Hayword's phone.

I glanced up at the people coming in as I heard Hayword say, "Hey, Brooke." One of the men walking past looked exactly like Ryan Nichols, Alberto's baby daddy. I blinked, and he was gone, or he morphed into another man. Christ on a stick. Now I was having hallucinations.

"Hayword, I feel strange," I said.

"What's wrong?" he asked.

"I feel panicky," I said. "Don't know why. Started in the car. Don't know why I'm calling you." Should be calling my sponsor. Or a doctor. Or something.

"Something's gonna happen," I said. "I'm sure of it."

"It already happened," Hayword said. "Probably all the media stuff."

I backed myself into a corner away from everyone. I whispered, "One of the media outlets mentioned Alberto. They fucking mentioned Alberto!"

"I know," he said. "I saw it."

"I forgot Alberto's birthday!" I said. "I fucking forgot his birthday."

"Oh Christ," he said. "I did, too."

"What a couple of lousy parents," I said.

"Because we forgot our dead son's birthday?" He sounded hurt.

"We're still his parents," I said. "You don't stop being a child's parent just because he dies. Hayword—" I felt like I was going to start crying. "Today. Today I saw Enrique. I can't tell you where. But I think seeing him brought up some old shit." To Hayword. I didn't normally spill my guts. Or as my therapist would say, I didn't normally "share." I knew I was supposed to—it was one of those things that could help me not drink. But I was not very good at it.

"I keep thinking of Ryan Nichols," I said. "In fact, I thought I just saw him. Can you fucking believe that? I think I'd kill him if I really ever saw him. Kill him fucking dead."

"Brooke," Hayword said, "you didn't see him. You're at a meeting? Why not go and talk. Is someone with you? Is Mark there? I'm gonna call AFT and see if they can pull some strings to stop the media from digging up our past."

I didn't tell him AFT had asked me to clean up this mess. I didn't tell him anything. It just felt good to hear his voice. We had been together for so long—before we weren't—and we had known each other for so long.

Or something.

"Breathe," he said. "Go find Mark."

"Why are you telling me to go find Mark?" I asked. "Isn't he the man who stole me away from you?" He hadn't, actually.

"No, I think that was Ryan Nichols," he said. "Or, more to the point, me. I pushed you away by being an asshole."

"You weren't an asshole," I said.

"But you always say I am," he said.

"You are now," I said, "but you weren't then." I laughed. "Love you, Hayword. Thanks."

Okay. I was feeling better. The people were all gone. The meeting must have started. I walked quietly down the stairs. The welcome was over, and now a woman was walking up to the front of the group to share.

I spotted Mark. He had saved a seat at the end of the row so I easily slid in next to him.

He took my hand and whispered, "Are you okay?"

I nodded.

The woman said, "Hello, my name is Nicole, and I'm an alcoholic."

"Hello, Nicole," we all said.

"Did you see that moon?" she asked. "Wow. Felt looney all the way over here."

We laughed. So I wasn't the only one. I began to relax. Nicole talked for a while about her struggles. Then she sat down and someone else came up. By the fourth share, I was completely relaxed. It wasn't so bad being in such a big group. I could be more anonymous than usual. The media talking about me or my dead son meant nothing. I hadn't done anything wrong, at least not today, and today was all that counted.

I closed my eyes and leaned against Mark. All was well in the world, all was well. I could almost take a nap. But then I remembered I should be paying attention. This wasn't just about me. It was about the other people in the room.

Except I had to pee. The next alkie hadn't gone up to speak yet, so I got up quickly and hurried to the back, found a hallway and then the bathrooms. Went in. Did the deed, quickly. Was tempted to turn my phone back on but didn't. Heard a muted "hello" from the crowd. Washed my hands. Left the bathroom, went down the hall, stepped into the gathering room again, the meeting place, the come to God or come to our senses room. Looked down and noticed I had splashed some water on my shirt near the waist, and I uselessly wiped it away.

Then I heard, ". . . found out my son died today. I don't mean he died today. I didn't know he was dead. Didn't even know he was a son."

I looked up.

I couldn't fucking believe it.

My knees almost buckled.

The room tilted.

I almost threw up.

Or maybe I did throw up.

Maybe I did buckle.

Maybe I grew a spine of steel and just stood there staring at Ryan Nichols, the father of my dead son Alberto. The man who left town without a forwarding address once I told him I was pregnant, like some kind of teenage boy who had gotten caught with his pants down.

He looked the same. It had been over a decade, but he looked the same. Maybe some gray. Yes, gray. Of course. But no pot belly. No wrinkles I could discern from here.

Or was I hallucinating? I blinked. Hard. No, everyone was looking at him. A woman got up and started to walk by me to the restrooms. I whispered to her, "Did that man say something about a dead son?"

She nodded—and frowned. She must have thought I was looney tunes.

"Do you remember what his name was?"

"Ryan," she said. "Or Bryan. Yep, that was it. Or Ryan."

I let her go her way.

"I didn't even know he'd been born," he continued. "Or that he was real. It's a long story."

I was riveted in place. It wasn't really a long story. He fucked me, I got pregnant, and he fucked me again by running away.

I stared at him. I couldn't hear what else he was saying. If I'd had a gun, I might have shot him. Or not. I wasn't a particularly violent person. Except my wit. My sharp wit. Could I cut him down with that? Could I ruin his life with that?

I could see tears in his eyes, but I couldn't focus on what he was saying. Tears? Twelve years too late. Maybe they weren't tears. Maybe they were some kind of lights. The weird full moon had caused the earth to open up and release all kinds of monsters into the world.

Not that he was a monster. As far as I knew.

I started to laugh. I did. Right out loud. In the middle of an AA meeting. Loudly. Everyone turned around and looked at me. I kept laughing. I couldn't help it. Ryan stopped speaking. He looked at me. At least I thought he was looking at me. I assumed he was looking at the crazy woman at the other end of the room.

I saw someone out of the corner of my eye get up. To take me away no doubt.

Did Ryan open his mouth and say, "Brooke?" Or maybe he said, "Brooke!" Or maybe it was an anguished cry indicating how fucked up his life had been since he left me. "Brooke."

I tried to stop laughing.

I finally choked out, "I'm so sorry. I'm sure I'll be black-balled from every AA group in LA and environs, but this man has no right to talk about my dead son. You have no right to talk about him, you asshole. He wasn't *your* son. He was *my* fucking son, and yes, he did die. You didn't know because you never bothered to find out if he'd ever even been born!"

I saw Mark now coming toward me. Someone else I didn't know, too. I heard someone else whispering, "I love coming to this group. It's fucking theater every time."

Heard someone else say, "Fucking full moon. Should never go to a meeting during the full moon. Every alcoholic has a little werewolf in their blood."

It was as if I suddenly had amazing hearing. A pin actually dropped somewhere in the room. Ryan blinked and the sound of his eyelids over his eyes sounded like sandpaper. He sucked in his breath as I talked, and I couldn't think what that sounded like. A death rattle?

Mark was next to me. He didn't try to stop me or touch me.

He was just there. My fucking stalwart man. My wing man. My troops.

The other person—was she male or female?—said, "You need to take it outside."

My spine of steel wobbled a bit then. Or the room stopped tilting.

Because I nodded. Then I headed toward the stairs, with Mark right beside me. I started up. Stopped at the third step. Turned around and said, "You are not his father, motherfucker. I hope you drink yourself blind tonight because of this."

I think everyone in the room gasped or choked. Even Mark? Maybe even me.

With my curse thrown, I hurried up the stairs, through the vestibule, and out into the night.

SIX

I started pacing the parking lot near Mark's truck as I pulled out my phone and called Hayword. I tried to look at Mark or the truck, but I could only focus on the darkness. It was so dark. I could not wait for spring. I could not wait for fucking spring.

"Brooke?"

"Hayword," I said. "Hayword, he's here. He's fucking here. And he's talking about Alberto as if he has a right to speak about him."

"Who is there?" Hayword said. It pissed me off that he sounded so confused. He should *know*. He should know. He should fucking know!

"Ryan Nichols!"

"Ryan Nichols?" I could hear in his voice that he didn't know who that was. That made me almost angrier at him than at Ryan.

"Oh my god," he said.

"Yes, yes," I said.

"He's at the AA meeting?" he asked. "Did he follow you?"

"No," I said. "He couldn't have. I've never been here before. Mark brought me, and Ryan—" I could barely say his name. Each time I said it, I felt sick to my stomach. Revulsion. Yes, that was it. I felt revulsion. "Ryan was inside before I was."

"Do you want me to come there?"

"No," I said. "I don't even know where here is. Somewhere in hell, I think." Or near Mark's house. Same thing? Yikes! Was that what I really thought?

"But find out why he's here," I said, "if you can. Is he in town for a job? Is he even still in the biz? I want to know why all the characters from my past are showing up today."

"They're not actually characters," Hayword said.

"Really, Hayword? Is that really what you want to say to me right this second?"

"Yeah, I know. Sorry."

"I'll talk to you later."

I ended the conversation and looked up. Mark was standing next to me. I hadn't known that. Had not been able to see him until this moment.

"I know him," Mark said.

I was so stunned I couldn't move.

"He lives in this area," Mark said. "Maybe for the last year or so. Has a house not far from mine. But he calls himself Bryan Nichols. I never made the connection—although even if he called himself Ryan I probably wouldn't have made the connection since I've only heard you mention his name once."

Yep. Once, when I told him that Hayword wasn't Alberto's biological father.

"I've played poker with him," he said. "Once or twice. I've seen him at a meeting now and again. Played basketball in his driveway. Doesn't say much. I think he lives alone. Gone a lot."

He kept talking, as though anticipating all of my questions.

"If I mentioned you," he said, "I probably only said your first name and there are lots of Brookes in the world."

Yes, that would have been my next question.

My heartbeat was starting to slow again. The world was beginning to look normal again. The big old moon in the sky was vaguely green. I had an urge to reach up and grab it, take it down, and eat it.

I heard footsteps and turned away from the moon.

"Brooke." It was Ryan. I stepped back as he got closer. "Brooke," he said again.

I remembered how Ryan used to whisper my name when we made love. I hadn't liked my name when I was a kid, had tolerated it when I was an adult, but when he said it, I had loved it. It was as if the wind itself were whispering it, and that wind loved and wanted me more than life itself.

"Stop saying my name," I said.

I could feel Mark next to me, could feel he wanted to say something, *do* something. But he let me do my thing, as always.

"Hello, Mark," he said. "I remember you mentioning a Brooke, but it never occurred to me it was this Brooke."

"Hello, Bryan," Mark said.

Ryan looked at me. "That's my real name. Bryan. When I'm working I use Ryan. Always thought that was more interesting." He smiled. Did he really think I would find this confession charming? "Although I've never heard of a director changing his name. At least not someone who is only a director." He shook his head. "I'm babbling. I'm scared. I don't know what to say, Brooke, except that I am so so sorry. I had no idea."

"What? No idea that you provided the sperm for a boy who was born and then who died some months later? That's because you ran away with your tail between your legs like some dog who had pissed on the carpet."

I really wanted to end this conversation.

I really wanted a drink.

"Yes, of course I'm sorry about that," he said. "I heard on the news today about the robbery, and they mentioned you and your son."

I shook my head. "They had no right."

"No," he said, "they didn't. They said he died of SIDS."

Why was I still standing there?

I nodded.

"When I heard that—" He shook his head. "I'm just so sorry, Brooke. You weren't a drinker then, I know, and I—I was always drinking. You just went along, I know."

"What the fuck are you talking about?" I asked. "I've never gone along with anything. I didn't drink then."

His head moved slightly, as though he wanted to correct me, but he didn't know how.

"Brooke, we drank every time we were together."

"We didn't," I said, "and even if we did, you think you were so special that you could force me to drink? You're at an AA meeting. You must know the drill."

"I know, I know," he said. "But the baby. Gawd. I was just stupid and careless."

"What are you talking about?" I said.

"You said he died of SIDS," he said.

I looked at Mark and then at Ryan again.

"So what? What are you trying to say?"

"When the mother drinks during pregnancy," he said, "their infant is more likely to die of SIDS."

I slugged him. In the face. I had never slugged anyone before so it turned into a kind of slap. But it was hard, and he backed away, moaned, put his hand up to his face.

And my hand hurt.

"You motherfucker," I said. "You learn my child died of

SIDS a few hours ago and then you come here to tell me you've figured it all out. I drank so my son died? You blame me for my son's death!"

"No," he said. "Me. I—"

"You cock-sucking motherfucking asshole." I was in his face now. "How about this? Maybe he died because his father was a cowardly bastard with defective sperm?"

"Brooke." Mark's voice.

"I did *not* fucking drink with you," I said. "At least not to excess. And I didn't drink when I was pregnant. So get the fuck out of my life. Get the fuck off the planet. We'd all be better for it."

I turned around. Thankfully the truck was right there. I opened the door and got in. Wished I had the keys so I could just drive away. Mark got in next to me, started the truck, and roared away. That's what it seemed like. I closed my eyes and listened to the roar.

I felt or heard a phone vibrating. I looked down at my phone. It wasn't mine. Mark was staring at the road as though he were in shock. The sound kept coming. I reached into my bag and pulled out the burner phone I'd told Enrique to call me on.

I pushed the button. "What?" I said.

"Brooke?"

"Yes, it's me, Ricky," I said. I had no inclination to be nice to anyone. Any milk of human kindness I'd had was gone. "What do you know?"

"I got it," he said. "The asshole was going to hock it."

"Oh Christ," I said. "Look, the police still think I had something to do with it. If I'm not off the hook soon, I'm going to tell them who it was."

"I can go to the police right now," he said. "I will tell them you had nothing to do with it."

"Too little, too late," I said. I rubbed my face. Although

maybe him going to the police was the best thing to do. I didn't know anymore. "Where are you? I need to pick up the bracelet and get it back to its rightful owner."

He gave me the address of some restaurant downtown.

"I'll be there as soon as I can," I said. "Don't leave the parking lot."

He told me what his car looked like, and then I hung up.

"Mark, I need to go into the city," I said.

He nodded. I told him the address and the name of the restaurant. He knew the place.

"You okay?" I asked.

He shrugged. "You?"

I blinked and looked straight ahead, trying to figure out where we were.

"Do you know where we are?" I asked.

"Of course I do," he said.

"You always know where you are," I said. "I admire that. I don't know where I am. I always feel like I'm lost. That's not even a metaphor. Although maybe metaphorically—"

"Brooke," he said.

"Babbling brook," I mumbled.

"What?"

"That's what my dad used to call me," I said, "because I talked a lot. At least my parents thought so. But since they barely said a word between them, I guess I would seem like a chatterbox. He was wrong, you know. Ryan Bryan asshole. I didn't drink. I don't care what anyone says. I didn't drink when I was pregnant. I mean, probably wine at dinner until I found out."

"It's okay," he said.

"Don't try to reassure me," I said. "There's no need. Can you believe the nerve of him?"

I did not cause my baby's death. I knew that. I didn't start drinking until after Alberto died. I mean, wasn't that *why* I drank?

"I know I stopped drinking when I found out I was pregnant," I said. I was four months pregnant before I knew. My periods had always been irregular, so it hadn't occurred to me, especially since I had always used protection with Ryan, and Hayword and I hadn't had sex for months.

Maybe Ryan and I had had wine when we went out. I closed my eyes and leaned against the headrest. But we hadn't really gone out. I had gone to Ryan's apartment, which wasn't far from the studio. We'd eat, drink some wine, and make love. Sometimes we watched old movies together, drank some wine, and made love.

I didn't remember ever being drunk with him. Intoxicated on love—or at least, on sex. But on booze? No. I didn't like to drink.

I had felt guilty then. I had believed in fidelity. Before Ryan, I thought Hayword and I would live together in happy monogamy for the rest of our lives. Only I had gotten bored with the Hollywood life, was definitely bored taking care of the house and the kids, and I was pissed at Hayword for not making all my dreams come true.

Even though I was a feminist. Even though I stood on my own two feet, as it were, and I took care of myself. Even though I did not expect my husband to satisfy my every need and desire, I expected my husband to satisfy my every need and desire. When I wasn't happy, I blamed him.

Who else could I blame? Not the kids. Not the dog. Certainly not me or the gaping hole in my soul.

Hey, that rhymed.

Gaping hole in my soul.

Perhaps I should write a hit song around that one line.

Gaping hole in my soul.

Summed up my life.

How quickly I fell back into the pity party for myself.

I chuckled.

"What's so funny?" Mark asked.

I opened my eyes and looked over at him. "Me," I said. "I was suddenly that drunk again, blaming everyone and everything for my problems. I guess I still have some unresolved feelings regarding Mr. Nichols."

Mark laughed. "You think?"

"Gawd," I said, "this town is just too fucking small."

"I hear ya," he said. "What are we doing anyway?"

"Getting back the stolen goods," I said. "You're about to become an accomplice. You up for it?"

"Been waiting my whole life for it."

Soon enough—since I'm skipping by all the boring stuck in traffic crap—we were in some parking structure next to some restaurant called Charley's Steakhouse or Charley's Blue Plate Special. I didn't know. I didn't care. Mark wanted to come with me, but I said no. I got out of the truck and looked around until I saw Enrique's car. It didn't take much doing. He was standing by his open door, waving wildly, and yelling, "Over here! Over here!"

So much for discretion.

I got into Enrique's dumpy little car. It smelled like stale clothes and rotten coffee. Or stale coffee and rotten clothes.

Enrique wasted no time. He pulled out the bracelet, which was wrapped in a white kerchief, and handed it to me. I opened the cloth on my palm. So this was what a ten thousand dollar diamond bracelet looked like.

"Doesn't look like that much, does it?" he said.

"No, not really," I said. "Could be glass for all I know. Did your friend know how much it's worth?"

"Naw," he said. "I didn't tell him because I was afraid I'd never get it back."

"Smart," I said.

"I know you think what I did was stupid," Enrique said, "but I've been desperate. I thought I was being clever. It never occurred to me anyone could get hurt. I am sorry."

"Should have probably run it by your AA group," I said. "They would have stopped you. Although I guess it's good you didn't. You didn't tell anyone, did you?"

I had never been part of a criminal conspiracy before. I didn't really know what to do and what not to do. How do people cover their tracks anyway?

"Naw, I didn't tell anyone," he said. "I don't think my friend—John Doe—did either. He doesn't have any friends anyway. I wiped off the prints. Should be good to go."

"Okay," I said. "I'm going to take it back to Juliet's."

"Thanks, Brooke," he said.

"Forget you ever saw me," I said.

I wrapped up the bracelet and stuffed it in my jacket pocket, and then I got out of Ricky's car and ran to Mark's pickup.

"Got the goods, baby?" Mark said.

"Funny guy," I said. "Yes. Now let's go to Juliet's."

"What's your plan?"

"I need to leave the bracelet in the restaurant somewhere," I said, "and make sure someone finds it who will give it to Donna and not steal it."

"How are you going to do that?" Mark asked. "You'll have to be there when someone finds it, right? So that you know it's found and no one stole it."

"Yes," I said.

"But *you* can't find it because they'll figure you just stole it and brought it back," he said.

"Oh crap," I said. "I had not thought about that."

"Why don't you go there now and tell Donna—is that the owner's name?—that you lost an earring last time you were there and look around for it. Something like that. Meanwhile, I'll put the bracelet somewhere. Maybe over by that potted plant near the buffet area. I'll wander away, and you can enlist Donna to help you find the earring. You can point her in the buffet direction while you look somewhere else. And then she'll find it."

"That's good," I said. "Do you have a criminal past I don't now about?"

"You're my criminal past, baby," he said, "and my criminal present."

"Stop that!" I said. "You sound weird when you do gangster."

"Why?"

"Because you sound too good at it," I said. "Remember, I've never liked bad boys."

"That's because you're the bad boy in relationships," he said.

"Got that right, motherfucka! Drive on, Macbeth!"

Okay. So we got there, and right away I could see that I was never going to be a great criminal either. I was nearly as dumb as Ricky. Juliet's is a restaurant: It's busy at dinner time. It was packed to the gills. One good thing, Mark had no trouble slipping by me to go plant the bracelet since no one was paying any attention to us. I finally caught Donna's eye, and she came over to me.

"Hello, darling!" she said. "How are you after the trauma drama this morning? And the news coverage. Wow! First you're a hero and then you're a thief. I could not stand being famous."

"I'm not famous," I said.

"You are now, honey," she said. She actually slapped me on the back. "And so is Juliet's. We haven't had a Wednesday night like this in—well, in ever. Thank you, stupid actors!" She clapped her hands together and laughed.

"So you believe they were actors, too?"

"Of course," she said. "For one thing, you said it, and I believe you. For another, real thieves would have taken the jewelry. So they pocketed one bracelet." She shrugged. "No big deal. They're out of work actors. They needed work, obviously, so they probably needed cash."

"About that," I said, "the reason the police think I had something to do with it is because of that missing bracelet. Is it possible the actor thieves left it here, dropped it or something? Did you look all over the restaurant for it?"

"Good lord, no," she said. "It didn't occur to me. Shall we look for it now?"

My. This was going to be a lot easier than I thought. Thank you, Universe. Make me a hero in the morning, a pariah in the afternoon, and a baby killer by evening: But make it all right before bedtime. My kind of day.

"Lead on," I said.

I followed Donna around the busy restaurant. She stopped to say hello to a lot of people, and I stood next to her, mute, feeling kind of silly—and nervous. At one point I caught Mark's gaze, and he nodded. I almost laughed out loud. What was this foolishness we were doing?

"This is Brooke McMurphy," Donna was saying before I had a chance to run. "She's the one who saved us all from those bad actors." She laughed. "I suppose they weren't *bad* actors since we believed they were robbers. But she got them out of the restaurant before anything went awry."

The people at the table nodded and smiled.

"Oh yes," one of them said. "I heard the police think you helped them rob the place." The group laughed. That made me look at them—really look at them. They seemed strange. Actually the entire restaurant felt strange.

"Must be that weird full moon," someone else at the table said.

"Or maybe we're all turning into zombies like the ones in your movies," another said. A woman? I tried to look at her, but I felt overstimulated. I couldn't concentrate. This was a familiar feeling. One of those feelings that drove me to drink.

Or so that was my excuse.

"Not zombie movies plural," someone else said. "Only one, and it was quite nuanced and funny. You should see *Love and Other Insanities*. Wonderful, too."

I looked at this person. A woman. She had long white hair and blue eyes. She looked vaguely familiar, but I didn't know why. She wore a blue sweater with a blue and green dragon arching up across it. The woman and I looked into each other's eyes, and I knew that she knew I was just about to go over some edge that would have been unimaginable just a few short hours ago.

"Thank you for those hours of entertainment," the woman said.

"That's kind of you to say," I said. "Thank you." And then to Donna, I said, "May we continue?"

As we walked around the restaurant, Donna looked behind potted plants and under tables, causing her patrons to laugh. Everyone was in such a freaking good mood.

Must be the food.

Or the moon.

Donna headed toward the buffet. Thank god. She bent over at the tall potted plant. She didn't come up right away. When she did, she was clutching something in her hand. She grabbed my hand and pulled me along until we were in the kitchen—where the kitchen staff didn't even look up at us.

"You won't believe it," Donna said. "Look!" She opened her right hand. She had found it—just where Mark had left it.

"So they really weren't thieves!" she said. "Wow. This is beautiful. Would you like to hold it?"

"No!" I said. "The police are already suspicious of me. I can't have my fingerprints on it."

"I hear ya," she said. "In fact, why don't you leave? I mean, I'm the one who found it. I'll call them straightaway and you don't have to have anything to do with it."

"I like the way you think," I said. I gave her a quick hug—I wasn't sure why she was being so nice to me—and then I hurried out of the restaurant.

Mark was standing by the pickup. I grinned. "Hello, Clyde."

He laughed. "Come on, Bonnie," he said. "Let's make our getaway."

"I'm with ya, baby," I said. And off we went.

SEVEN

In the morning, I awakened to sunshine—which wasn't exactly unusual in Southern California—but it was still glorious. I awakened to sunshine and quiet. Mark's side of the bed was empty. I had turned off my cellphone and unplugged the landline last night. No one could get a hold of me. I luxuriated in the blissful silence. Except for the seagulls. I could hear them. I smiled and buried my head in the pillow for a few more minutes.

I should get up. Do some writing. Greet the day.

Then I remembered yesterday. Remembered the "robbery," remembered recognizing Enrique, and then the events of the entire day came spilling out—like a sped up film. The climax came when Ryan Nichols suggested Alberto had died because I drank during my pregnancy.

Ugh.

Crap.

I had to figure out a way to get out of going to the party

tonight. I didn't know what I dreaded more: telling Fern I didn't want to go or actually going to the party.

Fucking Ryan Nichols. How life changed on a freaking dime.

I didn't want to think about *him*. Where was my man?

"Mark!" I called.

He didn't answer. Probably downstairs in the restaurant. I sighed. Wished I hadn't slept in. Would really love one of Mark's breakfasts.

I got up, slipped on a robe, and then opened the door that led down to the restaurant. We had agreed that we'd always leave the door locked so people couldn't mistakenly wander upstairs, but since the restaurant wasn't actually open, we weren't strict about it. I guessed Mark hadn't given it a second thought this morning.

I hurried down the stairs and went into the empty dining room.

"Mark!" I called.

No answer. I heard a radio playing in the kitchen, so I headed in that direction. I glanced out the window. What a great view his customers would have of the Pacific Ocean. And right now a flock of birds was circling the beach. I squinted. Couldn't tell what kind they were, but it was a huge flock. A few people on the beach had stopped and were pointing at the birds. The humans looked like stick figures in a diorama of the ocean beach. Strangely enough the birds looked as big as the people. Must have been my perspective, or something.

I hoped Daphne du Maurier's story "The Birds" wasn't about to come to life. I laughed. What a silly thought. Maybe the birds were circling because they didn't want to land on the radioactive beach with the radioactive ocean water.

I sighed. I really hoped that wasn't the case. I could ask David—he'd know. Poor stressed-out kid.

I pushed open the swinging kitchen door and found Sherry and Mark leaning over something on a side countertop. They were so close they were almost touching.

Sherry looked over at me and quickly moved away from Mark.

I felt momentary butterflies in my stomach.

Mark looked up at me. "Good morning, sleepy head." He came right over to me and kissed me. Didn't hesitate. Didn't look at Sherry. Wasn't a guilty bone in his body.

I looked at Sherry. Squinted at her. Narrowed my vision. Tried to ascertain what was up with her.

I didn't trust her or like her and I didn't know why.

But then, I didn't trust anyone, really. Except David. But he was a kid. I wouldn't burden him with the burden of me only trusting him.

Maybe Joanie, too.

Hayword to a certain extent.

Okay, Mark. About some things.

Lordy. Maybe I was more trusting than I thought.

Good grief.

But right that moment, I did not trust Sherry Burns.

"What are you two so intent on?" I asked.

"I'm looking over where the tables are," he said. "I'm still not certain it's working. I'm worried the wait staff won't be able to get around each table."

"Are you still doing a practice run on Saturday?" I asked.

"Sure," he said.

"I guess you'll find out then," I said. "In the meanwhile, have you had breakfast yet?"

Mark laughed. "What you really mean is will I make you breakfast?"

"That sounds great," I said. "I'll take the house specialty." I grinned.

"Actually Giovanni is fixing something so the electricity is off," he said. "Sherry, you need me here?"

"No," she said. "In fact, I don't think you need me here either. We're ahead of schedule. You're going to the farmer's market on Saturday and Sunday, right? So we're good to go." She smiled. "And Brooke, I didn't see anything about you on the news this morning." She looked at me as if she wanted to say more or hear more. Like she wanted to be my confidante. For a moment, I felt sorry for her. I was not the easiest person to get to know, especially when I had no desire to get to know the other person.

"Good to hear," I said. I was tempted to take Mark's hand, but I realized that gesture was too akin to a dog pissing on its territory so I refrained. Instead, I said, "Nice to see you again, Sherry." Then I left the kitchen.

I heard Mark say something to her—I don't know what—and then he was close behind me, grabbing my ass. I laughed, and we ran across the restaurant and up the stairs. Once we were in my apartment and the door was closed and locked, Mark said, "Sherry's nervous around you. Can't you give her a break?"

"Why is she nervous?" I said. "You two seemed pretty darn cozy when I came in. She looked a little guilty."

Mark laughed as he went into the kitchen. "She wasn't guilty. She was probably scared when she saw you. You are formidable."

"Good," I said. I got up on a stool at the bar between the kitchen and the living room. This apartment was a lot like my writing studio. I liked the coziness of both. "I hope she's scared of me. Then she'll keep her mitts off what's mine."

"What's that mean?" Mark asked. "What is yours? This building?"

"You know exactly what I mean," I said.

He frowned. "Are you telling me you're jealous of her? That doesn't seem like you."

"It doesn't, does it?" I said. "I'm feeling strange. Must be what happened yesterday."

"Have you been thinking about what Ryan said to you?" He cracked an egg into a bowl. Then another.

"Oh, Christ, no," I said. "I'm trying not to think about it."

"What about the police?" he asked. He whipped the eggs with a fork. "Are you off the hook?"

Ugh.

He looked over at me. "I bet you'd like me to stop interrogating you?"

"Yes, please." I smiled. "I'd really just like to go back to bed."

"Wish I could," he said. He poured the eggs into a pan. "I've got so much to do today. Ian has a soccer game tonight. Do you remember I'm staying at my house tonight because Ian is staying?"

"Yep," I said. "I remember. I'll probably stay at my studio after David's science report tomorrow. I need to get the script done by Saturday, so that'll force me to work."

He laughed. "Will that work?"

I shrugged. "I don't know." I grinned wanly. "I could be in denial. It's not like millions of dollars are riding on this or anything."

"It'll give you something to do on Saturday," he said. He spooned some takeout Chinese food onto the omelette. Smelled delicious.

"I really don't want you around for the dry run," Mark said. "It would make me too nervous."

"Hah!" I said. "I can't imagine you nervous."

He glanced over at me and then folded the omelette.

"Are you excited?" I asked. "Your dream is about to come true."

He slipped the omelette out of the pan and onto a plate and then brought the plate over to me. The omelette smelled lovely. Like soy sauce and ginger. I took a bite. Mmmmm.

"Wow," I said. "Will you marry me?"

I said it without thinking. But then a silence throbbed between us. I looked at Mark, who was watching me eat.

"Just kidding," I said. "You know, the whole bigamy thing. This is delicious. So, about your dream coming true?" I grinned. I did not want to talk about our relationship now. Geez, Louise.

"Sure," he said. He turned away from me and went back to the stove.

Talk about avoiding a question.

"Mark, come on," I said. "Be excited. I'm excited for you."

"And that's what counts," he said.

That almost sounded snarky. Mark didn't do snark. I felt another twinge, or something, like when I saw him standing so close to Sherry.

This was odd.

I should ask him about it. I should reassure him. Or do something human.

But I didn't.

"I better check my messages to see if the shit has stopped hitting the fan," I said.

I checked my voice mail on my landline. Three messages. First one: "Uh, this is Detective Baxter," he said. "I've called your lawyer, or the studio lawyer—whoever he is—but I wanted you to know we're dropping this. For now." I heard him sigh or breathe hard. Like he wanted to say something else.

I deleted the message.

Fern was up next: "Mom, you better not be using the robbery to get out of the party. I'm counting on you."

"Gee, thanks, daughter." I erased her messages, too.

Joanie: "Answer your damn phone, asshole."

I laughed and erased her message, too.

Sally had left two messages on my cell phone, telling me she thought all was well now. The big mucky mucks had calmed down. Now I just needed to get a final script to them and all would be well.

"Yeah, yeah," I said to no one. "I'll get you the fucking script." I just needed some time to sit down and think about zombies.

One message and a text from Irving Jackson. He repeated that he needed to talk to me. What the fuck did he want?

One message from Hayword, wondering how I was doing.

I called Hayword first.

"Hey, Brooke," he said. "Are you okay?"

"Yes," I said. "I'm so sorry I didn't call you back last night."

"I assumed you either killed Nichols or you didn't," he said. "And since you weren't on the news again, I figured you hadn't. In fact, I haven't seen anything about you on the news. Your 15 minutes are up."

"Thank god," I said. "David okay? I actually forgot to call him last night."

"Yeah," he said. "I told him you had called and were going to be incommunicado for a bit. He accepted that. Plus he got a text from you, so that was good. Having him become a teenager has been so much easier than when Fern became . . . well, any age."

I laughed. "Yes. You're meeting me at the school tomorrow, right? For the science project?"

"Sure," he said. "So do you want to talk about what happened last night?"

I shook my head. But I didn't say anything. I walked over to the window. It looked like the flock of birds that had been circling earlier had landed on the beach. Thousands of them. The beach was black with them. I squinted. The people on the beach seemed to be hurrying away from them, but they walked stiffly, almost like the zombies in my movie. I chuckled.

"What?" Hayword said.

"There are these birds on the beach," I said. "And the people are acting peculiar."

"I heard some strange things have been going on today," he said. "They're blaming it on a new wave of radiation from Japan. But I think that's highly unlikely. Some dolphins beached themselves down in Santa Monica, but they won't let people help them. It's as if they're refusing aid. Coyotes are doing something somewhere. I bet we'll find out they're all hoaxes."

"Maybe," I said, "but I'm seeing the birds." I moved the phone away from my mouth and called out, "Mark, come look at this."

Mark left the kitchen and came over to stand by me.

"So what happened when you saw Ryan?" Hayword asked.

I walked away from Mark. He glanced at me. I looked down at the phone.

"He implied Alberto had died because of my drinking," I said to Hayword. "But I pointed out I hadn't been a drinker until after he left me."

"What a fucking bastard." Hayword sounded pissed.

"I know. He's gone all this time and then shows up to blame me."

Mark looked at me again and then went back to the kitchen. Or somewhere. I didn't see. I didn't pay attention.

"I didn't drink back then," I said. "Right?"

"Even if you did," Hayword said, "that doesn't mean you caused it."

I nodded. Then I realized he hadn't agreed with me. Agreed that I didn't drink.

"Hayword," I said. "Did I drink or not?"

He made a noise. Then he said, "Do you want a real answer or do you just want me to make you feel better?"

"I want to feel better!" I said. "What do you think I've been trying to do for the last two years? No, longer than that. I've been trying to feel better for over a decade, give or take."

"I know, honey," Hayword said.

"Don't call me that," I said. I felt furious and weepy all at the same time. My knees wobbled.

"You'd been unhappy for a while," he said. "So you drank. And yes, when you were with Ryan, you drank."

"But I stopped when I knew I was pregnant," I said. "Come on."

"Sure," he said. "Sure. I'm sure you did. Of course. You were four months gone before you knew."

The implication being that Alberto stewed in my alcohol-filled womb for four months.

"No one says that anymore," I said. "Four months gone. I wasn't gone. I was pregnant."

"Well—"

"Hayword," I warned.

"Okay, look," he said. "Come home. You can spend the night, and we can talk."

"I can't have a sleepover with you," I said. "I don't think that would be kosher given I'm living with another man, and you must be dating someone."

"No," he said. "I'm not. I'm waiting for you to come to your senses and come home." He laughed, and I laughed with him. But I couldn't tell if he was joking or not. I glanced behind me, toward the kitchen, but Mark wasn't there. He was looking out the windows again.

"I'll meet you at the party tonight," Hayword said, "and then we can go home together afterward. Mark can come, too."

I laughed. Somehow the turn this conversation had taken was cheering me up. Was my husband actually flirting with me?

"That is not going to happen," I said. "For one thing, Mark is not coming to the party. For another, that would just be weird. I might come back to the studio, though, since I have to be in the area for David's science project tomorrow."

"Okay," Hayword said. "But I'll be at the party tonight if you want to talk."

"I think Fern wants me to talk to some young writers," I said, "encourage them or some nonsense. It would be better if I told them to run for the hills."

We said our goodbyes, and then I went to stand by the window with Mark. The birds covered the sand like a tattered black beach blanket. The humans had all scurried away.

"What kind of birds are they?" I asked.

"Black birds," Mark said.

"Funny."

"I'm serious," he said. "It looks like they're different kinds of black birds. Those walking over there look like crows. Over here are starlings, I think. Maybe those are cowbirds. The ones closer to us are grackles."

"You have amazing eyesight," I said.

He lifted up his right hand and showed me the binoculars. I laughed.

"What are they doing?"

"Just hanging out, as far as I can tell," he said. "Looking out at the water. Some of them are picking at the sand."

"As long as they don't block the driveway so I can't go to this stupid party," I said as I moved away from him and the window. Apparently I had decided it was easier to go to the party than tell my daughter I didn't want to go.

"I was thinking a similar thing," he said, looking back at me. "As long as they don't interfere with the opening on Sunday."

He faced the window again. "I guess that's what we all do. We're all NIMBYs. What if there is something catastrophic going on, and we're just fiddling while Rome burns?"

"Of course something catastrophic is going on," I said. "Haven't you been paying attention to the weather? To the oceans? Christ. We've all been fiddling."

Mark turned around and leaned back against the window. "Shouldn't we do something?"

"Yes! Of course!" I said. "But I haven't a clue what to do. So I'm taking my fiddle, and I'm going to the party. You wanna come?"

"I thought you told Hayword I wasn't going," he said.

"You never want to go to these things," I said.

"That's true," he said. "But if you asked me, if you really wanted me to go, I'd do it."

I rolled my eyes and sighed. "Mark, what the fuck? I'm not going to make you go someplace *I* don't even want to be. One of the reasons Hayword and I split was because I couldn't stand going to these bullshit things."

"Yet here you are going," he said, "and meeting Hayword there."

"I told you it was Fern," I said. "She begged me. The robbery thing traumatized her. The non-robbery thing. Why are you giving me a hard time about this?"

"I'm not," he said. He rubbed his face. He suddenly looked tired. "I'm just juggling a lot, I guess, and you know, you've got a history with Hayword. It would be so easy to fall back into familiar routines."

"Familiar routines? The last familiar routines I had with Hayword was living with him while fucking you."

He shrugged. "And fucking him."

This conversation was making my teeth hurt. I didn't understand it.

"Do you get the urge to go back to your wife?" I asked. "You had familiar routines with her."

"We've been apart for a long time," he said. "So, no, I don't get that urge. I want to see my son more, and I could do that if I were with her. But beyond that, no. But you work with Hayword. You guys talk to each other like you're still married."

"Because we are."

"Exactly," he said.

We stared at one another.

"I—I'm just not sure," he said. "I'm not sure that you're actually committed to us. Or if we were just easy after you got out of rehab."

"We live together," I said. "Your restaurant is practically in my house. That sounds like commitment to me."

"We don't live together," he said. "Some weeks we barely see one another. We've got three different residences! I want a life together. I want to cuddle with you every morning as we wake up together and every night before we fall to sleep. I want to read the Sunday newspaper in bed with you. I want us to plan our days together, our vacations, our lives together."

"No one reads the newspaper anymore," I said.

Mark just looked at me.

"I'm sorry," I said. "Inappropriate time to joke. I am absolutely committed to you. Come on, Mark."

"Brooke, you don't talk to me," he said. "Not about anything deep and real."

"You sound like a girl," I said.

"God damn it," he said. "Quit trying to make this into a joke. I'm trying to speak to you. To tell you what's in my heart and you're making a fucking joke out of it. You're starting to treat me just like you treated Hayword. Maybe not starting to. Maybe you always have. I'm not a spear-carrier in your life, Brooke. I've got my own life. You're either in it with me or you're not."

"I don't treat you like a spear-carrier," I said. "I'm not going to kill you off in the next scene."

He shook his head. "I just told you how I feel."

I nodded. "Okay. Okay. I—"

"I don't want to hear about you dealing with another crisis," he said. "Don't use that as an excuse. We'll talk about this after a, b, or c happens. That's what you always say. And then there's another drama."

Ouch. That stung. Was he implying I was a drama queen?

"It's not all about you, Brooke," he said. "It's not always all about you. Or your family."

"If this is about me not asking you to come to the party—"

"No, god damn it," he said. "You're still not listening. Just think about what I said. You don't have to have an answer. You don't have to defend yourself or your position. Just think about it. We'll talk next week."

"Next week?" I said. "Won't I see you before then?"

"Sure," he said. "We'll run into each other before then."

I made a noise. "Don't pout," I said.

"I'm not pouting!" he said. "We've got a busy few days coming up." He glanced out the window. "Besides, if the birds and other animals start coming after us, who knows what will happen?"

I went to Mark and put my arms around his waist and kissed his mouth. "But I want you with me during the animal attacks. Won't it prove my commitment if we're together when we're torn to bits by wild animals?"

"Not if they're black birds," he said. "We'd probably be pecked to death. Far less dramatic."

"Says you. Don't you remember *The Birds*? Gave me nightmares for weeks."

He put his arms around me, and we embraced, heart to heart.

"It's been a weird couple of days," I said.

"Understatement."

"Maybe the worst part of it is over," I said.

"Naw, the full moon is actually today," he said, "so my guess is the bird shit is really going to hit the fan today."

I moved out of the hug and looked at his face. "You don't believe that do you?"

He laughed. "Of course not. Unless it turns out to be true."

I pushed him away. "I've gotta go to work," I said. "If I don't get this screenplay done, more than shit is going to hit the fan."

EIGHT

I tried to write. Sat on my bed with my laptop in front of me, overheating on top of the bedspread. I had tried writing at my desk in the guest room, but I kept looking out the window and watching the flock of black birds. After a while, they flew up, divided themselves into other flocks, and flew away.

I had read reports on the interwebs from all over our area of birds and animals "acting strangely." On TV talking heads speculated that an earthquake was coming. Others blamed it on the moon or radiation. The strange was mostly animals gathering together. Coyotes and bobcats. Crows and cowbirds (although that wasn't particularly strange.) Dogs and cats.

"Dogs and cats living together!" I said as I scrolled through the articles. It all seemed pretty vague to me—and a stupid distraction when I should be working.

Nevertheless, I managed to piss away the day without talking to another human being—besides Mark when he came in the room to kiss me goodbye before he left for the day. I texted

David, asked him about his day. Texted Joanie. Sally. Fern. But I didn't talk to anyone. Didn't speak out loud.

I didn't try to locate Ryan Nichols. Didn't try to find out what he'd been doing for the last decade. Didn't try to get his phone number.

Even though I was tempted.

I was.

I didn't understand it either. I was furious with him. I still couldn't believe what he had said to me. I still felt mildly sick to my stomach that maybe I had remembered everything wrong. Maybe I had been drinking when I was pregnant—before I knew.

Even with all of that, I was tempted to find out more about Ryan. Tempted to find out how to contact him.

So that I could contact him.

Not to scream at him.

Although I might.

Not to tell him I hated him.

No.

Maybe I would scream at him. Maybe I would slug him. But part of me wanted to touch him. Part of me wanted to know what it would be like to touch him one more time. Would I feel that sexual electricity again? Would he feel familiar? Would it be like touching Alberto again? Would there be some kind of connection, some kind of sense memory of Alberto once I touched Ryan again?

I knew this sounded ridiculous. I didn't understand it. But there it was.

I hadn't had a drink in two years, so I could certainly resist trying to get in touch with my old love.

It was a strange few hours of resisting and trying to be creative. I didn't write a word. But I did resist searching for Ryan.

I felt strange. As if I wasn't all there. Or almost lonely. Yet I wasn't willing to do anything about the loneliness—if that was what it was—like actually talk to another human being.

When it was time, I ate something and then got dressed and headed for downtown.

Miraculously, traffic was light, and I watched the full moon rise above the city. It was so lovely I felt like howling, and I wished someone was with me to see it. Someone else in this city of many millions must be looking at the moon, too. Maybe even someone I loved.

And probably lots of people who annoyed the hell out of me.

The party was bigger than I had anticipated—too many people, big venue, lots of food, and a loud band—and I felt a twinge of shyness as I walked into the ballroom. Wished I had let Hayword take me, wished I had coerced Mark into coming with me, wished I'd come with Joanie. Something. But I didn't dwell on it. I sucked in my stomach, put on what I hoped was a bright smile, and off I went.

I made a beeline for Sally St. James. She smiled when she saw me, and we gave each other air kisses just to amuse ourselves.

"So glad you agreed to come," Sally said. "A friendly face, finally."

I kept my arm around her waist as we looked out at the spiffily dressed crowd. I smiled at this or that person, waved at one or two.

"You're the boss," I said. "Isn't everyone a friendly face?"

She laughed and made a noise. "I don't trust anyone. Do you? Your daughter. She's loyal. She's a good worker. But the rest? Come on. The bigwigs have been on my case. Didn't like the numbers from last quarter."

"I thought you had the owners—investors?—in your back pocket," I said. "Must be more than just a number thing. I thought AFT was all about the love of filmmaking."

"Easy for billionaires to say," Sally said. "But even billionaires worry about money. In fact, maybe they worry more than millionaires. I think someone has been badmouthing me. It's not you, is it?"

I dropped my arm, looked at her, and rolled my eyes. "Yes, Sally. I regularly hang with these unknown billionaires."

"I introduce you to them all the time," she said. "Why can't you remember them?"

"They have no interest in me," I said. "In fact, weren't they embarrassed that a zombie movie made them so much money? I think they'd just as soon I went away."

"Not true," she said. "We're counting on part two. How's that coming?"

I smiled and looked away from her.

"Brooke, I've got to have that in hand like yesterday," she said.

"I know," I said, "but haven't you heard about all the animals acting strangely, and then there's the radiation. And a green moon."

"What the fuck are you talking about?"

"The robbery and all this other weird stuff has thrown me off my stride," I said. "I'll get the script to you very, very soon. I promise. Have I ever let you down?"

"Sure," she said, "when you stopped fucking me. That left me very down, so to speak. Don't you ever miss the old days?"

"You mean when I was drunk and depressed and fucking everyone in sight?"

"Sometimes I miss a woman going down on me," she said. "I miss the curves. The juiciness." She sighed. "On the other hand, my husband can fuck like a banshee, and he never asks me what I'm thinking."

"How does a banshee fuck?" I asked. "I mean, aren't they dead Irish women wailing over dead people?"

"Way to kill the mood, Mac," she said. "Just saying if you ever want to have a quickie in my office, I'm up for it."

"I think this constitutes sexual harassment," I said.

"Oh good," she said. "Maybe they'll fire me then. Brooke, I haven't told you everything. I didn't want to worry you. Or I didn't want to talk about it." She lowered her voice as she smiled at this or that person walking by us. "AFT is in big trouble. They don't want to dump *Beauty and the Zombie*. I was wrong about that. There have been some financial . . . irregularities. The studio might be going belly up. They might have to cancel Hayword's movie—unless *Beauty and the Zombie Part Two* starts on time and the buzz is good. They think they can stall the creditors and maybe even the feds for 24 months, give or take."

"The feds?" I said. "What's going on? Is this you? Did you do something?"

"No!" She smiled and waved at someone across the room. "No. I'm not really sure who did what. They don't trust me. I don't know how much longer I'll be studio head. A lot is hanging on this little zombie movie, Brooke. The fate of the world as it were. At least our little world."

"Christ, Brooke. That's a lot of pressure."

"But you're almost done, right? You'll have it to me by Saturday?"

Hadn't written a word, beyond the initial treatment.

Fuck me.

"Sure," I said. "It's almost done. You'll love it."

Man, I suddenly wished I had a drink.

Buck up, Brooke baby. This is the adult world. Just do your job and everything will be all right.

Hah! What kind of bullshit advice was that? I really needed to get a better inner voice.

"By the way," I said, "did I mention that Irving Jackson has been trying to get a hold of me? Do you know what he wants?"

"That little weasel," she said. "I hired him, you know. I had faith in him, and now he's after my job. I bet you anything he's the one who's trying to take me down."

"What would he want with me?" I asked.

"Probably trying to figure out a way to fuck me up," Sally said. "He's not the man I thought he was. Be careful around him. In fact, I'd avoid him if I could. I'm trying to figure out a way to fire him."

"He's management," I said. "It's not like he has a union. Can't you just fire him?"

"You'd think," she said, "but some of the investors like him. I don't get it."

Just then we both saw Fern and waved at her. She looked all grown up in her black cocktail dress, holding a drink in her hand. Looked like hard liquor. Really wished the girl would stick to lemonade.

"Hello, Mom," she said. "Hi, Sally. Everything seems to be going well. Everyone is happy."

"That's great," Sally said. "Good job. Now just relax and have a good time. I better mingle."

Sally winked and then sashayed away; the crowd parted as she neared, like Moses approaching the Red Sea. I smiled. I did enjoy watching her walk.

I looked back at Fern. "Okay. Where are the writers you wanted me to meet?"

"They're not here yet," she said. "But Dad is on his way."

"He already knows how to write, dear," I said.

My daughter looked stressed, and her eyes were glittery. Drugs, alcohol, or both?

"What's going on with you?" I asked.

She shook her head, distracted. "Nothing," she said. "Nothing. Just trying to keep it all together. This party. You know. Let me go call. Go get a drink or something, Mom. I'll get back to you."

And then she hurried away.

Go get a drink? What was wrong with that girl? Was she purposely trying to turn me back into a drunk?

I saw Irving Jackson across the room, and I knew I should go over and see what the hell he wanted from me, but I decided I'd rather powder my nose. I headed for the bathrooms. What a relief it was to step out of the ballroom and into the relative quiet of the corridor.

A man in a suit was walking toward me. He smiled, was ready to talk to me, I could tell. Why didn't I know him? And then I knew him.

Christ almighty! What was *he* doing here? I hadn't seen him in 15 years, and now I saw him twice in two days?

"Ricky!" I said in a harsh whisper. "What are you doing here?" I looked around quickly.

"Hello, Brooke," he said loudly. "I haven't seen you in ages!" Then he whispered, "I was invited." We walked away from the bathrooms and stepped into an empty red and gold dining room that smelled like stale donuts.

"What do you mean you were invited?" I asked.

He nodded. "I've written a script," he said, "and AFT is interested in it. So they invited me to this."

"What?" I said.

Was he one of the writers my daughter had wanted me to meet?

"Ricky," I said, "my daughter Fern works for AFT. What if she recognizes your voice? You have to go! She was very traumatized by what happened yesterday."

"I'm glad you're here," Enrique said, ignoring what I'd just said. "Did everything work out with the bracelet?"

"Shhh!" I said. Why wasn't he understanding me? He

needed to leave. "Yes, the bracelet is back with its owner, and the police seem to be satisfied, at least for now. You've got to get out of here!"

"This is a business obligation," he said. "I can't hide for the rest of my life. No one saw me at Juliet's. No one will recognize my voice. It was deeper. Harsher. That was my character. He was a little taller, too, I think, don't you?"

"Ricky!"

"I needed to tell you something."

"Good grief. The suspense is killing me. What now?"

"Manny wants money or he's going to go to the police," Enrique said. "I don't have anything to give him. He wants his due."

"His due?" I said. "I'll give him his due by going straight to the police and telling them everything."

This entire debacle had absolutely nothing to do with me, yet it had turned my life upside down. And to top it off, now some asshole I didn't know was fucking blackmailing me.

That was not going to happen.

"Where is this little motherfucker?" I asked. "I'd like to tell him no to his face."

"He's not here," Enrique said. "He's working tonight at Juliet's."

"Then let's go," I said. "I want this done and over with because I am done and over with it."

"Sure," Enrique said. "But now? I just got here and—"

I made a noise. "Enrique, this is not how I manage my life," I said. "I stay far from drama. I certainly stay far from any criminal element. If someone thinks they can blackmail me, then I need to put an end to that particular thought form. I don't care if you just got here or not. Why would this little flea believe he could blackmail me?"

"He figures you wouldn't want the police to know that you

knew me," he said. "And he knows everyone who was involved."

I shrugged. "So? Everyone involved is you, your friend, and Manny, the one who is trying to blackmail me. I don't care about any of you."

I was speaking too loudly. Even though the dining room was empty, someone might hear me. I had to calm down. For one thing, Fern had left the ballroom and was walking toward me. She was actually smiling, nervously. She waved. I waved back. Enrique waved, too.

"Stop that," I whispered. "She doesn't know she knows you. You had your mask on."

He didn't say anything.

Then Fern was there.

"Hello, Mom."

She put her hand out. I started to take her hand and I realized my daughter had never reached for me in her life.

"Hello, Enrique." She took Enrique's hand. They held tightly to each other's hands and looked at me.

My eyes widened.

And then they narrowed.

"So you knew about all of this?" I said to Fern. "You brought me to Juliet's so I could be a witness to this stupid robbery? For what purpose?"

"Mom, shhh," Fern said. "Your voice carries."

"My voice carries! Fern! What the fuck is going on?"

"It was supposed to be harmless," she said. "We were trying to figure out a way to get Enrique and . . . his friend noticed. Manny tried to get Mahoney to come to Juliet's. When that didn't work, I suggested you. You and Dad both have new movies. We thought if you could see Enrique in a new light, you might hire him. And he is a brilliant scriptwriter. You could read his script, give him some advice."

"Then why didn't you just fucking *ask* me?" I said. I had definitely raised my voice. "Enrique, you could have called me. I would have found you work."

"I didn't want charity," he said.

"So robbing me is better?"

"It wasn't—"

"It wouldn't have been charity," I interrupted him. "I thought you were a good actor. But trying to scare me into hiring you, that's just bizarre! And to get me implicated in a crime, what the hell were you thinking?"

"Don't yell at him," Fern said. "It was my idea."

"I'll yell at anyone I want to yell at," I said. "Fern, you have no idea the backlash I've gotten because of this. Yesterday—" I couldn't tell her about the blowout at the Not Okay Corral yesterday (aka the AA meeting). She didn't know about Ryan Nichols. She didn't know Hayword wasn't Alberto's biological dad. I wasn't up to that conversation.

"The details don't matter," I said. "Just know that yesterday was not good."

"I know," Fern said.

Enrique nodded. "It's my fault. I should have thought it through."

"Damn right it's your fault," I said. "You're old enough to be her father!"

"No," he said. They both shook their heads.

"No, he's younger than Dad," Fern said. "But none of that matters."

"And you, Fern," I said, "you're supposed to be some kind of genius. This was just plain stupid."

"Let's not call each other names," Fern said.

"Yes, let's," I said. "This was a stupid plan. You're quite the good little actor yourself, daughter o' mine. And now what? Are you behind this plan of Manny's to blackmail me?"

Fern looked at her shoes. Enrique stared up at the ceiling.

"Look at me!" I cried.

"No," Fern said. "We have nothing to do with it. We tried to talk him out of it."

"So when you say Manny knows *everyone* who was involved," I said, "he's talking about *you*, Fern, isn't he? He knows I'm your mother and Hayword is your father and that maybe we have some scratch we can spare?"

She nodded.

"I'm not paying him off," I said.

"Then I'll go to jail," Fern said. "Enrique will go to jail! I'll lose my job."

"Maybe you should lose your job," I said. "I think you all need to get your heads examined. I mean, why the hell didn't you just ask me for a job, Ricky?"

"You hate all the Hollywood schmoozing," Fern said. "And I knew you'd be pissed that we were dating."

I shook my head. "And I wouldn't be pissed that you tried to have your boyfriend rob me?"

"It wasn't a real robbery," Enrique said.

I shot him a look.

"I thought it was a novel way to audition," Fern said.

"Did you come up with this when you were drunk?" I asked.

"I was trying to be creative," Fern hissed. She looked like she was eleven years old again, hurt and angry all at the same time. "I know everyone sees me as this automaton without a creative bone in my body."

"Criminality is not creative," I said. "It's ludicrous." I shook my head. "But it's all water under the bridge. We need to shut this guy up."

Oh Lord. I was sounding like some criminal from a noir film.

"Is he an actor?" I asked.

Fern and Enrique nodded.

"What does he want more?" I asked. "A job or the cash?"

"But if there's a job," Fern said, "shouldn't it go to Enrique?"

"I think that ship has sailed," Enrique said.

"Yep," I said. "First smart thing you've said."

"Hey, leave him alone."

I put my hands up. "Don't either of you dare tell me what to do, say or feel. Because right now I could say things to both of you that none of us would ever forget. You have no idea the can of putrid devouring monstrous worms you have unleashed. Find out what this guy wants: a job or cash. And don't just come out and ask. Be subtle. And get me an audition tape. His audition tape. Have him meet me tomorrow in the village near our house, Fern. At The Coffee Shoppe at eight a.m. sharp. And text me his exact name and address."

"Why?" Fern asked.

"Because I said so." I grinned maniacally—I hoped. Then I said, "I've got a goddamn plan, man. Now, if there are no real writers to meet here, I am leaving. I came here as a favor to you, Fern. Because you asked. See what happens when you just ask instead of concocting some elaborate scheme. It's so simple."

"Asking you a favor is like torture," Fern said.

"Obviously, you have never been tortured," I said. "I would do anything for you. I wish you'd understand that. Maybe it's time you get help for your mommy issues, Fern. They're driving me fucking crazy, and I can only imagine what they're doing to you." I shook my head. "We'll all talk later, I'm sure."

I walked away from Fern and her paramour. I wondered how long they'd been sleeping together. No. I shook my head. I was not going there.

Suddenly, just before I left the nearly empty dining room, Irving Jackson was beside me.

"Hello, Irving," I said, trying to muster all the cheer I could.

"I was just coming to look for you. I'm sorry I haven't returned your calls. Family and business stuff going on. How's everything?"

He smiled. "Everything is fine," he said. He put his hand on my elbow and deftly turned me around and steered me into the dining room. Enrique and Fern walked past us, and Irving nodded hello to them. He took me to a table and pulled out a chair for me.

"Irving, you seem so serious," I said. "What's going on?"

I sat in the chair, and he sat in one next to me. Sat a bit too close.

"I want you to help me push Sally St. James out of AFT," he said.

I laughed. "Okay. Right to the point. Didn't Sally hire you?"

"Yes," he said, "but now it's my time."

"Sally is one of my closest friends," I said. "I barely know you. Why on Earth would I help you do anything to hurt her?"

"Because I know what your daughter did," he said. "And my guess is you'd like to keep that quiet and keep her out of jail."

He looked straight at me and barely blinked.

I said, "What the hell are you talking about?"

"You know," he said.

So now Irving Jackson was blackmailing me over this stupid fake robbery incident? Christ. I should go to the police and tell them the whole thing: Couldn't be any worse than this bullshit.

"I don't know." I could play stupid as well as anyone. "What has she done? She's a grown woman, you know. Why aren't you blackmailing *her* over her supposed digression?"

"Because she has no power," he said. "You do." He shrugged. "Besides, she doesn't even know she told me. She was drunk. She drinks too much, you know. Like mother, like daughter, I guess."

I wanted to throw something at him. Instead, I smiled. "I don't drink."

"Anymore," he said.

"What did she tell you in her drunken state?"

"About burning down the house," he said. "Your house."

You have *got* to be fucking kidding me.

I laughed. I almost said, "Oh that." Instead, I let myself take a breath. Then I said, "She was a child when the house burned down. In her grief over the death of her brother, she believed she was responsible for the fire."

He looked at me and then slowly shook his head. "No. She burned it down. She told me about how she lit some things on fire in a waste paper basket and put it near the dryer. Then the house burned down."

"She is mistaken about that," I said. "It was an electrical fire."

"I have a cop on the police force," he said.

"Of course."

"He works arson and I had him look into the fire," he said.

I felt a wave of anxiety.

"He did say they believed it was an electrical fire, but if they had new evidence they might change their ruling. There was a note in the file about a fire in a wastepaper basket. If they investigated and ruled it arson—arson by someone who lived in the house—my guess is you'd have to pay the insurance company back, with interest. Plus there's the whole jail thing. I can encourage him to open the file again or throw the whole thing out."

I didn't say anything. Even if they decided Fern was guilty, she'd been a child. They wouldn't send her to jail now. Plus, what about statute of limitations?

"There is no statute of limitations on arson in California, by the way," Irving said, as though reading my mind. "I know I would do anything for my children, if I had any, so I'm guessing you would do anything to protect your children. After all, you've only got two left."

"If you want me to help you," I said, "you should probably shut the fuck up now. What do you want me to do?"

"Call Mr. Green and tell him you want Sally off your movie," he said.

"Who the fuck is Mr. Green?"

"He's the chairman of our board," he said. "Just tell him you're having trouble finishing the script because Sally is bothering you. Or something. You figure it out. Tell them you want me as your producer."

"Why?" I said. "I'm just the writer. You should talk to the director."

"I don't have anything on the director," he said. "Besides, you own a huge chunk of the movie. You've got the power."

"Then I'd be careful, Jackson," I said. "I could just as easily get you kicked out on your ass."

He smiled. "I don't think so. If I lose my job, I just go to my police friend, and then your daughter will be arrested. It's true she probably won't go to jail for long since she committed this offense when she was a child, but I'm betting she will do some jail time. She will lose her job certainly. And you'll lose your reputation."

I laughed. "I don't have a reputation to lose."

"You do, actually," he said. He paused. "Will you do as I ask? Will you call Chairman Green?"

I made a noise. "Why can't I just ask Sally if you can be my producer? She'd think it was strange, but she'd do it."

He shook his head. "No. I want to be studio head. I'm next in line."

"I don't think it works that way," I said. "I can't fuck over a friend. It's not right."

"It's Hollywood," he said.

I made a noise.

"There's more," he said. "Everyone in this town who has fucked you or been fucked by you is successful."

"What are you talking about?"

"Every director, every actor, every producer, writer. If you've had a relationship with them, they're doing well. No matter what I do, I don't seem to make it. So I want to make it with you."

"What? Are you kidding me? Is this a joke?"

He shook his head. "I'm dead serious. I want to come to your writing studio, your love nest—I've heard all about it. I want us to have sex. You won't be sorry. I am very good."

I stared at him. Had everyone drunk some kind of crazy ass juice in the last twenty-four hours?

"I am not going to have sex with you," I said. "Are you fucking crazy? I'm not going to screw Sally over. You can go fuck yourself."

"Your daughter is in big trouble," he said. "She drinks too much. She talks when she drinks and tells everyone your business. And her business. Probably AFT's business. That's going to get her fired if she isn't careful. She's going to tell someone else about the fire. You need to get her help. You need to keep her out of jail. I'm giving you the opportunity to do that. My police friend says he'll trash the file if I want." He shrugged. "Or he'll open it and investigate. I'll give him my statement about her confession. You help me get rid of Sally and you have sex with me in your studio, and I'll protect Fern. When Sally leaves, I'll make sure Fern keeps her job."

"I'm in a relationship," I said. "I can't have sex with you."

He smiled. "As I understand it, you're still married, and you live with a man who is not your husband. And before that, you pretty much fucked everyone in Hollywood."

"Not everyone."

"Everyone who is successful now," he said.

"What? You think my vagina is a success-maker or some-thing?"

"Maybe. Women are mysterious beings."

"What about your wife?" I asked. "If we have sex, I could then blackmail you by saying I'd tell your wife."

"She wouldn't care," he said.

That's what married men usually said.

"More importantly," he said, "I wouldn't care."

I shook my head. "Okay. Okay. But I've got too much going on now. Give me until Monday."

"No," he said. "That'll give you time to figure out how to get out of it. Tomorrow night. I'll meet you at your place at seven. I'll bring the wine." He smiled. "Oops. Maybe it's time for you to start drinking again."

Then Irving Jackson got up and walked out of the dining room.

I sat there alone, just for a moment. I laughed. Then I rubbed my face and said out loud, "What the fuck just happened here?"

NINE

I had to leave this place. This was a crazy fucking city. This was exactly why I hated Hollywood. Or the Hollywood life. Or whatever you wanted to call it.

I had to find some sanity.

I left the dining room and hurried back toward the ballroom. Needed to tell Sally where I was going.

I stopped at the threshold. Tell Sally? Maybe that wasn't the best idea. I had to figure out what to do. I was supposed to stab her in the back so Irving Jackson could get ahead. And I was supposed to fuck him because he believed I had a magical vagina.

Only in Hollywood.

Only in fucking Hollywood.

All at once I saw Fern standing next to Enrique and Sally across the room speaking with Irving Jackson who sipped on a martini like it was someone's cock. And there was Hayword— Hayword looking around the room for someone. For me?

My stomach lurched when I saw him. I wanted to call out to him. I wanted to beg him to save me from all of this bullshit. He knew about Ryan Nichols. He knew about Alberto. He knew it all. Except the part about his daughter confessing arson to a sociopath. And he didn't know about his daughter orchestrating the stupidest stunt in history for love because she couldn't ask her freaking mother for a favor.

I didn't have the stomach to bring him up to date.

I turned around and hurried out of the ballroom before Hayword could see me. Fortunately the valet was quick, and I was soon in my car heading for the beach. Mark wouldn't be there since he was staying in his house tonight—his turn with Ian. But I'd have peace and quiet. I'd have time to think about what to do next.

Have time to have a drink.

Yikes! Where had that come from?

I turned on the radio and headed home. I didn't like driving in the dark. Wasn't that a sign of getting old? Especially on these freeways where everyone was driving too fast, too fast, too fast.

Suddenly, about halfway home, the freeway was lit with red. Brakes screeched. Cars stopped. My side of the freeway became an instant parking lot. Cars on the other side whizzed by. I stopped, too, of course, thank god, and I didn't hear the sound of metal anywhere. No accident, maybe.

I saw people getting out of their cars and running forward.

"What the fuck?"

I put the driver's window down and leaned out. Couldn't see anything but people running. People ran past my car. Heard a few horns honking.

What were they running toward?

To save someone? To help someone? To gape at someone in distress? What was it?

I was tempted to get out, too, but my momma didn't raise

any idiots. I stayed in my car. A few minutes later people began running back, not as fast but as determined.

I shouted to someone passing, "What is it? What did you see?"

One woman just shook her head and kept running. But a man stopped and said, "It's a seal."

"A what? A seal? Like the seal of Solomon?"

"No, lady. Ain't no demons out and about. It's a frigging seal. Like from the ocean. It's there in the middle of the highway. Lucky no one hit it. Can't understand how no one hit it. But everyone is waiting. Waiting for the seal to keep going."

"Keep going? It's miles from the sea. Where on Earth could it be going?"

The man shrugged. "I don't know. But it's going somewhere." And off he ran.

I had to see this.

I got out of the car. Remembered to take the keys, remembered to lock it, but still, crazy ass me got out of the car and hurried forward. I waited for someone to stop me or call to me or call me names. Didn't happen. I counted the cars as I ran by, so I'd know where my car was when it was time to come back. One, two, three, four, five, six, seven, eight.

Then I was there, at the front of the row. Ahead was empty freeway for as far as I could see—which wasn't far because it was dark out. The front row of cars—four or five abreast—all had their lights on. I stood with half a dozen other people on the pavement. I didn't think I'd ever stood on the freeway before. It was strange. It felt otherworldly.

It felt end-of-worldly.

And there in the glare of headlights was a seal, looking preternaturally white in the artificial light. I blinked and saw spots—on the seal.

"It was moving quickly," someone said to me, as though

catching me up on the latest news, as if this had been going on for hours rather than minutes. "But it stopped."

"*She* stopped," someone else said. "It's a female. She was heading east. Her radar or whatever must be screwed up."

"I can relate," someone else said. Or was that me?

Then the seal did the strangest thing: She turned and looked directly at me. At me. She stared at me.

I looked at my human companions for the first time, and they looked back at me.

"She's looking at *you*," one of them whispered.

I looked back at the seal. I laughed, quietly. Couldn't be looking at me in particular. Must be the stress of the last day or more, me thinking she was looking at me. Maybe I was imagining *all* of this. It had been a rather odd twenty-four hours or more.

"Animals acting crazy last day or two," someone said.

I took a step closer to the seal. Don't know why. I wasn't particularly an animal lover. Didn't hate animals. But you know, they've got their tribes or flocks or whatever, and I've got mine.

The seal looked perplexed or frightened. Or lost. I heard her say, clear as day, "Where are you going? What are you doing?"

Okay. I didn't see her lips move or anything, but I heard the words. I glanced over at the woman next to me. "Did you hear that?" I asked.

"I sure did," she said. She looked over her shoulder and yelled, "Turn that radio down. We're trying to have a moment with the wild here."

Ohhh. It was the radio. I almost burst out laughing. Almost told the complete stranger next to me that I thought the seal was talking to me, because it would have been absolutely fitting: Where was I going? What was I doing?

For a moment there was silence. The cars were still racing

by on the other side, but here, all engines had stopped, and it was quiet.

"Honey," I said to the seal. "Darling wild thing, you are far from home. The ocean is thataway." I pointed west. "Is it the radiation? Is it pollution? Is there a big earthquake coming? Did you get in a fight with your mate? Or are you just trying to keep moving?"

The seal continued to stare at me until she burped or hiccoughed or whatever it was seals do, and she started moving across the pavement, awkwardly—probably painfully—undulating like a fish out of water. Or, actually, more like a seal out of water. Didn't she long for the ocean now that she was so far from it? Didn't she long for the freedom of the water?

Didn't she long for home?

I heard someone or something say, "You can't go home again."

I looked around, but no one was speaking.

"You go, girl!" I called out to the seal.

Yes, I fucking did. We all started clapping and hooting. Shouting, "We're rooting for you!" "Go home, ET!" "Send us a postcard." Probably scaring the shit out of her. Soon enough she was across the road. She disappeared into the darkness just like that, and I realized, "I'm standing on the freeway in front of a line of traffic that goes on forever. I'm gonna be dead if I don't get back to my car."

I heard engines start up. Sounded like a car race about to begin. I turned and ran back toward my car. Counting: one, two, three, four, five, six, seven, eight.

There it was. Unlocked it. Got in.

Start your engines, ladies and germs.

Off we all went again. Up to 70 mph in no time at all. As if it had never happened.

As if this incredible encounter had never happened.

How many things a day did we just take for granted? Driving these cars, for one thing. Talking to someone on a little box, for another. Or writing things on a little box and a second later, someone thousands of miles away could read what we'd written.

Those were just the technical amazements.

What about that wild creature on the freeway? How had she gotten there?

And why did she tell me I couldn't go home again?

I laughed and hit the steering wheel with the palms of my hand.

"Brooke, you crazy cunt, that seal was not talking to you."

Fucking stranger things had happened in my life. That was fer sure.

Well, maybe not.

Just like that, I was out of the blackmail funk, singing to some song as I headed home. I couldn't wait to take a shower, slip under the covers, and go to sleep. Wished Mark was going to be home.

Home? Home, home, home.

You can't go home again.

Soon enough, I drove up the private drive to my house. The porch light was on. Mark's truck was there. Yay! He must not be taking care of his son tonight as planned. I'd get to split the sheets with my sweetheart after all. I parked the car and then glanced at my phone. No messages from Mark. Wondered why he hadn't texted me he was going to be here instead of at his house as planned. Must have figured I wouldn't be home until very late.

I couldn't wait to tell him about the seal. I hurried up the back steps, opened the door, went into the laundry room and then stepped into the hallway that led to the bedrooms.

I heard voices.

Oh crap. Mark had company. I didn't really want to see anyone else. I would just sneak into the bedroom, text Mark I was there, and wait for the company to leave.

But I heard a woman laugh, and I froze.

It was more of giggle. The giggle of a woman who had either just been fucked or was about to be fucked.

I knew the sound well.

I heard water running. It was the shower. More voices again. A man. A woman. Murmurs.

Then the bathroom door opened, and Sherry stepped out. Completely naked. She didn't see me. She was so lost in what she was doing—or had been doing—that she didn't look around. She had no idea I was there. No idea. She was confident in her tight skin and unwrinkled face and her easiness in life as she fucked another woman's man that she did not, could not, see me.

"I need to get dressed, silly!" she said as she walked into my bedroom. "Before *she* gets back."

In that moment, I almost threw up, I almost killed them both, I almost went screaming through the house ready to destroy everything in my path.

Instead, I stepped back. Retraced my steps. Went through the laundry room. Stumbled down the steps and out to my car. Suddenly remembered Hayword fucking that blonde up against the copier or filing cabinets or whatever it had been after Alberto died. Thank god, I hadn't actually seen Sherry and Mark fucking one another.

I threw up. Splattered my lunch all over the pavement.

I got in the car and drove away. I was so shocked and angry and pissed and horrified, I could barely see. It was dark, it was dark. I couldn't keep driving. Where could I go? They had been fucking in my house. My own fucking house. How could Mark do this to me?

Fuck. I thought I knew him. I thought he was the stalwart man.

I started laughing. Could this night get worse? Fern and Enrique, then Irving Jackson, and now Sherry and Mark.

Mark was actually fucking that stupid airhead?

All right, all right, all right.

I should call my sponsor. Yes, that was it. Should call her.

Didn't want to.

I wanted revenge.

I was suddenly so angry I felt like the car could not contain me. I was on the freeway. Wasn't sure how I'd gotten there. Maybe I should go fuck Hayword now. That would teach Mark. Of course, when we'd first gotten together, Mark and I had sex for a year during which time I continued to fuck Hayword. He was used to that.

Besides, if I fucked Hayword, he would think I wanted him back.

Maybe I did.

Maybe I did want our old life back.

I didn't know. Didn't know.

Where *was* I going? What had I been doing for the last couple of years?

I had changed my entire life so that I could be sober. So I could be a good mother. A good person.

Yet everything was the same: except the details.

Except the fucking details. I wasn't drinking. But I was doing everything else to keep the rage down.

And why? Why? It hadn't done any good! Fern was fucking up her life, and she had fucked up mine by blabbing to Irving Jackson. Now Mark, my stalwart man, was cheating on me with the manager of his restaurant. The restaurant that was situated in my building. How messy was this going to be?

Christ. What now? What now?

Don't cry for me, Argentina.

I could go fuck Ryan Nichols. Yes, that was it. Lure him into my web again. Fuck him like crazy and then go tell him to fuck himself.

Good lord. Really needed a new set of curse words.

I shook my head. Okay. Okay. I'd go to my bungalow. The former love nest. I'd stay there the night. I needed to go to David's science experiment tomorrow morning. After I met with one of my blackmailers.

And then tomorrow night I had to meet Irving Jackson and let him fuck me.

No fucking way.

No cock-sucking way.

No damn way.

No darn way.

Hell no.

Maybe I should just stop cursing.

Heck no.

I giggled.

Man, I needed a fucking drink. Wanted a fucking drink.

Fuck, fuck, fuck.

I could not handle the next twenty-four hours without a drink.

I could not.

Handle.

The next.

Three minutes.

Without.

A.

Drink.

I got off the freeway and drove toward the village.

My head ached. My stomach hurt. My ears rang.

A coyote ran out in front of the car.

I braked, but he, she, it kept going. She had no messages for me.

I opened the window and howled. The coyote didn't even pause to listen.

Howling snob.

Wait. Coyotes yipped and wolves howled. Right? When I was growing up in the Midwest, we didn't have wolves or coyotes, so how the hell would I know?

Crazy talk, crazy thinking.

Just like that I was crazy again.

How easy they tumble.

Since the car was stopped, I pulled out my phone and called Joanie. She'd get drunk with me.

No, no. She'd help me get revenge. No drinking.

"Aren't you supposed to be at some swank par-tay that you should have invited me to?" she said when she answered the phone.

"Damn straight I should have invited you," I said. "Should have, could have, would have. I need your help."

"Who do I have to kill?"

"Um—" That was an idea. Naw. That would just land me in jail because I would fucking brag about it. "Can you get your hands on knock out drugs or date rape drugs or whatever they are? Something that I can give someone that won't kill him, but I will be able to fool him into thinking he had sex with me?"

"Do tell," Joanie said. She sounded far too interested.

"It's a long story," I said. "Upshot is that some asshole thinks my vagina is magic."

"From what I hear, it just might be," Joanie said. "If I was interested, I'd certainly be interested, if you know what I mean."

"Everyone on the planet knows what you mean," I said. "Probably the zombies from another planet in my movie know what you mean."

"I've known people who have been in your vagina," she

said. "I've heard it is nice, but I'm not sure anyone has ever classified it as magical."

"Joanie! Fucking focus!" I said. "This man is blackmailing me. He wants to hurt Fern."

"Nuff said. You nearby? I can meet you at the love nest in thirty."

"Writing studio," I said.

"I thought it was an art studio," she said, "aka love nest."

"Now that I'm not pretending to do art there," I said, "it's a writing studio."

"Where you actually write?"

"That's not the point," I said. "How about we call it the fucking bungalow. I'll meet you there in thirty minutes."

"We're calling it the 'fucking' bungalow? I thought you didn't do that anymore."

"Joanie!"

"See you then. Drugs in hand."

I called Irving Jackson. I made a face when I heard his voice. Made my fucking skin crawl.

"Can you be here in an hour?" I asked.

"Sure," he said. "What changed your mind?"

"I haven't changed my mind about anything," I said. "I just want to get it over with. Bring a bottle of wine."

"Got it. Glad to help the wicked."

Shut the fuck up, you moron. You threaten me, that's one thing. But you threatened my family. I. Will. Take. You. Down.

I ended the call before I said all of that to him. Because I was going to say it to him one way or another.

Now. What about Manny? Fern had texted me his full name and address.

I called our cop friend Philip.

"I need a favor," I told him.

"Of course," he said.

"I need to get some dirt on a John Manuel Reilly. He presently works at Juliet's. They call him Manny. I can give you his address."

"I can't, Brooke," Philip said. "I can't just violate someone's civil rights because you don't like him."

"I don't even know him," I said. "He's trying to blackmail me. He knows something about Fern, and if I don't give him money or maybe a part in a movie, he's going to the police."

"Blackmail is against the law," Philip said. "You should be going to the police about this."

"You are the police," I said. "Besides, if I went to the real police, or the other police, Fern could be in trouble."

"Legal trouble?" he asked.

"I think so."

"Don't tell me anything else," he said. "This is the last fucking time I'm doing this. For either of you. Last night Hayword got me to track down Ryan Nichols, some guy who worked in your first movie. I'm not the fucking phone book."

"Did you give him his address?"

"No," he said. "This Ryan guy must be in some guild or union. He can track him that way."

"Okay, last time I ask," I said. "Last time either of us asks."

"Give me this guy's address." He sounded disgusted.

I gave him the address.

"Can you get back to me before eight tomorrow morning?" I asked. "I'm meeting him at The Coffee Shoppe."

"Jesus H. Christ," Philip said.

"Please."

"Don't beg," he said. "It's so . . . not like you. Speaking of strange. Have you seen what's been going on with the animals? They're calling it the zombie animal apocalypse. I've heard your movie mentioned several times in relation to this."

What? "Why my movie?"

"Maybe because it was the most successful zombie movie of all time," he said. "You've surpassed *Night of the Living Dead* and *The Walking Dead*."

"The animals who are being weird aren't dead," I said. "They're not coming back from the dead. They're just acting strangely. Actually saw a seal on the freeway tonight. No one hit it. It was odd."

I didn't mention that the seal had talked to me. Or that I *thought* it had talked to me.

"So they're alive," he said. "*The Living Dead*?"

"Isn't that what we all are?" I said. Then I laughed so I didn't sound melodramatic. "Thanks, Philip. I appreciate all you do for us. You want a part in my next movie?"

I knew he didn't want a part. He was the only person in this whole damn town who didn't want a part in a movie. Okay. Slight exaggeration. As far as I knew, Mark didn't want a part in a movie either.

My stomach lurched. *Mark*. Fuck. I had almost forgotten about all of that.

"Naw, not this time," Philip said. "Later." He was gone.

I called Hayword.

"You okay?" he asked. "I've been looking all over for you. They said you left suddenly."

"I'm fine," I said. "You know how much I love those gatherings. I'll tell you the rest later. Hayword, I was just talking to Philip. What the hell you doing looking for Ryan? What were you thinking?"

"I don't know," he said. "I wanted to tell him off. Tell him how he ruined our family and ruined you."

"First off," I said, "all those TV shows about someone ending up dead always start off like this. Some guy finding someone's address and then going to confront him. Never turns out well."

"It probably usually turns out well enough," Hayword said. "I think those so-called news shows just retell the same murders over and over. Most of life does not end in murder or in the end of the world. You and David need to understand that."

"Off topic, Hayword!" I yelled. "And secondly, you wanted to tell Ryan he *ruined* our family. No way. I don't want him to think he was that fucking important."

"He *was* that fucking important!"

I rubbed my face. Oh god, oh god, oh god. Okay. If I can't drink, could I please have a hit of acid? Or maybe that had already happened. Maybe the past two days were a result of a hit of acid I hadn't known I'd taken.

"Man, I wish I did drugs," I said.

"Don't even joke about that," Hayword said.

"Who's joking?"

Dead silence.

I laughed. It was a hoarse strained laugh, but it was a laugh.

"All right," I said. "No joking. But you can't talk to Ryan, and you really can't tell him he ruined my life. He didn't ruin my life, Hayword. *I* fucking ruined our lives. And actually I didn't ruin our lives. We had Alberto. We got back on track after the affair."

"But you see me and that woman," Hayword said. "I know you still do. Every time we made love afterward, you saw me fucking her. You couldn't get it gone. If you and Ryan had never been together, I would have never cheated."

He was right. I had never been able to stop seeing him fucking the blonde. Seared into my memory. I thought memories were supposed to fade with time. Not that one.

"So you fucked her because I fucked Ryan?" I said. "I don't think so. All those years I was fucking everyone and their mother, you never cheated on me. So why her, why then?"

Were we really having this conversation now over the phone while I was in the car, stopped off the side of a dark road?

"I have no idea," he said. "I really don't know. I was angry, and I was grieving. You wouldn't talk to me. You wouldn't listen to me. And she was there."

Convenience. Was that why Mark had fucked Sherry? She was convenient?

Bleck.

"Is that what you told her?" I asked. "You said my wife won't listen to me?"

"No," he said. "I didn't tell her anything. I was so sad, Brooke. I loved that little boy, and yet, I didn't feel like I was entitled to my grief. Because he wasn't mine. I never felt like he was mine. You seemed to hate us all."

"I didn't hate you all!" I felt like I was going to throw up. Why were we having this conversation now? I wanted to scream.

"I had lost my son," I said. "I couldn't be there, for anyone. But I certainly didn't hate you or the kids."

"Before that," he said. "Before that, you had lost Ryan, and you blamed us all. Or that's what it felt like. He left you, so you left us."

"I don't know what the fuck you're talking about," I said.

"I know!" he said. "You always say that. None of us is able to have an opinion about any of this—about Alberto's death—because you're the mother, you're the one grieving."

"What do you mean 'none of us?'" I said. "David and Fern didn't know about Ryan."

"They knew Alberto was dead and you disappeared," he said. "Even before Alberto died, you disappeared."

"What are you saying? I wasn't there for you so you fucked someone? I wasn't there for Fern so she burned down the house?

I wasn't there for David so he got neurotic? I wasn't there for Alberto so what? He died?"

"No," he said. "That's not what I mean."

Another coyote crossed the road in front of me. Or maybe it was the first one coming back. It stood in my light beams and watched me. Then she sat on her haunches, easy with herself, and looked casually from side to side. Peering into the darkness, I supposed.

I took a deep breath. "You know, Hayword. I can feel myself becoming really pissed—and I was already pretty pissed. I've got a lot of balls I'm juggling right now."

That didn't sound quite right.

"Can we have this heart-to-heart later?" I asked. I didn't really care if he agreed or not because I was not going to keep talking about it.

Silence.

A sigh.

"We all have a right to our grief," Hayword said. "Even Ryan."

I screamed. I let out the loudest scream I could manage, and it came bouncing back into my own ears. I dropped the phone and raised my hands. I could hear Hayword's squeaky voice calling to me. I leaned down, picked up the phone, and ended the call. And then I said, "Shut up, you motherfucking cuntsucking asshole."

I leaned back in my seat.

Then I picked up the phone and texted Hayword, "I dropped the phone. My apologies. Text me Ryan's number and address if you found it. I'll go tell him he's entitled to his fucking grief."

I looked at my watch. I had time to stop at The Coffee Shoppe and get a drink. A drink of coffee. Tea. Whatever. I had time for a pause before I either killed Irving Jackson or made incriminating photos of him that I could use against him forever.

Not that I wanted to do that. But I wanted him out of my life. Two hours ago I hadn't even known he was in my life, except peripherally.

I looked ahead. The coyote was gone. Just like that. Hadn't she a message for me, too?

TEN

I drove into the village and parked in front of The Coffee Shoppe. The neon OPEN sign glowed unnaturally in the foggy night. Five minutes ago, it had been a clear and beautiful night. Now fog clouded everything.

I got out of the car and went into The Coffee Shoppe. Glanced around. Two other people were there. One with her back to me. The other person was a twenty-something with ear-buds on while she read a book. She glanced up at me, but I could tell she didn't see me. She turned the book over and set it down while she took a sip of coffee. *Call of the Wild*. Really? Someone was reading Jack London on this foggy night? Fitting, I sup-posed.

"It was a dark and stormy night," I murmured.

I went to the counter and ordered a coffee. The barista was young, tattooed, with a pierced nose, pierced ears, and a pierced belly button. Yep, I could see the pierced belly button. I hadn't noticed her in here before.

"You from Portland?" I asked.

She grinned as she handed me the coffee and I gave her money. "Yeah, what gave it away? My dashing good looks?"

"Of course," I said. "That and the salmon swimming up your arm."

"We're all swimming upstream, sister," she said as she handed me my change.

I nodded, took the money, and sat at the nearest table. Something weird about The Coffee Shoppe tonight. I had been here hundreds of times. Always seemed perfectly normal. Now I felt like I was in a George Romero movie. I looked around again. Everything was in color, not in black and white. We weren't in *Night of the Living Dead.* I closed my eyes and tried to breathe deeply. It was difficult. My stomach was in a knot. A million knots. How could my life have unraveled so quickly in such a short time?

"Hello, there." The voice was calm, quiet, gentle. I opened my eyes, and the woman from Juliet's was there: the friendly one with long white hair, blue eyes, and dragon sweater. Only she wasn't wearing the sweater tonight. She carried a bag on her shoulder and held a book in her left hand, using her middle fingers as a bookmark. I couldn't see the title, but the cover looked red.

"Hello," I said. I started to stand, but she waved me off.

"Don't get up," she said. "I'm just leaving. But I wanted to formally introduce myself. I'm Gabriella. I live around here. Just so you don't think I'm stalking you or anything."

"Now I do," I said. I smiled. I remembered how calm and pleasant she'd been at the restaurant. How familiar she'd seemed. Maybe I had seen her here before and had forgotten.

"Are you all right?" she asked.

"Why? Do I not look all right?"

She smiled. "You look a little bit shaky, actually," she said.

"It's been a strange couple of days," I said, "and it's about to get stranger."

She nodded. "With the robbery and all," she said. "I bet. And the world has been a bit strange these last couple of days. Forcing us all to walk on the wild side a bit, I suppose."

I motioned to the chair across from me. She said, "Just for a bit. I don't want to bother you."

"What do you mean: forcing us to walk on the wild side?"

"Don't you ever feel like that?" she said. "As though we walk through the world believing we're not a part of it. Believing we don't live and die. That we are tame beings instead of wild beings. That's what makes us sick: believing we are tame. Striving to be tame."

"But being wild is chaotic," I said. "It's dangerous. We've created civilization, so we don't have to live like animals."

"Of course we live like animals!" she said. She laughed. "We *are* animals. As animals, we create art and beauty and buildings and structure. We listen to the cosmos and create music. We listen to the earth and we tell stories. It's like your movie."

"*Love and Other Insanities*?"

She smiled. I swear her eyes were twinkling.

"No, love," she said. "*Beauty and the Zombie*. They were the living dead until she dug her toes into the earth and let the sun bath her in its light. It was the connection between the light and the dark, the earthly with the heavenly. It was really quite spiritual. They became human again when they became human again."

I laughed. "No one has ever claimed *Beauty and the Zombie* is a spiritual movie."

"An earthly spiritual movie, of course. They got down and dirty while bathing in the light. They became *earth*lings, truly, while also accepting their heavenly nature, as it were."

"I don't believe in heaven," I said. "But today, I believe in hell."

"It doesn't matter what you believe," she said. "Heaven is just a word to convey a concept. Don't get so caught up in semantics. It's one word that probably came from another word that meant something else. Everything is always changing meaning, isn't it?"

She said all of this so gently, without any judgment, it seemed.

"Everything isn't semantics," I said. "Some things are real. Some things are horrible."

"It's true," Gabriella said. "I saw this interview with a woman who was the sole survivor of a plane crash not too long ago. The plane crashed in the jungle. Statistically she was sitting in the least safe place. Yet she was the only one who survived the initial crash. You know why?"

I shook my head.

"She was the only one not wearing a seatbelt. When the plane disintegrated, she fell free. So there she was, after the crash, in this jungle, surrounded by the dead, including her fiancé, and she said she accepted the situation straight away. She didn't think why me? She accepted it and tried to figure out what was next. And she noticed the beauty all around her. She noticed how beautiful the jungle was. She didn't focus on the death and destruction—she didn't deny it either. She accepted it, and she accepted the beauty of the jungle. And she survived."

I squinted. Why was the woman telling me all this?

"No matter how hard we try," she said, "we can't be safe. Sometimes trying hard makes us unsafe. Sometimes we need to get a new perspective."

I sighed. Perspective? I couldn't see it. I really was getting blackmailed by two different people. My husband and lover had cheated on me. My son had actually died. *That* was my perspective.

"I just saw a seal on the freeway," I said, apropos of something. Or nothing. "She was traveling away from the ocean. She wasn't walking on the wild side. Or hearing the call of the wild. She was scooting across a highway. What the hell was that about?"

"I have no idea," Gabriella said. "She must have heard the call of something."

Why was I asking her? Just because her name was Gabriella didn't mean she had the ear of God.

Not that I believed in God.

I did believe I was having a strange night, and I needed to get going. I had to pick up knockout drugs from a girlfriend so I could blackmail my blackmailer.

"I can see you need to go," Gabriella said. "I hope I haven't taken up too much of your time."

"It was nice running into you," I said as we both got up. Amazing how we could still maintain our civility even in times when the shit was hitting the fan.

"Just remember," she said, "things are not always what they seem."

"You got that right," I said.

We shook hands, which seemed strange, and then she was out the door. I soon followed, but I didn't see her anywhere. She had disappeared into the fog. In the distance, I could hear a coyote yipping.

I got into the car, then checked my phone messages. One from Jackson: He was stuck in traffic and would be a little late. One from Joanie: She was at my bungalow. One from Hayword: Where the hell was I? One from Mark. I stared at his name, stared and breathed, stared and breathed. But I didn't look at his message. Didn't want to hear or read anything he had to say.

Nothing from Phil Case telling me all I needed to know about Manny, the other guy trying to blackmail me.

I drove slowly through the fog to my bungalow. Felt like I was driving through the end of the world. By the time I got there, Joanie was leaning against her car in my driveway, looking like some tarted-up ghost in the fog, her ruby red lipstick shiny in my headlights, her short blue dress sparkling prettily, ready to dance to whatever tune the universe was playing. She had no idea what it was like to be discreet, apparently. We were about to commit a freaking crime. I hadn't wanted any of the neighbors to see her at my house. Of course, in this weather, no one could see anything. I nodded to her as I got out of the car, and we hurried into my darkened house. I switched on the light over the kitchen sink. We stood close to each other while she showed me the pills on her palm.

"This one will just knock him out," she said. "This one is like a memory loss pill. It will eventually knock him out, but you can have fun with him if you like, and he'll never remember the next day."

"I don't want to have *fun* with him," I said. "You mean fuck him? Good gawd. No! I mean, I thought about it. Because that's what he wanted and it might solve the immediate problem. But I'm not a drunk anymore. I can't do shit like that. At least I can't do shit like that and forget about it."

Joanie laughed. "Fortunately, I can still do embarrassing shit and forget about it."

"What embarrassing shit do you do?" I asked.

"Fuck my husband," she said. She threw her head back and cackled. Then she said, "Oh, and this pill is if you just want to get high yourself."

I looked at her. What was wrong with the people in my life? First Fern, then Irving Jackson, and now Joanie? Everyone wanted me to drink and drug again?

She returned the pills to a plastic baggie and gave the baggie to me.

"Let me know if you need any help later," she said, "like moving the dead body. I've done it before. I can do it again."

"Funny lady," I said.

"I'm not joking."

"If I could get away with it," I said, "I would consider it."

She shook her head. "No, you wouldn't. I would. But not you. I'll hang out at The Coffee Shoppe for the next hour or so, just in case you need me."

We hugged each other, and then she was gone. I took the baggie into my bedroom and hid it under one of the pillows on the bed. Then I went into the living room and sat on the edge of the couch, waiting. I could hear the kitchen clock tick, tick, ticking. I could hear my heartbeat. My breath. My everything.

I did not like it.

This stillness.

This waiting.

Waiting for death?

I felt that undeniable urge. No. No. It was deniable. I could deny it.

I was not going to drink.

Was. Not. Going. To. Drink.

Unless Irving Jackson brought wine. Then I might drink. Come on. Wine was not actually drinking, was it now? It was just wine. *Christ.* Yes, speaking of Christ, he drank wine. In fact, didn't he turn water into wine? Must have thought there was something divine about it.

Finally, I heard a knock at the door.

"I love the smell of napalm in the morning," I murmured as I got up to answer the door. It was time to tank this motherfucker.

I opened the door and smiled.

Irving Jackson stood on my threshold, dressed in a cream-colored suit, like some kind of natty Grim Reaper. Or Darth Vader in normal drag. He grinned, and I could see the whites of his pearlies. He looked like the proverbial cat and I was the canary he was about to eat.

Well. Not if I could help it.

"Come on in, Irving," I said.

"It's so dark," he said.

"Oh, yes, sorry," I said. "I just got here. Let me lighten it up." I turned on a couple of the lamps in the living room.

"Much better," he said. "Very cozy."

I smiled. How dare he comment on what my house looked like. As if he had a right to an opinion about anything of mine.

He held out a bottle of wine to me. I took it and went into the kitchen.

"Make yourself at home," I said. I opened a drawer and pulled out a corkscrew. I hesitated. If I smelled the wine, I was afraid I might gulp the entire bottle down. I bit my lip.

Wine would make these next moments easier, wouldn't it?

I got a wine glass from the cupboard and carried the bottle and the corkscrew into the living room. Irving was sitting in my chair, the one where I usually sat to figure out what came next in whatever narrative I was spinning at the time. I didn't want him there.

"Come sit on the couch," I said. "There's not room for me in that chair."

He looked surprised, but he smiled and got up and went to the couch. I put the glass on the end table and handed him the bottle and corkscrew.

"Could you open this for me?" I asked.

He didn't ask me why. He just did it. I sat on the couch next to him, but I leaned away as the cork came out. I could still smell it a bit. Loved the sound: gulp, gulp, gulp as he poured the wine into his glass. He set the bottle on the end table.

"You're not having any?" he asked.

"You know I don't drink, Irving," I said. "So, listen, I've started composing the email in my head to Mr. Green, and I've already left him a voice mail, asking for a meeting on Monday. I have some ideas on how to get Sally out."

"Excellent," he said.

His excellent sounded so diabolical that I almost laughed.

"And the other thing?" he asked.

The other thing being sex.

I nodded. "Yes, the other thing," I said. "Let me go put on something less comfortable but more arousing." I smiled as I rose from the couch.

"I like what you have on," he said. He reached for my hand, and I let him have it. Actually wished my hand would drop off my arm once he had it in his grasp.

"Trust me," I said. "You'll like this. Besides, you wanted the full Brooke McMurphy treatment. So I'm gonna give it to you."

I leaned over and picked up the bottle of wine. "Maybe I'll just have a nip."

"That's my girl," he said.

Oh my gawd. Did he just say "that's my girl?" Really, I should just fucking kill him.

"I ain't anyone's girl," I said through gritted teeth. "Even when I was a girl, I was nobody's girl. Don't fucking forget that." I smiled.

"Whatever gets you through the night," he said. "I'll be here, waiting."

I took the bottle into the bedroom, closed the door behind me, and sat on the bed. I brought the wine bottle up to my mouth, and I breathed in deeply. I smelled fruit. Sourness. I almost coughed. Then I looked at the label.

"Cheap bastard," I whispered.

I reached under the pillow, grabbed the plastic bag of pills, and opened it. "Okay. This pill to get high. This one to make him pass out. This one to get him to do whatever I wanted and then pass out. Yep. That's the one."

I took the pill out, got up and went to the dresser. I set the pill on the plastic and then—as quietly as I could— pounded the bottom of the wine bottle onto the pill to crush it to powder.

I looked at the wine bottle, took another sniff. Maybe I could just have a swallow. I felt so thirsty I almost ached. I knew just a gulp would help. It would slake my thirst, as it were. Satisfy my longing. Fill the void.

Fill the fucking abyss.

Maybe I could just sit here and drink half of the bottle. Hell with a gulp or a swallow. The whole thing.

I had every reason to drink it, didn't I? No one understood the pressure I was under. No one understood what it was like to be me. To feel like me. First, my daughter was so afraid of me that she had staged a mock robbery to get me to notice her boyfriend. Then I was at once hailed and then pilloried in the press. No big deal, that. It passed quickly but not before my ex-lover discovered his child was dead because of the news reports about me and my personal life. I got to curse him in front of the world, and now I was probably banned from every AA group from here to Mexico and back up to Canada. And some punk kid was trying to blackmail me into giving him cash or a job or he'd tell the world that Fern had been involved in the faux robbery. Not to mention the asshole sitting in my living room waiting for me to come and fuck him. On top of it all, the love of my life Mark Pantano was fucking some bimbo who could barely walk and talk at the same time.

I turned the bottle around and around in my hand.

The love of my life.

Didn't I used to think Ryan Nichols was the love of my life? Hadn't I lain in bed at night, next to Hayword, thinking that I had never loved anyone as much as I loved Ryan. When I found out I was pregnant, I was horrified, terrified, and happier than I'd been when I was pregnant with Fern or David.

I loved David and Fern when they were born, but I hadn't liked being pregnant with them. I was afraid I'd be a bad mother.

Lo and behold, I had been right about that. A good mother didn't drink herself into a stupor because things went wrong.

Although the thing that went wrong was huge.

Except, according to Ryan, according to Hayword, I was drinking before Alberto died.

I shook my head.

Why would I have been drinking then?

I'd been sad.

Why?

Ah, yes, the abyss in my soul.

Why should I be different from everyone else in the world?

Naw. That was too facile. Not everyone felt that way.

But they had to. Weren't we the first to know what was happening all over the planet? In an instant. Weren't we the first to witness the destruction of our world? Because of us, the seas were rising, the climate was fucked, the oceans were filled with trash and radioactive whatever, and on good days, people could leave their homes and walk the streets of Beijing wearing masks as they made their way through the polluted air. The polluted air that made its way to our shores in the good ole U. S. of A.

All of that should be a fucking crime.

I heard last week the air in Paris was more polluted than the air in China.

Let's have a contest to see who has the worse air.

The Parisians had fought the Nazis only to die from polluted air?

What the fuck?

I had birthed three children into this world.

No wonder I drank.

Used to drink.

Thinking about this was not helpful. What the fuck was I supposed to do? We were living in whackadoodle times. I could only observe it. Write about it? Drown my sorrows?

Yes, that was the answer. Drown my sorrows.

In lovely alcohol.

The crazy ones were the ones who saw the world as it really was. Were the ones who saw it and faced it straight.

What had Gabriella told me tonight? About the sole survivor of a plane crash. She had survived because she faced the truth. She faced reality.

And then she saw beauty.

She didn't pretend the horror wasn't there.

She didn't sink into delusion.

I felt like I was going to throw up again.

I faced reality. Every day. *I did. I did.*

So where was the fucking beauty?

I glanced at the clock. Shit. I'd been in here for twenty minutes. Jackson must have thought I'd fallen asleep.

I opened the door a crack and shouted out, "I'll be right there. Had a little woman thing going on!"

He didn't answer. Good. Maybe he had gotten drunk and passed out on one glass of wine. That would be all right with me.

I closed the door again. I took the wine bottle into the bathroom and poured most of it out. I went back into the bedroom and swept up the crushed pill into my palm. Then I carefully brushed the powder into the wine bottle.

I took the remaining pills into the bathroom and dropped them into the toilet and flushed them away.

I wiped the powder off the rim of the wine bottle.

I stopped. Wait.

What the hell was I doing?

This didn't make any sense. I rubbed my face.

What *was* I doing? I couldn't fix this. If Fern had burned down the house, maybe she needed to face the consequences. Maybe I should just tell the police everything about the fake robbery. Maybe I should just stop trying to fix and control everything. Maybe I should trust someone to . . . to what? To tell them what I was really feeling?

I shook my head.

Maybe, maybe, maybe.

Wished someone loved me enough to make this all go away.

I laughed. Or whimpered. Such a child's wish.

Was I actually really in that thing called reality looking for the love of my life. Still?

Ryan Nichols hadn't been the love of my life. Mark wasn't the love of my life either. I leaned my head back. Neither was Hayword.

The real love of my life had been Alberto.

My little dead boy.

I had been bereft when Ryan left me. Felt like a rose crushed under his heels. Ground into the earth. All the color gone. All the meaning gone. I had felt like a teenager again then. Awful, awful, awful. Hayword had waited for me to come back to him. And Fern and David. All of them wanted me to be home again, home in myself.

But I had left home long ago.

You can't go home again.

You have to be in your body when you're giving birth. You have to be. Unless you're drugged out of your mind, I suppose. But I wasn't drugged. I didn't drink a drop once I knew I was pregnant. When I went into labor, I said no to every drug they offered. Alberto was the easiest birth of any of the three kids.

When they put him in my arms, when they laid him on my chest, I fell in love. Instantly. I knew he was the reason I was put on this earth. And I didn't even believe in that kind of thing. Any pain I had felt about Ryan leaving me, any pain from the birth itself, any pain I had felt my entire life was meaningless because my life now had meaning. Because I had my baby boy.

Alberto was the love of my life.

Yes.

I wanted to wail.

But I needed to go drug that motherfucker sitting in my living room. Get him in my bed. Get him stripped. Get him in compromising positions and take photographs. Use the photographs to blackmail him. Shame him. Show them to his wife or Mr. Green. Tell everyone he had been blackmailing me.

No.

"This is stupid," I said. "Stupidest thing I have ever done."

It was a scheme a drunk would have concocted. I was still thinking like a drunk, acting like a drunk.

Everything is not as it seems.

"No fuck."

I picked up the bottle, strode across the bedroom, and opened the door.

"Jackson," I said as I stepped into the hall and headed to the living room. "This is all complete horse shit."

Irving was sitting on my couch, naked except for a black garter, black fishnet stockings, and a pair of black stilettos. And he was asleep.

"Were you wearing those under your clothes?" I asked.

He didn't say anything.

"Jackson? Your bare ass is on my couch. I'm gonna have to burn that couch now, man. Such an asshole. You blackmail me and then you don't have the decency to stay awake."

He didn't move. I stood just a few feet from him.

"Irving!" I yelled. I didn't want to get any closer. It was bad enough seeing him naked and flaccid from across the room. Didn't want him to wake up and get an erection.

"Jackson! Wake up. I'm not doing this. I'm not writing to Mr. Green. I'm not fucking you. Well, pretending to fuck you actually. I was never going to do that. Jesus H. Christ. Wake up!"

Crap.

I went over to him, hesitated, and then shook his arm.

Something not right here.

I turned on the lamp closest to him.

His eyes were slightly open. He was vaguely blue and cool to the touch.

"Fuck, fuck, fuck."

He was dead. Dead, dead, dead. Dead as a doornail. Dead as an almost naked asshole fucking up my life even in death.

I knew he was dead, but I checked his pulse at his cold neck and his wrist.

Crap. He must have died as soon as I went into the bedroom. No sense doing mouth to mouth on him now.

Was there?

"Christ, Christ, Christ." I got my phone and called Joanie. "Get your ass up here!"

I threw the phone down, and then I grabbed a pillow and put it on the floor beneath Jackson. I went to his feet and pulled on them gently—"Ugh!"—until his limp, heavy body slipped off of the couch and onto the floor. I thought his head would hit the pillow—that's why I put it there—but his ass hit it and dragged it with him so his head bounced on the carpeted floor. If he wasn't already dead, he now had a cracked skull.

I quickly positioned him so he was flat on the floor. Then I did my resuscitation ABC's: checked his airway, checked his breathing, and checked his circulation by trying to find his pulse again. Dead, dead, dead. Breathed two long breaths into him, then I did fifteen compressions.

Wasn't I supposed to call the ambulance first, before I did this?

But he'd clearly been dead for a while.

Could you bring someone back from the dead after twenty minutes?

You couldn't. And I couldn't have them find him in my house dressed only in fishnet stockings.

How the hell had he died? Had there been something in the wine? They'd think I killed him.

I checked his pulse again. I tried compressions three more times. About that time Joanie showed up.

I let her in.

"Oh my," she said as she surveyed the scene.

"I tried mouth to mouth," I said.

"Ew," she said. "Don't ever kiss me again then. You've been making out with a dead guy. I've seen dead and this guy is long past dead. One of the pills kill him outright or did you give them all to him?"

"No!" I said. "I didn't give him anything. I went into the bedroom and kind of got waylaid as I went down memory lane. Half 'n hour later I came out and he was like this."

"Call the paramedics," she said. "They won't be able to revive him, but they'll haul his sorry ass out of here."

"Not like this," I said. "I gotta get him dressed. It's quicker if we both do it."

She nodded. "Okay, well, we're even then. You helped me when I was naked with my toe up the faucet. I'll help you dress a dead guy."

And then we just did it. We pulled off his fishnets.

"I didn't know they still made these," I said.

Joanie said as we took off his stilettos, "Where you been? The Junk Shop has them right in the village."

I grabbed the garter, stilettos, and fishnets and ran into the bedroom and put them in my dirty clothes basket. Then I ran back into the living room and helped Joanie put on Jackson's pants—sans underwear because he didn't have any.

"Man, he is really a dead weight," Joanie said.

We put on his shirt next. We left off his jacket. I unbuttoned his shirt after we buttoned it.

"What?" Joanie asked.

"I want it to look like I tried to resuscitate," I said. "Which I did."

Joanie put her hands over his eyes and closed them.

"Why the hell didn't you do that five minutes ago?" I asked.

She shrugged.

I picked up the phone again, called 911, told them someone was dead at my house. After I hung up, I washed out Irving's wine glass and put it away. I poured the rest of the wine down the drain, rinsed the bottle, and scrubbed the sink. Then I stuffed Jackson's girdle, hose, and stilettos into a paper sack along with the bottle and the empty pill baggie. I took it all out to Joanie. "Just put the clothes in your closet, as if they were yours, if that's okay. You can throw them out later."

"Sure," she said. "I love fishnet stockings. The shoes might be a little big for me."

"Get out," I said. "I'll call you later and let you know."

She nodded.

"Thanks, Joanie."

"This will be okay," she said. "You didn't do anything wrong."

"I know," I said. "But it feels weird. I'm not sorry he's dead. I'm just sorry he's dead in my living room. I had just decided I wasn't going to lie or bullshit about anything, and now this."

"Ah, the Universe provides," Joanie said.

"I can't tell the paramedics he was here blackmailing me to have sex with him. Christ."

"He was here for a business meeting," Joanie said. "Period."

"Are you still here?" I said. "Go, go."

She left, and I was alone with a dead guy.

ELEVEN

Then I remembered the drug dust on my dresser top. I ran into my bathroom, grabbed a wet washcloth, then wiped down the dresser, rinsed off the cloth and hung it in my bathroom.

"You didn't do anything wrong," I told myself. "You didn't do anything wrong."

My clothes! If I was going to pretend this had just been a business meeting—which is what I was going to do—I probably shouldn't be dressed in party clothes.

I quickly stripped off my dress, threw it into the closet, then pulled on jeans and a shirt. I wiped off the little bit of make-up I had on and then looked in the mirror. I was white as a sheet. A white sheet. I pinched my cheeks.

I went back into the living room and glanced around. Everything looked normal. Except for the dead guy.

Heard sirens. Suddenly I flashed right back to the night Alberto died. Flashed on finding Alberto in his crib. Blue. Cold. And then the sound of sirens. I had continued hearing the sirens even after the paramedics came into the house, even after they gently pulled Hayword away from Alberto, where he had been performing baby CPR. He'd known how to do it. I hadn't. I hadn't known what to do.

Although later, later, after everyone was gone and I was alone in the house—even though the rest of my family was still there—later, I took a drink. Many drinks. Just to block out the sound of the sirens from my ears.

Now I felt like I was going to throw up for the second time that day.

Instead, I opened the door.

Things got a little fuzzy after that. Or foggy. Busy? The paramedics did their thing. Asked me questions: Had he taken any drugs, drunk any alcohol, complained of anything?

"I don't know," I said. "It was a business meeting. He might have taken something before he got here, but he seemed fine." I was tempted to tell them the whole long made up story: We'd been at an industry party together, and he was nervous about *Beauty and the Zombie Part Two*, so we decided to work on the script for a bit tonight.

But I didn't say any of that.

The guy was dead. Declared. The police arrived. Different police than I'd talked to yesterday, of course. Different jurisdiction. I wasn't a criminal, but I was an alcoholic, so I was—by nature—good at lying. Lying is the second language of addicts, after all. If anyone doubted my version of anything, I couldn't tell.

Before long, they were all gone. Dead guy. Medics. Police. They had said they'd notify the family. Said something about an autopsy.

Gone.

I stood in the middle of my living room.

I wanted to burn down the house.

"Bleck."

Was it too late to have someone come in and clean? No bodily fluids or anything. Just . . . ickiness.

I texted Miranda, my cleaning guru. Begged her to come first thing in the morning.

Crap. Tomorrow morning. I had to go to David's science project presentation in the morning.

I went into my bedroom and phoned Joanie.

"Thanks," I said. "I'll call you tomorrow."

"They know what killed him?" she asked.

"No, heard someone mention maybe a heart attack. They have to do an autopsy."

Then I called Sally St. James.

"You still at the party?" I asked.

"No," she said. "I'm home fucking my husband. You wanna join us?"

I wasn't in the mood.

"Irving Jackson is dead," I told her.

"Really? How do you know?"

"He died at my house," I said. "At the bungalow."

"Your love nest?" She sounded surprised and angry.

"That's not what was going on," I said.

"What other reason would that slimeball have for being there?"

"I'll tell you about it later," I said. "But he's dead. I don't know what killed him. They've taken him to the hospital, and they're going to notify his family."

"Brooke, what the hell is going on?"

"Can we talk tomorrow?" I asked. "You wouldn't believe the day I've had."

"Sounds like Irving had quite a day, too," Sally said. "I'm sorry he's dead, but I can't say that I'm sad to have that thorn out of my side. Is there anything I need to know about this before I call our media department?"

"No," I said.

"They're gonna want to know why he was at your house," she said.

"He was helping me with *Beauty and the Zombie Part Two*," I said.

"He was not," Sally said.

"Wasn't he AFT's creative director or some such?" I asked. "He was helping me be creative."

"What the fuck, Brooke?"

"Sally, you've just got to trust me," I said. "The line can be 'while working on a script with screenwriter Brooke McMurphy, creative executive Irving Jackson passed away.' Blah, blah, blah."

"All right," she said. "I do trust you. Talk to you tomorrow then. By the way, you okay?"

"Sure," I said. "Why not? I've been fake robbed, blackmailed three times now, caught my lover fucking around on me, cursed my baby's father, and now had a guy die in my living room all in less than 48 hours. Good times all around."

"What? Mark?"

"I'll talk to you tomorrow, Sally."

"You want me to come over?"

I thought about it.

"No," I said. "I don't think so."

"The script still on schedule?" she asked.

"Jesus, Sally."

"I'm sorry," she said. "I don't care about me, not really."
Bullshit.

"But your whole family is wrapped up in this company."

"Not David," I said. "Maybe he'll save us all. Man, I am tired."

"Get me that script and all will be well in the world."

"Guess the mourning period is over?"

"Why would I mourn Irving Jackson?" she said. "He was not a good guy."

"No shit," I said.

"Talk to you later," Sally said.

Then I was in silence again.

I looked at my list of texts. Mark had texted three times. Was he feeling guilty or had he figured out I'd been at the house? I sighed. I didn't have the energy to deal with that drama yet. Fern had texted, too. Nope, didn't have the energy for that drama either. Phil Case left a voice mail. "Call me."

I called Phil.

"What the fuck, Brooke?" he said. "One of the guys in your neck of the woods said they found a dead man in your house. Are you a one woman crime wave?"

"Hey, I wasn't the fake robber yesterday," I said, "and Irving Jackson just died. I didn't do anything to him."

"What happened?"

"He came over to my place, and he died. I was in the other room when he died. I was gone for a bit, and when I returned, he was very dead."

"You were gone for a while?"

"We had gone to an industry party, separately," I said. "The studio is nervous about my new film. I haven't finished the script, and it's supposed to be done in the next couple of days. They're ready to shoot. Jackson wanted to help me with the script."

"At your house late at night?" he said. "I remember what you used to use that place for."

I was silent for a moment. Then I said, "What do you mean?"

"Come on," Philip said. "I'm one of Hayword's best friends. He knew what you were doing. I knew what you were doing.

The entire fucking world knew what you were doing. I thought you'd given that up once you got sober."

Who the fuck was he to ask me these questions?

I took a deep breath. I still had to protect my family. Had to protect myself.

"Phil, I promise you that nothing like that was going on," I said. "But more importantly—since having sex isn't against the law—nothing illegal was going on. Unless dying is illegal. Now, did you find out anything about John Manuel Reilly?"

Phil made a noise. Trying to convey disgust, perhaps. Then he said, "He's got an outstanding warrant in Ohio."

"For what? Anything I can blackmail him with?"

"As I mentioned in a previous conversation, blackmail is illegal. But no, the warrant is for parking tickets. His parents live in Ohio. If he goes home he could go to jail, though. He got these tickets in a town where the fine keeps multiplying and they put people in jail until they pay it. He's racked up eight thousand dollars in fines. Hasn't been home in three years as far as I could tell. Been trying to get his SAG card for a while. Hasn't been able to get a gig, and even if he got one, he couldn't afford the initial dues. Doesn't seem like a bad guy, just kind of an ordinary loser. Does that help?"

"Not sure," I said. "Thanks. Man, I swear. I don't think I know what I'm doing. I forgot Alberto's birthday, Philip. Forgot it. Once I remembered I'd forgotten it, everything has gone to shit."

"I forget my kids' birth dates all the time," he said. "My wife always has to remind me."

"Seems like I should remember my dead child's birthday," I said. "Seems like a good mother would remember that kind of thing."

Oops. I hadn't meant to say that last part out loud.

Philip didn't say anything.

"I know you don't like me," I said. "I know you think I ruined Hayword's life. That I'm a bitch and a slut. And a drunk who is only temporarily reformed. I know that. In spite of all that, you try to help me whenever I ask, and on behalf of my family, I appreciate that."

I heard him sigh. "Brooke, I don't hate you. I don't think you ruined Hayword's life, and I certainly don't believe any of those other things about you. In fact, I think you're one of the bravest people I've ever known. Now, if you need help kicking this Manny kid's ass, let me know. I'll be there."

"Thanks, Phil."

The house throbbed with quiet. And the ghost of Irving Jackson past?

I phoned Hayword.

"Can I spend the night?" I asked.

"At home?" he asked.

"Yeah, at your house."

"At *our* house?"

"Whatever," I said. "May I spend the night?"

"Um, sure. Come on over. Where are you?"

"The bungalow. Hayword?"

"Yeah?"

"Can I sleep in our bed? With you? No sex. Just you and me in bed together."

"You mean like when we were married?"

"Funny guy," I said. "And we're still married."

"Might confuse David," he said.

"Let's not tell him."

A few minutes later, I walked into my old house. I felt such relief as I went through the front door. I stood in the kitchen for a moment, breathing deeply some smell I couldn't quite place, until I realized I was smelling oranges: an orange about to cross over into rottenness.

I went up the stairs, taking two steps at a time. I started to announce, "I'm home!" But I realized that would definitely send mixed messages.

"Hey, you guys!" I called. "You forgot to change the locks. I was able to get in."

David was out of his room and at the stairs before I got all the way up. He grinned.

"Hiya sailor," I said. We gave each other a big hug. He was nearly taller than me. I frowned. When the hell had that happened?

"Why are you here?" he asked.

Hayword came out of our old room. He was grinning, too, like a child on Christmas morning. Perhaps sleeping in the same bed was not a good idea, no matter how needy I was.

"I came to see my best buds," I said. I put my arm around David's waist. "How's the science project coming?"

"All finished," David said.

"You wanna tell us about it?" I asked.

He smiled and shook his head. "Nope. Just wait until tomorrow. You'll be so surprised."

I glanced at Hayword. He shrugged.

"David," I said, "I'm spending the night. I might be in your father's room for a while."

"You mean your room?" David said.

"What?" I asked.

"Your room," David said. "That room is *your* room. *Yours.* The two of you. It's your room."

"Technically it's not *my* room anymore," I said. "It's your father's room."

David shook his head. "No. It's *yours*."

I felt like my head was going to explode. Why was he insisting on this now? I hadn't lived here for nearly two years.

"We don't need to have this discussion now," I said. "I—we

didn't want you to be confused. I need to talk to your father about some things, so we might be in his room—our room—tonight. But it doesn't mean anything. We're not having sex. It's nothing like that."

"Why not?" he said. "Why not have sex? You're married. Mark doesn't have anything to say about that. So, you know, he's in the wrong here because you're already married."

Hayword and I looked at one another.

"It's difficult to argue with that," Hayword said.

"You're not helping," I said. "Maybe this was a bad idea. I just had a terrible day, and I wanted to be with family. I didn't want to be alone."

"Where is Mark?" David asked. He almost sounded angry. I thought he liked Mark.

"It's his night to be with his son," I said. I wasn't going to tell David the rest of the story. That could come later.

"Anyway, are you cool with your dad and me hanging out for a while, and I may spend the night? It doesn't mean we're back together or anything."

"No shit, Mom."

I stepped back from him. "Whoa! Where'd that come from?"

"Sorry," he said sheepishly. "I didn't mean to channel Fern."

"Good," I said, "cuz I couldn't deal with more than one of her."

"Go ahead and stay," David said as he turned and walked away from us. "Have sex if you want. Just don't be loud. I'm already screwed up enough as it is."

"But you're our normal kid," I called. "The one and only normal one. Our hopes and dreams are pinned entirely on you."

"Then you're screwed," he said.

I ran after him and tickled him. He laughed. I tickled him all the way to his bedroom. Then I hugged him again, kissed him, and left his room.

"Close the door on your way out so I'm not privy to your marital perversions," he said.

I closed the door. "Privy, eh? Where did he come from?"

Hayword held his hand out to me. I took it. "Okay. Let's get this pajama party started. Ice cream or coconut fake ice cream?"

"Hell," I said. "Let's just eat anything and everything with sugar in it."

"Deal," he said.

We went downstairs. I sat on a stool at the island while Hayword pulled out chocolate and vanilla ice cream and vanilla fudge almond Coconut Bliss from the freezer. He found fresh strawberries, too, and soon piled ice cream, Coconut Bliss, strawberries, chocolate syrup, and bananas into two bowls. We took our goodies into the living room and curled up on the couch together.

I looked around and couldn't believe that less than an hour ago, give or take, I'd been taking fishnet stockings off a dead man and then dressing him again. Made me shudder.

"Hayword," I said. "Can I tell you what's been going on without you freaking out?"

"Way to start a conversation, Brooke," I said. "But yes, you can tell me anything. I've been seeing a therapist, you know. Learning how to be a grown up. It's art therapy, but she calls it something else. Learning to be a grown up by painting like a child. I hadn't realized how strange I had gotten. How wrapped up in this life of ours. This life of mine. It was so important for me to be noticed. To be successful. Everything else just paled. Even you and the kids. I couldn't hear you when you said this wasn't the life you wanted. I couldn't hear it because it was as if you were speaking another language. I thought this was paradise. Or thought I would be happy once I achieved my goals. I don't know. I can't really describe it. I'm just sorry I wasn't what you needed. I'm sorry I was a bundle of nerves—a tender bundle of nerves you had to watch over. Or whatever it was you did."

"Hayword, I was fucking drunk," I said. "I didn't watch over anything."

"Yes, you did, Brooke," he said. "You watched over all of us."

"Not all of us," I said. "One of us died." I shook my head. "God. When will that go away? Not Alberto. I don't want him to go away. But I'd like the hurt to go away."

"Maybe it will never go away," he said. "Maybe it's a kind of sacred wound. When we decide to love, it's incredibly brave, because it's all temporary. We're all temporary. Maybe love is temporary. And so we are opening ourselves up to being wounded. Once we love and then we lose love, we should get a purple heart, or something, to let everyone know we were brave enough to love. I mean, how cool is that?"

"That's very cool," I said. "Wow, Hayword. Did you think of that yourself?"

"Sure," he said. He put a spoonful of chocolate into his mouth. A bit dribbled onto his chin. "I've had a lot of nights alone to think about our lives."

I reached over and wiped the chocolate off his chin with my forefinger and then sucked the chocolate off my finger.

"That robbery yesterday," I said, "or the fake robbery. Enrique deChamp was one of the fake robbers. It turns out Fern planned it all as a way to get me to notice Enrique, so I would put him in the next *Beauty and the Zombie* film—even though I'm not the fucking director, even though I don't make those kinds of decisions. She couldn't just ask me. She had to concoct this elaborate scheme."

Then I told him the rest of it. All of it. The various blackmails, the seal on the highway, all about finding Mark with that bimbo woman, about Irving Jackson and my magic vagina, talking to Phil Case, Joanie bringing the pills, me almost drugging Jackson, finding Jackson dead and then dressing him. The paramedics.

Hayword didn't say anything. Although he did stop eating his ice cream about the time I mentioned fishnet stockings.

"Oh, and you already know about me seeing Ryan Nichols yesterday. And the worst part, the worst part of it all—besides contemplating how fucked up our daughter must be—is realizing I forgot Alberto's birthday."

"Man, I'm sorry," he said. "What a fucking day." He set his bowl down. He reached for me and pulled me up onto his lap. He wrapped his arms around me, and I wrapped my arms around him. I curled up on his lap, just like I used to when we were younger, when we were new together, when I actually went to him for comfort and solace. In the before time. Before Hollywood, before kids, before Ryan. Before we . . .

Before we what?

Didn't matter. I closed my eyes and held him. Breathed deeply his familiar smell. For the moment at least, I was home.

Before I knew it, I fell asleep.

TWELVE

I awakened to laughter. David and Hayword were giggling about something. Just like old times. Was I dreaming? I opened my eyes to sunshine, and I felt a wave of relief and happiness. I was with my family again, in my house, and all was well, all was well, all was as it . . . had never been in this house.

"Hop on the reality train, sister," I mumbled to myself. I had been an unhappy drunk in this house. I had been a lousy wife and a lousy mother in this house.

I pushed the quilt off of me and sat up. I was on the couch in the living room. Must have slept through the night here. That was not how I had planned on spending the evening, but it was probably for the best. Who knew what would have happened if Hayword and I *had* gotten into bed together. Old habits died hard.

"I hear moaning," Hayword called from the kitchen. "The dragon awakes."

"Not the dragon," I said. "The dragonslayer."

Hayword brought me a cup of coffee. David followed him into the living room. I took the cup from Hayword gratefully.

"Dragonslayer?" David said. "What did the dragon ever do to you?"

"This particular dragon tried to screw with my kids," I said.

David raised his eyebrows. I took a sip of the coffee and waved a hand in front of me.

"Pay no attention to me," I said. "I'm just babbling."

"I'll take David to school," Hayword said, "and I'll meet you at his presentation at ten? Your other thing is at eight?"

I nodded. "How are you doing, sweetheart?" I asked David.

"Great!" he said. "I'm ready to give this presentation. It will blow your mind. Come on, Dad. I don't want to be late."

David kissed the top of my head. "See you later, Mom."

Hayword leaned down and kissed me on the forehead. "You okay?" he asked.

"Did it all really happen?" I asked.

"It was on the news," Hayword said, "so I told David about it. About Jackson being at your house for a business meeting."

"I never liked that guy," David said.

"I didn't know you had met him," I said.

"A couple times," he said. "He was always asking me questions. I never thought he really wanted the answers. He was pretending to be a nice guy when he so clearly was not."

"You're right," I said. "He was not a nice guy. I never knew that before. I just thought he was, well, kind of a nothing."

"Really?" David said. "You think of people that way?"

"Um, well, I hadn't realized that until this moment." I looked up at my son. I felt like I had a hangover. "I will try to do better."

David and Hayword left, and I was alone in my old house.

I felt like a stranger in a strange land. And a familiar in a familiar land. Whose familiar was I?

I was tempted to go online and see what they were saying about Irving Jackson's death. Hoping they didn't mention he died at my house. Hoped they didn't mention the fake robbery again. But I didn't do it, and I didn't wander around my old home like some kind of ghost come to wail over a former life.

No matter what had happened last night, I still had some little weasel I had to deal with this morning.

I checked my phone. Four texts from Mark. I hesitated and then I read the latest one. "Where are you? I called to say goodnight and never heard from you. Love." Second one: "Miss you. Wish you were here. Love." First one: "Ian and I went to Wally World. Ate too much cotton candy. I'll let you guess which one. Love." I smiled. And then I remembered what I had seen. Remembered the naked woman talking about me, in my house, after fucking my man.

In my freaking house.

I would lay waste to her later. She was so fired. And Mark? What was I going to do with him? He was opening a restaurant in my building in two days. I could sell him the building. Move back here. Live in the bungalow.

The bungalow where Irving Jackson had died dressed in fishnets and a garter. Was I ever going to get that image out of my brain? The feeling of my lips pressed against his dead lips as I tried to bring him back from the dead?

I went upstairs to my old bedroom. The bed was made. Either Hayword hadn't slept in the bed last night or else he had actually made the bed. He was a fairly neat man, actually. I was the one who didn't give a shit about things like made or unmade beds. I couldn't remember if I'd always been that way. I mean, I must have taught my children how to live in the world, how to make their beds, put away their toys, set the table, things like that.

Hadn't I?

I sat on the edge of the bed. How many nights had I slept in this bed? How many times had I made love to Hayword in it? No one else but Hayword. I'd never brought another man to our bed—or another woman, for that matter. I wondered if he'd had sex with anyone else in it, since I had left.

I made a noise and got up. This was stupid.

I went to the closet and slid open the door. My side of it was still empty. He hadn't even pushed his clothes over to fill it. I looked up on the shelf. I'd left behind some boxes of stuff. And one precious item.

I dragged the chair from the dressing table over to the closet and stood on it. Then I reached to the back of the shelf until my fingers touched metal. I put my hands around what I knew to be a small urn, and I pulled it down off the shelf.

Alberto's ashes.

In the beginning, Hayword and I had planned on going out to sea and scattering Alberto's ashes in the Pacific. But we didn't do that. Then we thought about taking his ashes all over the world with us. Until I realized that was macabre. And stupid. Alberto was not in his ashes. I couldn't press the urn against my chest and feel his little heartbeat one last time. I had tried that with his little body after he died.

I had tried.

Now I pressed the urn against my chest anyway. I closed my eyes.

I tried to remember what it felt like to hold Alberto. Tried to remember that smell. The glorious smell of his newness. His Alberto-ness. He had been the happiest being on the planet Earth. Always felt like a kind of betrayal to him that I could not be happy after he died. Not that I ever really tried. Except lately. Yes, lately I had been trying.

I looked down at the urn. We should really do something with his ashes. Maybe next year.

I got back up on the chair and pushed the urn to the back of the closet again.

Enough of this. Wasn't my home no more, no more.

Time to go.

I went downstairs, finished my coffee, grabbed an apple from the table, and left the building.

I didn't look back.

I drove down the hill and into the village. Parked the car in front of The Coffee Shoppe. Wasn't sure what I was going to do or say.

The fog had lifted, and it was a sunny cool day. Everything seemed so different from last night. Chirpy, almost. I felt a spring in my step. Heard a crow cawing from somewhere. When I looked around for her, all I saw was blue sky. Suddenly I had an idea. I pulled my phone out, turned on the record function, and slipped it into my pocket.

Then I opened the door to The Coffee Shoppe. A bell tinkled as the door moved outward. I hadn't noticed that before.

Inside, The Coffee Shoppe seemed normal and perky, as usual. The weirdness from last night was gone, and Portland with the tattoos was nowhere in sight. I glanced around and immediately saw a young man with blond hair and black roots sitting in a corner. Must be Manny. He looked completely out of place here. Couldn't quite put my finger on why.

Maybe because he was a criminal and the other customers were not.

I sauntered over to the table, stopped, and looked down at him. "Gonna fake rob anyone today, Manny?"

He smiled. As if he were charmed by me.

I wasn't trying to charm him.

He held out his hand to me. "Nice to finally meet you, Ms. McMurphy. But I didn't fake rob anyone. I wasn't even there."

"Save it," I said. I sat across from him without shaking his hand.

"You want me to get you a coffee?" he asked.

"What? So you can charge me for it? No. Let's get down to business here."

He shrugged. "Okay. Things haven't been going well for me."

I thought, "Probably because you're a dick," but I didn't say anything.

"I'm always on the lookout for opportunity," he said, "and this opportunity just landed in my lap."

He had pretty blue eyes, but his mouth was a little crooked. His hair was dirty. He should really do something about those black roots. He could very easily play a scuzzball on screen.

"What opportunity?"

"You know," he said, "finding out it was your daughter who helped plan this thing."

"What thing?" I asked. I leaned back. I'd just play dumb.

"The fake robbery," he said. "We never guessed people would get so upset about it all."

"You thought people would enjoy getting robbed?"

"It wasn't a real robbery," he said, "although now I can see that they wouldn't have known that until it was all over. So I understand. But I've got rent to pay like anyone else, and I need a job."

"Go work at McDonald's," I said.

"Like that will pay my rent," he said. "Come on. You and your old man must be flush."

I made a face. Who talked like they were in some noir film?

"I figured you'd pay me ten thousand to keep my mouth shut," he said. "Otherwise I'd go to the police."

"You were involved just as much as anyone else," I said.

"They'd cut me a deal," he said. He shrugged. "On all the police shows I've seen, that's what they do."

I stared at him. He was looking at his fingers. He didn't understand how ridiculous he sounded.

"If I gave you ten thousand dollars to keep quiet," I said, "if I gave in to your blackmail, who's to say you wouldn't just come back for more?"

He looked at me. "Who's to say? But if you don't, I will go to the police."

I heard the bell at the door tinkle or twinkle. What was the word? I had a headache. Needed a fucking drink. I suddenly felt like a songbird in a cage. And this kid wanted to keep me in one.

A shadow fell across me. I looked up. Hayword stood on one side of me, Phil Case stood on the other. Neither said a word. They just looked tough. My own personal Wookiees.

Perfect timing. I knew exactly what to do.

I turned back to Manny and smiled.

I reached into my pocket and pulled out my phone and put it on the table. "This is Brooke McMurphy signing off." I pushed stop and then put the phone back into my pocket.

"This is how it's going to go, John Manuel Reilly," I said. "I just recorded you trying to blackmail me. That's a crime. The police know all about the fake robbery and they know about everyone's involvement. This is Detective Philip Case." I held my hand up in Phil's direction. Phil took out his badge and flashed it. Still didn't say a word, just held out the badge for a long time, long enough for Manny to see it was real. "And this gentleman is Mr. Smith. He's a hit man for Louie Berlugetti. Gangsta supreme. Mr. Berlugetti is a private man. Keeps his business neat and tidy. He is a personal friend of mine. Half of Hollywood is mobbed up, you know, and the other half is going down on the half that is mobbed up. It's a nasty business. You've stepped right into it." I stood up, and then I leaned over, resting my hands on the table. "Here's the thing, you little shit ass motherfucker, you've tried to fuck with my family. You've tried to fuck with my children. I make a mamma grizzly bear look like a soccer mom. The last man who tried to fuck with my family ended up dead. You hear about Irving Jackson? Yes, that guy. You aren't getting a fucking dime from me. Ever." I felt rage surging through my body. Pent-up rage. Pent-up anger and frustration. Hadn't realized I had so much fucking anger and grief. If this boy said one wrong word to me, I was certain I would club him to death.

I took in a breath, and then I said, "If you go quietly, I won't tell my friend Louie about you. Detective Case here will pretend he never heard of you. Go back to Ohio for a while—you'll find Mr. Berlugetti paid off your tickets at my bequest. You can come back here one day if you like, maybe even work in the movie business if you've got any talent. If you've got any talent for keeping your mouth shut and keeping away from me and my family. You got that?"

He looked like he had shit his pants.

He nodded.

"Good," I said. "We'll be watching you."

I turned around and walked across the restaurant. I heard Phil and Hayword following me. The door tinkled as I opened it. I went to my car and leaned against it.

I was shaking with anger. I tried to breathe it out, breathe it down and out.

"Who the fuck is Louie Berlugetti?" Phil asked me.

"I made him up," I said. "Sounds like a gangster, doesn't he?"

He laughed and then put his hand across his mouth to keep from laughing.

"That was perfect, guys," I said. "Thank you so much."

Phil shrugged. "Blame Hayword. He called me last night and we concocted this. Couldn't let the dame have all the fun."

Hayword and I laughed.

"If he truly goes to the cops," Phil said, "I don't know if I can do anything."

Hayword came and stood next to me. He put his arm around my waist and I leaned into him. Let Manny see that I was on good terms with Berlugetti's hit man.

"Thank you for everything," I said to Phil.

He shrugged. "What are friends for? And remember, I don't want any details." He leaned over and kissed my cheek. Then he walked away.

"You want a ride up to the school?" I asked Hayword as we moved away from one another.

"Sure," he said. "So you see me as a hit man, eh?" He grinned. "That's kind of sexy."

I got into the driver's seat, and he slid into the passenger's seat.

"Why would you think being a murderous thug was sexy?" I asked.

"Blame it on TV."

I pulled out my phone. "Better call Fern and let her know."

Hayword's phone rang as I called Fern.

"Mom?" she answered.

"I think we took care of it," I said. "Just stay away from Manny. If he asks any questions about me, play up the murderous rageful aspect of my personality."

"Done," she said.

I heard Hayword saying something like, "I'll ask, but I don't think she wants to talk to you."

"Fern, we're going to have to talk about all of this," I said. "I have a lot to tell you."

"Okay," she said. She did not sound okay. I ended the call.

Then I phoned my business manager. I instructed her to pay off some parking tickets in Ohio, anonymously, so that Manny would think the gangster did it. I texted her Manny's name and the name of his town.

"Who were you talking to?" I asked Hayword as I started up the car.

"Mark," he said.

"Mark who?" Really, for a second I didn't know who the hell he was talking about. He gave me a look. "Oh. He called *you*?"

"He said he's been calling you and texting you," Hayword said. "He was worried. I told him you were at our house last night."

"Good," I said. "I hope you told him we fucked each other's brains out."

Hayword didn't say anything.

"Sorry," I said.

I drove us out of the village and up the canyon road to David's school.

"I would have," Hayword said.

"Would have what?"

"Fucked your brains out," he said.

I laughed. One thing about Hayword, he could almost always make me laugh.

"In fact, I'd be willing to try right here and now."

"Thanks for the offer," I said, "but we've got a science experiment to watch."

Hayword and I got to the gym a few minutes before David was due to give his presentation. Each kid had fifteen minutes for his or her experiment, and god bless the school, they didn't make the parents sit through every student's experiment. All of the kids in David's class had their booths set up in various places throughout the gym.

David grinned and waved as we walked toward him. I refrained from hugging and kissing him, but he gave us each a big hug.

Then we heard a bell ring, which startled me. In the corner of my vision, I thought I saw kids moving away from their booths, but I didn't pay much attention.

"Hello everyone," David said. He cleared his throat and smiled nervously. "Today my experiment involves gases." His voice shook slightly. "We are surrounded by gases. If it weren't for gases, we would die. The atmosphere we breathe is 78 percent nitrogen, 21 percent oxygen, .9 perfect argon, and .03 carbon dioxide. Each one of these is clear and odorless. We breathe other things all day, too, and they affect us in different ways. Some things we breathe in we can smell. Like flowers, for instance."

He was smiling and pointing to things on a large screen next to him as he occasionally moved something on his laptop. He was showing us a bouquet of roses now. "Scent is the first sense activated when we're born." A baby was on screen. "Some scents make us feel good." He pointed to the baby. "Some don't." The screen flashed a photo of garbage.

"Some gases we smell," he said. "Some we don't, and yet they affect us." He picked up a jar from his table, took off the lid, then set the jar, open, on the table.

"For instance, the gas in this jar will fill the gym in seconds," he said. "It's gas produced from an odorless flower in the Amazon. The scent from this flower is a renowned love potion. When people breathe in the molecules from this plant, they often feel quite loving, and they're able to express their true feelings to one another."

Parents looked around the room at one another. I noticed the other kids were all standing by the gym doors, like guardians. I vaguely wondered what was up with that. David was watching us—the adults. He had a twinkle in his eyes. I was glad he was spreading love. I saw people hugging one another. I looked at Hayword and rolled my eyes. He laughed and grabbed my hand and pulled me to him. He whispered in my ear, "He's doing this to get us back together. I bet that's why he wanted to make sure we came together."

I nodded, and we moved slightly apart.

"It would be all right with me," Hayword said quietly. "I wish you would come home."

"Hayword," I said. "It's not like I've been on vacation. I've moved out. I've moved on."

"But we really never tried a normal life," he said. "With you sober. Just home with us. As a family. Maybe it would be great. I mean, last night felt so normal."

"We never wanted normal," I said.

"Then right," Hayword said. "It felt right."

That was true. When I was in trouble, last night when I felt alone and friendless, I headed back home. I headed to my family.

I looked at Hayword. I did love him. I loved being in the same house as David. But I didn't want that life. Didn't want that vacuous life. I wasn't that person anymore. I hoped. I was someone now, wasn't I? I mean, I wasn't just a big abyss of grief and nothingness.

"I'm glad you're all enjoying the Amazon Love Plant," David said. He put the cap back on the jar.

"Awwww," several people said.

Then we all clapped.

"Thank you," David said. "You could see how even though you didn't smell anything, your mood changed, didn't it? You felt more affection."

I shrugged and then nodded. I supposed he was right. He began wiggling the top off another jar.

"Now what's in here is a thousand times more powerful," he said, "and will move across the gym in seconds."

I heard the gym doors open. Then heard them close. I glanced over. The kids were gone. Heard another strange sound. Like something dragging across metal.

The top came off the jar. David set the lid aside.

"Inside this job is a particular type of ionizing radiation in a gaseous form. It's like the radiation from the Japanese power plant. Only this is more concentrated. It can disable in minutes. But it's been designed to affect only some people. It's a manufactured nuclear weapon. One of the other kids here got it for me—from his dad."

Suddenly the air seemed to go out of the room.

What had my son just said?

The eyes on the principal widened. Several parents raced for the gym doors.

"They're locked!" one of the parents shouted as she reached the door. "They've put chains across them."

What the fuck? I looked over at David. He was still smiling, like some maniac from a bad TV show.

"We've locked all exits," David said. "You shouldn't worry, though. This weapon only affects some people. The symptoms are a racing heart. Next is itchy skin. Then throat tightening. And trouble breathing."

I saw one man start to scratch his neck. Then he stopped and looked horrified.

"Are you one of those lucky people who won't be affected?" David looked around the room. His gaze stopped on us, for just a moment, and then he continued glancing around.

One woman began to weep. Another man kept scratching behind his ear. The rest seemed to be waiting, paralyzed with fear? Why did no one reach for a cell phone?

Wait.

I knew my son.

He was not a monster.

Was he?

"David," the principal said. "You must stop this."

David nodded. He put the lid back on the "nuclear potion."

"It's too late!" someone said. "Look, I've got the rash!"

David then took the lid off of the Amazon Love Potion. "Here, this will counteract the radiation."

I could hear the chains sliding off of the doors. Then the doors opened, and the kids came back into the gym.

"No, go back," one of the parents shouted. "It's contaminated."

"Yes, it is," one of the students said. A girl. Tracy someone. "It's all contaminated."

The other fifteen students or so came and stood around David.

"This was a community experiment," David said, "designed by all of us."

One of the boys—Jeremy Fox—picked up the love potion bottle.

"There was no love potion," Jeremy said, "although some of you were effected."

Another one of the girls—KateLynn Morris—picked up the radiation bottle. "There was no radiation in this bottle," she said. "If there had been, we all would have been doomed because radiation does not discriminate. It cannot. Everyone is affected by radiation. Right now radiation contaminates our ocean. Radiation contaminates our air."

"Air pollution doesn't discriminate either," Betsy Day spoke up. "We are all affected by what is going on in the world today."

"And we feel as though you, our parents and teachers, are fiddling while Rome is burning," David said. "We want you to do *something*. We want you to stop the radiation and the pollution and all the crazy stuff that's going on."

The gymnasium was spooky silent.

Dead quiet.

The kids stared at us.

I thought of that woman who had survived the plane crash. She hadn't worn a seat belt. She acknowledged the truth. Acknowledged the horror. And saw the beauty anyway.

I said, "How?"

The kids all looked at me. For a second I felt like they were those children from *Village of the Damned.*

"How what?" one of them asked.

"How do we stop it? How do we fix it?" I asked.

The kids glanced at one another. Then David looked at me and said, "We don't know. That's why we did this. We want you to figure it out."

I shrugged. "Obviously we haven't figured it out. The thing is, some of us are still trying to figure it out. Some of us aren't. We each have different abilities to respond, depending upon our circumstances in life, depending upon who we are, how we're feeling, etc. Responsibility. Our generation tried to change the system, and then we tried to live with the system. Didn't work. We're living in whackadoodle times, kids. We can't escape that fact. So what do we do? We look around. We face the truth and figure out how we can respond. As we respond, we also enjoy the beauty around us. I mean, really, what else can you do? If you wait for someone else to fix it, you're fucked. If you try to ignore it, you're fucked—or you're a drunk. Figure out how you want to respond, then respond, and enjoy yourself as best you can. You bitch-slapped us here today. You got us to think in a surprising and wonderful way—and a dangerous way, I might add. You're lucky no one collapsed with a heart attack."

"That could still happen!" one of the parents shouted.

Nervous laughter all around.

The principal said, "I should suspend you all, and if your parents want me to do that, I will. If not, we will have a conversation with the entire class about ethics. I want each of you to write a detailed essay about this experiment and how it has affected you—and what you're going to do to change the world. Now say goodbye to your parents and let's get back to work."

"Wow, Mom," David said. "It was like you were Mom again."

"You mean because I could put more than two sentences together?" I said.

"No, because you knew what to say," he said. He smiled. "What'd you think?"

"Very effective," I said. "You are a bad, bad boy."

David stood between us with one arm around my waist and one around his father's.

"So did you two decide to get back together," he said, "so we could live happily ever after?"

"Is that why you did this?" Hayword asked.

"I did it so they'd kick me out of school," he said, "but then everyone else wanted to do it with me, so odds were they weren't going to kick us all out. Are you coming home, Mom?"

"If you're asking me if I'm moving back to your house," I said, "no."

At least I didn't think so. Right this moment, I felt like I could go back. It would be okay, right? I could undo some of the damage I had done all those years I was drinking.

"Why the hell do you want to get kicked out of school?" I asked. "I thought you loved school."

David rolled his eyes. "Mom. I am always the outsider. I hate school. Or I did. Planning this faux killing spree really bonded us."

"Do not call it that when you talk to the principal," Hayword said. "Really, David, this could have gone really wrong."

"But it didn't," David said. "It didn't." He grinned. "It will not show up on my disaster app."

I laughed. I couldn't help it. My boy had been nervous about one catastrophe after another for almost as long as I could remember.

"Please think about coming home," David said. "I miss you. Dad misses you. If we had a dog, the dog would miss you. Can we get a dog?" He grinned.

I sighed and looked at Hayword. He shrugged and shook his head, trying to tell me he hadn't put David up to it.

"I better go," I said. "I have to finish the script. The fate of the world hangs on it."

"The fate of the world?" Hayword said. I could see the anxiety in his eyes. His insecurity was always just below the surface.

"Just a figure of speech. I'll talk to you both later."

I kissed David on the cheek and gave Hayword a quick peck on the lips. We were both surprised by it. I laughed, uncomfortably.

"Habit," I said.

"Don't try to break that one," Hayword said.

I backed away, and then I left the love-potioned radioactive gym and headed out to my car.

THIRTEEN

The day seemed brimming with spring. The sound of birds came from everywhere. Hopefully they weren't gathering in the trees à la *The Birds* to swoop down and peck my eyes out.

I breathed deeply. Okay. Now I needed to call Sally and then Mark. I'd have to deal with the whole thing with Mark before I started writing the script. The script, the script. How was I going to write that stupid script?

I jogged across the road toward my car.

Then I saw Mark leaning against my car, his arms crossed. He smiled when he saw me.

I felt butterflies in my stomach. He was so beautiful.

"There you are!" he said, dropping his arms, coming toward me. "I've been worried sick."

"What are you doing here?" I asked. I tried to get to the driver's side of my car, but Mark was standing in my way.

"What? Brooke, look at me. What's going on? I've phoned

you, texted you, called your husband, for god's sake, and he said you wouldn't talk to me. Why?"

"Get the fuck out of my way," I said.

Startled, Mark moved, and I opened the car door.

"Why don't you ask your naked fuck bunny Sherry," I said. I slid into the car seat and started to close the door, but Mark held it open.

"What the hell are you talking about?"

"Don't play innocent with me," I said. "I got home from the party early last night and there was Sherry, walking around in my house, naked, after taking a shower, trying to hurry and get out before I returned and caught you two together."

"What? Sherry was in our house naked?"

"Let me close this fucking door," I said, trying to jerk it out of his hand.

"No!" he said. "Get out here and tell me what the fuck is going on."

Disgusted I got out of the car.

"I went home," I said. "My home, by the way, not *our* home. Left the party early. I saw your truck, and I was so excited that I'd get to see you, surprise you. So I went in the back. There Sherry was, naked, talking to you about getting dressed before the bitch got home. The bitch being me. I always knew she was after you—or after something of mine. Worthless piece of trash."

"That wasn't *me*!" Mark said. "I lent Giovanni my truck because his broke down. That SOB. I'm gonna kill him. How dare he do this to my sister."

"What are you talking about?" I said.

"What are *you* talking about?" he said. "You thought I was cheating on you? You believed that and you didn't have the courtesy of asking me?" He was pissed. I hadn't seen him pissed before.

"You were naked!" I said. "I—I couldn't ask you. I couldn't confront you. I'd seen Hayword fucking someone, and I never got over it. I couldn't go through that again!"

"It never occurred to you that it wasn't me?"

I looked at him. I was so relieved it hadn't been him that I wanted to fling myself into his arms. I wanted to forget the entire thing. Let's fire Sherry and move on.

"No," I said softly, "it never occurred to me. My daughter had told me she'd seen you and Sherry together and you looked really cozy together."

"I was with Ian last night," Mark said. "Just as I said I would be. Giovanni's car died, and he needed to finish up some things at the restaurant, so I told him to take my truck. Brooke, I would never cheat on you. It's not in my nature."

He looked so desperately hurt and angry all at the same time.

"I know it's not," I said.

Then why had I so readily believed it? What was wrong with me?

"And you went home," he said. "You went back to Hayword."

"No," I said. "I went to the bungalow because Irving Jackson told me if I didn't have sex with him he was going to tell the police that Fern burned down our house in Brentwood."

"What?" Mark said.

I shook my head. "No, no. That can all wait. Mark, I'm so sorry. I don't know what to say. It was such an awful day yesterday. You wouldn't believe what happened. When I came home and saw Sherry and heard them—and thought it was you—I just . . . I have no explanation. I felt like the whole world had crashed and burned."

"Did you have sex with him?"

"Who?"

"Irving Jackson, whoever the fuck he is."

"No." I shivered. "No."

"But you invited him to the bungalow," he said.

I sighed. "It's such a long story. I was planning on black-mailing him. Not sure how." I rubbed my face. "It was a stupid plan, and if I had told someone besides Joanie about it ahead of time, I might not have gone through with it. In fact, I wasn't going to go through with it, but when I came to tell him, I found him dead."

"What?"

"I told you. It's long and complicated. My guess is he died of a heart attack or a stroke or something. I'm really hoping that's what it was. I don't think I'd like to be involved in a murder investigation."

"I really don't know what to say," Mark said.

"Can I hug you?" I asked.

Mark shook his head. "No. I don't think so. I don't know what I'm feeling. You dumped me, just like that, right out of your life. Making it clear that our home is not our home but it is your home." He put a hand up. "I need to go fire Sherry and Giovanni and tell my sister. I will talk to Sherry and Giovanni first, to see if they are actually having an affair."

"Come on, Mark," I said. "If you came home and saw Hayword naked, for instance, and heard someone else in the shower and my car was there. Wouldn't you assume it was me? Would you actually wait and try to talk to me?"

"Yes, I would. Jesus, Brooke."

"I told you she was fucking bad news," I said. "Please get all the locks changed in the house ASAP."

"Yes, your majesty," Mark said. "Let me get that done for you right away."

"For us," I said.

He shook his head. "Naw. Ain't my house."

"Mark," I said. "Please have some understanding. It's been crazy."

"That's what you *always* say," Mark said. He shook his head. "Of course no one else matters when things are crazy for *you*."

"That's not fair!" I said. "I've been putting out fires to protect my family. It's not about me! I know you've got the restaurant opening. I know that's stressful. But you seem to be handling it."

"I'm glad you're okay," he said. "Now I guess I'll go figure out the rest of it. I'll talk to you later."

"Um, can you get someone to come and clean the house?" I asked. "I want everything Sherry touched scrubbed or thrown out. I don't think my cleaning lady from here will go that far."

Mark nodded.

"I'll see you tonight?" I asked. "Oh wait. I can't. I need to finish up this script. And you didn't want me around for the soft opening."

"I'll stay at my place," he said. "Maybe I should postpone the opening."

"What? Why? You've been looking forward to this!"

He looked at me. "No, I haven't. I don't give a shit about any of this. I did this for you, Brooke. I did it because it was clear you're not comfortable being in a relationship with a mere plumber. But a Hollywood chef? Yeah, you can handle that."

"You are out of your fucking mind," I said. "I don't care about Hollywood. I don't care about appearances. I only care about your happiness."

Mark laughed. "Yeah, right."

"Everything okay?" Hayword was walking toward us.

"Of course she runs to you as soon as anything goes wrong," Mark said.

"What are you talking about?" Hayword asked.

"She sees Ryan at an AA meeting and she calls you," Mark said. "She thinks I'm cheating and she goes straight to you."

"She didn't," Hayword said.

"It's like you're still fucking married," Mark said. "Oh wait! You still are! *I* am the interloper."

"Mark—" I started.

"I've been a part of this weird triangle for three years," he said. "That is three years too long. I've had enough. You two figure out your shit. I'm outta here."

He started to walk away.

"Goddamn it, Mark," I said. "This isn't you! You're just upset."

He stopped and laughed—it was more of a snort—really. "I'm *just* upset. You bet I am. How would you know if this was the real me or not? Do you have any idea who I am? Or Hayword? How about your kids? We've all got our roles in your life, right? And they're all about not rocking the boat and doing exactly what you'd like us to do. We're not fucking spear-carriers in your life, Brooke. When you're not around, we don't just disappear from the world and we turn on again, like little dolls, when you want us."

"Are you spear-carriers or dolls?" I said. "You're mixing metaphors here, Pantano."

"Brooke—" Hayword.

"Perfect," Mark said. "That's fucking perfect."

This time he kept walking to his car. Then he drove off.

I turned and looked at Hayword. "What was that?"

"He has a point," Hayword said. "I hate to admit it. I mean, I'd love to say screw him, come home with me and life will be great, but he's got a point."

"I don't understand this," I said. "I did not cause this! I didn't do anything wrong. Except maybe I should have double-checked to see who Sherry was fucking. Apparently it wasn't Mark."

"I gathered that," Hayword said. "And again, darn. Although I hope you detect the sarcasm. I need to get to work. Give me a ride down the hill?"

"I thought you liked Mark," I said.

"Brooke, you don't seem to understand that other people in the world—besides you—are going through difficult and confusing times."

"No shit, Sherlock," I said. "Come on. I'll take you to your car. Then I need to write another hit movie. That'll make everyone happy. That'll save our particular world."

"Why do you keep saying that?" Hayword asked. "Is there something going on at AFT?"

"You mean besides one of the execs dying in my house after he tried to blackmail me? No, nothing else."

Hayword and I didn't say much to each other as I drove him down to his car.

Before he got out of the car, he said, "I'm glad our child didn't actually dose us with fatal radiation. Always a good day when that happens."

I nodded. "Yes, always a good day then."

He was gone, and I headed to the bungalow. I hesitated before I opened the front door. I shouldn't have. Miranda had come and gone, and she'd done a fabulous job. She not only cleaned houses: She *cleaned* houses. Did feng shui. Performed cleansing ceremonies. Etcetera. When I walked through the door, I felt no death hangover. No visions of Irving Jackson danced through my head. She'd left a vase filled with yellow sunflowers on the table. Sunlight streamed through the picture windows that looked out over the backyard.

"Thank you, Miranda," I said. She was going to get a big bonus for this.

I closed the door behind me. I needed to eat something and then start writing. I went to the fridge. Miranda had stocked the fridge, too, with all my favorites. How had she known? Organic fair trade chocolate bombs from Vita's, along with various salads and hors d'oeuvre. A mushroom quiche. Chilled Martinelli's organic sparkling apple cider.

Wait a minute. That quiche plate was from my house at the beach. Miranda hadn't filled the fridge. Mark must have been here.

I closed the fridge and walked over to the table. A small card rested against the flowers. I opened it.

"Good luck. I know you can do it. Picked the flowers myself. Your neighbor is pretty pissed at me. Reheat quiche at 375 for 15 or eat at room temp. Love, Mark."

I pulled out my phone and texted Mark. "Thx for flowers & food. For everything. Let me know if I can help w/ restaurant. Or anything."

I slid the quiche in the oven and then put my laptop on the coffee table in front of the couch. I read over my treatment.

"Ugh," I said when I'd finished it. If it had been on a piece of paper, I would have balled it up and thrown it across the room. As it was, it was light and dark on my computer screen.

"This script has to save the world." I shrugged. "Let's not be a drama queen, Brooke. It's only a movie."

In the last movie, scientist Colleen Kelly falls in love with the zombie alien leader, Thomas. She convinces the world that the aliens aren't bad—they just have a wasting disease. Turns out the zombie aliens, including Thomas, are trying to wipe out the human race. Colleen goes on the run from the zombies and humans with her friend Marissa. They try to develop a cure but fail.

One day, figuring it's their last day, they stand barefoot on the earth as the sun comes up. Some kind of chemical combination occurs between the sunlight and the earth that cures them, and the world is saved. Thomas is put behind bars with the other zombie aliens. Colleen declares she never loved Thomas while he whispers that he really loves her. The last shot of the movie is of Colleen standing on a hilltop—and she is very pregnant and very afraid.

"Okay," I said. "Now what?"

I started typing. "Black screen. We hear Colleen screaming in terror. At first we think she's being hurt, but then the camera fades in to a hospital room where Colleen is giving birth to a beautiful baby boy. He looks completely human except when he opens his eyes: They are all shiny blue. Colleen names him Adam."

"No, too corny," I said, as I deleted the name.

"Colleen names him Aiden. The boy grows quickly. He ages a year for every month. He's very bright. He learns to read within days of his birth. Very soon he's doing math and physics. By the time he is eighteen months old, he is an adult working by his mother's side. The world is still devastated from the zombie invasion, and the humans are trying to put their world back together. Meanwhile the humans don't know what to do about the zombies who have survived and are imprisoned. In some countries, they have been put to death. Not all zombie aliens participated in the invasion and not all of them knew about the plot to kill off the human race. Should those aliens be put to death, too?

"Other zombie-human babies have been born, with varying abilities. Some are strong. Some are extraordinarily smart. They are ostracized, and legislation is introduced in the United States to incarcerate them all. Colleen works to prevent this from happening. Meanwhile, Aiden tells her he is homesick and wishes to return to the alien world—the alien world he has never seen. He becomes so depressed that Colleen takes him to prison to visit Thomas. She doesn't want to see Thomas, but she doesn't want to leave her son alone with him.

"Thomas seems the same as the last time Colleen saw him. He tells his son that he can't return to the home world because it is no longer livable. They destroyed their world and then came here to make it their home, but they were wrong. What they had done was very wrong and now they needed to repair any damage done to Earth. He hoped his son would work with Colleen to heal the damage.

"Colleen believes Thomas is bullshitting, but she's grateful for the speech. Before they leave, Thomas gives his son a ring with a swan carved in bone on it—a blue green swan. 'To remind you of me,' he says, 'and to remind you that everything wasn't terrible about me. Your mother loved me once enough to give me this ring—this ring that belonged to her father. She told me their crest was a swan. She told me the swan is a fearsome guardian.' Colleen is touched Thomas remembers her words. Aiden puts on the ring."

I stopped typing. "Crap. What next?" I needed an action scene now. I looked outside. The morning light spotlit a dog lying on the grass in my backyard. I squinted. No, not a dog. I got up and went to the window.

It was a bobcat. It turned and looked at me, saw me, and then looked away. What an exquisite-looking animal. Its pointed ears reminded me of something out of a fairy tale.

"You're welcome to stay," I whispered. I had never seen a wild animal like this near any of my houses.

I went back to the couch and stepped back into my imaginary world.

"Colleen and Aiden go back to their lives in the lab. Overnight, it seems, the animals begin to act strangely. First the domestic animals attack their owners, in some cases killing and eating them. When doctors examine the animals, they discover they have the animal version of the zombie disease. Soon enough it spreads to the wild animals. The world is once again thrown into chaos.

"The governments believe the zombie-human children are responsible for this new variant of the old disease. These children—who have all now grown quickly into adulthood—are ordered into camps. Aiden becomes convinced he can come up with a cure for the animals—and maybe even a cure for his own people. 'They aren't really evil,' he declares to his mother. 'It's just the disease.'

"Aiden goes on the run with his girlfriend, the zombie-human Molly. She is also a scientist. Soon the full forces of the government are focused on finding Aiden and Molly. Thomas sends a message to Colleen that he must see her. Reluctantly she goes to the prison again.

"He's bribed the guard to allow him to talk to Colleen privately. He tells her he is in telepathic communication with Aiden and has been since he was born. He knows where he is and can help her find him before the government does, and he has a cure for the animal plague. The same thing happened on their planet, and they discovered the cure too late. But it's in a ship that's hidden from the humans. Only he—Thomas—can retrieve it.

"Colleen doesn't know what to do. It's probably a trick. He might get to the ship and use the weapons on it to destroy the Earth or signal to any zombie aliens that are off-world. But she's desperate. The world is in such chaos, and her son is in danger. She agrees to help Thomas escape from prison."

I stopped typing. "How the hell are they going to escape from Alcatraz?" My fingers tapped the keys lightly as I tried to think of a way. Then I start typing.

"The government has used some zombies in experiments. Colleen arranges it so that Thomas is temporarily released into her custody on the ruse that she will experiment on him. Getting him off of Alcatraz is full of suspense. They're almost caught several times, but finally they are off the island, and now they, too, are on the run. Thomas takes her to the ship and arranges— telepathically—for Aiden to meet them. Of course they have to battle their way through crazy domestic and wild animals to get to the ship which is buried in the desert.

"Once in the ship, Colleen is certain Thomas will betray her. He powers up the ship and discovers that the information on the cure is gone. Colleen wonders if it was ever there. Suddenly three alien ships appear in the sky above them. Thomas swears he didn't call them. Just then Aiden arrives with Molly. They claim they have the cure. The army shows up then, too, demanding they all surrender. The alien ships begin firing on the army. Thomas tells Molly, Colleen, and Aiden to run. But first Thomas tells Colleen he loves her, and they kiss. He tells her that he believes these are the last of the alien ships. If he can get rid of them, Earth will be free. Colleen wants to stay, but Aiden drags his mother away. Once the three of them are off the ship, Thomas brings the ship's power online all the way and he fires on the zombie ships all at once, blowing them to bits.

"Just as Colleen and Aiden are about to go back to the ship and get Thomas, the ship rises up into the air. When it is high above them, the ship explodes. Colleen is bereft, but she sees the army has turned their attention to them. They demand that the three of them put up their hands and surrender. Aiden starts to walk toward one of the soldiers, holding something in his hand, 'We've found the cure. We've got to get it out right away.' A single shot rings out, and Aiden falls to the ground. Colleen runs to his side. 'It's up to you now, Mom,' he says. 'You've got to save the world.'

"Aiden dies, and Colleen screams. 'He was trying to save us!' she cries. 'Save us!' Months later, we see Colleen standing by Aiden's grave. Molly is next to her for a few moments, but then she kisses her and walks away. 'Well, baby boy,' Colleen says, 'the cure worked. Things are settling back to normal, whatever that is. They've released the zombie-human children from incarceration. Although you aren't really children. I'm not sure what to call you. Your father saved us, and he is now regarded as a hero.' She shrugs. 'Of sorts. Now, I better leave and get back to work.'

"She turns and walks away, but the camera continues to frame the grave. A few moments after Colleen walks away, a hand and arm burst from the ground at Aiden's grave. On one of the fingers of that hand is the swan ring. Hold for several beats. Fade to black.

"The End."

I laughed and pumped my fist into the air. "Yes!" I sighed. "Now for the script."

I ate part of the quiche, and then I started typing.

"So glad Colleen is gonna get her baby boy back," I whispered.

That's what I loved about fiction.

FOURTEEN

Once I got going on any writing project, I was a dynamo. I could write faster than anyone I knew, and what I wrote was good. Screenwriting is dialogue, basically. I mean, sure, you've got to think about shots and place and things like that, but it's really all character, from my viewpoint, and what they say to one another. And what they don't say. Those silent moments. The pauses. Sometimes it feels like the pauses are everything. Although in a movie like this, the pauses were certainly short and sweet.

Anyway, I wrote quickly. I didn't think about anything else as I wrote. I was in the world of chaos and zombies, and horror—and I was in the world where Colleen Kelly gets to work beside her baby boy. Where she gets to love him and try to save him. In the end, he dies, but he is saved, too. Perhaps. I suppose another screenwriter could be fooling with the audience. But I wasn't fooling. I could already imagine what happens next. As he bursts through the earth and calls out for his momma.

As I wrote, I saw several deer come into my yard, and another bobcat. Lots of birds. None of them were zombie animals. No one was attacking any humans. They weren't attacking one another either. I got up now and again and watched them.

I called Sally when I broke for dinner or lunch or whatever it was.

"Irving died of a heart attack," Sally said. "As far as they can tell. They'll do a tox screen, but they're pretty sure."

"Thank god," I said.

"His wife called," Sally said. "Wanted to know if you and Irving were sleeping together. I said as far as I knew you couldn't stand the man."

"You said that to his widow?" I said.

"She didn't seem that upset," Sally said. "She said she found something of yours in his belongings. She wanted your address for the messenger. I gave it to her. Hope that's okay."

"How do you know she's not some nut case come to kill me for being with her husband?"

"I thought you weren't *with* him," she said.

"I wasn't. But he was blackmailing me. He wanted me to help overthrow you, and he wanted me to have sex with him."

"Ew! And you agreed?"

"I pretended to agree," I said. "He died before my stupid plan could come to fruition. I found him dead dressed only in a garter, fishnet stockings, and stilettos."

"Double ew. How am I going to get that picture out of my head? Thank you very much. Would you have gone through with it? What was he blackmailing you with?"

"Not gonna tell you that over open airways," I said. "But no, I wouldn't have gone through with it. Now I need to finish this script."

"I'll see you Sunday," she said.

"Sunday?"

"Mark's opening," Sally said. "Sheesh."

"Oh, yeah."

"Email me the script as soon as you have it."

I called Joanie, too. Thanked her. Told her she could trash Jackson's um, clothes. "He died of a heart attack," I said.

"Oh good," she said. "So no murder investigation? Those are no fun."

"You've been involved in a murder investigation before?" I asked.

"Sure," she said. "What do you think happened to my first husband?"

"He was murdered?"

"No, but I had to go through a bit of white-knuckle interrogation before they figured that out," she said. "Taught me not to marry someone quite so old next time. His kids didn't want me to get anything. Even accused me of sexing him to death, if you know what I mean."

I groaned.

"My advice, don't ever let anyone die while you're having sex with them," she said. "It's not very sexy, no matter what the movies say."

I laughed. "Oh my god, Joanie. I want to hear that story but not now. I've got to finish work. Love you."

I ended the phone call and went back to the couch. Being friends with Joanie was like peeling an onion. There was always something underneath and it made you cry. Or laugh.

She was a good friend, though, and I was lucky she was on my side.

Just then I heard a knock at the door. I got up, looked through the keyhole, and then opened the door.

Mark stood on my steps with a manila envelope in his hands.

"This was on the top step," he said, holding it out to me. He looked uncomfortable, nervous.

I took the envelope. "Wonder why they didn't ring the bell," I said. "Come on in."

I set the envelope on the coffee table and sat on the couch.

"Can I get you anything?" I asked. "Please sit. Thanks again for the quiche and the other goodies. I've been snacking on them all day. The script is going well. Even faster than usual."

My stomach was doing flip-flops. Mark looked so delicious standing there in a T-shirt and jeans. I wanted to rip off his clothes and take him to bed.

Or at the very least, I wanted to put my arms around him.

"I'm sorry I was so pissed," he said. "I was worried about you all night. That got my adrenaline pumping. And then to have you treat me like I was nothing to you—that was tough."

"I'm sorry," I said. Felt weird sitting while he stood. "Hayword said you had a point about the way I treat people."

"Hayword says it so you listen?"

"What? No! You're both saying similar things, so I'm trying to understand. I will figure it out. Eventually. I need to finish the script, and then we'll figure everything out."

"You always say that," Mark said. "There's always something going on and after that something is finished, you say, we'll figure things out. But then something else comes up. That's what alcoholics say. They'll stop drinking when things settle down. Or people who smoke. Whatever. It's an excuse."

Mark sat in the chair opposite the couch.

I sat cross-legged on the couch.

"You're right," I said. "It is an excuse. It's because I don't really know how to have deeply personal intimate relationships. Haven't you figured that out? I don't want to talk about our future or even our now because then I have to think about it. Hayword wants me to come home. David wants me to come home. You want me to be with you. I'm satisfied loving you all."

"And having us all do exactly what you want," Mark said.

"Yes, I guess. Is that so odd? Don't you want me to do what you want? I mean, you want me to divorce Hayword and be with you. Marry you."

"But I'm not threatening to leave you if you don't do those things."

"Sure you are," I said. "You said this morning that you were gone until we figured it out."

He shrugged. "Okay. So you may have a point. But I'm not trying to control you. I just want to know where I am in all of this. We seem to be ships passing in the night lately."

"I thought I had made my decision!" I said. "I moved out, didn't I? I moved away. I live with you. You're opening a restaurant in my house."

"You made it abundantly clear that it's *your* house," he said, "not *our* home."

"I was just pissed."

"It's not an equal relationship," he said. "It never has been. I want it to be. Otherwise, it's not healthy for me. I almost took a drink today. I try to live my life so that doesn't happen. Look, if you don't trust me, I don't think we can stay together. If your heart is at home with Hayword and David, then you need to do that. Just tell me. Talk to me about it. I'm a big boy. I want us to be together, but if we're not, I won't die. It won't be the end of me."

"Really?" I said. "But I want you to feel like it would be the end of you. I want you to love me that desperately."

"That only happens in the movies," he said, "and to teenagers. I have a child, I have responsibilities. If you break my heart, I will mend and move on. I mean, you thought I was cheating on you. Did you curl up into a ball and die?"

"No," I said. "But I did throw up. That counts."

He laughed. He glanced outside. It was twilight now, but I

could see the animals moving around, like strange little shadows—ghosts of what they had been.

"What is going on? Are those people?" Mark asked.

"People?" I said. "No! They're animals. They've been there all day."

We went to stand at the window together.

"I feel like something big is going to happen," Mark said. "Something is about to snap or break."

"Me, too," I said. "Just so many weird things. The animals, the blackmail, Ryan. You. So I'm keeping busy trying to save my family."

Mark nodded. He put his arm around my waist, and I leaned against him.

"Ian is going up to Oregon with his mom for a week," he said. "I'm glad. I felt relief when she called and asked if it was okay. I just took them to the airport. And I'm postponing the opening of the restaurant."

"No!" I said. "But you have all that food. What a waste."

He shook his head. "No. It'll be okay. It's better to figure out what's going on here, between us, and with your family and mine. Better to get that figured out. I talked to Giovanni. He finally admitted it was him with Sherry in our—in your house. I told my sister. She was devastated. And yes, I fired Sherry and had the locks changed. Remind me to give you the keys before I leave."

"Are you staying?" I said. "I mean, at the house. You seemed so finished with me this morning."

"I was hurt and pissed, Brooke," he said. "What did you expect? I still want some definition. Can't you come to me when something's going on, not to Hayword?"

"No, not always," I said. "We share children. What was going on with Irving Jackson had to do with Fern. I would have told you, but I thought you and Sherry were . . . together. Anyway. Can we start the day over? Or the last 48 hours? If you're not having the soft opening tomorrow, do you want to stay here with me?"

He shook his head. "No. You've got a script to finish by tomorrow. I've got people to call. But Sunday, you and I are sitting down for a talk. Until then, why don't you and your family come for a late lunch tomorrow, after you're done working? We can celebrate you finishing the script, and we'll eat some of the food. I'll make it a feast."

"Really?" I asked. "Hayword, too?"

"Yes, of course," he said. "I mean, he's your husband." He gave me a look. I put my arms around him and hugged him.

"I love you," I said.

He didn't say anything. He put his arms around me, and we held each other. Until I sighed. Until I relaxed. Hadn't realized how tense I'd been.

When we finally let each other go, I went to the table and picked up the envelope and opened it. Inside was a file folder from the LA Police Department. I opened it. One sheet of paper, essentially. About our house fire. Investigators determined it was an electrical fire. They had found some evidence of fire in a trash can, but the fire hadn't gone outside of the can. Case closed. Just like Phil Case had told us. I had seen a form like this before—when we had to settle an insurance claim.

"What is it?" Mark asked.

"I'm not sure," I said. I turned the folder over and found a large post-it note. I read it out loud. "My husband was a prick. Said he was using this to blackmail you. Now it's all yours."

I handed the folder to Mark.

"There's nothing here," Mark said. "There's nothing he could have used against you."

I nodded. "I need to show this to Fern. She has to understand she didn't burn the house down. Maybe that will give her some peace."

Mark nodded. "Okay. Tomorrow at two. Text me how many will be there. Now I've got stuff to do."

He kissed me on the lips. I pulled him close to me and continued the kiss.

He pulled away and looked at me. "Sherry? Really? She reads *Hollywood Gossip* throughout the day and then tells me about it."

"You hired her," I said.

Then he was gone. I texted my family. "Be at the restaurant at 2:00 tomorrow or be square. It's a celebration."

I smiled as I sent the invite. Maybe everything was going to be all right after all.

I wrote for several more hours. Then I slept for a few more.

Dreamed Alberto was Aiden standing on the shoreline looking out at the Pacific Ocean. His hand was raised in a fist above his head. I could see the swan ring. "Momma," he whispered. "Run!" Then a wave the size of the world rolled over both of us. I awakened gasping for breath.

"What the fuck was that?"

I made myself coffee, ate some quiche and chocolate, and then peered out into the darkness. Couldn't tell if the animals were still there or not.

I kept writing.

And writing.

And writing.

Until Aiden's fist came bursting up through the earth.

Then I laughed.

Never had written anything this quickly in my life. Wouldn't tell anyone that—besides my family and Mark. Let the world believe I toiled over it forever.

I attached the treatment and the script to an email to Sally with this message: "I haven't proofed it yet, but here it is."

I clicked on send.

"May it save the world!"

I looked out the window. The animals were gone—except for one. The bobcat was now sitting on my back porch.

I opened the door and looked out at her. "Do you have any messages for me?" I asked.

The bobcat stared at me. Perhaps she was asking, "Do you have any messages for *me*?"

"Run," I said.

FIFTEEN

Soon enough, I was on my way back to the beach and the restaurant. I had butterflies in my stomach. I couldn't remember any time we'd all been together. Maybe never? Wasn't sure it was a good idea, but we were doing it. Everyone had said yes. Even Fern—although she was bringing her boyfriend. Her *old* boyfriend, Enrique, who was partially responsible for all the turmoil I'd been going through for the last few days. Ah well. Be flexible, eh?

It was another beautiful warm sunny day. Hayword's SUV was already at the restaurant when I arrived. And Fern's car. Mark's truck. I opened the restaurant door almost reluctantly. I heard voices—laughter. Then I saw them all standing around a food-laden table. They turned and looked at me. Everyone smiled. Except Fern. Her face didn't move. Couldn't tell if that was good or bad. David was the first to come over to me.

"So you made the world better for zombies today," he said as he hugged me.

"Yep, I did."

I put my arms around him and gave him a bear hug. He was so grown-up, especially for a 14-year-old.

He took my hand, and we walked over to the rest of the group. Mark kissed me on the cheek.

"Heard you had a little trouble here," Fern said. She even hugged me.

"That's an understatement," I said. "Where's Ricky?"

"Something came up," she said, "but he sends his regards."

Hayword came over and kissed me on the cheek. I kissed him back and let go of David's hand to squeeze Hayword's. I didn't want him to feel like a third wheel. Or fifth wheel. Whatever it was.

"Wow, Mark," I said. "This is gorgeous. What a feast! I'm so sorry you didn't get to open today."

He shrugged. "Maybe it all happened for a reason. That's what some people would say."

I looked at him. "Would you say that?"

He smiled. "Probably not. But maybe. Let's just say it's all for the best. Now let's eat."

It was a round table so we didn't have to think about who sat at the head of it. My kids sat on either side of me which left Mark and Hayword sitting next to one another.

We ate omelettes, quiches, homemade sausages, crepes stuffed with fresh fruit, scrambled tofu, baked potatoes, hash brown potatoes, hash brown sweet potatoes, all kinds of salads and side dishes. Mark got up and opened one of the big windows so we could hear the seagulls and smell the ocean. David talked about his experiment at school, and Fern listened, dumbfounded. Mark seemed a bit surprised, too.

"Lucky they didn't haul you off to jail," Fern said.

"Me? I heard about you staging a robbery at Juliet's," he said.

"What?" Fern said. "Who told him?"

Hayword shrugged. "Your mother and I have decided it's best not to keep secrets. Anymore."

"Really? I don't remember that," I said. "Must have been something I agreed to in my sleep. Mark, this is all so delicious."

"It's really good," Fern said. "I didn't know you were such a good cook."

I laughed. "Why did you think he was opening a restaurant then?"

"Because you wanted him to," Fern said.

I frowned. "Really?"

"Sure," Fern said. "You seem to have this ability to get the men in your life to do whatever you want. How do you manage that? You treat them like shit, and then they still follow you around like lap dogs."

"Fern," Hayword said. "She never treated me badly. And I'm no one's lap dog."

Mark didn't say anything. He just shook his head.

"Are we going to spoil Mark's wonderful meal by arguing?" I asked.

"I wasn't arguing," Fern said. "I was actually curious. How do you get men to love you when you aren't very nice to them?"

"Wow," I said. "First, I don't believe I am unkind to anyone. I love and I am loved back. I'm quite fortunate. But I've had my heart broken." I look over at Hayword, trying to ask him silently if it would be all right now to share this secret. He nodded. I glanced at Mark. He knew what I was up to, too. "For instance, Alberto's father broke my heart. Crushed me. I thought I'd die. But I didn't. Life went on."

Fern and David looked at Hayword and then back at me.

"You cheated on Dad before Alberto died?" Fern asked. "How could you do that?"

"Our marriage really isn't any of your business," Hayword said. "Or our sex lives before, during, or after our marriage. That's between us. What your mother is trying to tell you is that she's had her heart broken, too. We all have. Your mom has always been honest with me."

"Even while she was sleeping with someone else?" Fern asked.

He nodded. "And my behavior wasn't always exemplary."

"It could never equal what she's done," Fern said.

"I think you should start giving your mother a break," Hayword said. "Yes, she drank. Yes, we had some hard times, but she was a good mother."

"She was a fucking drunk," Fern said.

"I don't want to listen to this," David said.

I put my hand over his. "Fern is entitled to her opinion."

"She is," Hayword said, "but she needs to hear the whole truth. About how you got drunk, Fern, and told Irving Jackson that you'd burned down our house. He used that information to get a police file, and he told your mother that he would expose your secret to the world unless she helped him get rid of Sally. He was trying to force your mother to have sex with him."

Fern looked at me. "So that's why he was at the bungalow? Did you kill him?"

"No!" I said. "I wouldn't do that for you or myself or anyone else. Christ. I was trying to figure a way out, and lo and behold, he died. Instant karma? His wife sent me the file he was holding over my head, the one from the police."

Fern stared straight ahead.

"Fern," I said. "Listen to me, Fern."

"What?"

"There was nothing in it," I said. "Dad had Phil Case look into it. There's nothing to it. There was an electrical fire. It was just a weird coincidence that you'd started a fire in a wastebasket. That fire went out. Coincidences happen all the time. And this was one. The house burned down because of electricity. You didn't do it. You may have wished it, but you didn't do it. You have got to let go of this. You aren't an arsonist. You didn't cause your brother to die. None of what happened to this family was your fault. Or David's fault. Or Alberto's. Maybe it was no one's fault. Maybe it's just life. You can put the blame on us." I put my hand over hers, and she didn't pull away. "You can blame me. But stop blaming yourself. Let this go. Let yourself be happy."

"You didn't burn the house down," Hayword said. "You didn't cause Alberto's death. It wasn't your fault Mom drank or that we split up."

Fern moved her hand away to wipe the tears off her face. She began to sob quietly.

I reached into my purse at my feet and pulled out the folded paper from the case file. I unfolded the paper on the table and pointed to "case closed."

"Maybe the spirit of fire heard my prayers," Fern said. "Maybe that's what caused the fire."

"Then the spirit of fire shouldn't be answering children's destructive prayers," I said. "Even if that were true in any world or any dimension, it still wouldn't be your fault. We can't be blamed for what we wish. Good grief. How many politicians would be dead if wishes like that came true?"

Fern looked over at me. Her face was streaked with tears and mascara.

"Why do you wear makeup?" I asked. "You're so beautiful."

"Shut up," she said, wiping her face with her napkin. "Do you ever wonder what it all means?"

I shook my head. "No, never. That way lies madness, darlin'. Complete and utter madness."

"I don't believe you," Fern said. "I see it in your eyes."

"What?" I asked.

"Substance," she said. "You've got substance. Depth. I look in the mirror and see only hollow places."

I shook my head. "Darlin,' we've all got hollow places. Why do you think I drank? We just all try to do the best we can. Try not to hurt other people. Try to be kind and do good work."

"Really?" Fern said. "Is that what you do?"

I laughed. "Yes, baby girl. Believe it or not, that's what I try to do. I'm sorry if it doesn't seem that way. I apologize to all of you if it doesn't seem that way. I think after Alberto died I was so afraid of another loss that I just tried to control everything and everyone. Including you all." I looked around the table. "I'm sorry. I know you've got your own feelings and foibles and wishes and they don't always coincide with mine. I understand that intellectually, and I'll try to live by it more literally."

"Mom, I'm sorry Irving did that to you," Fern said. "I'm sorry about the fake robbery."

"You don't know all of it," David said. "When she found him dead, he was only wearing a garter, fishnet stockings, and stiletto heels."

Fern's eyes widened—as did mine, I'm sure.

"Hayword! You told our son that?" I cried.

"Fishnet stockings?" Mark said.

"Joanie told me," David said. "She'll tell me anything. I just offer her chocolate and champagne."

"Oh my word," I said. "Now you're going to be scarred for life."

David shook his head. "Why? I've heard worse. At least you weren't . . . you know, with him."

I laughed. Mark sputtered on some cider he'd just sipped.

I held up my glass filled with apple cider. "Here's to not having sex with a naked dead guy dressed in fishnet stockings."

"I am not toasting to that," Hayword said. "How about here's to honesty."

I shrugged. "Mine was more imaginative." We held up our glasses and clinked them together. Then we drank.

"Mom, look," Fern said. She pointed out the window.

The tide was out, and the beach was covered in white birds: large and small, just as it had been covered the other day with black birds. We all got up and went to the window.

"The big birds are swans," David said.

Mark came up behind me and put his hands on my shoulders.

"Wow," Hayword said. "I wonder where they've all come from."

"Brooke had all kinds of animals at her house yesterday," Mark said.

I nodded. "Bobcats. Deer. Raccoons. Birds."

David said, "There were elk and coyotes at our house last night."

"What do you think is going on?" Fern asked.

"I have no idea," I said.

"Look, one of the swans!" Fern said, suddenly excited. "It's blue and green. Like the swan pin." She tapped the swan pin she was still wearing with the fingers of her right hand.

I squinted. She pointed out the window again, trying to help me see it. Yes. There. It did look like a blue and green swan. Which was impossible.

I had to get closer.

"Must be full moon," Hayword said. "That's a pretty low tide."

"Yesterday, I think," Mark said.

As a group, we hurried outside, went down the steps to the yard and then more stairs that led to the beach, and then down an incline until we were on the sand. The wet sand seemed to stretch to forever. The birds did not move and the swans made a kind of clicking noise as we walked. Other human beach-combers stood amongst the birds, too, looking dazed.

David, Mark, and Hayword stopped amidst the birds as Fern and I went forward, looking for the blue green swan.

"There," Fern said, pointing again.

We hurried forward. The sand was wet beneath our feet, and we sank a bit. For a moment, we hesitated. The swan was so beautiful. A real life blue and green swan.

Only, no such thing existed.

I blinked and realized the swan was caught in something. Fern glanced at me. She saw it now, too.

As we neared the blue and green swan, she didn't move. She was stuck inside some kind of blue green plastic. It was around her neck and digging into her skin. The rest was draped over her beautiful white body. The plastic was bloody where it choked her neck. Her beak was open as she gasped for breath.

"Oh my god," Fern said. She dropped to her knees beside the animal. "Mom, we've got to help her."

"Shhh," I said soothingly, to the bird. "It's okay, it's okay. We want to help you."

The swan moved nervously. I glanced behind me. Hayword, David, and Mark were coming nearer. I held up my hand to them, and they stopped.

"Do any of you have a pocket knife?" I asked.

"I do." Mark.

Mark pulled out a Swiss army knife. "It's got a knife and scissors," he said. I went and got it from him, then went back to the swan. I looked at the plastic. I couldn't figure out how it had gotten over her head.

"Shhh," I said. "Fern, try to keep her calm. Talk to her. Maybe pet her, if that's what she wants."

"How will I know what she wants?" Fern asked.

"Ask her," I said, "and see what you hear."

Yeah, I don't know where that came from, but Fern whispered to the swan. Then she pulled a kerchief from her back pocket and slowly and gently wrapped it around the swan's head, covering her eyes. I motioned the men over to us.

"Quietly," I said, "and quickly. Hold her down and still."

Fern cooed to the swan. The men fell on the bird, gently, almost tenderly, and she didn't move. I used the scissors to cut into the plastic. I heard the humans breathing around me, felt the heartbeat of the swans—of all the swans. The beach was so still. The ocean was such a long way off. At first the plastic wouldn't move, wouldn't give, but then it did, and I was able to cut enough away to slip it over the swan's head. Which I did, carefully, slowly.

"Take off the blindfold," I said. I stepped back. Fern slipped off the kerchief and then stepped back. I nodded to the guys. "Let her go." As one, the men stepped away.

The swan tottered a bit. Then she almost shuddered. She flapped her wings. She looked at us and seemed to bow, to acknowledge our existence. I laughed and looked at my daughter. She was smiling, too. Mark glanced at me and smiled and nodded.

The beach breathed again. And then as though they had all gotten a message from God or the Queen Swan or the Wind, every single bird on the beach lifted into the air. As if they had come to this beach and this time and place just for us to save this one bird. For a moment, the sky was a beautiful moving white quilt. I put my arms across Fern's shoulders as we watched. The birds circled us and then flew east.

"Go east, young woman."

Suddenly I remembered my dream from early this morning—where Alberto had screamed, "Run." I looked out across the beach. Where was the ocean?

This tide was too low even for full moon low tide.

"Run!" I cried to my family as I grabbed Fern's hand. "We've got to run!"

SIXTEEN

I'm not sure exactly what happened next, or in what order, but we ran. Not an easy thing to do as we climbed a small hill and then two sets of stairs.

"Grab as much non-perishable food as you can," I shouted when we got to the restaurant.

"What's going on?" Mark asked as the kids and Hayword began filling bags with food.

"David," I said, "have you heard about any earthquakes?" I looked at Mark. "He's got a disaster app on his phone."

"No," David said.

We got the food and a case of bottled water and headed for the SUV, after Mark locked the door.

"We're all going together?" Mark asked.

"Yes," I said. "Get in."

Then Hayword drove us away from the sea.

"The wild animals were at my house," I said. "I bet that means it must be safe there."

"Even safer up at the big house," Hayword said.

I didn't look back at the ocean or my house. Fern and David looked at the sky and watched the swans heading east.

"Mom, tsunamis come after an earthquake," David said. "Not before."

"I had a dream last night," I said. "Alberto told me to run. So I'm running. And the seal told me to go east."

"The seal?" Fern asked.

"Long story," I said.

Strangely enough, we didn't run into any traffic. At least nothing to speak of. The kids barely said a word. Mark and Hayword sat in the front together, figuring out the best way to go. I didn't care, as long as we were all together. David kept looking on his phone to see if anything had happened. I got a text from Sally telling me they loved the script and they'd go ahead with it as soon as possible.

We stopped at my bungalow. I packed a bag while the others filled any empty containers they could find with water. I packed extra clothes for Fern. Mark and Hayword turned off the gas. We locked the doors, and then Hayword drove us up the hill to our house.

We got out of the car and looked around.

It was a perfect beautiful blue day. Nothing going on.

Hadn't it been a perfect beautiful blue day when Alberto died?

Or had it been night?

I phoned Joanie. "I think something is going to happen," I said. "You alone?"

"Yes," she said. "Hubby is out of town."

"Come on over," I said.

We went through the house and filled up more bottles and containers with water. Hayword made certain the generator was working and ready to go. The kids filled up the bathtubs with water. I could hear them splashing each other and laughing as I went into Hayword's bedroom. I pushed the chair over to the closet, stood on it, and got Alberto's ashes.

I hopped off the chair. I heard Joanie downstairs. "This is awkward," she said. "Husband and lover. Or is it civilized?"

"We've just been waiting for you to make it a foursome," Hayword said.

I laughed.

Then I felt dizzy. I looked over at the window. The curtains were moving.

I wasn't dizzy.

"Run!" I screamed, holding the urn close to me.

Fern and David came out of the bathroom as the ground swayed, as the house swayed. We ran together down the stairs, barely able to keep ourselves upright, and then we were outside with Mark, Joanie, and Hayword, standing away from the house, between it and the pool house. Hayword took a hold of the kids, and Mark reached for me. I set the urn on the ground and reached for Joanie. The six of us held onto each other as the ground beneath us shook, as it undulated. The air seemed filled with static. Or electricity. I felt tense, as though white noise was roaring in the background, only I couldn't hear any. I looked up. The trees around us swayed. Only the sun seemed still. Birds flew up from the trees, soundlessly, and then disappeared into the blue.

"It's lasting so long," Fern said.

I heard windows breaking. I closed my eyes. I could almost imagine I was riding a surfboard. I kicked off my shoes and felt the cool earth beneath my soles. Could almost feel the waves beneath my feet. Or was that the tectonic plates? I smiled. Didn't matter. I was riding the waves. I moved away from my family and held out my arms, balanced myself on the earth.

"Come on, darlin's," I said. "Feel the ground!"

And just like that, they all took off their shoes. David fell to the ground as it continued to move like a live thing beneath us. He got back up. We all heard a tree crack and then fall in the woods behind the house.

"We're surfing the earthquake," I said. "Riders in the storm."

"Mixed metaphor, love," Hayword said.

I laughed. Mark went along with it, too. Surfing the Earth.

Joanie watched us and shook her head. But she was barefoot.

"I was never a very good surfer," she said.

"Mom," David said. "The urn fell over."

I looked behind me. Hayword leaned over and picked up the urn. The cap had come off.

"Part of it spilled," Hayword said.

And then, just like that, the quake stopped.

Fern ran over to her father and took the urn from him. Then she began running around the yard with the urn. As she ran she slowly tipped it over and the ashes spilled out in a line behind her.

"Goodbye, Alberto," she called. "We love you!"

We watched her run and run, long after the urn was empty. I hadn't seen her look that free since she was a girl, since before Alberto died. Then she stopped and grinned.

We all clapped. Spontaneously, happily. I held my arms open, and Fern ran to me. Just like she had when she was a girl. And she grinned, happy to see me, happy to fall into my arms, which she did, and I held her tightly, I held onto her for dear life. I kissed her hair and told her I loved her. Soon David was hugging us, and then Hayword, Joanie, and then Hayword pulled Mark in. Until we all started laughing, and Joanie declared it was all too kinky for her.

In the near distance, we could hear sirens and fire alarms and car alarms.

"Man," I said, "I can't wait until this full moon is done and over."

"That was a big one," Joanie said. "I better go home and see what's up. I left Marie there all alone. She's been in a staring contest all day with a bear in our back yard." She blew us a kiss and then wobbled away.

"What now, Mom?" David asked. "I can't get any service on my phone. Do you think the world ended?"

The survivor on the plane had looked around, faced reality, and saw beauty, too. Beauty was part of the reality of survival. Was that what Gabriella had been trying to tell me?

Beauty does exist, even in awful times. Even in whackadoodle times.

"The world hasn't ended," I said. "Look around. We're still here, and we're still together."

"This is about the time in a movie when zombies would come out of the woodwork," David said, "or out of the woods."

"Not in my movies," I said. "In my movies, the zombies and humans all live happily ever after."

"Only after the zombies almost destroy the world," Fern said.

We all walked toward the house.

"Are we the zombies or the humans?" David asked.

"Only time will tell," I said.

"I vote for zombies," Fern said.

"You would," David said.

They ran toward the house.

"Wait for your dad," I said. "It might not be safe."

I watched the three of them cross the threshold and go into the house.

Mark stopped me and put his arms around me.

"That was intense," he said.

"The life of a repo man is always intense," I said.

He looked down at me. "What?"

"Oh god," I said. "You've got to start watching more movies. Didn't you ever see *Repo Man*?"

He smiled. "I was just teasing you," he said. "I knew what movie it was from. Now I need to call Ian and let him know I'm okay. I'll go see if I can get phone service anywhere."

"Okay," I said.

And then Mark was gone, and I was standing in my old backyard, alone. In the sunshine, under the blue sky. I looked at the grass where Fern had strewn Alberto's ashes. I waited for a beat. But no arm came bursting up through the sod.

Thank goodness. I would not want life to be like any of my movies.

"Love you, sweetheart," I whispered before turning around and going toward the house to join my family.

Turned out the earthquake was a pretty major one. Pundits started calling it the earthquake the animals predicted. Some even called it the Zombie Animal Earthquake, which I didn't really understand since none of the animals died and came back to life. After the quake, a tsunami hit our shores. It didn't reach the restaurant but it was pretty high and pretty bad.

LA was knocked off its foundations by the quake. Many buildings destroyed. Because of retrofitting and new building codes most people survived. Most buildings, too.

But the chaos was extreme for a time. We didn't have electricity for days. Fortunately the generator kept the food safe for us. We weren't able to get down to the village for almost a week because of damage to the road. Trees were down everywhere. We were lucky.

We all rallied around each other. We came out of our shells, out of our houses, and helped each other out. Our house—Hayword's house—had some damage, but it was structurally sound. The bungalow had absolutely no damage while other houses around it fell apart. The beach house and restaurant had some structural damage.

Despite all of this—or maybe because of it—my family and community seemed to grow closer. Mark and I stayed in the bungalow, and Fern moved in with David and Hayword since her apartment was all but destroyed. The five of us spent so much time together that we actually began to feel like we were a family. Even Mark's son Ian started joining our little crew.

It's only been a few months since the quake, but filming on the movie started on time. The financial problems at AFT either resolved themselves or else they stopped talking about them because Sally hasn't brought them up since. AFT will use part of the profits from the movie to help those who were affected by the earthquake.

Hayword and I decided that we're going to start a foundation in Alberto's name with the profits from *Beauty and the Zombie Part Two*. We're not sure what the foundation will do. David wants it to be used to save the world. We told him we needed to be more specific than that.

"Okay, save this world," he said. "Planet Earth."

We asked Fern if she wanted to run the foundation. She has a certain facility for business. Why not? So she's going to start taking some classes on running a nonprofit and see if she likes it. She's also promised to go back to therapy. We'll see. She wants to take acting lessons, and this fills me with dread.

Hayword and I haven't divorced yet. I'm not sure why. But Mark and I are actually talking about our relationship. I don't leave the room when these conversation start, no matter how much I'm tempted.

Hayword thinks we should tell Ryan Nichols about the foundation once it's up and running. Since it's in his son's name. I dunno. Alberto was never his son. He was always Hayword's. David wants to call it the Alberto McMurphy Lightman Back from the Dead Foundation. We told him to think again.

They've already asked me to start writing the third *Beauty and the Zombie* movie even though they haven't completed filming on the second one. I've got an idea for it, though. It's called *Beauty and the Zombie Part Three: Whackadoodle Times*.

But first I'm looking forward to seeing Part Two. Especially the last scene. I want to see Colleen walking away from her son's grave. I want to see his arm come up through the Earth, I want to know he will live again. I understand he's part zombie, so he'll be part of the living dead. And he's fictional.

In other words, I know my son will never be coming back to life again.

Still, when no one is around, I stand in the backyard of Hayword's house—or our house—in the spot where Fern spread Alberto's ashes. I'm not waiting for Alberto to burst forth from the Earth or anything. Or maybe I am. Who knows? But I do talk to him. I do whisper to him, and I listen for his voice in the wind. Sometimes I close my eyes and see him as I did in the dream, with his fist raised above his head, and he is whispering to me, he is calling to me. "Momma. Run!" I'm ready. I'm ready to run. If that's what's needed.

Until then. Until then I'm ready. Until then, I'm ready to stay.

WHACKADOODLE TIMES THREE

For Mario

ONE

I know precisely when things went whackadoodle again. Eartha did not show up on my doorstep offering perfect margaritas. No fake robbers burst into the restaurant where I was breakfasting with my blackmailing daughter. Nope. It was a perfect February day in the canyon at my old house. They were all sitting outside enjoying the sun, and I was cleaning up after the dinner party. I picked up a wine glass on the counter that had a splash or two of white wine sloshing in the bottom of it. Instead of tossing the wine into the sink and putting the glass in the dishwasher, I brought the glass up to my lips, breathed deeply the scent of fermenting grapes, leaned my head back, then drained the wine into my mouth.

I didn't swallow right away. I waited a beat. A nanosecond. An eon.

Then I swallowed.

It tasted like Nirvana.

If Nirvana was a place where addicts went to drink warm white wine that tasted vaguely of someone else's lipstick.

Addicts always have an excuse for relapsing. My excuses could have been that the biosphere was crashing and burning, I believed Mark and I were finished once and for all again, my first son David would turn 17 soon and his anxiety was still full-blown, and my second son Alberto would be a teen now if he had lived.

Or my excuse could have been that my ex-husband Hayword had arranged this dinner party so we could all meet his new girlfriend Patricia who was now listening with rapt attention to my son talk about climate change like she was his new momma come calling. David kept talking about some strange lightning storm coming this week that they were predicting could kill us all. And p.s. Hayword isn't really my ex-husband. We have not officially divorced. Still.

Or maybe my excuse could have been that I was late delivering the screenplay for *Beauty and the Zombie Part Three: Whackadoodle Times.* Sally St. James kept telling me that the fate of our entire studio rested on my shoulders. Again.

But I ain't gonna make any excuses. Even though any one of those would have been good ones. The truth is I swallowed that wine because that's what a drunk does. Even one who has been sober for five years.

Give me some credit though. I didn't pick up another half-ass half-filled glass of wine or start desperately rummaging through the cupboards looking for liquor. I stood in the kitchen breathing, leaning against the white cupboards, my hands on the wooden countertops, my fingers holding on to the edge for dear life.

I could hear them outside laughing and talking: David, Hayword, dearest wanna-be-momma Patricia, and my best friend Joanie. My daughter Fern was off somewhere. She had stopped by the bungalow a couple days ago when I wasn't home. She left me a note on the kitchen countertop, next to a bottle of Martinelli's sparkling apple cider (already opened) and a piece of cherry pie from Nellie's. Two of my favorite things to consume. She had sounded fine in the note.

In fact, my whole family seemed fine without me. I breathed. What a relief. What a relief. What a fucking relief. They were fine without me.

What we had all feared had come to pass: I had taken another drink.

And the world had not ended.

"What are you doing in here?" Joanie asked, suddenly in the kitchen, suddenly beside me, opening up the refrigerator with the hand that wasn't holding a drink.

"I'm cleaning up," I said. I let go of the countertop and began putting dishes in the dishwasher once again.

Joanie closed the fridge and picked up one half-empty wine glass after another and gulped down the contents before handing me each glass. "See," she said, grinning. "I'm helping, too."

I didn't say anything. I could hear my heart beating in my ears. Or was that the alcohol pulsing through my veins, singing, "More, more, more?"

Joanie stood too close to me. She was always too close. She had no sense of personal space. Never had. Sometimes that made me love her all the more. Now, I could smell the alcohol on her. Not on her breath. Was she sweating it?

"Are you doing anything to prepare for this lightning storm?" Joanie asked. "They say we should all stay indoors once it starts and stay until it ends. Will it burn down our houses? Will our phones die?"

"Why are you asking me? Do I look like a weather vane?"

"They say that just before, during, and after a lightning storm, all things can change. For the better and for the worse. They say magic can happen and wishes can come true."

"Who is they?" I asked.

"You know," Joanie said. "They who know everything."

"Oh, *they*."

Joanie gave me a look. "What do you think of the new bride to be?" she asked, in an almost-whisper.

I nearly dropped the empty glass in my hand. Instead I dropped it into the dishwasher and looked at my friend. "What are you talking about? They're not getting married. I bet they haven't even slept together yet."

"Why not? Can Hayword still get it up?"

I rolled my eyes. "How would I know? I haven't had sex with him in years."

Joanie looked out the window over the sink. "He is still a good-looking man."

"Quit lusting after my husband," I said.

"Ex-husband," she said. No one knew we weren't divorced yet. It was no one's fucking business.

Joanie looked at me. "What's wrong with you? You've been nasty all day."

"Why did he invite us all here?" I asked. "To meet his fucking girlfriend? I don't want to meet his new fuck buddy."

"I thought you said—"

I put my hands up. "There's too much going on. Can't he keep it in his pants until we get this film finished?"

"Hey, you brought Mark around all the time, and Hayword never said anything."

"That's because Harwood is a fucking saint," I said. "And I am not."

"Brooke."

"I took a drink," I said. "I wasn't thinking, and I took a gulp of wine."

Joanie put her glass down and put her arms around me. "Oh, baby," she said.

I wondered if this was what it was like to be caught in the Iron Maiden.

"Get off me," I said, a little harsher than I meant.

Joanie let me go.

"Do you want to go to a meeting?" Joanie asked.

I was sorry I had told her, but then she had helped me dress a naked dead man, and I had pulled her toe out of a bathtub faucet, so we didn't have many secrets between us.

"No," I said. "I took the one sip." Ahhh, now it had gone from a gulp to a sip. "I want to forget about it. It'll be OK."

"It's Mark, isn't it?" she said. "He was so good for you. Have you broken up again? Now that the restaurant is closed it must be weird living there."

I sighed. "It was never right after the earthquake," I said. "I was in the bungalow more than I was at our place." I shrugged. "We are so different. It was bound to happen."

"Wait," Joanie said. "Does Mark know you are broken up?"

I snorted.

"Come on," she said. "You don't like goodbyes or endings or any of that. I could see you sneaking out and—"

"Shut up," I said. I ignored her question. Because I didn't know if Mark knew. Once the restaurant closed, he went back to being a plumber, and his clients were closer to his old home. So he often stayed at his old house. I often stayed at the bungalow. We texted. But we hadn't actually spoken in days.

"Hollywood sucks the life out of you," I said.

Joanie laughed. "Give me a break. You are enjoying the fame and the game."

"No, I am not. For one thing, I don't have the fame. And I've never been game."

Truth was life had been more fun when I was drunk. Hadn't it? I squinted. That couldn't be true.

"Where's Marv anyway?" I asked. "Are you still married? I

haven't seen him in ages. Maybe years. Did you kill him and bury him in your backyard?"

Joanie laughed. A screechy nervous laugh. She picked up her glass and emptied it into her mouth. And swallowed.

"If this was a horror movie," I said, "you would now be a suspect in a murder plot."

"I didn't murder him," Joanie said. "But I haven't heard from him for a while. I think he might want a divorce. We had a big fight before he want on a trip. He left three weeks ago, and I haven't heard from him. You know he goes to visit his brother in Mali every few years. He doesn't communicate much when he's there. I think he and Marty go out and pick up women."

"In Mali?" I asked. "That's a long way to go to commit adultery."

"Adultery?" she said. "No, he just has a few fucks. He's careful. I'm sure."

"About as careful as you are," I said.

"Hey!" she said.

I shrugged. "Truth to power, sistah. Well, truth to slut. From slut."

Joanie laughed. "Anyway, I finally called his phone, and he doesn't answer. I left a message with his brother and didn't hear back. Finally got his brother's house, and they said he was out on safari, or whatever they call it. I asked about Marv, but the houseboy, or whatever he was, didn't seem to know what I was talking about. So I'm a little concerned."

I stared at her. "A little concerned? Jesus. Your husband has been missing for three weeks!"

"Hey, you know we live very separate lives," she said. "We like it like that. I was giving him space, and I thought he was giving me space."

"Did you check his credit cards," I asked, "to see if he was using them and where?"

"Check his credit cards?" she asked. "How would I do that?"

"Jesus, woman. Aren't they your credit cards, too? You'd look it up online."

"You are harshing my mellow. He's been gone for this long before. I'm sure he's fine."

"How are you going to explain it to the police if he's not?" I asked.

"What do you mean?" She suddenly looked alarmed.

"If someone has hurt him and you never filed a missing person report, won't they suspect you of foul play?"

"You've been watching too many crime shows, Mac," she said. "Let's forget about it. Are you staying at the bungalow tonight? Come up to the house tomorrow, and we can go through Marv's papers. You're better at this sort of thing. I bet you'll figure it out."

"Better at what sort of thing?" I asked.

"Sneakiness," she said.

She left the kitchen. I felt a tinge of dizziness, like the beginning of an altered state of consciousness. I glanced around the kitchen. Were all the glasses emptied? Yes. Fuck. But that bottle of wine didn't look quite empty. I hurried across the room, picked up the dark bottle, put it up to my lips and opened my throat. Liquid red gold flowed into my body. I gulped and gulped.

When I stopped, I let out a long sigh, wiped my mouth, and poured the rest of the wine down the drain.

"Hey, that's good wine," Hayword said, as he came into the kitchen. "I would have put a cork in it so I could have it tomorrow."

"Too late," I said. "It's all gone."

The monster was now coursing through my whole body. I felt free and devastated all at the same time.

I leaned against the counter again and smiled at Hayword.

"Soooo," I said. "Must be love."

He looked at me, frowned a bit, and then shrugged. "You mean Patricia? She's fun."

"Unlike me," I said.

Hayword went to the sink and began putting dishes in the dishwasher, taking over my unfinished job.

"What's going on, Brooke?" he asked. "You don't like Patricia?"

I shrugged. I had my hand up, as if it now contained a glass of wine. What *was* going on? I wanted to scream, "Please, help me, Hayword. It's happening all over again." But I didn't.

"No one is funnier or more fun than you," Hayword said.

Joanie was right. Hayword was still good-looking. That had never been the problem. The problem was that he had always been insecure, was always looking for adulation or—approval. At least that was what he was like when we were married. Now that he was a successful producer, he wasn't quite so needy. Maybe he would be better in bed now. Not that he had ever been bad.

I walked up to him and put my hand on his back. We shocked each other and both jumped. He turned partway around and looked at me. "What was that?"

"I dunno. I guess we have electricity." I smiled. I felt more dizzy. I blinked hard. It was almost as if someone else had control over my body.

Almost.

Hayword laughed. "Like the kind of electricity in an electric chair, the kind that kills? I would agree with that."

"Hey, we weren't bad together," I said. "Don't rewrite history. Except for the part when you fucked some blonde bimbo after our son died."

"And you fucked every hair color under the sun," he said. "We're lucky we don't have an SDS."

"An SDS? Wasn't that a terrorist group in the sixties?"

He frowned and looked up as he tried to remember. "Oh yeah. STD."

I laughed, and he grinned.

"I'm feeling a little dizzy," I said. "Do you think you could drive me home?"

Hayword glanced outside.

"You'd be in and out before anyone knew you were gone," I said.

He looked at me, his expression saying the same thing I was thinking. What was I doing?

"Please," I said. "I don't want to worry about going around those curves and ending up careening off the mountain."

"Let me go tell Patricia I'm leaving," he said.

"No need," I said. "You'll be right back. I promise."

He hesitated, and then he nodded. We went out the front door together and got into Hayword's little sports car. I thought it was ridiculous for a man his age—or any age—to be tooling around in something like this. I didn't know the model. I didn't care. I drove a sedan. Just like any sensible person would.

I texted David. "Dad's taking me home. Don't worry if he doesn't get back right away."

Crap. I was feeling cranky again.

I needed another drink.

Hayword drove quickly down our canyon road—but not too quickly. He didn't look at me, but he kept asking me questions.

"How is Mark doing?"

"Fine." I wasn't gonna tell him nuthin'.

"I haven't seen Fern lately," he said. "She doing well?"

"You don't know? She is your daughter."

"She's your daughter, too," he said. "So how is she?"

"How would I know?" I said. "She did stop by my house on Friday when I wasn't there. Left me a little present. I think she's trying to be nice. You should see her sometimes. You're at the studio more than I am."

"Yeah, how is the script coming along?"

"Just fine." My buzz was starting to wear off. Maybe that was a good thing. Maybe that would stop what was about to happen.

We were almost at my bungalow.

"You love this Patty woman?" I asked.

"Patricia. And no."

He drove up my drive and stopped the car. He didn't turn off the engine.

"You're not gonna walk a girl to the door?" I asked.

"You're not a girl," he said, "and usually you don't want me anywhere near this place."

"Well, I fucked a lot of people here," I said. "I didn't want you to have any bad memories."

We got out of the car, walked up the steps together, and went into the bungalow together. It smelled like cinnamon inside.

"Why would I have bad memories?" Hayword said. "You never fucked me here."

"We can change that tonight," I said as I walked back to the bedroom. I switched on the light and began stripping off my clothes.

"Um, wait, what? Mac, why are you taking off your clothes? Stop it."

I smiled. "Come on," I said. "For old times' sake. You can go back to Patricia, and she'll never know."

"I'll know," he said.

"Have you fucked her yet?"

"That's none of your business."

I pulled my pants off—and now I was standing in front of Hayword naked.

I walked to him and put my arms around his neck. He didn't move. He looked down at me.

"What's going on?" he asked gently.

I leaned against him. I could feel his erection.

"What about Mark?" he asked.

"What about Mark?" I said. "It's only us here, Hayword. Like it used to be when we were kids writing *Love and Other Insanities.*"

"Is this love or insanity?" he asked.

"Does it matter?"

He put his arms around me, and we kissed. It felt so familiar. A few moments later, he was naked. We were on the bed together. As soon as his penis was inside me, I felt the same way I had when I took the drink: wonderful and devastated all at the same time. What was I doing? What was I thinking? How on Earth had this all happened?

"It's always only been you, Brooke," Hayword said as we moved together.

Oh fuck.

What had I done?

TWO

Strangely I dreamed of Katherine and Oscar, the couple
who had produced and financed our first movie *Love and Other
Insanities* all those years ago. In the dream, they kept telling me
everything was going to be OK.

I woke up to a pulsing headache. I sat up slowly. The room
tilted a bit. I put my head in my hands. Was I such a fucking
amateur that I had a hangover from the equivalent of a glass or
five of wine?

"Fuck, fuck, fuck," I murmured.

I heard a stirring in the bed.

Then I remembered what had happened. Shit. Everything
was not going to be OK. What I had done? Jesus H.

I got up, grabbed my clothes, and hurried out of the room. I
closed the door softly—I hoped. My head was throbbing too
loudly for me to know for certain. I switched on the light in the

living room, got quickly dressed, and then sat on the sofa. It was 9:30 p.m. It was still the same day I had taken a drink.

I looked around the room. I felt terrified.

I breathed deeply. Once. In and out. Twice. In and out. Looked around.

So much had happened in this house over the years.

The lovers I had brought here while on a drunk I had pretty much forgotten. But this was where I had written the first two *Beauty and the Zombie* scripts. This was where Fern had told me she thought she had burned down our house. This was where I found a movie executive dead—and dressed only in fishnet stockings. This bungalow had survived an earthquake and a wildfire. It had survived me being a drunk for many years. It had survived me being sober for many years.

But it had never felt like home.

I rubbed my eyes. I tried to remember the last time I felt at home anywhere.

I couldn't.

No place felt like home.

Ugh.

Why had I taken that first drink? Why on Earth had I slept with Hayword? We had survived the fire at our first house. We had survived the wildfire and earthquake here. We had finally come to terms with the death of our son, Alberto. We had come through my alcoholism. Well, Hayword and I were almost divorced, so we hadn't come through it as a couple. But we survived. We were friends.

Hayword and I not being divorced was a constant source of tension between Mark and me. He didn't understand why Hayword and I were still married. I didn't understand why it mattered. It wasn't as if Mark and I were going to get married. You got married if you were gonna have babies. Otherwise, why bother?

Christ.

I had taken a drink. I had slept with Hayword.

What now?

I was supposed to be working. My script for *Beauty and the Zombie: Whackadoodle Times* was overdue. Sally St. James kept bugging me about it. It was our studio now: Sally, Hayword, and I owned it. Sally and Hayword ran it. I was the talent, so to speak. Back to Life Studios we called it. *Beauty and the Zombie Three* would make or break us.

I had worked under a deadline before. I had done it drunk; I had done it sober. I could do it now.

Yet for some reason I had barely written a word of it.

That could not be why I picked up that drink.

It could not be why I slept with Hayword. Could it?

Fuck. Why was I asking myself these stupid questions? Again. I was going in circles. I drank because I was a fucking addict.

I grabbed my purse and keys and stepped outside onto the porch. Then I realized I had left my car at Hayword's house.

Fuck, fuck, fuck.

I went back into the house, set down my purse, and tiptoed into the bedroom. I closed the door enough to shut out the light. Then I went to the chair where Hayword had thrown his trousers. I reached into the front pocket and felt around until I found his keys. As I pulled them out, the keys jangled, and Hayword made a noise. I stayed very still and listened to the darkness until I heard him sleep-breathing. Then I left the room and the house again, closing the doors quietly behind me.

I took Hayword's car down to the village. I felt stupid driving a little sports car. It seemed dangerous. I didn't feel drunk any longer, but what if I was? What if I got stopped and got a DUI? It would be all over the papers.

I parked in front of one of the small markets in the village that sold liquor. An all-nighter. It was only 9:30 p.m.—not 2 a.m.—but the lights in the store were still too bright for me. I put on my sunglasses and went to the cooler first and got a jug of orange juice. Then I went straight to the vodka. Still remembered where it was. I plopped them both down on the countertop. A pale woman rung them up without touching them. Unless she did it very quickly. I gave her the money she asked for.

"Early breakfast," she said. "I remember those days."

I looked at her through my sunglasses.

"Yes," I said. "I'm an alcoholic, and this is what I have for breakfast, lunch, and dinner. Well, it's what I used to have. Haven't had a drink in five years until tonight. Tonight I decided to celebrate."

"Celebrate what?" the woman asked as she slipped the vodka in a bag and then put that bag into another one with the orange juice.

"The fact that the world is just too fucking scary," I said.

The woman laughed.

I took the bag from her and asked, "What's so funny?"

"How can the world be scary to you?" she said. "You have everything."

"You don't know anything about me," I said.

She nodded. "Yes, I do."

I squinted. Did I know her? She looked vaguely familiar.

"You're an alkie, too," I said.

She looked at me. I nodded. "Don't mind me. I'm not a good alcoholic or a good sober."

"I'll go to a meeting with you."

"What? You're standing behind that counter selling poison

to people, and you're offering to go to a fucking meeting with me? How hypocritical are you?"

"It's not poison to everyone," she said with very little expression. I suddenly felt like I was in one of my movies. Was she a zombie, too?

"Be careful of the paps," she said. "They like to follow celebrities after they've bought liquor. I've seen it happen several times."

"Paps are such assholes," I said. "But I'm not a celebrity. No one is gonna follow me. Thanks. Stay sober."

I hurried out to the car. What I used to do was drain out half the orange juice and then pour the vodka into the jug. Instant screwdriver. In case any paparazzi were hanging around, I decided to wait. I drove carefully up the winding road back to my house.

I went inside quietly, listened for any movement, didn't hear any, so I tiptoed into the kitchen. I got a glass and filled it 2/3rds with orange juice. Without hesitation, I took the seal and cap off of the vodka. I unscrewed it, and I poured it into the glass until the glass was full. I opened the pantry door, moved some boxes around, and hid the vodka behind them all. I put the vodka-spiked OJ in the fridge, next to the almost empty bottle of Martinelli's Fern had left me. Then I stood over the sink, and I drank the vodka-laced orange juice, slowly, until I emptied the glass. I rinsed it out and stood at the sink.

It was as if a decision had been made a long time ago that I was going to drink again, and tonight was the night. I didn't get it. I didn't understand it. But I didn't fight it. It was a relief not to fight it.

I felt like I was going to throw up.

Liquor on an empty stomach. Gawd.

I scrambled a couple of eggs. Then I sat on the couch and ate them while I became drunk again. I felt sick and dizzy, but I didn't feel anxious. I didn't feel stressed. I didn't feel much of anything.

I heard my name from far away. I opened my eyes to daylight. I blinked. My head throbbed again. My eyes finally focused. Hayword was leaning over me. I had fallen asleep on the couch.

"It's OK," Hayword was saying. "It's just me."

"What? Yes." I sat up.

"You looked so scared just now," he said. "Why didn't you wake me?"

"What? Oh, I was a little hungry," I said. "I must have fallen asleep after I ate."

He sat on the couch next to me and put his hand on my arm. I wanted to slap it away.

"What happened yesterday?" he asked.

"Um, weren't you there?" I said. "We had sex."

"It feels like—it feels like you seduced me," he said.

I did slap his hand, and he pulled it away.

"What the fuck are you talking about?" I asked. "I didn't seduce you."

"I think you wanted to have sex with me for some reason," he said. "And it happened."

"You didn't want to have sex with me?" I asked.

I got up and moved to the chair. I pulled my feet up underneath me.

"Of course, I did," Hayword said. "I love you. That has never gone away. But I didn't think you felt the same way."

"I honestly don't know what happened," I said. I knew I should tell him that I had started drinking again. I knew I should go to a meeting right then and there. If I wanted to get sober again, I had to be honest.

But I didn't know if I wanted to be sober again. It was a lot of fucking work.

"I was jealous of Patricia," I said. "I guess."

He nodded. "I'll have to tell her this happened."

"Why? Are you two exclusive?"

He shook his head. "We haven't even slept together yet."

"I knew it," I said.

"What?"

"Nothing."

"And Mark," Hayword said. "We'll have to tell Mark. I wouldn't want to betray him."

"Betray him?" I said. "I don't belong to him or to you. I can fuck whomever I like."

"That's all it was?" he asked. "A fuck? You wanted to keep me on the hook for yourself like some little lap dog."

"You are mixing metaphors," I said. "Or whatever. I'm sorry. I don't know what's going on."

He looked away from me and shook his head. "We just left the house. We didn't tell anyone. They must have been worried sick."

"I texted David last night."

"That's something." He looked at me again. "I don't know what's going on with you, but I hope you're OK. I hope I didn't screw anything up for you. I had waited a long time for you to want me again, and that was . . . irresistible."

Oh crap. What a piece of scum I was. He was having all of these feelings, and I was having none. I knew what to do. I leaned toward him and held out my hand. He took it, and I squeezed his.

"You've always been a hunk in my eyes," I said.

Hayword chuckled. "OK. Knock it off. I'll take you back to

the house and you can get your car. I can make you breakfast after I take David to school. Remember his car is in the shop."

I had forgotten how charming he could be.

"I do need my car," I said, "but I've got that script to work on, so I better come right back here. Hey, I dreamed about Katherine and Oscar just now. Isn't that strange? I always liked them. They liked us. Thought we would go all the way together."

Hayword nodded. "They have their OK Studios out in the country now."

Ah, that's why they kept telling me everything was OK.

"It's a really nice place," Hayword said. "I think you'd like it."

"You've been?" I asked.

He nodded. "I've kept in touch over the years. They tried to keep in touch with you, but you were never interested."

I nodded. I had no memory of that. Another one of my failings, I supposed.

I wasn't in the mood.

"I should probably give them a call," I said. I smiled. I would never call them. What would I say? "Hey, you haven't heard from me in 15 years, but here I am now."

A few minutes later, Hayword drove us back to the house. David came out before Hayword stopped the car. He cocked his head slightly as he looked at us.

Fuck.

We got out of the car.

"Hi, darlin'," I said. "It's nice to see you, but I gotta get going."

David held up his hands and blocked the way to my car and to the house.

"Where were you?" he asked.

"Your mom wasn't feeling well," Hayword answered.

"And you couldn't text or call Patricia?" David asked. "That was so rude, Dad."

Hayword looked at me. I shrugged. "It was a family matter," I said. "She'll get over it."

David said, "You say that like she doesn't matter."

I bit my tongue so that I didn't say what I wanted to say: She didn't matter.

"She's a human being," David said.

"What are you so mad about?" I asked. "You met her all of once."

"It's a crappy thing to do," David said. "Like something you would do when you were drinking."

I could feel Hayword's eyes on me. I looked up at David.

"I am sorry," I said. "It was rude. I'll call her and apologize."

"Are you drinking, Mom?" David asked. He occasionally asked me this when I was doing something he didn't like.

"Of course not," I said. "I can stay if you like. Dad offered to make breakfast."

"I already ate," David said. "Dad, we need to hurry or I'll be late for school. And you haven't done anything to the house for the lightning storm. They said we should put up storm shutters and make sure everything is grounded."

"It's just a storm," Hayword said. "Everything is grounded. We have storm shutters. We have a generator."

"We could all be fried," David said. "In the Luxembourg storm, 300 people died."

"That was 200 years ago," Hayword said. "And munitions blew up. We don't have any munitions."

"You don't know," David said. "For all we know one of our neighbors is a rightwing white supremacist with a barn full of explosives."

"Then they'll die in a fiery blast, and we will be fine," Hayword said. "Besides, the guy predicting this could be all wrong. Normally they can't predict electrical storms."

"The *guy* has been studying climate change for decades, and he found some unexpected atmospheric parameters that allowed him to develop a prediction model for lightning storms," David said. "When he applies the algorithm to current conditions, he can predict lightning storms with 94% accuracy within 4-5 days. I looked it over. It seems solid."

Of course David had looked over the evidence. Good for him. I had not realized how worried he was about this.

"It's going to be OK," I said.

"You don't know anything!" he said. He turned and went into the house. He sounded like Fern.

"When is this storm supposedly coming?" I asked Hayword.

"Wednesday or Thursday," he said. "Is David right? Are you drinking? Did you just stand here and lie to our son?"

"I did not," I said. "I am not drinking."

He nodded. "Ahhh, the literal defense. Fuck." He leaned his head back. "You were drinking. I should have known. Well, I'm not doing this again, Brooke. I can't. I won't. I can't believe you made me a part of your sickness."

I laughed. "You were always a part of my sickness, Hayword. You know that. The death of our son. You fucking someone else."

"I'm not falling for that," he said. "You had a hole in your soul as wide as the Grand Canyon before any of that happened. If you remember, he wasn't my son. You had fucked someone else and gotten pregnant."

"How dare you say he wasn't your son!" I said a little too dramatically. "I knew it. You never loved him."

Hayword made a noise. "This is old stuff, Brooke. We've been over it. We've healed it. It's finished. Don't start it again. Your outrage is about as fake as . . . as you are."

My stomach knotted. For a moment, I felt like myself again: full of guilt and doubt.

"I know," I said. "I know. I don't know what's wrong with me. I don't know what happened."

Truth peeked out again.

"Please," I said, "don't leave me."

Oh fuck. What was that? I sounded so pathetic.

"You left me a long time ago," Hayword said. He shook his head. "I'll take you to a meeting, but beyond that, you are on your own."

"Really? I make one slip in five years and suddenly I'm evil and worthless, and you're gonna cut me loose?"

"You got drunk and you fucked me," he said. "It wasn't because you loved me or wanted me. You wanted to take me away from Patricia, as though I were your plaything that had gotten away. You wanted to show me that you could have me if you wanted. That's cruel, Brooke. That's fucking cruel. The woman I loved would never have done anything like that. Ever."

I stared at him. Then I sighed. I was as perplexed as he was.

"The woman you loved died a long time ago," I said. "Ain't that the truth? We've been waiting for her to come back all these years that I've been sober, haven't we? But I just kept going from one emergency to another. Getting through one thing only to go through another. And now that things are almost normal, I realize . . . I am not."

"Sounds like a crock of shit to me," Hayword said.

Wow. He was angry.

"Are you going to a meeting or not?" he asked.

I laughed. "You just said you didn't want anything to do with me. So whether I go to a meeting or not is none of your fucking business."

"Don't forget David's car is in the shop," Hayword said.

"You need to pick him up after school. He's got a club until 4:00."

I got into my car and drove away. I didn't want to look back, but I did. Hayword was not staring after me. He had walked into the house and closed the door. I could almost feel him slamming it.

I began to cry. Or rather I tried to make myself cry. Didn't work.

What had happened?

It didn't matter, didn't matter.

I needed to go to a meeting. And listen to the pathetic stories of all the people who were as pathetic as I was? I shook my head as I continued up the road a bit and then drove into Joanie's driveway. She ran out her front door toward my car. I slammed on the brakes. As usual, she was barely dressed, wearing something beige and mostly sheer with red high heels. I turned off the car.

"Mac!" she yelled as I got out. "You were right. I looked at the credit card statements."

She looked terrified. I sighed. OK. We would deal with her fake drama first.

"And?"

She grabbed my hand. "Marv hasn't used them. Mac, he must be dead!"

THREE

"Did he take out any cash before he left?" I asked.

"Just a thousand dollars," Joanie said. "Pocket money, you know."

"OK."

"Where is he?" she asked. "What's happened?"

"How would I know? Maybe you should call the police."

"But you said they're going to ask why I didn't call before."

We walked into the house. Her housekeeper Maria was nowhere in sight. We sat in the living room. A plate of scrambled eggs and a martini glass rested on the glass coffee table. Huge picture windows looked out at the back of her property. She picked up the martini glass and emptied the contents into her mouth.

"Oh," she said. "I'm sorry. Should I hide the martini glass or get you a drink?"

I blinked. Really? She would get me a drink? I didn't know if that was awful or generous.

"No," I said. "I'm good. So when did you last see Marv? Did you check if he took his scheduled flight?"

She shook her head. "I have no idea how I would actually do that. That morning he came into the bedroom and kissed me goodbye."

"Did he say anything?"

"He said he'd see me in a month," she said. She closed her eyes. "And then we fucked. Oh no. Wait. That wasn't him. No, Ronnie came that morning. Literally and literally. It was her day."

"Her day?" I had met Ronnie. Back when I was drinking and fucking everyone, I had fucked her, too. She was young and bored. And pretty good in bed. I hadn't known she and Joanie were a thing.

"Um, I thought you leaned toward the tall dark and penis laden," I said. "Ronnie?"

Joanie shook her head. "Something about her. She's got a tongue that will not quit."

I didn't like the idea that Joanie and I had had sex with the same person. It felt incestuous. Or something. Icky.

"Anyway, Marv kissed you goodbye."

"Said he was taking the Jag to drop it off at the dealer's," she said. "I had forgotten that."

"I assume the Jag is gone," I said.

"I assume so," she said. "It's in the other garage at the bottom of the property, where we used to keep the horses. He has a few of his more expensive cars there."

We looked at each other.

I said, "People go down to that garage regularly, though, right? Your landscapers or workmen or you?"

Joanie shook her head. "No. It's Marv's garage. No one goes down there. I've been there probably twice in twenty years."

Oh fuck, fuck, fuck.

"We better call the police," I said.

"No," Joanie pleaded. "Not yet. Let's at least go to the garage. See if he took the Jag like he said."

"Joanie, he could be there. Dead."

"No," she said. "Maybe he got into an accident on the way to the airport, and he's lost his memory."

"And his ID?"

"Please," Joanie said.

"Get some shoes on at least," I said.

"These are shoes," she said.

I rolled my eyes. She ran upstairs. A few minutes later she came down dressed in slacks and a shirt and wearing flats. She looked unlike herself.

"Wait," I said. "Don't you have security cameras all over the place? We can look at those."

"No," Joanie said. "We keep them up, but they don't work. They were always a pain in the ass."

We went out the back door and walked down the long manicured lawn.

"This looks too perfect," I said. "Do you use chemicals on it? David would be so disappointed."

"I don't know," she said. "Like I pay attention."

"David says that's what's wrong with the world. People don't pay attention."

"I love David, but he should enjoy himself more."

"Hey, leave him alone," I said. "He's perfect the way he is."

"He's an anxiety bomb waiting to go off," Joanie said. "Did you go to a meeting?"

"Not yet," I said.

We neared a low wooden building. Looked like a four car garage. Joanie peeked through the window on the side door.

"The Jaguar is in there," she said. She looked at me. She bit her lip.

"Open the fucking door," I said.

And so she did. We were hit with a wave of stink. Dead body stink. Shit, shit, shit. Joanie turned around and threw up. I covered my mouth and looked inside. I could definitely see a figure in the driver's seat of the Jaguar. I backed out of the garage and shut the door.

"Was it Marv?" Joanie asked.

"I don't know," I said, "but someone is dead in there. Did you bring your phone?"

She shook her head.

"Did he kill himself?" she asked. "Did someone kill him? Did he have a heart attack and die there?"

"I don't know," I said. "We need to call the police."

She nodded and started to cry.

"I'm sorry, Joanie."

"He was a good man," she said.

I didn't say anything. I didn't know if he was a good man or a bad man. I took her hand, and we walked back up toward the house. I did not want to stay for the coming shit storm. I needed to go to a meeting. Or go get a drink.

We went back into the house. I picked up her phone on the coffee table and held it out to her.

She said, "Wait. Let's think about this. I don't know if he left a will."

"You don't know if he left a will?" I repeated. I was astonished.

"What if he didn't leave me anything?" she said. "His kids could take it all. I need time to move some cash around before I call the police."

"Joanie!" I said. "You have to call the police now."

"You didn't call the police when your guy died in fishnet stockings," she said. "I helped you dress him before you called the police."

"OK, yes. But he wasn't my guy. If you move money around the day you call the police, they'll know something is up."

"Well, we can wait a few days. I'll tell the police I was worried he had left me, so I wanted to make sure I got my share, in case they ever ask. They won't ask. Marv has money in places that no one knows about, except me. Unless he mentions it in a will. I need some time."

"You're comfortable leaving a dead man in the garage?" I asked.

"Have some respect," Joanie said. "That dead man is my husband. And yes, he's been there for three weeks. Another couple days won't hurt anything."

"Oh my gawd. I feel like I'm in a Faulkner story. Or one of my movies."

"He's not coming back from the dead," Joanie said. "I want to get my fair share before his greedy children take it all."

"We need to call the police," I said.

"And you need to go to a fucking meeting," Joanie said. "But you aren't going and I'm not calling the police."

We stared at each other.

"Jesus, Brooke," she said. "Why don't you have a drink? You were so much more fun when you were a drunk."

I raised my eyebrows. Gotta admit: That stung. It was what I always feared.

"It's true," she said. She picked up the martini mixer on the coffee table and poured the liquid into her glass. She wiped her lipstick off the edge, and then she held the glass out to me.

"We have to walk on glass around you all the time," she said. "So that we don't upset you so much that you drink or fuck or whatever. It's exhausting. And you're always so sure of every-thing, that you're right, that AA saved you. It's pompous. It is fucking boring."

I took the glass from her and emptied the contents into my mouth and swallowed. Martinis were never my drink, but what the hell.

"I think you meant you all walk on eggshells around me," I said.

"What?"

"You walk on eggshells, not on glass," I said.

She shook her head. "Whatever. Just don't tell anyone. Let me take care of this myself."

I laughed. "When have you ever been able to take care of things yourself?"

"Look around," she said. "I've got everything I ever wanted. I did that."

"You married this," I said. "What did you ever do to earn it?"

"I fucked him," she said. "That's what I did."

"Your grief is touching," I said.

We were supposed to be best of friends. What had hap-pened?

"Mac," she said, her voice suddenly soft and friendly again. "I'm in shock. I don't mean anything. Please, don't call the po-lice. Let me get things in order, and then I'll call the police. I promise."

"Hey, it's not my funeral," I said. I tossed the martini glass toward the fireplace. It shattered on the stone floor. "Oops. I'm so clumsy. Now see: That's glass. Try walking on that instead of eggshells."

I hurried out of the house and got into my car.

"What the fuck," I said out loud as I drove quickly away. I always knew Joanie was a little different, but this was downright dangerous. She could go to jail. Now that I knew about it, could

I go to jail, too? For what? Not disclosing a dead body? I would tell them I was doing research on my next script. No, no. If this blew up, got in the media, it could ruin the studio. Who would want to work for such a sleazy outfit? I laughed. That hardly made a difference these days, did it?

It was just after 8:30. I had time to get to a 9 a.m. meeting, one I rarely attended. Wouldn't see anyone I knew. Didn't want to tell anyone I was drinking. Didn't want to tell anyone *else*. Not yet.

So I drove to the bungalow and got my screwdriver breakfast from the fridge and put it between my legs as I drove out of the canyon and into another one. Parked in the church parking lot. Saw a lot of pickups. I gulped some of the vodka orange juice. I already felt high from the martini. I guessed my tolerance for alcohol was low these days. That was good. I didn't need as much.

I groaned. I did not want to do this. I needed something else. Hayword wasn't gonna fuck me now. Maybe Sally would be up for it. No. She was married, had kids, and we worked together. *Come on, Brooke.*

Mark. We weren't officially over, right? I bet he'd take me back. He wouldn't care if I was drinking. He hadn't before. He minded it, but he liked fucking me better when I was drunk I bet. After all, he was a drunk, too. One who hadn't had a drink in how many years? I didn't know. We never talked about it. He went to his meetings. And I went to mine. When I went to mine.

"Brooke," I whispered. "Go to the meeting. Go to the meeting."

I watched the people filing through the open door to go downstairs to the meeting room. Suddenly I recognized one of the people heading toward the door. I hadn't seen him in a few years—not since I screamed at him in another parking lot after another AA meeting. I had been so pissed at him. Ryan Nichols: Alberto's baby daddy.

I pressed on the car horn. Everyone looked my way, even Ryan. I opened the window so that my face was visible. Everyone else kept walking. Ryan stopped and stared at me.

I felt a lump in my throat. I had loved him so much at one point in my life. I had risked everything for him. Even my health: We hadn't used protection, and I had gotten pregnant. Then he left me. It was crazy what I had felt for him. Stupid. I couldn't imagine it now. Seemed like it happened to another person.

I waved him over. He hesitated and then started walking toward the car. As he got closer, I saw that he had aged very well in the intervening years. He was still gorgeous, and I remembered we had had a lot of fun making Alberto—even though we weren't trying to make a baby. We had done it up, down, turned around. He was very good at pleasure.

"Hello, Brooke," he said, stopping a few feet from the car.

"Hello, Ryan," I said. "You wanna blow this meeting and take a drive?"

"Um, why? So you can kill me?" he asked.

Last time I had seen him I had called him every name I could think of and then some. I hated him so much for leaving me and for not even knowing Alberto had been born.

But now . . . I didn't feel anything.

So I laughed. I hoped it was a charming laugh.

"No," I said. "I want to be spontaneous. Come on. You owe me for deserting me when I was pregnant."

He flinched.

"I swear," I said. "I have no weapons."

Ryan got into the car. We looked at each other.

What the fuck was I doing?

Maybe I should kill him, make him pay for what he did to

me. To us. I could put him in the garage next to Marv. I laughed. I wasn't a killer. I was a lover.

"What's so funny?" Ryan asked.

"You got in the car with me," I said. "You're done for now."

I tore out of the parking lot. For a second, I wished I had Hayword's sports car.

"Do you know this area?" I asked.

"Sure," he said.

"Take me some place beautiful then," I said. "Where we can see the world."

"OK," he said. And he told me where to go as we talked, interrupting every once in a while to tell me to turn here or there. It was a beautiful blue day, but I noticed none of it. I kept thinking about how close Ryan was to me. Thought about how many times we had been naked together. How he had ruined my marriage to Hayword. No, it had already been ruined. I was tired of being Hayword's cheerleader back then, his midwife, his mother. We had our life in Hollywood that seemed so . . . vacuous. Even more so after the success of our movie *Love and Other Insanities.*

I hadn't much liked life in the Midwest either, before Hollywood. I thought life in Michigan was provincial, claustrophobic.

Maybe I just couldn't be happy anywhere.

"How are the kids?" Ryan asked.

"You mean the ones who aren't dead?"

"Jesus, Brooke."

I laughed. "This is who I am," I said. "You must have always known that. A fucking bitch on wheels. Isn't that what they used to say?"

"I don't know who says that," Ryan said.

"I remember you said it more than once when you were fucking me," I said.

"It was a compliment," Ryan said.

I laughed. He chuckled.

"The kids are fine," I said. He didn't need to know. "How are you? Married with children now?"

"No," he said. "Just trying to stay sober and live day by day. I've gotten some work directing low budget movies."

"Good for you," I said.

"That sounds so patronizing," he said. "I know you own a studio now with Sally St. James and Hayword. You two still together?"

"We haven't been together since I got sober," I said. "But yes, we run the studio together. Sort of. It's a small studio."

"Your zombie movies are blockbusters," he said.

"They aren't zombie movies," I said. "They are more rightfully called the living dead."

"Aren't the main characters called zombie aliens?"

"Yes, but when you say it out loud it sounds stupid."

He laughed. "I liked the movies. Especially the last one. Made me cry. The shot of Aiden's arm coming out of the grave. Her dead son coming to life. Beautiful. I can't wait for the next one."

I groaned. I didn't want to talk about this. I wanted to fuck. I wanted to fuck Ryan and then leave him.

"Is Aiden going to be alive in the next one?" he asked.

"That's a secret," I said.

"Because you don't know?"

I glanced over at him. Maybe he wasn't as stupid as I thought he was.

"Because in real life, dead sons don't come back to life," I said. "My son didn't come back to life. So, no, I don't know what to do next."

Shit. I hadn't realized that was the crux of my problem. How was I going to bring a dead half-zombie alien/half human back to life again? Again.

"I would love to have that problem," Ryan said.

"Would you now?"

Suddenly the road turned and ended in a small parking lot, and we were somehow up on a hill or ridge looking out at the Pacific ocean.

I gasped. Even my alcohol-addled brain registered the beauty.

"How'd you do that?" I said.

He shrugged. "I found it one day when I was drunk. Almost went over the edge. That was the day I decided to go to rehab." He nodded, smiling at the memory.

I leaned over and kissed him. I practically fell into him. He did not pull away. We crawled into the backseat and began making out. I felt a rush of adrenalin and pleasure. I liked his smell. I liked his taste. I put my hand between his legs and felt his balls but not his penis. He tried to slip his hands into my pants.

"No," I said. "I can finger myself. I want to fuck you."

He kept kissing me, we kept rubbing each other. I felt like I could come any second. But he stayed as soft as over-done noodles.

I straddled him.

"Let me do you," he said.

"No. I want your dick." He had never been particularly adept at any oral or digital sex, if I was remembering correctly.

"Brooke," he whispered. "I can't."

"Why? Did they cut it off? Are you sick? Are you impotent?"

He nodded.

"What are you saying yes to?"

"I haven't had an erection for years now," he said.

"Really?" He couldn't have told me that before we drove up the mountain and I got all hot and bothered?

"After I got sober," he said, "it never got really hard again. And after a while, I couldn't get it up."

"Did you try any medication?"

"Once or twice," he said. "It got hard, but that was about it. I didn't feel anything."

"Who cares if you felt anything?" I said. "You could still give someone a good ride."

I was starting to lose my buzz and my desire.

"Honestly, Brooke," he said. "It got really bad after that time I saw you at the AA meeting. I had just found out that Alberto had died, and then you went after me. I stopped dating pretty much. And then, you know, it wouldn't get hard."

I laughed. "Are you blaming me for this? That's giving me a lot of power. Maybe you brought me up here to kill me?"

"Um, can we not talk about killing while my hands are in your pants?"

"Don't you want me," I asked as I kissed his ear. "You always wanted me."

Until I got knocked up.

I bit his ear.

"Ouch," he said.

I moved away from him and reached for my OJ jug. I took a swig. Then I held it out to him. "You want some?"

"What is it?"

"Orange juice," I said. He started to take it from me, but I pulled it back. Then I said, "It's got vodka in it."

We stared at each other.

"I'm sorry I left you," he said. "I'm so sorry about Alberto. I wish I had known him."

"He was a good boy," I said.

A tear rolled down his cheek. Or was it my cheek?

Ryan took the jug from me. His hands were shaking as he

brought it up to his lips. And then he took several gulps and handed the jug back to me. I put it on the front seat again.

Then we began kissing. I pulled off my pants. I couldn't believe I was doing this. It was like something out of a dream. I opened the glove compartment and dug around until I found a condom. Then I straddled Ryan and undid his pants, unzipped him. He was hard as a rock. We pressed against one another. I put the condom on him. I was still proficient at that. Then I put his penis between my legs and pushed myself down on it. It hurt both of us a bit. He began to cry, and I moved up and down on him until we both had an orgasm, almost at the same time.

I wondered for a moment if it had been like this when we made Alberto. No. Ryan had never cried back then. And he had liked fucking me from behind most of the time, sometimes with me on my hands and knees like I was a fucking dog. Or he was a fucking dog? Never understood that. Did men have some secret fetish about acting like dogs or animals? Or was it that they didn't want to see our faces, they wanted to fuck us for the holes in our bodies?

So now on this mountainside, I was fucking Ryan because of all the holes in his body. Right? The holes in his soul.

Or maybe I was trying to fill up the monstrous hole in my own soul.

Naw. I couldn't have a soul. I had just handed an alcoholic a drink. And then I had fucked him.

I didn't know what was worse: Him leaving me after he found out I was pregnant. Or this, this moment, as I got off of him.

"Good news is there won't be an Alberto two," I said as I pulled my pants back on.

"Oh, great. Good news." He wiped the tears from his face and then zipped up his pants.

"See," I said, "you're cured. Now you can go fuck to your heart's content."

He stared at me. He looked absolutely ruined.

"I guess you did bring me up here to kill me after all," he said.

I opened my mouth to deny it. To tell him he had just had a great fuck and a good time. But I couldn't quite bring myself to say anything.

"Come on," I said. "I'll take you back to the church."

We got in the front seats again, and we drove away.

FOUR

We hardly said a word to one another as I drove back to the church. Every once in a while, Ryan picked up the jug of orange juice vodka and took a gulp. He stared out the window, mostly. I had thought revenge would feel a lot better than this—if that was what this was.

I stopped the car at the back of the church. Ryan opened the door to the car, got out, and walked toward the building. He did not look back.

I sure knew how to win friends and influence people.

I parked in the lot for a bit and checked my phone. I had texts from Sally, Fern, and David—and four from Mark. Nothing from Hayword. That meant he was still pissed. Nothing from Joanie. Maybe she had come to her senses and called the police about Marv. Dead Marv.

I read Sally's messages first.

"The investors want to talk to you," she wrote. "Can you come by today?"

Oh fuck. I had forgotten about investors. I had agreed to be a part of Back to Life Studios so I didn't have to deal with this kind of thing.

I texted back. "No. I'm busy. Another time?"

The phone rang almost immediately.

Fuck.

"Hi, Sally," I said. "How's it hangin'?"

"I don't know," she said. "I haven't seen it for a while."

"Trouble in paradise?" I asked.

"I dunno," Sally said. "Jonathan has seemed distracted lately. Won't tell me why. But who cares about real life. Why can't you come in today?"

"I've got things to do," I said.

"Like what?" she asked. "Are you working on the script? Because that's the only thing you should be doing."

"You aren't the boss of me," I said mildly.

"If we don't get this movie out, we're dead," Sally said, "and we will not come back to life. These guys are willing to give us some money."

"Can't I just fuck one of them?" I asked.

Sally laughed. "I have fucked you, and it ain't worth millions of dollars. Besides, we're respectable now. We don't do those kinds of things."

"Did you ever do those kinds of things?"

"Never," Sally said. She did not sound sincere.

"Spill," I said. "I'm in the mood."

"No," Sally said. She sighed. "It's a fucked up town, and we've all done some fucked up stuff."

"Not me," I said. "I am pure as the driven snow. I miss snow. Do you ever miss snow?"

"I'm from California," Sally said. "I don't miss any fucking snow. Come in and tell these guys about the movie."

"I want it to be a surprise," I said.

"So far that's working," Sally said. "The cast doesn't even have a treatment. We're filming in a month. Didn't we go through this last time?"

"And it all worked out," I said.

"I'll see you at Rio's at noon," Sally said. "I made a reservation."

"I can't make it downtown by then," I said.

"Do your best," Sally said. "And bring some pages."

She hung up.

"Well, fuck you, Sally," I said to the phone. "Fuck you, fuck you, fuck you."

I read Fern's text. Something about the character Molly in the movie. She made so many typos that it was difficult to read. David texted to say hello. "It was a good day today," he wrote. "I'm hearing some good ideas to combat climate change from the other kids."

I texted back, "You don't need to save the world."

He wrote back immediately. "Someone has to. You and Dad certainly didn't."

No, we had not saved the world. When had David turned into a little brat like his sister Fern? Fern was always mad at me. Now David was the same. Alberto would have been a teen now if he had lived. I wondered if he would have hated me, too.

I texted Joanie. "How's it going?"

"All good," she said. "All good. Sorry about the martini. I didn't mean to able you."

"Enable me."

"What?" she texted.

"You said 'able you.'"

"What's the difference?"

I sighed.

"Two letters."

"You at a meeting?"

I answered, "Yes, I am at a meeting."

This was exhausting. Best to ignore her.

I texted Hayword. "Are you up for a nooner?"

Why was I saying such things? I must have lost my mind yesterday. Was it the full moon? Had there been an alien invasion like in *Beauty and the Zombie?*

Hayword responded: "Your nooner is with Sally and our investors."

"I've never liked a crowd during sex," I texted.

"Have you gone to a meeting?"

They had all apparently forgotten how this works: They couldn't nag me into getting sober.

"I'm in the church parking lot right now."

Hayword didn't say anything, and that was pretty much the end of our conversation.

By the time I got back to the bungalow, I felt completely sober. I took a quick shower and put on jeans and a nice shirt. How else does a famous scriptwriter dress? I didn't drink anything. I hadn't been drunk for any Back to Life business, and I wasn't going to start now.

I got in my car, got onto the highway, and drove toward LA. When I neared Mark's exit, I remembered he had texted me, too, and I hadn't read them. I didn't know why. When we closed the restaurant, we both agreed to go back to our old houses for a while and reassess. He missed his friends and his mom. Beach life was too quiet for him. Me, too, really. I had thought I wanted to get away from all the bullshit of Hollywood, and once I was at the beach, I twiddled my thumbs. I waited for the next big catastrophe. I had fun when we were making movies, Hayword, Sally, and I. Otherwise, I was kind of antsy.

And once Mark and I got used to each other and weren't fucking every minute—and I wasn't drinking—life seemed kind of dull.

That was shocking to me. I got the quiet life I wanted, and then I didn't want it.

I needed to check in with Mark, but not this minute. I was going to be late getting to lunch as it was.

A valet parked my car, and I hurried into Rio's. I saw Sally at her favorite table with two young guys. My heart sank. I wasn't going to be seducing either of them. As I walked toward the table, I remembered Sally had said they were two tech guys who had made a lot of money doing something or another. I didn't care. Just give me your money.

The boys rose when I got to the table. The shorter one with blond hair and very white skin pulled out my chair, and I sat in it. The taller one with black hair and browner skin smiled. Sally introduced us. Damon Friend was the blond; Paolo Allende was the black-haired one.

I said, "It's cold and flu season so I don't shake hands. But I'm glad to meet you. Damon Friend. What a great name. Did you make that up?"

He smiled. "No, my parents were hippies. They wanted to be everyone's friends, and they loved Damon Runyon and Damon Knight's work."

I nodded. "That's interesting. Two very different writers."

"Guys and dolls, and it's a cookbook," Paolo said.

Damon rolled his eyes. "He's not a reader. He's more of a visual guy."

"Yep. I'm the movie guy," Paolo said. "I loved all your movies."

"Are you related to the writer Isabel Allende or her uncle Salvador Allende?"

"I wish," Paolo said. "Wouldn't that make a great movie?

Tech entrepreneur is related to the great writer Isabel and the president the CIA assassinated?"

"He hasn't read a word she has written," Damon said. "Just so you know."

I smiled. I could like these kids.

"I ordered you a BLT," Sally said. "They have the best BLTs in the world here. Turkey bacon. Organic beefsteak heirloom tomatoes. Lettuce to die for. And gluten-free bread. Brooke loves them. Don't you, Brooke?"

I frowned. Sally sounded anxious. I grinned. "Whatever you order me, I will enjoy. Even got me some sparkling water while you all drink champagne. How fun."

"Well, you are driving," Sally said, giving me a look.

"I'm happy to hear you're interested in investing in Back to Life Studios," I said. "How can I help? As Sally has mentioned, I'm sure, I'm pretty much the writer. I leave the schmoozing and boozing to Sally and Hayword."

"Hayword is going to try to stop by," Sally said.

I frowned. "Really?"

"*Love and Other Insanities* is one of my old time all time favorite movies," Paolo said.

"It's not that old," I said.

"It's over twenty years old," Sally said. "They were about two. It's old to them."

"Ten," Paolo said. "I was ten. We know Katherine and Oscar Bernstein, by the way. They speak so highly of you. They said without you and Hayword's *Love and Other Insanities*, they wouldn't be the success they are today or have the catalog they have."

Weird. Their names had come up twice in one day.

"How kind," I said.

"I would love to have their catalog," Sally said.

"I heard rumors they might be retiring," Damon said, "And

looking for someone to run the studios. Have you been out to their place? It is amazing."

"I have," Sally said. "Many years ago. My kids loved it. I'll have to check that rumor out. Or not." She shrugged. "I already have my dream job." She sounded like she was trying to convince herself.

Paolo said, "And the *Beauty and the Zombie* movies are so intense and so real," as if the conversation had never moved away from him. "I root for Colleen and her son Aiden—and Thomas. They are great characters. We're glad to hear that the old cast is returning."

"We start shooting in a month," Sally said.

The waitress brought our food. I was starting to get a headache. It was a little too noisy in here, and these kids were a little too intense.

We ate quietly for a few minutes. Then Damon said, "I met your daughter Fern the last time I came to the studio. She seemed nice."

"Fern nice?" I said. "Are you sure it was her?"

Sally St. James shot me a look.

I said, "I'm kidding. She's a treasure."

"She knows the business," Damon said.

"It is a family business," Sally said.

"I asked Fern about the story for the third movie," Damon said, "but she said she didn't know anything about it. You keep it pretty close to the vest."

"That's right," I said. "Plus we don't want it to get out and ruin the surprise."

"Is Aiden alive in the third one?" Paolo asked. "He'd have to be, wouldn't he? That was his hand that came out of the grave. That must feel so sweet, so cathartic, to make him alive, especially after what happened to your son Alberto. I figure the whole series is an homage to him, right? Aiden equals Alberto. The names both start with 'a.' They both died."

I stopped chewing. Sally's eyes widened. It seemed as if the whole restaurant stopped and we were all frozen in time and space.

I looked at Paolo. He was still chewing, completely oblivious.

"This time of year must be particularly difficult," Paolo said. "With Alberto's birthday and all."

I stared at him. Alberto's birthday? What was he talking about? It wasn't February. Wait. It was February. I closed my eyes. Fuck. Yesterday was his birthday. What the flying fuck? I had forgotten his birthday. Again. We had all forgotten his birthday. I felt like I was going to throw up.

"Paolo," Damon said. "That's pretty personal stuff."

The world began to throb. Or was that my head?

"I do my research," Paolo said. "They should know that."

"Who the fuck are you?" I said. I looked at Sally. "Who the fuck are these punks? Are you sure they don't work for the tabloids?" I looked at Paolo again. "Who the fuck are you to even say my son's name?"

"I-I thought it was common knowledge," he said. "And it happened so long ago. I figured it had been talked about before, in relation to your movies."

I pushed my chair away from the table and stood. I wanted to punch Paolo.

Just then, Hayword showed up. He looked at me. He was still angry with me. But then he must have seen my face— truly—and he knew something was wrong.

"What's going on?" Hayword asked.

"They were talking about Alberto's death," I said, "ten seconds after meeting me. Like it was fucking nothing. Mentioned his birthday yesterday." Hayword and I reached for each other's hands and hung on tightly.

Damon was standing now. Paolo looked perplexed.

"He didn't mean anything," Damon said.

"This meeting is over," I said.

Hayword and I hurried away. I was shaking as I walked out into the bright blue day. Handed the valet my ticket. He brought the car. Hayword and I got inside, and I drove down the block and parked it. We sat in silence.

"We forgot his fucking birthday," I said. "Again. We did that a few years ago. How come now?" I put my head on the steering wheel. "I guess that explains some things."

Hayword stared out the window. After a minute or two, he said, "I didn't forget his birthday. That's why we had the picnic yesterday."

"What?" I looked at him. "But you never said anything. And Fern wasn't there. We usually have a cake or a ceremony or something, all of us."

"We haven't done anything for a while," Hayword said.

"You should have said something. I forgot."

"Because you were drinking," Hayword said.

"No," I said. "No!" I was drinking now, but I wasn't then. I wasn't yesterday. Until I was.

That must be why I started drinking. It wasn't because my brain was fucked. Or I was fucked. I was still mourning the death of my baby son. I nodded.

"I'm sorry about yesterday," I said. "I don't know what happened."

I didn't look at Hayword, but I could see he was shaking his head.

"Did you call Patricia?" I asked.

"It's none of your business," Hayword said.

My phone buzzed. I looked down. "Get your ass back in here." From Sally St. James.

"Sally," I said. "She wants me back inside. Do we really need these guys?"

Hayword shrugged. "We're a small company. We need the cash. Of course, normally we would have a script and know how much the production will cost."

"I've given you the treatment," I said. "They're making the sets."

"To answer your question then: Yes, we need the money."

"Why aren't you outraged that he asked about our son?"

"Why are you?" Hayword asked.

"It was such a shock," I said. "From strangers. We don't talk about it."

"It was a shock that he knew Alberto's birthday and you didn't?" he asked.

"Wow," I said. "That's mean."

"Takes one to know one," he said.

"Get out," I said. "I'm not going back to that meeting. If we need the money, you and Sally can get it. It's your job, not mine."

"They want to schmooze with you," Hayword said. "They want to see pages."

"When does anyone show investors pages?" I asked.

"All the time," Hayword said.

"I'm not showing pages to anyone," I said, "until I'm ready."

"Because you don't have any or because you don't want anyone to see them?"

"Hayword," I said. "Can't you trust me on this?" I put my hand on his arm. "It's the middle of the day. We could go home and fool around."

Hayword pulled his arm away. "I guess this means you're

still drinking," he said, "because you'd only want to fuck me if you were drunk." He opened the car door.

"Not true," I said.

"You used to say that I acted like a child," he said. "I always wanted to be comforted. I wanted someone to hold me up and tell me things are gonna be OK. You said as adults we had to do things we didn't necessarily want to do. But when do you do something that you don't want to do?"

"All the time. Every minute of the day."

"Bullshit," he said. "We all work around you and your eccentricities."

"My eccentricities?" I said. "You mean my alcoholism?"

"Everything has to be your way," he said. "Otherwise you're going to break. We're all walking around trying to make sure we don't do anything that would cause you to break."

What was he talking about? Had he and Joanie gotten together to bitch about me?

"We need the money and you don't want to talk to these investors because they said something that hurt your feelings. How old are you?"

He got out of the car, shut the door, and walked away.

I didn't understand why he was so mad. I spent my life trying to fix all of their messes. Not the other way around.

I texted Sally, "Hayword is coming. I am not."

She texted back. "Don't be a fucking baby."

"Talking about my dead son = deal breaker."

I turned the phone off and then started the car.

"Fuck." I growled, turned the car off, got out, and practically ran to the restaurant. Nobody calls me a baby and gets away with it. I shook my head. I better never put that line in a script.

When I got to the table, Hayword was just sitting down again. They all looked up at me.

"You, Paolo, or whatever the fuck your name is," I said. I

was talking rather loudly. "Don't mention my son's name again. Learn some manners. I don't know you, you don't know me. What if I brought up the fact that you're impotent most of the time even though you're only in your thirties."

Paolo looked around the restaurant. Then he looked at me, "But that's not true. It only happened—"

I held up my hand. "Boundaries, son, boundaries. Unless I'm fucking someone, I really don't want to hear about their potency problems. And even then, I don't want to hear it. Now I appreciate that you both like our films. That's great. We like fans. In fact, I could write in minor roles for you both, like extras, if you invest, if you'd like that."

Both their faces brightened, as if they were 10 year olds about to eat a trough of ice cream. Or whatever it was that caused 10 year old faces to brighten.

"That would be great," Damon said.

"Only you," I said, looking at Paolo, "your character will be an asshole. You good with that?"

Paolo nodded. "Absolutely."

"Good," I said. "Now I've got pages to write. And no, you're not gonna see them. Maybe in a few days I'll send you a scene or two. Maybe. If you don't piss me off."

I glanced at Sally. She winked at me. I sighed. Sometimes I did really miss fucking her. I glanced over at Hayword, but he didn't look at me. He was the fucking baby, not me.

I turned and walked away. I needed a drink or a fuck. Or an AA meeting. I'd take whichever came first. So to speak.

FIVE

For some reason, the freeway was not busy. I drove my car north like a bat out of hell. I didn't care if a cop stopped me. I felt free. Empowered. I had had a drink and the world had not ended. I was still here. My family was still safe. I had probably even saved the investment deal for Back To Life Studios with those punk kids. Whatever their names were.

I wasn't drinking now, but if I wanted to drink, I could. It would not be the end of the world. What a glorious feeling. The sky was blue. No catastrophic lightning storm in the works. I could almost smell the ocean. *I had had a drink and the world hadn't ended.*

Granted, I had fucked my almost ex-husband and my ex-lover all within the space of about twelve hours. That was excessive even for me. I still wasn't sure why I had done it—or done them. It didn't matter. Nothing mattered but the sheer pleasure I felt right that second.

I was coming up to the exit to Mark's house, so I took it. I wanted to spread around this feeling. And Mark and I had not had sex for a while.

I grinned as I drove toward his neighborhood. He would be glad to see me. No doubt. Of course it was in the middle of the day. He would probably be out working.

I turned down his street. I could see his driveway. His truck was parked there. Good. I wasn't sure how or why we had grown apart. He had stuck with me through everything. I thought the restaurant was his dream, but I was wrong. He only did the restaurant because he thought I would rather be with a chef than a plumber. He didn't realize I didn't actually care one way or another. I didn't know what I wanted to be when I grew up, so I thought I would help him be who he wanted to be. Turns out, being a plumber, hanging out with his friends, spending time with his mother, and being with me was what he wanted.

I parked my car in his driveway, glanced in the mirror, and then opened the car door, got out, and went to the front door. I had a key, but I knocked anyway. Then I tried the door. It was unlocked. I opened it and called, "Mark, it's Mac."

No one answered. I stepped inside and closed the door behind me. I felt a twinge of anxiety. I really didn't want to walk in on Mark on top of someone or in on someone on top of him.

"Mark!" I called again.

I walked into the living room. Everything looked the same as the last time I had been there. When had that been? Months? I went down the hall toward his bedroom. I steeled myself for what I was about to see. Mark was in bed, but he was by himself. And the room stunk of booze. A mixture of booze, urine, and vomit.

"What the fuck?" I said.

I hurried to the bed. Mark was snoring. Thank god. He was

alive. Mark had been sober all the years I had known him. I shook him.

"What?" he mumbled. I shook him again.

"Mark! Wake up!"

He opened his eyes and pushed himself up. He blinked hard. "What? What?"

Good gawd, he stunk. And he looked like hell. I backed away from him.

"Mac," he said. He sat on the edge of the bed. "Finally. I've been texting you. I called, too. Where have you been?"

"I thought we were taking a break from one another," I said.

"A break?" He looked at me. "I don't remember that. I thought you were living at the bungalow for a while until we figured out where we wanted to live. Together."

I frowned. "Really? That's not how I remember it. But that doesn't matter now. What happened?"

He groaned. "I drank. Something terrible happened, and I picked up a drink. I'm so so sorry." He put his head in his hands and began to cry.

What the fuck? I had never seen Mark like this. He was always so dignified. So in control. So competent.

I did not like seeing this.

"Do you have any alcohol in the house?" I asked. Just in case I needed a quick boost. "You know, so I can throw it out."

"I dunno," he said.

I was not in the mood for anyone else's drama. I was supposed to be in love with this man, but I just wanted to run away.

What was wrong with me?

"I need to talk to you," he said. "Why didn't you answer your texts?"

"Mark, it stinks in here," I said. "Why don't you splash your face, and I'll meet you out in the living room."

He nodded. "I won't be long."

"Are you still drunk?" I asked.

He breathed deeply, stared at the wall for a second, and then said, "A little."

I left the room and closed the door behind me. I went to the kitchen and looked around. A bottle of whiskey. Two shot glasses. Someone had been drinking with him. And beer cans. What on earth had happened to him? What had happened to us? We had been together, and then suddenly we weren't. We had always led pretty separate lives, but after the earthquake a couple years ago—and then the second movie coming out—we just didn't seem to connect as much. Or something.

I opened the whiskey bottle. The smell nauseated me. I quickly put the cap back on. I opened the cupboards and looked around until I found a chocolate bar. 70% dark cacao. I quickly unwrapped it and began to eat it. If I could have had an orgasm while eating it, it would have been the perfect end of a really weird day.

Mark walked into the kitchen as I finished the chocolate bar. He was dressed in a clean white t-shirt and blue jeans. His hair was combed away from his face. He was as handsome as ever. I was so tempted to ask if he wanted to get naked, but I stopped myself.

Mark went to the sink, took the cap off the whiskey, and poured it down the sink. He threw the bottle into the recycle box and turned on the water until we couldn't smell the whiskey any longer.

"Do you want to talk about it?" I asked.

Mark shook his head. "Now you want to talk?"

"Are you mad at me?" I asked.

"No," he said. "I'm mad at me."

I took out my phone, turned it on, and waited. I heard the ping of several text messages and a voice mail. I searched for Mark's texts.

From Mark: "Please call. Having a difficult time."

I glanced up at Mark and then looked down again. Second message. "Brooke, please call me. I left you a voice message."

Third message: "I want a drink."

Fourth message: "I need you. Where are you?"

"Fuck," I whispered. I listened to my voice messages. One from David wondering where I was yesterday. One from Sally St. James asking when the manuscript would be finished and telling me to call her ASAP, from today. One from Mark: "Have you dropped off the face of the earth? Where are you? I need you." Two days ago.

"I'm sorry, Mark," I said. "I didn't see any of these."

"Why were you ignoring me?" he asked.

"I wasn't," I said. "It was Alberto's birthday yesterday. I guess I've been kind of depressed. I was ignoring everyone." That wasn't true, but I didn't want a big scene now. Obviously I had failed him when he needed me.

"What happened?" I asked for the 17 millionth time. I leaned against the counter; he leaned against the fridge.

"I didn't like us being separated," he said. "It stressed me out. I couldn't get a hold of you."

"But you knew where I was," I said. "You could have come over."

"Why? It seemed like you wanted me gone. You got all of your possessions out of our apartment when I wasn't there. It was as if we were breaking up."

Well, it did feel that way.

"Weren't we?" I asked. "I mean, you wanted to move back home."

"I wanted you to come with me," he said.

"Mark, we've had that conversation a thousand times," I said. "I wasn't going to move here. I wouldn't be happy here. It's too far from my kids."

"The beach was just as far," he said.

"But there was the beach," I said.

"And here there was me," he said. He shook his head. "You could never let go of the life you had with Hayword, no matter how messed up it was. You never even divorced him. How do you think that made me feel?"

"I thought you were over that," I said. "I thought we settled that years ago."

"You settled it by not talking about it," he said. "I was just supposed to accept it. Just like Hayword was supposed to accept you and me fucking. And you fucking everyone else under the sun."

"Hey," I said. "That is all water under the bridge."

"I need a meeting," he said.

"OK," I said. "We can talk about this later."

He looked at me. "I'm not blaming you," he said. "I was just trying to explain how I was feeling. Like I was never good enough for you, in your eyes."

"That's your shit," I said, "not mine."

"I took a drink yesterday," he said.

What the fuck was in the air yesterday that we both started drinking?

"Then Clare came over," he said. "And we had sex."

Clare. Who was Clare? Was that his ex-wife?

Mark was watching me. Did he want a reaction? Not want one? Was I relieved? Was I horrified? I didn't know. I felt so little. When had this started? When had I started feeling so little? Was there something wrong with me?

"I'm so sorry, Brooke," he said. "I know it's not an excuse, but I was drunk."

"Don't we do what we really want to do when we're drunk? It just gives us an excuse?"

He shook his head. "No. I wanted you. And then she was here."

"She was here?" I said. "So a woman showed up. She has the right orifices and you fuck her? Wow. I bet she'd be glad to hear that you fucked her because she was here."

"She was here," Mark said, "and she was listening to me. She was seeing me. She wanted to be with me."

OK. That was worse. He fucked her because she wasn't me and she showed up.

I wanted to scream, "Guess what, you cheating motherfucker: I was with Hayword yesterday. Sexually speaking. And then this morning, I fucked Ryan. So I've got you beat!"

But I didn't say it.

"Do you want me to look up some meeting times for you?" I asked.

Mark shook his head. "No, I know when and where to go. Will you come with me?"

Why did he ask me that? We never went to the same meetings together. Or rarely. Did he know I was drinking, too?

I wanted to say, "You stuck your dick into another woman. No, I don't want to go to an AA meeting with you."

"Did you at least use protection?" I asked. Pot calling the pan something or another.

"I don't know," he said. "I can't remember."

"Fuck," I said. "No, I'm not going to a fucking meeting with you. I'm sorry I didn't answer your phone calls or texts. But I can't be with you now. I can't help you through this. I thought you were the one person who would never betray me, and look what you've done."

"I didn't betray you," he said. "I had sex with another woman. I thought you didn't want me any more."

I stared at him. I wanted to feel something: love or hate or outrage. But I didn't feel anything.

"Maybe I don't want you any more," I said. "Especially now that you've got some other woman's cum all over your dick."

With those loving and caring words, I hurried out of the house. I got into my car and drove away. Only down the block. I stopped to make a few calls. Now I felt something. Now that I was away from him, I was angry.

Only I wasn't certain why.

I called our offices. Caryn, our receptionist slash secretary, answered.

"Hi, Caryn," I said. "Can you get me the home address of a Ryan Nichols? He should be in the Director's Directory."

"Sure," she said. "Sally said if you called she wanted you to call her."

"OK," I said. "Will you text me Ryan's address?"

"I will," she said. We ended the call.

I breathed deeply and then phoned Sally. When she answered, I said, "Are they giving us the money?"

"Yes," Sally said.

"So I saved the day."

"It didn't need saving until you started calling people names."

"He was wrong," I said.

"He's a stupid kid," Sally said. "A stupid rich kid. And there are some caveats on the investment."

"Like what?"

"They need to see some pages," Sally said.

"They are fucking children," I said. "They wouldn't know a good script if it hit them in the face."

"Let's not hit them with anything," Sally said. "They want to see some pages in a week. By next Monday."

"Even I'm not that fast."

Silence. And then, "Does that mean you don't have any pages done?"

Crap. "Um, no. I have pages. I have lots of pages. I've just got some personal stuff going on."

"You've always got something going on, Mac," she said. "What is it now?"

"Don't talk to me like I'm two years old," I said.

"You've had two years to write this fucking thing," Sally said.

"Mark cheated on me," I said. OK. That wasn't what was causing me stress or a delay in the manuscript, but I wasn't going to tell her I was drinking. Or had drunk. Drank?

"That sucks," Sally said. "I'm sorry to hear that. What are you gonna do? If Jonathan cheated on me, I would kill him and the bitch he cheated with." She sounded angry.

"Guess you've thought about this," I said.

"Lately he's seemed so distance," Sally said, "so I've been wondering if he's cheating. Been thinking about what I'd do. When I think about everything I've given up to have this family."

"You mean like fucking me?"

Sally laughed. "We were over long before Jonathan. Besides, you told me I was a pain in the ass."

"It's true," I said. "In general women are more of a pain in the ass than men. Thank god I never fucked Joanie. You wouldn't believe the mess she's gotten herself into."

"Do tell."

Oh shit. It was a secret.

"I better wait," I said. "I'll tell you when I know more."

"There's something else the boys want," Sally said. "Damon wants Fern to be involved with the project."

"You want me to pimp out my daughter to get this investment?"

"Of course not," Sally said. "But she's closer to their age, and Damon likes her. What could it hurt? She does work for the company. Why not?"

"It's up to her," I said. "But what do you know about them? Are they drinkers? Druggies? Misogynists?"

"Do you know the answers to those questions for everyone your daughter dates?"

"Dates? I thought she was going to be *working* with them. If they are working together, they cannot date until the project is finished. Make sure that's clear."

"All right," Sally said. "Jesus. But we start filming in a month. If I don't have the script by next Monday, we will have to hire someone else, and we'll lose these investors."

"You can't do that," I said. "I'm part owner, and I have to agree to that. And I don't."

"Just write the fucking script!" Sally said. She sounded angry again. Why did everyone sound so angry with me?

Because everyone was angry with me.

"Fuck off," I said.

And that was the end of the phone call. Just then, Caryn sent me a text: Ryan Nichols' address. He still lived close to Mark.

I put the address into my GPS and headed out.

I didn't know what I was going to do when I got to his house. I felt out of control and peaceful and horrible all at the same time. It was as if I had been tied up in knots for years, and now I was coming . . . undone.

A few blocks and a few minutes later, I was walking up the sidewalk to Ryan's nondescript one-story ranch house. When I got to the door, I rang the bell. Ryan answered. He looked surprised to see me. Or shocked. Or afraid. He also looked drunk.

I said, "You promised that we would be together forever."

He took a deep breath. "I obviously didn't mean it."

"I was in such grief when you left," I said. "I'm sure that

grief affected Alberto. I'm sure that stress contributed to his death from SIDS."

"So you're saying I'm the reason our son died?"

I felt a twinge of fury. (Can one have a twinge of fury?) How dare he call Alberto *our* son.

"Yes, I am blaming you," I said.

"What can I do about it now?" he asked.

"Nothing," I answered. "Just don't do it to anyone else, ever again."

"I was young and stupid," he said. "And I was afraid. I didn't know anything about raising a kid."

"So you just left?"

"It was a complete asshole move," he said. "Do you want to come in for a beer?"

I shook my head. "I'll go to a meeting with you."

"I've already been," he said. "It didn't help."

"It doesn't work that way," I said.

"How would you know?"

"You got coffee?" I asked.

He nodded, moved out of the way, and I stepped into Ryan Nichols' house. I followed him into the kitchen. Somehow we bumped into each other. We started kissing again.

I pulled away and asked, "Do you have any chocolate?"

"No."

I shrugged. "OK. I guess we better fuck then."

And that's what I did for the rest of the afternoon: Alberto's baby daddy and I had sex. Several times. Apparently I had actually cured him of impotence by getting him to drink. Or something. Neither of us drank anything, but he went into the bathroom a couple of times and came out happy. I figured he was taking something.

"Let's not use protection this time," he said mid-afternoon.

"We can make another baby, to make up for what happened to Alberto."

"You don't trade dead children for living children," I said. "That's disgusting."

"That's not what I'm saying. We could have another one. And do right by it. I wouldn't leave this time."

I laughed, grabbed my shirt by the bed and put it on. "And what, we'd live here and live happily ever after? I am not that woman you left behind a decade and a half ago. I am meaner and leaner."

"Obviously," Ryan said. "I don't care."

"You don't want to have a baby with me," I said. "You don't know me. You're just higher than a kite."

"I know," he said. "But I can fuck like a stud again. It's great. You ready to go again?"

"I have to get a drink." I got out of bed and stumbled to the kitchen, half-dressed. I looked around for some liquor and found an open bottle of vodka. I took a gulp. I loved the way it burned my throat. I hurried down the hall again. Ryan came out of the bedroom and pushed me gently up against the wall.

"Here," he said. "For old time's sake."

"Fucking standing up or against a wall?" I said.

"Both," he said.

He picked me up by my thighs. I put my arms around his neck as he maneuvered his penis into my vagina. I loved feeling the wall against my back, Ryan's dick inside me, the vodka in my belly. I moaned with pleasure.

Then something turned. In my stomach. "Oh no," I said, a second before I vomited all over Ryan. Yep. Right in his face and on his bare chest.

He screamed and dropped me. Fortunately, I landed on my feet, and I ran to the bathroom. Where I threw up again.

I heard Ryan in the hallway. "What the fuck?" he was saying.

I wiped my mouth and stood. I reeked. I turned the water on in the shower and stepped into it. I let the water run over me, washing away all the vomit and all the sin. I didn't know why I threw up. Maybe I had developed an allergy to vodka?

I came out of the bathroom, all dry and clean, as Ryan was walking down the hall toward me. He was dressed. He must have showered, too.

"Sorry about that," I said. "You might have a bad batch of vodka."

"This is certainly your day for revenge," he said. "You got me to drink again, and then you vomited all over me while we were having sex. I don't know how much worse this day can get."

I laughed. What an asshole he was. Why had I come here?

"I'm sorry for what I did to you all those years ago," he said. "I'm sorry about Alberto. But this, whatever this is, is crazy. I need to go to a meeting."

I suddenly felt very naked. I took the towel off my head and wrapped it around my body.

"There's a meeting down the street in about 15 minutes," he said. "I'm going. Do you want to come?"

"Sure," I said. "Text me the address, and I'll meet you there. I need to get dressed."

"OK. Lock the door when you leave."

Then he was gone, out of sight. I heard the front door open and close. I went to the bedroom, retrieved my clothes, and got dressed. My stomach still felt strange. I needed something to eat. I opened Ryan's fridge. It was nearly empty except for some cold cuts. From Ruby's. Very expensive. She made great bread, too. I looked around the kitchen until I found half a loaf of her Como bread. Also expensive. I made a sandwich and ate a few delicious bites. I put half of it in my purse. I dropped the par-tially-eaten half into the sink, where Ryan would see it.

Then I took some red lipstick from the bottom of my purse. I pulled the top off as I stood in the living room looking around. I turned the lipstick so it was all the way up. I liked the color scheme in Ryan's house. One living room wall was dark turquoise. I stood on his couch and leaned forward. Then, using my lipstick as a pen, I wrote on his wall in big capital letters "LOSER." I turned the lipstick back down, put the top on again, and dropped it on the couch. The lipstick was contaminated now. I wouldn't use it again. I supposed my vagina was contaminated now, too, again, with Ryan cooties.

Oh well. I wasn't leaving that behind.

I left the house and drove away.

SIX

I drove right by Mark's house. I thought about stopping to see if he was all right. His truck was there. But I kept going. My phone rang soon after. I pulled over to the side of the road.

It was David.

"Mom," he said. "Where are you? You were supposed to pick me up from school."

"What? Why?" We had bought him a car as soon as he got his license so that we wouldn't have to be there to pick him up.

"The car is in the shop," he said. "Dad reminded you."

Shit. He had reminded me.

"I'm sorry," I said. "I had a meeting downtown, and I forgot. I'm still in the city. I'll never get there in time. Aren't you there kind of late?"

"I had my climate change study group," he said. "Do you ever listen to a fucking thing I say?"

"David," I said. "Language, please. I'm sorry. I'll call your dad and see if he is at the house."

"Don't bother," David said. "I'll do it." And the call ended.

"He fucking hung up on me," I said. "That little shit."

I had always liked David. Of course I loved all three of my children. Alberto never got old enough for me to dislike him. But Fern had. I did not like her. We had our moments over the years where it seemed like we had reached a rapprochement. Then something would happen or the winds would shift, and she hated me all over again. I still loved her, but who wants to be around someone who is so disagreeable all the time?

David had always been agreeable until now. He had been worried most of his life about something. He was afraid. He had lots of anxiety. But he liked me. He never hated me. He never accused me of ruining his life. Fern had accused me of ruining her life since she first became a teenager. Now that she was grown up, in her twenties, working a real job her mother and father got her, she was still testy. Now David was apparently following in her footsteps. I did not like that.

I called David. He answered with, "What?"

"Listen, David," I said. "I am sorry I didn't pick you up. But that's no reason to act like a little shit. I get enough of that crap from your sister. You speak to me respectfully or don't speak to me at all."

"You mean I have that choice?" he said.

Little fucker.

"What could I have possibly done to make you so angry with me?" I asked. "We had a great relationship and then suddenly the past few months, you've been treating me like crap."

"I suppose you're going to use that as an excuse for why you started drinking?" He said it combatively, but I could hear the fear hidden behind the words. He was worried he had caused my relapse.

Maybe I could use his treatment of me as an excuse for my drinking.

Jesus.

No, no. Through it all, I had been a good mother. I never let them know how I was really feeling. Never let them know how drunk I was. I was a good mother no matter what. Right? That was a good thing, not telling them anything about how I felt or what I was going through. Besides, I was a drunk ages ago; I had been sober for years now.

"No," I said. "And I'm not drinking." Not now. Hadn't had a drink in hours. OK, I had had a drink, but I had vomited it all up. "Besides, I wouldn't blame you for my drinking."

"See, you're still lying," David said. "I know about all the men you slept with when you were a drunk."

All the men *and* women. I thought he already knew that. Hadn't we talked about it?

"You cheated on Dad over and over," he said. "It wasn't just Alberto's father."

"That was so long ago," I said. "I'm a different person. I've made amends."

"You haven't made amends to us," David said. "I don't remember you ever making amends to the family."

"I did," I said. "I'm sorry if you don't remember, but I apologized to all three of you. Why is this coming up now?"

"Because I know now what you did," David said. "And I can't believe Dad just forgave you and now you're sleeping together again."

"Who is telling you all of this?" I asked.

"It doesn't matter," he said.

"It most certainly does matter," I said. "Who is saying these things to you?"

It had to be Fern or Hayword. Hayword was the only other person who knew we had had sex.

"Your father should not be talking to you about these kinds of things," I said.

"It's not Dad," David said. "I found a site on the dark web. It's called the Whore of Hollywood, and it has a list of all the people you've had sex with."

"What?" I said. Oh my gawd. This couldn't be true. No, no, calm down, calm down. No one in the world knew everyone I had had sex with. Not even me. I certainly had never written anything down.

"Are there pictures?" I blurted out.

"No!" David said.

"You believed something on the dark web?" I said. "Why didn't you just ask me about it?"

"How could I ask my mother if she is a whore?"

"For one thing, you would never ask that of anyone. That's a derogatory term usually used against women."

"Men can be whores, too," he said.

"The word comes from the Horae, or hours," I said. "The Horae were sacred priestesses who knew the mysteries of sex and helped teach men about them so they would be better lovers."

"Is that what you were doing?" David sounded disgusted.

"No," I said. "The point isn't what I was or wasn't doing. Whore is now a misogynist term used against women to try to take our power away. Send me the link. Or whatever it is you do to get on the dark web. I need to figure this out."

"Does that mean you didn't cheat on Dad?" David asked.

"That's a complex question," I said. "You know that Dad wasn't Alberto's biological father."

"Yeah," he said, "but I thought he was the only one."

"It's really none of your business."

"That means yes, you cheated on Dad."

"That means it's none of your fucking business!" I said. "Do you want me to call a car service for you or can you find a way home?"

"I'll find a way," he said.

I immediately called Hayword. I was surprised when he answered.

"I was supposed to pick up David," I said. "But I forgot. Are you at the house? Can you pick him up?"

"Where have you been all afternoon?" he asked. "Did you find another old beau to fuck today?"

I gasped. How could he know? He couldn't, he couldn't. He was just being mean.

"I was at a meeting," I said.

"Which one?" He didn't believe me.

"Can you pick him up or not?"

"I can and I will."

I ended the call. I looked at the clock. If I got on the freeway now it would be hours until I got home. I hung my head. I was closer to the studio, traffic-wise. Maybe someone was still there who could help me with this Whore of Hollywood website. I glanced at my phone. David had sent me a link. I didn't dare look at it.

It took me a while to get to our offices, but finally I drove into the lovely complex of old bungalows that were now offices, mostly for movie people. We called our offices a studio, but we didn't actually have any places to make movies, not like the old MGM studios: We just had offices. When we made a movie, we were mostly on location.

I used my key to go through the front door of Back to Life Studios. Caryn was still at her desk, but the doors were locked. She smiled when she saw me. "You decided to avoid the traffic, too," she said.

I nodded. "It's been a clusterfuck day," I said. "Hey, Caryn, is there anyone here who could help me get onto the dark web? Is that what it's called?"

"I could," she said. "I keep an eye on it in case anyone is saying bad things about our actors or directors. I have an anonymizing tool on my computer. It's part of my job."

"Oh," I said. "I had no idea." I really was fairly ignorant about our operations. Why was that?

"I'm sorry I didn't know that," I said. I showed her my phone. "My son says there's a website there called the Whore of Hollywood, and it's all about me. It has a list of people I've had sex with. Although that's impossible. I mean, it can't be true. But I need to see it."

"Sure," Caryn said. "It'll take me a minute."

I nodded. "Thanks. I'll go to my office," I said. "Haven't been there in a while."

I walked down the narrow hall. I liked the light yellow walls and the prints of flowers and beaches penned in by tasteful frames. It was all lovely and soothing. My office was decorated in pastels. I only had one painting on one wall: It was a colored egg with a deep blue background. The name of the painting was Creation.

I glanced out the window. Darkness was falling.

I sat at my desk and smoothed my hand across the wooden top. It was such a lovely desk. Why didn't I ever come here?

"It's nice, isn't it?"

I looked up. My daughter was standing in the doorway.

"Hello, Fern," I said. "I didn't know you were here."

"And I didn't know you were here," she said. "May I come in?"

"Of course," I said.

She was holding a file folder. She stepped into the office and closed the door. She then closed the blinds so no one from the hallway could see us.

"We don't bug our offices, do we?" she asked as she sat in the chair on the other side of my beautiful wooden desk.

"Not that I know about," I said.

She was being quite pleasant, but she usually was at the office. I will give her that: She was professional.

"Mom, I tried to take care of this myself," she said. "But I haven't been able to. I apologize for bringing it to you, but you're the only one I can trust. You're the only one who will understand."

"Uh-oh," I said. "This doesn't sound good. You're buttering me up."

"I'm being blackmailed," she said. "They're telling me that they will publish these photos if I don't pay them a million dollars."

"What?" Was this a joke?

"Is this another one of your pranks?" I asked.

She frowned.

"Like the staged robbery in the restaurant?"

She shook her head. "No, Mom. I'm having an affair with a married man. I love him. He's promised to leave his wife. But if she finds out now, it could ruin everything, for all of us."

"For all of us?" I asked.

She put the folder on the desk and pushed it toward me. I did not want to open it. Did not want to see my daughter having sex.

I sighed and opened the folder. There in living color was my daughter, naked, astride a man's lap. The man's face was scrunched up in passion, I supposed, although he looked like he was taking a shit. The man was Jonathan, the husband of Sally St. James.

"Fuck," I said. "You've really screwed the pooch this time, sister."

SEVEN

"Who is blackmailing you?" I asked.

"I don't know," Fern said. "The photos just showed up on my desk."

"So someone in our company is blackmailing you?"

"I don't think so," Fern said. "There was a postmark. Later I got a text. I know I screwed up. But what do I do now? I don't have a million dollars." She looked at me.

"You think I have a million dollars just in my wallet for the taking?" I asked.

"If these get published in a tabloid, our company will be ruined."

"Sally will kill you," I said. "She suspects Jonathan is cheating, and she said she would kill him and the bitch who was sleeping with him. That's a quote."

Fern squirmed in her chair. "That's just something people

say. She wouldn't really hurt me. People don't kill other people because of an affair."

I raised an eyebrow. "Apparently you don't watch a lot of TV. Of course people kill each other over shit like this."

"Mom, you're scaring me."

"You should be fucking scared," I said. "You come in here all calm, asking your rich momma to bail you out. How could you sleep with Sally's husband? That's a horrible betrayal."

Fern's eyes widened. "You are talking to me about betrayal? How many husbands did you fuck?"

"None," I said. "Except my own. I would never do that to another woman."

"I don't believe you," she said. "I've seen the list. Some of those men were married."

I slapped my hand on the desk. "It was you who told David."

She shook her head. "David told me about the list, and I checked it out."

"Did you talk to him about the list?"

"You mean about your former sex life?" Fern said. "No! That's not a conversation I want to have with anyone, especially not with my little brother."

"I don't believe you," I said. "He's been treating me like shit for months now, and I knew someone must be poisoning him with bad mommy stories."

"He's got his own bad mommy stories," Fern said, "from all the years you lived with us when you were drunk on your ass and fucking everyone but daddy dearest."

I sucked in a breath and got to my feet. I had never wanted to hit one of my children more than I did at that moment.

"I am not giving you a million fucking dollars," I said. "Or even a penny. Sally won't split up the company for this. But we will fire you for it. So good luck. Now get out of my office."

Fern got to her feet, snatched the file from my desk, opened the door and left. She tried to slam the door, but is was partially pneumatic or something. But she was gone. I stared after her. That conversation had been mildly satisfying. I had always wanted to say, "Get out of my office." Like in the movies. Or on TV. Now I had.

I was as bad as all of them. All of them who loved this cesspool called Hollywood. I had been sucked in. I had been enjoying myself for the last few years, because of the success of *Beauty and the Zombie.* It had been fun to be rich and semi-famous and sober. I rubbed my head. None of it was real. We made these ridiculous movies while the world fell down around us. Only the disasters reminded us that it was all going to hell in a handbasket: the earthquakes, fires, floods, viruses. No disasters now to blame anything on, no disasters to finally wake us up. Just me drinking. And now Fern fucking her boss's husband.

I sat down again. I really couldn't let those photos get out.

There was a knock at the door. I heard Caryn's voice. I told her to come in. She walked in carrying her laptop which she put on my desk. The screen was covered in a kind of dark purple with the words "Whore of Hollywood" scrawled across it in the same font as the *Beauty and the Zombie* title credits. I leaned forward. In white letters below the Whore of Hollywood I read, "Brooke McMurphy pretends she is the perfect mother and wife, but those in the know know that she has slept with more men than the whore of Babylon. She's ruined many marriages. Was yours one? Here's the list."

I blinked, and the afterimages stayed. "White lettering on a dark background. Amateur shit. And I slept with just as many women as men. Well, OK, not quite as many."

I looked up at Caryn. She smiled wanly. "Sorry," I said, "but accuracy is important in these things."

"Certainly."

I leaned closer to read the list of names and squinted. Yes, him. Yes, him. No, not him. No, gawd, no, not him no matter how drunk I was. Ryan Nichols' name was there. All in all, I read about 30 names. Most of them I knew. About half of them I had probably had sex with during those years when I was a drunk.

"Thank you, Caryn," I said. "Is there any way you can find out who put this up? Can we get it taken down?"

She shook her head. "I doubt it. I can do some searching though, bring in some of my buddies, if this is important to you. But no one will see this, most likely. If it's not true, who cares?"

"My children have seen it," I said, "and there's enough truth to it that they believe it." I looked up at her. "I used to be a drunk."

Caryn nodded. "Been there, done that. I've been sober for three years."

I smiled. "Congratulations." I figured she wanted me to say how long I had been sober, but I didn't want to tell anyone else that I had started drinking. Why confess to a lapse? I wasn't drinking *now*. I wouldn't drink any more. There. I had decided. No more drinking.

"Yes, do whatever you can to find out who put it up," I said. "If you can get it gone, that would be great."

"If we find out who it is," Caryn said, "we can threaten legal action. Sometimes that's enough."

"Great," I said. "Thank you. Keep this between us and your crew for now. I want to see if I can keep it quiet."

"Of course." Caryn took her laptop and left the office, letting the door close softly behind her.

Now what? I needed to find out who was blackmailing Fern. Phil Case, our old friend who had worked Major Crimes for many years in Los Angeles, had retired last year and set up shop as a private investigator. He had pulled our familial bacon out of the fire more than once. Maybe he could do it again.

I left my office—phone in hand—and walked down the hall to Fern's office. The door was open. She was sitting on her couch, texting.

"Texting your lover?" I asked.

She looked up at me. "Shhh," she said. "You don't know who's here."

I rolled my eyes and shut the door.

"Did you tell Jonathan?" I asked.

She shook her head.

"It's not him blackmailing us is it?" I asked. Fern had a bit of a history with boyfriends using her to get to us.

"No," she said. "He is successful businessman."

"He's got kids, you know," I said.

"So did you," she said.

I sighed. "No one broke up my marriage with your father."

"Ryan Nichols did," she said.

I had never heard her say his name out loud, at least not since I told her about him a few years earlier.

"He didn't," I said. "Your father and I stayed together to raise our family. We loved each other. We still love each other."

She made a noise.

I sighed. "Why do we always have to go over old ground? It's in the past. All of this."

"Why do you still mourn Alberto?" she asked.

"That feels like a particularly nasty question," I said.

"I don't mean it that way," Fern said. "You want to know why I keep bringing up the past. Alberto is in the past, and you still mourn him."

I leaned against the wall. "OK. I'll give you that. But you're still so angry about things that happened years ago. You blame me for everything bad in your life. You've got to take responsibility for your life. My parents were clueless, but I know they did the best they could."

"You did not do the best you could," Fern said. "As a mother."

"And as a daughter, you haven't done the best you could either," I said. I put up a hand and shook my head. "I'm not going to do this with you. I'm going to call Phil Case and see if he can figure out who is blackmailing you."

"But then other people will know," Fern said. "Please don't tell Dad. I don't want him to know."

"People are going to know," I said. "It's a crime to blackmail someone."

"I just want to pay it," Fern said. "And get the photos back."

"Back from where?" I asked. "If the photos are online, they are there forever. Maybe if we find the guy, though, we can get him prosecuted."

"I don't want Jonathan to know about it," Fern said. "I love him, Mom."

She looked at me with pathetic puppy dog eyes. Good grief. She was too young to be that madly in love. Of course, I had been younger than she was when Hayword and I got together. I don't think I was ever madly in love with him, though. Not crazy, like I had been with Ryan. Thank goodness. How can you build a life when you're sick with love all the time? I shuddered.

"He will leave me if this comes out," Fern said. "And he can't go through a divorce right now. They have a prenup."

"What does that matter if they're both rich?" I asked. "Or if he's so in love with you."

Fern shrugged.

"How long has this been going on?" I asked.

"Six months," she said.

"And the blackmail?"

"About two months ago," she said.

"And you're just taking care of it now?"

"I was stalling for time," she said. "I paid him a little here and there. But then he texted me that he wanted the money this week or he was going to the tabloids."

"Six months," I said. "Jesus, Fern. He's old enough to be your father. He has children."

"You already said that!" Fern said. "I'm hoping to have my children with him."

"Are you pregnant?" I asked.

"No," she said. "Not yet."

I wanted to shake her.

"You are a talented woman," I said. "You're interesting and beautiful. There are unmarried men out there who would love to spend time with you. Just today Damon Friend said he wants you to be part of the *Beauty and the Zombie Part Three* team."

"That's work," she said. "And I'm already a part of that team. Have you finished the script? Does Aiden come back from the dead?"

I wished people would quit asking me that question.

"I'm just saying that you don't need this guy. It's beneath you to be doing this. You're a modern woman. Be your own person with or without a significant other."

"Like you?" Fern asked. "You were going to leave us for Ryan Nichols."

"No," I said. "I was willing to leave Hayword, not you or David. You would have come with me."

Fern laughed. "Never. We would have never left Dad."

I stared at her. She looked me right in the eyes.

I nodded. She was right. The kids would not have left Hayword.

"Besides," she said. "We were a unit, the four of us and then the five of us. If you left one of us, you left all of us."

"And now that's what you want Jonathan to do," I said. "You want him to break up the family unit."

"Sally already did that by being a bitch," Fern said.

"Oh, Jesus H. Christ," I said. "You fell for that old saw? I taught you better than that."

"No, you didn't!" She was standing now and yelling. "You taught me how to be a drunk and a whore."

That's when I slapped my daughter across the face. Hard. It left a red mark.

"Don't you ever talk to me like that again," I said.

We stood a few feet from one another, breathing hard. Tears flooded her eyes, and she looked like she wanted to kill me. I'm sure I looked the same. I couldn't believe I had hit her. Given all the other things I had done that day, I shouldn't have been surprised.

"I'm going to call Phil Case now and see if he can clean up another one of your fuck-ups, daughter dearest."

I left her office. I felt like I was going to throw up. I wondered if this was some weird hangover or was my body feeling something I wasn't willing to process: sex with my ex, finding a dead body, sex with another ex, not sex with another ex who was now drinking, realizing I had forgotten my dead son's birthday, finding out my daughter was having sex with someone else's soon to be ex, and hitting my daughter. Good grief.

Once in my office, I curled up in one of my cushy chairs and phoned Phil Case. I was surprised when he answered.

"Hi, Phil. It's Brooke McMurphy. Long time."

"Hi, Mac. What did you do now?"

"Funny shit, Phil. It's not me. I want to hire you. You keep everything private, right?"

"Sure," he said, "unless I get called to court and then all bets are off."

"I don't think this will go to court," I said. "My daughter is being blackmailed. They've got what you might call compromising photos."

"Like what?" Phil asked. "Speeding? Killing someone? Fucking someone?"

"The latter," I said. "And she's fucking someone she shouldn't be."

"Like the boss?"

"Like the boss's husband," I said.

"That's not good," he said.

"It would not be good for the studio if these got out."

"Where are you?" he asked.

"I'm at the Back to Life offices," I said. "Where are you?"

"I'm downtown," he said. "I can drop by now. Be there in ten."

"OK. I'll let you in."

I went out to reception. It was dark. Caryn must have gone home.

I walked to the kitchen and searched the cupboards for something to drink. I didn't find anything besides tea and coffee—and a chocolate bar. I unwrapped the bar and ate it in about ten seconds flat.

I went to reception and sat in Caryn's chair. It was dark outside now, twilight. Not my favorite time of the day. I hadn't seen Phil for a while. I liked him. Didn't think he liked me. He was a good-looking man. Kept himself in shape. At least he did when he was on the job. Not sure about now. But he was married. So that was out. Why was I even thinking about him in that way? How many times had I had sex today? Had I become some kind of nymphomaniac over night?

Suddenly Phil was there, outside. He smiled, and I got up and unlocked the door, and he came inside. He looked even better than the last time I had seen him. I locked the door again, and we embraced. I probably held on a little longer than I should have. I had to get a hold of myself.

"Hi, Phil," I said. "How's retirement treating you?"

"My wife left me, and my kids hate me," he said. "Other than that, it's all good."

"Oh, shit," I said. "That sucks. I thought you two were the perfect married couple."

We started to walk down the semi-dark hall.

"Why would you say that?"

I shrugged. "I guess because you weren't divorced."

"Then you and Hayword must be the perfect couple since you're not divorced."

"Shut up," I said. We passed my office and went to Fern's. Her light was on. She was sitting on the couch, still, only this time she had a drink on the table in front of her. Looked like some kind of hard liquor.

She no longer had a red spot on her cheek. I flinched slightly, thinking about it. I hoped this day would end without me killing anyone or ruining anyone else's life. Fern stood and held her hand out to Phil.

"Hello, Mr. Case," she said. They shook hands.

"Please sit," I said.

Phil sat on the couch next to Fern. I sat in the chair. We all stared at the folder on the coffee table.

"Do you really have to look at those?" Fern asked. "It's so embarrassing."

Phil said, "It's possible I can tell something about the person blackmailing you from looking at them. What kind of photos are they. Professional. Amateur. From a phone or a camera. Where they were taken. I've seen a million crime photos. These won't bother me."

"At least these aren't photos of dead people," I said. I didn't know where that came from. They both looked at me and then away.

"Where were you?" Phil asked.

"Just some hotel," Fern said, "that Jonathan found. I can get you the name."

"And the curtains or blinds were open?" Phil asked.

"They must have been," Fern said. "I didn't even think about it. We were six stories up."

Phil nodded. I rolled my eyes. First rule of having illicit sex: Close the fucking curtains.

"Do you remember what was across the street?" Phil asked. "An apartment building? A hotel?"

Fern shrugged. "I don't know. I wasn't paying attention."

Second rule of having illicit sex: Pay attention to your surroundings. I should write a book: *How to Have Illicit Sex and Get Away With It.*

"OK," Phil said. "Are you ready to show me?"

"Do I have to stay and watch you look at naked photos of me?" Fern asked.

"Yes," I said "If I have to stay, you do, too."

"I'm not a child," Fern said. "You can't tell me what to do."

"I might have questions," Phil said. He picked up the file folder and began flipping through the photos. It didn't take long. Then he shut the folder.

"May I see what he said when he contacted you?"

Fern picked up her phone, scrolled at bit, and then handed it to Phil. He wrote down something and then handed it back to her. He asked her the name of the hotel, the date they were there, and the room number. She told him.

"I can't tell you anything for certain," Phil said. "I need to do some investigating, but I'm pretty sure you were targeted. These look professional to me. My guess is that it's a paparazzi. Have you had run-ins with any pap in particular?"

"I don't think I'd know one if I saw one," Fern said.

"Any reporters?"

"No," Fern said. "I don't think so."

"How about you, Mac?"

"Me? No. I ignore the paparazzi. When I got out of rehab a few years ago, they covered me, but that's about it."

"What about the new movie?" he said. "I've been hearing rumblings that it's about to start and there's no script."

"What would that have to do with anything?" I asked.

"Maybe the studio is trying to create buzz with a scandal?"

"Hayward and I and Sally are the studio," I said. "We don't want anything like this out."

"OK," Phil said. "Let me run some things down. Fern, I'd advise you to tell your gentleman friend what's going on. See if anyone has been after him."

"I don't want to tell him," Fern said.

"It's probably going to come out one way or another," Phil said. "That's the way these things are."

Fern looked terrified. "I need to get going," she said. She picked up the folder and grabbed her purse. Phil and I got up and left the office. Fern followed us out and locked her door.

"Keep in touch," I told Fern. She didn't say anything. She just hurried by us.

Phil and I went to my office. "You want me to get you some water or coffee?" I asked. "I could probably scrounge some up."

"Naw," he said. "I better get on this. The guy wants an answer by this week or he's going to publish. My guess is that he's a paparazzi just trying to make some extra dough before he turns over the photos. They're going to get published one way or another. At least that's my guess."

"Can't you find out who it is," I asked, "and then go intimidate him?"

"Blackmail is illegal," he said, "but taking and selling photos isn't. I'll try to find out who he is. Maybe you can threaten legal action."

"That's the second time I've been given that advice today,"

I said. I sat on the couch. Phil sat in the chair kitty-corner from me.

"Oh?"

"There's a website on the dark web that purports to be a list of all the men I've had sex with," I said. "It's call the Whore of Hollywood."

"Ouch," Phil said. "That doesn't sound good. Is it real?"

"You mean the list?" I shook my head. "No, it's not. But my kids believe it's real. When I was drinking my appetite for all things was voracious."

Phil nodded. "I remember."

"What do you mean you remember?"

"Hayword had to talk to someone," he said.

"Jesus," I said. "And to think I was going to try to seduce you. Now I just feel icky."

Phil laughed.

He thought I was kidding.

"Have you talked to Hayword lately?" I asked.

"A couple weeks ago," he said. "He was dating someone. Really liked her." Phil looked at me.

I said, "Don't say anything to Hayword about this. I'll tell him when it's time."

"You're my client," Phil said. "I can keep my mouth shut."

"You want to go have dinner? The traffic will still be too bad to go home."

Phil said, "Sure. But don't make any moves on me. I'm weak. My wife left me for a younger man. Any attention is quite gratifying."

We both stood. "I won't make any promises," I said.

EIGHT

It was good having a nice normal dinner with someone out-side the business and not part of my family. Phil talked about missing his old life. I talked about missing a time in my life when I was relaxed. Although I couldn't remember when that was.

I didn't drink. I didn't try to seduce him. I went home alone to my dark bungalow, took off my clothes, and crawled into bed. I hoped I would wake up and this was all a dream.

I dreamed of Alberto. He was far away and waving to me, waving me toward him.

When I woke up, my heart was racing. Was Alberto telling me to come toward him, toward death? Because that was where he was. He was dead.

I shuddered. It was daylight. I had made it through the night. I remembered the vodka bottle was still in the cupboard. I longed for a swig, but I stayed away from the cupboard. I got dressed. Then I scrambled a couple of eggs and ate them with bacon and toast. I felt like shit.

I sat at the table looking out at my backyard. What was happening to me? Why had I suddenly gone off the deep end? Was it the fact that no one in my family seemed to want anything to do with me? Now I knew why: They were mad at me over the Whore of Hollywood list. And currently, no doubt, Fern was mad at me for hitting her. She had a right. I should have never done that. Bleck. What now? I wished I believed in therapy, because I could use a good shrink. Or a good drink.

It wasn't that I didn't believe in therapy; it was just that it never worked for me. Yes, I drank because my kid died. And I fucked around because my kid died, and I was mad at Hayword because he cheated on me. And yes, I couldn't seem to move out of that hole of grief. Until I did. I went to rehab, and I hadn't had a drink since, not through two successful movies, not through my make up and break up and make up with Mark. Not through the earthquakes and floods and fires. Not through finding a dead guy right in this living room.

I was going in circles. This was not productive. I could figure this out. I could stop it. I could stop drinking and fucking.

The doorbell rang.

Crap.

If someone was selling me religion, I would slap them across the face, too.

"Brooke!"

It was Sally. Oh fuck, oh fuck, oh fuck. Had she found out about Jonathan and Fern?

"I'll be right there," I said. I glanced around the place. No sign that I had been drinking yesterday. I opened the door. Sally strode in, tall, thin, and so white—and gorgeous, as usual.

"I brought croissants," she said. She walked to the kitchen in two strides. "Unless you're not eating gluten or butter. I can't keep up with everyone these days."

"There's strawberry jam in the fridge," I said.

"No need," Sally said. "The croissants are filled with chocolate. Mine's filled with chocolate and vodka." She took down two small plates and put two croissants down on each. "This is mine," she said pointing to the right plate. "I need to wash up. You have coffee?"

She swooped into the bathroom. As soon as she was out of sight, I switched the right plate with the left one. Then I poured her a cup of coffee. I picked up the left plate (the former right one) and returned to the table. I wanted the vodka-laced croissant.

Sally came out of the bathroom. She looked at the remaining plate. "Did you take the right one?" she asked.

"I took the correct one, yes. And there's your coffee."

Sally brought her plate and coffee over to the table. I bit into the croissant. All that doughy goodness, all that butter and chocolate. Where was the vodka? I couldn't taste it. I took several bites as we stared out the window together.

"Was there really vodka in yours?" I asked.

"No, and there isn't any in yours," Sally said. "I wanted to see if you'd switch plates, and you did. I put a tiny smear of chocolate on mine. See." She pointed. "If you'd been smart, you would have changed the croissants, not the plates."

"What the fuck?" I asked.

"I wanted to see if you were drinking," Sally said.

"You could have asked."

"Are you drinking?"

"None of your business," I said.

"See," she said. "There's no vodka in anything. What can I do to help? Is it bad? Do you need to go into rehab?"

She was being awfully nice.

"No," I said. "I've got it under control."

Sally raised an eyebrow. "We could fuck. Would that help?"

I looked at her. "How would that help?"

"I dunno," she said. "I'm just so good that you would be cured of all that ails you."

I laughed. "I don't know what ails me. Brain chemistry. I still don't understand why I did it." I put my head in my hands. "And then Hayword and I had sex."

"Oh lordy," Sally said.

"And then I went to Ryan's AA meeting," I said. "And we had sex. Many, many times. Until I threw up on him."

"Oh my word!"

"In-between all that, I learned that Mark had cheated on me," I said.

"Did he cheat before or after you cheated on him?" Sally asked.

"What does that matter?" I said. "He cheated first. But I haven't been around. We have barely seen each other for weeks. We haven't had sex for weeks and weeks. I mean, not that that's everything. But for us, it was a way we got close. I started wondering why we were even together. It was so boring out there on the beach. But back here, with Hayword and the kids, it reminded me of the old days when I was drinking and carrying on. I missed it."

"Not really," Sally said.

I looked at her. "I missed people wanting me and wanting to be around me. It feels like the world is ending and everyone is mad at me."

"The world is ending," Sally said. "It's always ending."

"But this feels so big," I said, "and David keeps asking me why we didn't stop climate change when we could. I don't have answers for him. And there was David liking Hayword's new girlfriend. There was Hayword liking his new girlfriend. I thought what about me, even though I don't think I really thought that. But, maybe. Then I took that drink."

"You took that drink so it could be all about you again."

I stared at her. Oh, fuck. Was that it?

"Maybe," I said. "I dunno."

"How about we take your mind off of all of that?"

"I like the idea of fucking," I said.

Sally smiled. "It would be a pity fuck," she said. "Besides, I'm still hoping Jonathan and I can work on our marriage."

Her marriage. Christ. I had forgotten about that.

"I hope so," I said.

"Maybe working on the script would help you," Sally said.

I nodded. "OK. You run along, and I will do that."

Sally laughed. "Let's do it together. Come on. Get your laptop. We can brainstorm."

"Let me finish these delicious non-alcoholic croissants first," I said.

"Stalling," she said.

We talked and ate and drank coffee. Eventually I went to the couch, and she sat in the chair. I sat cross-legged and took my laptop from the coffee table and put it on the cushion in front of me. I wondered how long I could pretend that I had pages.

"Do you want to read me what you have?" Sally asked.

I shook my head.

"I assume the first shot is of Aiden's arm coming out of the grave?"

"We see Molly walking away from Aiden's gravesite," I said, "and Colleen is talking to Aiden, like in the end of the last movie. Then she walks away, and Aiden's arm bursts up through the earth." And then what, and then what, and then what? I felt like I was going to cry.

I looked down and tried to breathe deeply.

I needed a drink, I needed a drink, I needed a drink.

Well, perhaps need was the wrong word.

"Alberto's birthday was Sunday," I said. "That's when I drank. I forgot his birthday." I looked over at Sally. "I forgot. Instead of celebrating it, I got drunk and fucked Hayword and then Ryan."

OK. Technically I really hadn't been that drunk. I had been drinking.

"Oh, Mac," Sally said. "I'm so sorry."

I nodded and closed the laptop.

"Don't use Alberto as some bullshit excuse," Sally said. "You're not reading me pages because you don't have any fucking pages. Don't lie to me. Don't bullshit me. This company is my whole life."

"Really? What about your children and husband?"

"Besides them, of course, smart ass," she said, waving a hand. "No excuses. Not a single fucking one. Not Alberto's birthday. Not you fucking everyone you meet. Not drinking. I want to see the whole script by the end of the week. End of fucking story."

Sally got up.

"This visit started out so nice," I said, looking up at her.

"This is what you get for turning down my offer of sex," Sally said. She leaned down and kissed my forehead. "Now be well. No fucking around, literally. And keep in touch. Love you."

"Love you, too."

When she got to the door, she turned around and said, "Is Aiden going to live?"

I looked for something to throw at her, but everything was breakable and/or valuable.

"Leave me alone," I said.

Sally St. James left the building.

I did try to work after she left. I swear I did. But all I could see was Aiden's arm reaching out from beyond the grave, and I didn't know what to do with that. It was such a good ending. Positive, in a way. Because we left Colleen knowing that there was some hope that her son was still alive. Or alive again. So how could I follow that up? How could I end such a successful series on a high note, on a good note, making everyone happy?

I rolled my eyes. It was impossible to make everyone happy. Everyone I knew wanted Aiden to be alive somehow. Dead is dead in this world. But *Beauty and the Zombie* was about . . . zombies. It would be possible for them to come back from the dead. In fact, couldn't Colleen's true love Thomas come back from the dead? No. He had exploded with the ship.

As far as we knew.

Yes, as far as we knew.

That vodka bottle was still in my cupboard. I should throw it out. The question was: Should I drink the contents first and then throw it out? Since I hadn't had another drink in almost a day, didn't that mean I wasn't really a drunk? Maybe I could have one or two drinks now and again and all would be well. Like a normal person.

Some normal people could drink poison and survive; others couldn't.

Perhaps that was the wrong attitude: It wasn't poison. It was bliss. It was heaven. It was Nirvana in a bottle. Not the band but the state of being. Was I allowed to use that term? I wasn't Buddhist, so was it cultural appropriation? I knew a lot of Buddhists. They wouldn't give a shit if I used that word. And who I knew and what they thought was all that mattered.

I laughed. My ridiculous state of mind was apparently continuing.

Phil phoned just then.

"Hey, thanks for a nice dinner," he said. "It's the most relaxed I've been for ages. I don't know why Hayword says you're such a pain in the ass."

I laughed. I knew Hayword would never talk shit about me or his kids to anyone. "Very funny. I had a good time, too. So did you figure it out?"

"It was so easy," Phil said. "I tracked down who bought the burner phone that sent the text. I was right. It was a freelance photographer, one of the local paparazzi. Lance Johnson. You know him?"

"I don't think so," I said. "A few years ago there was a faked robbery at a restaurant where I was. After that, the outlets did stories on my rehab, showed some bad photos. But I don't know who was involved. Do you want me to go talk to him? Or do you think we should call the police?"

"If you call the police, it will get out," Phil said, "but that is what I'd advise. If he's a blackmailer, who knows what else he'd do."

"Let me think about it," I said. "Can you text me his phone and address."

Silence.

"Just for my information," I said. "I'm not going to do anything."

"I've known you a long time," he said.

"Not that long," I said. "Besides, have I ever hurt anyone?"

"Well—"

"Physically, god damnit. I've never hurt anyone physically."

"OK," he said, but he didn't sound convinced. "I'll watch him for a few days. Find out who he really is. See if there's anything we can use against him."

"That sounds good," I said. "I like that."

"By the way, Hayword called a little while ago."

"You didn't tell him about you working for me?

"Of course not," he said.

"Did he say anything to you?" I asked. "I mean, why was he calling?"

"We're friends," Phil said.

"Don't be coy," I said. "Did he tell you we'd slept together?"

"He did indeed."

Phil sounded like he was trying not to laugh. I could feel my face turning red.

"That's horrible," I said.

"He's trying to figure things out," Phil said. "He needed someone to talk with."

"I'm trying to figure things out, too," I said. "But you don't see me running around blabbing to everyone about my sex life."

"Maybe you should talk to someone," he said.

"Like you?"

"Good gawd, no," Phil said. "I don't even like you."

"I knew it!" I said. I couldn't help it: I chuckled.

"He's worried about you," Phil said. "He says you're drinking again."

I made a noise. For a little bit, Phil had been interesting. Phil had not been a part of any of the bullshit that was my life. Now . . . ugh.

"I'm not drinking," I said. "Thanks for the information, Phil. I've got to go."

"Mac, don't be like that."

I rubbed my face.

"I actually do like you," he said, rather gently. "I always have. Most people do. But you run from intimacy like a stallion running from a vet trying to geld him."

"Oh good grief," I said. "Don't pretend you're some country bumpkin."

"OK. You run from intimacy like a criminal runs from a cop," he said. "That has no punch to it."

"I've been intimate with many many people," I said. I knew what he meant, but this conversation was pissing me off.

"And I asked you to find my daughter's blackmailer," I said, "not psychoanalyze me."

"I wasn't doing that," he said.

"What did you tell Hayword?" I asked.

Phil didn't say anything for a moment. Maybe now he was pissed. "I told him people sleep with their exes all the time. It was no big deal."

I breathed a sigh of relief.

"Do you sleep with your ex all the time?"

"Are you kidding?" he said. "I've seen the dick she's sleeping with and I have no idea where his dick has been . . . so no. Besides, she humiliated me. I have no desire for her. I can barely look at her."

"I'm sorry," I said. "That must suck. Hayword has always been good to me. He's stayed a part of my life no matter what I've done."

"He's not a saint," Phil said.

"He only cheated on me once," I said, "with the blonde. And I think they only did it once."

"Yeah."

"Did you cheat on your wife?" I couldn't even remember her name. What was that about?

"No," he said. "Never did. Never had a desire to. Thought men who did that were dogs."

"How about women who did that?" I asked.

"Never had a name for them," he said. "Wasn't my business."

"I bet," I said.

We were quiet for a moment.

"You trying to be my girlfriend or something?" I asked.

"Naw, just trying to pretend to be a friend."

I laughed. "I don't have many of those. Thanks, Phil."

"Now are you gonna tell me or what?"

"Grrrr," I said. "I'll tell you the same thing I told you last night: You'll just have to wait and see when the movie comes out whether Aiden lives or dies."

"OK, OK."

"Hey, Phil, did you ever think that Aiden was like a stand-in for Alberto?"

"What? No, why? Was he?"

"I never thought about it," I said, "but one of our potential investors suggested it might be so."

"They are good entertaining movies," Phil said, "and they are layered with a whole lot of other meanings. That's what makes them feel deeper than just zombie movies. But I don't try to figure those kinds of things out. That's not the kind of mystery I try to solve."

"Huh," I said. "You are much more interesting than I would have guessed."

Phil laughed. "Most people are."

"Most people are fucking assholes," I said.

"Wow," he said. "That seems especially bitter."

I looked down at my phone as it wiggled in my hand. Hayword was calling.

"Phil, I'd love to continue this gabfest," I said, "but Hayword's calling. I'll get back with you. Thanks again. Don't forget to text me the photographer's address."

"OK. Later, Mac."

"Hi, Hayword," I said. "What's up?"

"Have you talked to Fern lately?"

"I saw her last night," I said. "Why?"

"I can't get a hold of her," he said, "and she was supposed to be at a meeting this morning. She's a no-show. That's not like her. Sally's out of the office, and I can't get a hold of anyone else who knows Fern. I'm down in Palm Springs meeting with potential investors. It would take me two hours to get back. I'm worried, Brooke. Could you go check on her?"

"I'm sure she's fine," I said. She probably was still upset about last night's meeting.

"She would have called," Hayword said. "It was a marketing meeting I asked her to go to. She wouldn't miss it."

He really gave that girl much more credit than she deserved.

"Hayword, I'm probably an hour from her apartment myself," I said. "I don't know what the traffic is doing."

"She stayed in the guest house last night," he said. "At our house."

That was a surprise.

"Was she drunk?" I asked.

"Asks the kettle about the pot. But, I don't think so. She seemed sad. I left really early so I didn't get to see her."

"OK. I'm on my way."

"I'll text her that you're coming," he said.

I grabbed my keys, put on my shoes, and was out the door. Up the winding road I went. Soon enough, I was at Hayword's house. He called it our house, but it wasn't mine, not any more. I never had any real attachment to it until we sprinkled Alberto's ashes on the backyard during an earthquake. Now I thought of it as the family home.

George, our neighborhood handyman, was climbing a tall ladder to our roof when I got out of my car.

"Watcha doing, George?" I asked as I hurried toward the door.

"Hayword asked me to put up a lightning rod because of that storm," George said.

"I thought I was the only lightning rod this family needed," I said.

George chuckled and continued up the ladder.

I used my key to the house to open the front door. As it creaked open, I heard Joanie's stiletto heels on the drive. I glanced behind me. Her car was parked at the end of the drive. She tottered toward me, waving, and clutching a huge peach-colored purse that kept dragging on the ground. She was high or drunk.

"Brooke, Brooke, I've got to talk to you," she said.

"I don't have time," I said. "I'm looking for Fern."

I went into the house. Joanie was right behind me.

"Fern!" I called. No answer.

I shut the door, walked through the house, and out the back door.

"You haven't called the police, have you?" Joanie asked. "You haven't told anyone? I was gonna go down and double-check that it was Marv's body in the car in the garage, but I got scared. I've never seen a dead body. Well, not a dead body of my husband who's been rotting there for a month."

"Joanie, shut up," I said.

I hurried across the patio and the yard to the guest house. I suddenly had a sick feeling.

I knocked on the front door.

"Fern!" I called. "Fern!"

No answer.

Joanie looked through the window.

"She's on the floor," Joanie said.

I opened the door and ran inside. Fern was on the rug next to the couch, unconscious or dead. I knelt next to her. "Fern!" I called. "Fern!"

Her lips were blue. Like Alberto's had been when he died. She seemed so small, like a child.

I felt for her pulse. If there was one, it was faint.

"What's happened?" I yelled. "Fern!" I slapped her face. "Fern!"

Nothing.

Joanie was next to me, looking around for something in her purse while she called 911. She didn't seem drunk or high any more.

"A woman is unconscious," Joanie said. "I think she's overdosed. I'm going to give her Narcan."

"What?" I said.

The whole world had slowed down. Joanie seemed to be talking very slowly.

"It won't hurt her if she's not overdosed," Joanie told me. "I take opiates sometimes, and my nurse friend got this for me." She pulled out something that looked like nasal spray. She put it up Fern's nose.

Fern gasped almost immediately. Or murmured. Something. She was alive.

"Mommy," Fern whispered.

I took my daughter in my arms and pressed her against me. *Live, live, goddamnit, live*. She felt so tiny.

"I told Jonathan," Fern whispered. "He broke up with me." She began to cry. "You were right, Mommy. I'm not good for anything."

No! I never said that. Never even thought it.

"Hang on," I said. "I'm here. Hang on."

"I saw Alberto, Mommy," she whispered. "He said to tell you hello."

"It's all right, darlin'," I said. "Everything is going to be OK."

NINE

I don't remember a lot about the next 24 hours. They took Fern to the local hospital. I followed the ambulance, after grabbing Fern's old battered purse from the floor near her. It was one of my old purses that I had given her years ago. Maybe even a decade ago. She was a strange child.

I thanked Joanie for saving Fern's life.

"Remember that," Joanie said, "whenever you get the urge to rat me out."

"Rat you out for what?" I asked her. "You haven't done anything wrong."

"Just remember that."

George was gone by the time I came out to my car again. I glanced at the roof, but I couldn't tell if he had done anything or not.

Hayword eventually met me at the hospital. He had to fly in because the traffic from Palm Springs to Los Angeles to the village was so bad. I told him about the photos, the affair, and the blackmail. When we went into Fern's cubicle, Hayword embraced her, and she sobbed while he held her. I took her hand and wouldn't let go.

I had thought she was so grown up for so long, but she was really still a girl.

"I don't know how it happened," Fern said. "I just ended up with Jonathan a few times, and he was funny. He didn't drink, so I thought that was good. But then he offered me some pills. He said he took them for his back, but they also made him high. I thought because they were prescribed it would be OK. I know, I know. I didn't realize they were opiates until I'd been doing them for a few months."

Hayword and I glanced at each other.

"I knew it was wrong to be with him," Fern said. "But he was so nice to me. He seemed to really like me. That's so alluring because no one likes me."

I wanted to say, "That's not true, Fern." But I didn't know. Maybe people didn't like her. I often didn't like her.

"That's not true, Fern," Hayword said. He gave me a look like "what the fuck?"

"People like you, Fern," I said, a little too late. "You were very popular in high school."

Fern laughed. "That was a long time ago. Besides that was because I'd give a hand job to almost anyone." Hayword groaned. Fern said, "Sorry, Dad. I don't do that any more."

No, she just ate opioids and had sex with married men. But who was I to judge?

"None of it matters," I said. "You just need to get well."

"I didn't try to kill myself," Fern said. "I took too many. If they think I tried to off myself, they'll put me in the psych ward."

"Maybe that would be a good thing," Hayword said.

"No, Daddy, please," she said. "I will go to rehab."

"I'm so sorry you are going through this," I said.

"You're not going to yell at me about bad choices?" Fern said.

I squeezed her hand. "No. You can blame me. You probably inherited my brain chemistry. There is a place in Tucson that deals with drugs and alcohol abuse as well as depression and eating disorders. Honey, you are skinny as fuck. You having trouble eating? I'm so sorry that I didn't notice. I'm so sorry I slapped you yesterday."

"What?" Hayword said. "You hit her?"

I nodded.

"I deserved it," Fern said.

"No, you didn't," I said.

"If I can get into the place in Tucson," Fern said, "I'd like to go. But what should I do about the photos? I want to tell Sally what happened. I want to apologize."

"You leave the photos to me," I said. "I will tell Sally, too, for now. You can talk to her when you're better. Right now, though, you need to get better."

After that, we all talked to doctors, and I called the rehab in Tucson and got her a place. Turned out it wasn't against the law to overdose, so we didn't have to deal with the police. Fern convinced the docs that her overdose was a mistake. I didn't know if that was true or not, but right then I went with it.

We brought Fern home that night. She slept in her old room. David sat in the chair in her room until she fell asleep. Then he came downstairs and sat with Hayword and me.

"She'll be all right," Hayword said.

"She's never been all right," David said. "Not since Alberto died. I don't think any of us have been."

"I'm sorry about that," I said. "I'm sorry that your entire

childhood has been about trauma." All I seemed to be able to say was "I'm sorry."

"It's not your fault," David said. "At least not all of it."

I laughed. "Thank goodness for that."

"Can I go tomorrow when you take Fern to Tucson?" David asked. Fern said she wanted her dad to drive her. It was an eight hour drive, give or take the traffic. I offered to come, but she wanted me to be here to take care of the photos. She kept using that expression. "Take care of the photos." Like she expected me to put out a hit on the photographer or something.

Maybe that was a good idea. Every time I closed my eyes, I saw Fern lying dead on the floor of the guest house.

"You've got school," Hayword said. "I won't be back for a couple of days."

"I'll stay here with you if you like," I said.

"Yes, I would like that," David said.

"Did you tell your dad about the Whore of Hollywood list?"

David's face reddened. "No."

"What?" Hayword said.

"On the dark web someone put up a list of men and said I had slept with them all. The website is called the Whore of Hollywood."

"And did you?" Hayword asked.

"No!" I said. I gave him a dirty look. How could he ask such a thing in front of our son?

"I saw the list today," I said. "I don't know who would do such a thing. Did you put it up, Hayword?"

"No!" This time he gave me a dirty look.

"I wouldn't have a clue how to do something like that," Hayword said. "And I've never seen a list."

"That's why David's been so angry with me," I said. "He's mad that I cheated on you."

Hayword nodded. "We had some bad years, your mom and

I. That's all water under the bridge. We both made mistakes, but we love each other, and now we're friends." He shrugged. "It worked out."

"What do you mean you both made mistakes?" David said. "Did you cheat on Mom?"

I put a hand up. "David, our marriage is our business."

"I wish you would either be married or be divorced," David said. "It is confusing."

"It's complicated," Hayword said.

"No, it's not," David said. "That's what adults say when they don't want to do something. Climate change is complicated. No, it's not. We're burning the planet up. Whether you get a divorce or not is complicated. No, it's not. You either love each other and stay married or you don't and you get divorced."

"I don't think we're on the same scale as climate change," I said, "but I get your point. Your dad and I will talk about it."

"I've heard that before," David said.

"David, come on. I saw my daughter dead today. Can you give us a break?"

David sucked in his breath. "She was dead?"

I thought he knew that. Hayword and I looked at each other.

"The important thing is she is alive now," Hayword said.

"Is your car back from the shop?" I asked.

"Yes."

"So you can get to school tomorrow?" I said. "I might go into the office early."

"OK by me," David said.

"I'll be here when you get back from school."

David kissed us both good night, and then he went to bed. Hayword and I went up to Fern's room. She opened her eyes.

"How you feeling?" I asked.

"Like a truck hit me," she said. "I'm ready to get better."

I kissed her forehead. "Good. I might go to the office early in the morning. Do you want me to wait until you leave?"

"No," she said. "I know you've got things to take care of for me." She said it almost proudly. As though her life's goal had been achieved.

"That's right," I said.

She closed her eyes and snuggled under her covers.

"Will you say goodnight like you used to when I was little?" she asked.

I glanced up at Hayword. He shrugged.

"I'll start," Fern whispered. "See you later, alligator."

I bit my lip. "After while, crocodile."

"Take good care, grizzly bear," she said.

My lost little girl. "Bye, bye, butterfly," I said.

"Toodle loo, kangaroo," my first born murmured, a smile on her lips.

"See you soon, my raccoon," I said.

"Love you always," she whispered.

"And forever," I said.

I kissed her on the head again.

Then Hayword and I left the room. We kept her door open, but we went into our old bedroom, where Hayword slept now, and closed the door. I sat on the bed and began to cry. He put his arm across my shoulders.

"What's wrong?" Hayword asked. "Fern is OK. She's gonna be OK."

"Fern and I never said that to each other when she was a kid," I said.

"You didn't?" Hayword said. "It seemed so familiar."

"It was a scene from *Love and Other Insanities*," I said, "when the main character—Charlie—tucked her daughter in at night. Remember I named the daughter Fern, as a kind of homage to Fern, something she could see as she grew up, so she knew we loved her. Hayword, she just asked me to do something from a movie. Do you realize she is nostalgic for a mother that never existed?"

Hayword kissed the side of my face. "We all are, darlin', we all are."

Hayward and I made slow quiet love, and then we fell asleep in each other's arms. I woke up around midnight, wide awake. I slipped on my clothes and checked on the kids. Both were alive. Both slept.

I went downstairs and looked at my phone. I had several texts. Sally and Phil asked me to call in the morning. I did not look forward to talking to Sally. I also had a text from Mark. And one from Ryan.

I looked at Mark's first. "Can you come see me?" Sent hours earlier. Fuck.

I read Ryan's. "How could you do this to me?" Three hours ago. "Please come back." I stared at the phone. I thought of all those years ago when I was pregnant with Alberto. I would have done almost anything to have Ryan beg to see me. Now, I just felt numb.

I went back upstairs into Hayword's room. He was sleeping soundly. I kissed his face and put my cheek against his. He whispered in his sleep, "I love you," just like he used to do when we were together. I whispered back, "I love you, too."

Downstairs I stared out into the darkness. This was where we had spread Alberto's ashes. This was where Fern had died and come back to life this morning. This was where my family lived. It was where they belonged.

It was not where I felt I belonged.

I left the house and got in my car. Crap. Fern's purse was in my backseat. I'd never returned it. Oh well. She didn't need it now. I drove away. For a moment I thought about going to Joanie's, but she had a dead man in her garage. Didn't want to sleep there. I couldn't go to Sally's. Not until I told her what was going on between Fern and Jonathan. I got on the freeway and drove and drove.

I got off at Mark's exit. Went to his neighborhood. Drove up his drive and parked next to his truck. I sat in my car in the dark for a bit. I didn't know why I was here. Didn't know what to do. But he had asked me to come, and he had been so good to me.

I used my key to get into the house. I walked down the dark hallway to the bedroom. It no longer smelled of alcohol and urine. Or whatever it had stunk of before. I could smell Mark. I could smell his beautiful self. I took off my clothes down to my underwear. Then I got under the covers and into bed, and I spooned up behind Mark. He felt warm and familiar. I slipped my arm around him and laced it through his. He squeezed it. I breathed deeply. There. There. There. In a few moments, we were breathing together. I had loved him so much. And then, I just couldn't stand it. Love always meant loss. Always. If I kept loving him and something happened to him, where would I be?

Just as I was falling asleep, Mark turned around, and we wrapped our legs and arms around each other. "I love you," he whispered. "I know," I said. "I love you, too." *As much as I am able, I love you.* After a while, he fell asleep and then turned away from me.

I got out of bed and went to the kitchen. I opened the fridge. No booze. Opened the cupboards. No booze. Good. Good. Mark would be all right. I always knew he would be OK no matter what. Or at least that was what I used to think. Now . . . I hoped he would be all right.

I looked around. I didn't belong here either.

I took the key to his house off of my keychain, and I put it on the counter. Then I left again.

I drove to Ryan's house, which wasn't far away. I still had this gnawing in the pit of my stomach. Or ache. I got out of the car and walked up the sidewalk and rang the doorbell. Ryan opened the door almost immediately.

As soon as I stepped over the threshold, he put his arms around me. I folded myself into him, letting him envelop me.

"Thank you," he said. He no longer smelled of alcohol.

When he let me go, I said, "I'm sorry about the other day. I guess I've gone a little crazy. What can I do to help?"

He leaned down and kissed me. I gently pushed him away.

"I vomited last time we had sex," I said.

"I didn't take it personally."

"I just had sex with my husband a few hours ago," I said.

"I don't care," he said. "I can't stop thinking about you. About us."

"I think you're a complete asshole," I said.

"I am."

"Are you using?" I asked.

"Not for 24 hours," he said, "but I've got drugs and I've got alcohol. I've been staring at them. You came just in time."

"I'm not your get out of jail free fuck card," I said. "You texted me. I thought you were in trouble."

"I am."

He took my hand and led me into the kitchen. On the countertop were bottles of booze, mostly small bottles, like they have on airplanes. He had some bottles of pills and what looked to be a rock of cocaine.

"Jesus H.," I said. "What is going on here?"

"I gathered together all of the alcohol and drugs," he said. "I've been trying to decide if I should use them or not. What do you think? Do we drink and drug or throw it all out? I've been having this debate all night."

"What do you want?"

"I want to use!" he said. "But let's throw them out."

He looked at me eagerly. Please, don't let me be the cause of this, I thought.

"Let's throw them out," I said.

One by one we opened the bottles and drained them into the sink. The smell of alcohol was difficult to resist. I wanted to chug them all. Instead we rinsed each bottle out and threw them in the recycle bin. We put the pills and cocaine down the garbage disposal. I had no idea if that was all right or not. But we did it. Ryan sang and danced nearly the whole time. I was reminded of why I had fallen in love with him all those years ago: He had a happy carefree spirit. I did not. I wondered if Alberto would have been like me or Ryan?

"Anywhere else?" I asked. "Any hiding places?"

"No," he said. "This was it." He grinned. "It's all gone. I can start fresh again."

"I'm glad," I said. I wasn't sure if I was glad. I wasn't even sure why I was here. Did I belong here with this old, old lover? Someone I had loved and then loathed?

"Will you stay?" Ryan asked. "Look. I'm hard as a rock. I could go all night long."

I laughed and shook my head. "I am so glad for you."

"Glad for you, too," he said. He took me in his arms and kissed me. Part of me felt like that woman of 15 years ago who was so in love with him, and part of me felt like the me of now who didn't know him at all. I embraced him and kissed him.

"Let me tuck you into bed," I said. "And then I'm leaving."

"Awww, OK," he said.

Once we got to his bedroom, he stripped naked and then got into bed. "I am tired," he said.

I pulled the sheet and blanket up to his chin. Then I kissed him on the lips.

"Good night, Ryan," I said.

"Will I see you again?" he asked.

"I have no idea."

"Then stay."

I was tempted, but I turned off the light and left the room. I went to the kitchen to turn off the light there. I looked around. I certainly did not belong here. I reached for the light switch and spotted an unopened bottle of some kind of booze that had gotten pushed behind a roll of paper towels. I grabbed it, took off the cap, and started to pour it down the sink. Instead, I lifted it to my mouth and guzzled it.

Vodka.

I rinsed the bottle out and put it in the recycle bin. Then I left the house. I sat in the car. Fuck, fuck, fuck. I could feel the alcohol having its way with me.

I picked up my phone and called Phil. He answered sleepily.

"It's 3 a.m. and I don't do booty calls," Phil said.

"Very funny," I said. "Where do you live? Can I come over? I drank some vodka. My daughter died and came back to life today, and I drank some goddamn vodka. You're the only one at this moment that I know who I haven't fucked or fucked over. Can I sleep on your couch for a couple hours?"

"Sure, kiddo," Phil said. "I'll send you my address."

TEN

I woke up on Phil's couch. The clock by the front door said 11:00, and the AC was on already. It was freakin' February, and we had to use air conditioning in the morning. I threw off the blanket and sat up. I could hear Phil whistling somewhere in the near distance. Probably in the kitchen. Last night—this morning—I hadn't told Phil anything when I arrived. He had shown me the couch and handed me a pillow and a blanket. I lay down, and that was all she wrote.

Now I grabbed my phone and texted Hayword. "I couldn't sleep. I'm not drinking. Do you need me to come home?"

He immediately wrote back. "No, we've been on the road for hours. All seems well. Hey, have you seen Fern's purse?"

"No," I lied. "Maybe she left it in the Garden House. I'll check when I get back. Have a good trip."

"Love you," he said. It was automatic, something we had

said to each other for decades, until we hadn't. Was love on the table now, again?

"OK," was all I managed to say. "Keep in touch." And I pressed off.

"It's slop!" Phil called.

I stood, shook myself, and walked toward the sound of his voice.

"I gotta pee first," I said as I walked into the open kitchen that had tall white cabinets, white countertops, and a black and white checked tile floor. It felt very homey.

Phil pointed, I went to the loo, and then I returned to the kitchen. He was sitting in a booth in a nook on one side of the kitchen. The windows looked out on a shady side yard. I sat in the booth across from Phil. On a peach-colored plate in front of me were two fried eggs, fried or baked breakfast potatoes, fat sausages, probably Wonder bread—toasted and buttered—and slices of peaches. I stared at the plate.

"What?" Phil asked. He was already chowing down.

"It's a little greasy," I said.

He laughed. "I ain't your chef boyfriend," he said. "Eat it or not. I don't care."

"You sound cranky," I said. I slowly put a forkful of eggs in my mouth. They were quite good.

"Yummy," I said. "Thanks for letting me stay here. You are a good girlfriend."

He shrugged. "I do my best."

I felt slightly awkward. It had been a long time since I had had a man as a friend.

"So what do we do here?" I asked. "Am I your boyfriend? Do we watch sports together? Give each other hand jobs? Bitch about women?"

Phil rolled his eyes. "You actually think men masturbate each other?" He shuddered.

"Well, Phil, some men do do that."

"I mean heterosexual men."

"I dunno. I'm not a man."

"We're human beings," he said. "Just like you."

"I doubt that."

Phil looked at me, and I grinned. "I'm just teasing you."

"You are pretty chipper for someone who said her daughter died yesterday."

"Oh yeah," I said. "I had almost forgotten about the cluster-fuck of days I've had. Our family has had. Fern overdosed. Fortunately Joanie was there with some Narcan. Saved her life."

"Joanie? Your neighbor. I think I met her a couple of times. She's cute."

"Cute?" I said. "She's a grown up ass woman. She's not cute. Although she's a lot younger than you are, so you shouldn't be lusting after her."

"I wasn't lusting," he said, "and she's not that much younger."

"I'm younger than you," I said, "and she's younger than I am. By a little."

"She looks a lot younger," Phil said.

"Because she's had a ton of plastic surgery. You could probably rip out those breasts and play ball with them."

Phil made a face. "Now why would I want to do that? See, this is why people don't like you. You always gotta argue."

"Don't say people don't like me," I said. "I might start to believe you. I could introduce you to Joanie."

"She has a husband."

Oh, fuck. I had forgotten that no one knew he was dead.

"Oh yeah," I said. "Well, she fools around a lot."

"I don't," Phil said.

"Anyway," I said. "Fern and Hayword are on the way to rehab in Tucson. I need to be home by the time David gets home from school. This whole thing has gotten him upset."

"I can imagine," Phil said. "What do you need from me?"

"Let's go confront the blackmailer," I said. "He's the reason my daughter almost died. I can't kill him—I guess. But I want him ruined."

Phil nodded. "I understand. How could you ruin him?"

"I don't know yet," I said. "You said you could go talk to him and see what his reaction is."

"Sure," Phil said, sopping up the broken yolk with his Wonder Bread and then eating it. "You can't go with me." I could barely understand what he was saying with his mouth full.

"Is this Wonder Bread?" I asked. "I haven't had Wonder Bread since I was a kid."

"No, it's just white bread," he said. "From a neighborhood baker. He has his own sourdough starter that he treats like a living thing."

"It is a living thing."

"What I'm saying," Phil said. "And he uses old flours."

"Old flours?" I said. "Heirloom? Heritage?"

"Something like that," he said. "He lets the dough rise and fall naturally. Keeps people from getting sick on bread."

"As I live and breathe," I said, "I would have never guessed you were a foodie."

"I'm not a foodie," he said. "I'm an eatie. You pay attention to the world and you know it ain't goin' so well. So I try to be responsible."

I smiled. "I love when people surprise me."

"That is so fucking condescending," Phil said.

"That's my jam," I said.

"You can't come with me," Phil repeated.

"I can come but stay in the car," I said. "I promise on my mother's grave that I won't cause any problems."

"Your mother isn't dead last I heard."

I shrugged. "She will be someday."

"We'll all be dead one day," he said. "So swear on your own grave."

"No! That's just asking for trouble. My mother can take care of herself."

"All right," he said. "The blackmailer doesn't live far from here. You keep down, and you keep shut up."

I rolled my eyes. "OK, boss."

We ate the rest of our meal in silence. When we were finished, I said, "That was really good. I almost feel normal."

"And what is normal to you?" Phil asked.

I thought for a moment. "I don't know. Normal seems to be that I'm always on the verge of disaster. Trauma is around every corner."

"You sound like a lot of cops," Phil said. "They get so used to trauma that it feels better when they're in the midst of some kind of shit storm. They're always fucking up in their lives—because disaster feels normal. Fortunately, I am not that way. I'm glad to be retired. I don't need the trauma or the drama."

"No," I said. "That's not right. I like peace and quiet."

Although I did get nervous when everything in my life calmed down. Didn't everyone? Because it couldn't last, the good times, right? Something bad was always around the corner.

I said, "I'm not like those cops. I want everything to settle down. It just never does."

"I hear ya," Phil said. "But I've never known you when things were settled down."

"Are you saying I cause all these things that happen in my life, like my kid dying?"

"Jesus, no," Phil said. "We all have real things happen in our lives, horrible things." Phil gulped the last of his coffee and then he said, "So, you ready to go find this dirt bag?"

We took Phil's car. The dirt bag lived in a house on the edge of a nice part of the city.

"I guess blackmail pays well but not that well," I said when Phil pointed out the house. We parked down the road a bit.

"Stay low," Phil said.

"What are you going to say?"

Phil shrugged. "I'll wing it. People talk to me."

That didn't sound like much of a plan. I picked up my phone and called Phil. He answered it. "Yes?"

"Keep it on," I said. "I want to listen to it all."

Phil made a face, but he put the phone in his pocket. "Whatever you hear, you stay the fuck in this car."

"Yes, grandpa," I said.

Then he got out of the car and began walking down the street.

"Can you hear me?" he asked.

It was muffled, but I could hear him.

"Yep," I said.

"Don't talk," he said.

"Yeah, right," I said.

I watched him walk up to the house. Heard the doorbell ring from his phone.

Door squeaking open. Children's voices in the background laughing. Then a man's voice. "May I help you?"

"Are you Lance Johnson?" Phil.

"Yes." He hesitated.

"I am Phil Case," Phil said. "I'm a private investigator. May I speak with you in private?"

"We're just about to get ready to go to church," Johnson said. I could see a man stepping outside. Closing the door. He was probably in his forties, red hair, a complexion that was not suited for Los Angeles.

"What is this about?" Johnson asked.

Phil had stepped back a bit. Must be his training as a police officer.

"You've been blackmailing a client of mine," Phil said, "and I wanted to talk to you about it before we report it to the police."

"Which client?" the man asked.

I covered my mouth so I wouldn't gasp. He was doing this to more than one person?

"How many people are you blackmailing?" Phil asked.

"I wouldn't call it blackmail," Johnson said.

This guy was a talker. Good.

"I offer people a chance to buy back photos they don't want made public."

"Photos you've taken," Phil said.

"Most of the time," he said, "but not always. They all know that if they go to the police, I will hand over the photos to the tabloids. That's our deal."

"Deal?" Phil said. "I don't think any of them willingly made a deal with you."

Johnson laughed. "You'd be surprised. I have one girl who gave me the address of what hotel she'd be at so I could take photos of her and her married lover. Then she asked me to pretend to blackmail her, and we could split the money. She said 80/20. I said 50/50. She works for a studio, but she has a drug problem."

I was getting sick to my stomach. Obviously he was talking about Fern.

"The joke's on her, though," Johnson said, "because I've got the photos and I will release them if she doesn't come up with the money."

"You seem pretty proud of yourself," Phil said.

"A guy's got to make a living," Johnson said. "I've got two daughters and a wife. None of them contribute a dime. But praise Jesus, they are all good girls."

"Phil," I whispered to myself. "Ask him who the woman is, ask him who the woman is."

"So if someone named Fern Lightman asked you to track me down," Johnson said "tell her she still has a few days to get me the money. Otherwise, I'm sending those photos everywhere. The photos of her mother, too. I'm sending them everywhere, too."

"Photos of her mother?"

"Yeah, that writer. Brooke McMurphy. It's all legal. Fern let me in so I could install cameras in McMurphy's house and car. Fern said she was part owner of everything so it was OK." Johnson laughed. "I tell you one thing: She is not a very good daughter. Can you imagine doing that to your mother?"

"Did you give her the photos you took of her mother?"

"No, not yet," Johnson said. "I haven't seen her yet. I'm meeting her at my office at 4 p.m. Bad traffic time, but I'll get something more out of it. She's a great roll in the hay despite everything. She's meaner than hell. If my wife ever found out, I'd be done for. But you gotta do what you gotta do. Good talking with you, man. Just tell whoever it is to buy the photos from me, and then we're all good."

And then Johnson went back into the house.

It took everything in my power not to jump out of the car and run after him. To kill him. Or at least slay him with my wit.

As Phil walked back to the car, he took out his phone and hung up on me. A few moments later, he got into the car.

He looked at me. "I-I don't know what to say, Brooke. I'm speechless."

"What a fucking piece of shit," I said.

"Who? Him or your daughter."

I stared at him. "Both."

ELEVEN

I was so angry I was speechless. No, that's the wrong word. I was enraged. I saw red. No, I saw scarlet. That's how pissed I was. I wanted to call Hayword and tell him to drop Fern off at the side of the road. But no, no, I couldn't do anything yet. I had to think, think.

Phil tried to talk to me, but it was as if I couldn't hear anything except the voices in my own head. How could Fern do this to me, her own mother? Every time I thought we had come to some kind of understanding, she would do something to blow it all up. She burned down our house—or she didn't. The jury was out on that now as far as I was concerned. She staged a robbery in the restaurant where we were having breakfast to get her then-boyfriend a job. And now . . . this. What was *this?* Was she trying to get revenge on me for something or just make a boatload of money?

"She's an addict," I heard Phil say. "Her brain isn't right."

I looked over at him. It seemed like he was in the passenger's seat, and I was in the driver's seat.

"You should understand that," Phil said.

No, Phil was driving. Thank god.

"Why should I understand that?" I asked. "Because I'm a drunk? I never hurt anyone except myself."

Phil made a noise and shook his head.

"What?" I said. "And be careful with your answer because I want to punch someone, and you're the only one near."

"Like you scare me," he said. "You hurt everyone around you. Your husband especially. Your kids."

"But never on purpose," I said. "I didn't have a plan. It just happened."

"And Fern's worse because she had a goddamn plan?"

"Fuck, yes," I said.

"What are you gonna do?" he asked.

"You mean after I kill her?" I said. "I'm gonna bury her body where no one will ever find it."

When we got back to Phil's house, I felt a bit more grounded. My anger had dulled enough for my feelings to be hurt, for a moment, and then I was angry again.

Phil got into my car and dug around until he found a tiny camera where one of the plug-ins was.

"The photos were automatically sent to the satellite and then probably to Johnson's computer," Phil said, pointing to something on the camera. "But there's also a memory card, for extra protection in case anything went wrong."

"But we know he got photos," I said, "because he mentioned them. Nothing went wrong from his point of view."

Phil pulled out the memory card and handed it to me.

"What am I gonna do with this?" I asked.

"You can see what he has if you like," Phil said. "I can put the memory card in my camera and then download it onto my computer."

"I don't want you to see these," I said.

"OK, then *you* can put them in my camera and download them onto my computer. You know what a computer is, right? And you know what downloading is?"

"Shut up," I said. I snatched the memory card from him. We closed the door to the car and walked toward Phil's front door. "Although really, I don't know the difference between uploading and downloading. You?"

"Absolutely no clue," Phil said.

Phil put the card into his camera and showed me how to download the photos onto his computer, without him looking at them. Then he left his office and closed the door behind him as one after another of the photos came up in a line on the screen.

Ryan and I sitting together in the car. Looks like we are talking. I hold up the vodka-laced OJ jug. He drinks. I pull off my slacks. Good god. Close up of my bare ass. They say the camera adds twenty pounds. This camera added a hundred pounds. My ass was too close to the camera. Oh fuck. Ryan's erection. Me putting a condom on his dick. Me sitting on his penis. Nothing sexy about it. And no mistaking who we were.

If these photos were published, my family would be destroyed. For my children to know I was fucking Ryan hours after I had slept with their father. Gawd.

Not that I cared about what Fern thought at this moment, but there was David to consider. And Hayword. The media would dig up the story of Alberto, his death, our house burning down, me later going into rehab. I did not want to relive that courtesy of the 'bloids.

Plus, this would not be good for Ryan. Especially if someone figured out he was an alcoholic, and the OJ was really a screwdriver. He would look like a victim, and I would look like . . . what I was. An enabler. Or worse.

Jesus.

Fuck, fuck, fuck.

I could see it now in the tabloids: First photos of Hayword and I doing it with the timestamp plain and visible while our private parts would be covered with a black line? Then photos of me and Ryan, only hours later.

I deleted the photos from Phil's computer and took the memory card from his camera and slipped it into my front shirt pocket.

I went into the living room where Phil sat with his feet up on the coffee table. He looked up at me.

"That bad?" he asked.

"You have no idea," I said as I sat in the chair opposite him. "I was having sex with an old love hours after having sex with Hayword."

There, I had said it out loud.

"That's what Johnson has photos of?" Phil asked.

"Yes," I said. "It's not a good way to figure out I need to lose about 30 pounds either."

Phil laughed. I guess it would be funny if it were happening to someone else.

"What about the camera in the house?" Phil asked.

"It'll show Hayward and I having sex, I assume," I said.

"You think it would hurt Hayword if those photos were published of you and this other man?" Phil asked. "Even though you're separated. I don't think it would be a big deal."

"It would be to my family," I said. "The other man was Alberto's father, the one who deserted me when I got pregnant all those years ago."

"Jesus," Phil said. "How did you happen to get together with him again?"

I groaned. "It's too sordid to talk about."

"Remember I was a police officer," he said.

"I went crazy a couple days ago. That's all. And right now I need to remove that camera from my bedroom and then figure out what to do next."

Lance Johnson thought he was meeting Fern at 4:00 today at his office. I looked at the clock. I needed to delay that meeting until I figured out what I was doing.

"Phil, can you tell me where to look for the camera in my house?" I asked.

"I'll find it for you," he said.

"You are being so nice. Don't you have some work to do?"

He laughed. "This is work," he said. "I'm charging you for every minute."

"OK then," I said. "I'll meet you at my bungalow around 2:30. I'll text you the address."

He nodded. "I expect food!" he called after me as I headed for the door.

"I don't do booty calls," I said.

I heard his chuckle as I headed out the door.

I hurried to my car and texted Phil the address. Then I dug Fern's phone out of her purse. I looked through her contacts. There was Lance Johnson's name, plain as day. I texted him from Fern's phone, "Got tied up today. Can I meet you tomorrow morning at your place? I'll have the money."

I held my breath, hoping that Fern had not gotten a hold of him some other way. I stared at the screen.

"Come on, you dirt bag," I said.

"10 a.m. Be there or don't you dare," he wrote.

I texted a thumbs up emoji.

"Phew." I now had a few hours to figure this out.

I texted Sally, "I need to see you. Where are you?"

"My house," she texted right back.

I put her address in my GPS. Shouldn't take too long. No major traffic jams.

"Can I come over? We need to talk."

I was already on my way. I heard the phone beep with her reply, but I didn't look. I didn't want to be discouraged. This was going to be a terrible conversation that could ruin our friendship as well as our business.

I had to do it. I couldn't go forward until I knew what Sally wanted and how she would react.

I was almost there when the phone rang. My car answered it.

"You driving?" Hayword asked.

"Hands-free," I said, "remember, you made sure my car had it. Are you in Tucson?"

He hesitated. Then he said, "Not yet. Fern wanted to stop at Quartzsite to look for some rocks. We kind of lost each other."

"She's probably off buying drugs," I said.

"No," Hayword said. "She's been so loving and sincere."

Just like last night when she was so loving toward me. Fake, fake, fucking fake.

"We're supposed to meet at this little café," Hayword said. "It'll be all right."

"A little café in Quartzsite?" I said. "That sounds doubtful. Be careful, Hayword; all is not what it seems."

"What do you mean?" he asked.

"I'll talk to you about it later," I said, "when I know more."

"OK," he said. "I love you."

"Why are you saying that now?" I asked.

"Because I do," he said.

"Look, we had sex a couple of times," I said. "It was nice. But we're not getting back together or anything."

"Our daughter died yesterday," he said. "I figure I want everyone in my life to know when I love them. And I fucking love you. Even though you are such a pain in the ass. Maybe because you are a pain in the ass."

"Fuck you," I said. "I fucking love you, too, but it doesn't mean anything, except that I love you and I'd protect you with my last breath."

"Yeah, me, too," he said. "Call me."

He was right: Fern had almost died yesterday. She hadn't faked that. Joanie had given her the Narcan. The paramedics had taken her away.

I squinted. Only the doctors never told us anything specific. Because she wasn't a minor. Her records were private.

Could she have faked her overdose and her death?

Fuck. Could that be true? What was real? How could she have pretended to die in front of me, after I had already lost one child?

I turned into Sally's long paved drive. It wound up and around a hill. True Beverly Hills style. Her place made ours look like a log cabin. I parked the car and walked up the palatial steps to her huge wooden front door. I rang the bell. A tall thin white woman dressed all in black opened the door. Was she the maid, the housekeeper, Sally's new love interest?

"May I help you?"

"Sally's expecting me," I said. "I'm Brooke McMurphy."

"Ah yes," the woman said. "Come in."

I stepped over the threshold, and she closed the door behind me. She led the way across Sally's huge living room and down several steps toward the patio.

"I love the zombie movies," the woman said solemnly.

I wished people would stop calling them that.

"Can you tell me if Colleen's son Aiden will come back to life in the third movie?" she asked.

I almost burst out laughing as I followed her. She didn't even turn around and look at me as she asked the question.

"I guess we'll have to wait and see," I said as I followed her outside.

She pointed to Sally who was sitting by the pool under an umbrella.

"Dead or alive," the woman said as she walked by me. "I'd fuck him."

I stood with my mouth open for a moment as she went back into the house.

"What the fuck?" I whispered. Then I walked down the steps and across the grass to the pool where Sally lounged. She was wearing a one piece black bathing suit that made her white skin look even whiter. She tilted her head and her black hat up when she saw me. She smiled, but her eyes looked dead. Uh-oh.

"Lovely to see you so soon again," she said. "Why aren't you working?"

"Why aren't you?" I asked. I sat in the chaise lounge next to her. I felt entirely overdressed.

"I can have Maude get you a bathing suit," Sally said.

"So that's Maude," I said. "Is she new?"

"New to this world or new to us?"

"Either or both."

Sally laughed. "Yes and no."

Didn't matter.

"I need to talk to you about some things," I said. "I don't know where to begin."

"I know you fucked Hayword and Ryan," she said. "And you forgot your dead kid's birthday. Again." She was flipping through a magazine like this was nothing.

"His name is Alberto," I said.

Sally looked over at me. "What?"

"My dead kid's name."

She blinked. "OK. You forgot Alberto's birthday. Again."

"What the fuck, Sally?"

She threw the magazine down. "If you're trying to tell me that your whore of a daughter fucked my husband and someone took photos of it and they're blackmailing your daughter with them, I already know." She was trembling. "Jonathan told me this morning. You should have told me."

"I just found out," I said.

"When?"

"When?"

"Yes, when did you fucking find out?"

"I-I think it was Monday," I said.

"And here it is already Wednesday," Sally said. "How could you not tell me?"

Wednesday. Wasn't that the day of David's lightning storm? I looked up at the sky. Blue, blue, blue.

"I was trying to figure everything out," I said.

"Figure out what?" Sally said. "How you could get away with it? How you could get your daughter off the hook?"

"How not to hurt you," I said. "How not to destroy our friendship. Fern overdosed yesterday and died. Apparently she was distraught because Jonathan broke up with her when he found out about the blackmail, Monday night. Joanie gave her Narcan. She's on the way to rehab today. I hired Phil Case to find out who was doing the blackmailing. It's a pap, Lance Johnson. But he said Fern hired him."

Sally drew in her breath. "What?"

"That's all I know right now," I said. "I wanted to let you know. I'm going to Fern's apartment right now. I haven't spoken to her since I found out she had something to do with it. Apparently she's a drug addict, and she needs money. I guess. I don't really know."

Sally picked up her phone and shouted into it, "Get my asshole of a husband out here."

A few moments later, Jonathan stepped out of the house and

walked toward us. He looked smaller. Or something. Much diminished since last I saw him in real life. Strange not to see my daughter naked on top of him.

"Hello, Brooke," he said.

Sally waved to him, as if to keep him from getting any closer.

"When did you break it off with the whore Fern?" Sally asked.

"Hey," I said. "Just call her Fern. A woman calling another woman a whore diminishes us all."

Sally gave me a look—I can't describe it more than to say it was as if we were complete strangers and she hated me thoroughly.

"When did you break it off with the cunt slut Fern?" Sally asked.

Jonathan looked from Sally to me and then back again. "As I told you, she broke it off from me. She told me a month ago that she was being blackmailed with photos of us, and she needed a million dollars. When I told her I didn't have it, she broke it off. Not right away but soon after."

"She didn't realize that Jonathan hasn't worked for a while and that I've been supporting his ass," Sally said. "He told me about it last night because Fern told him the photos would be published unless I could give her money to give to the blackmailer. Jonathan doesn't care about the photos, and neither do I. What do I care if Fern's reputation is in pieces?" She shrugged.

Sally waved Jonathan away. He turned and left. I had more questions, but apparently she was done with him.

Sally found a cigarette somewhere and lit it.

"I thought there was something in your prenup about not smoking," I said.

"There's also something about him not fucking someone

young enough to be his daughter. Almost young enough." She took a long drag on the cigarette.

"I'm so sorry about this, Sally."

She looked at me. "You should be. It's all your fault. Fern despises you. She blames you for everything. Couldn't you see that?"

"I thought that had all gotten better," I said.

"And these movies are paeans to your dead son," Sally said. "Fern has no place in your life. So she emulates you. Fucking everyone and drinking like a fish."

"I never slept with married men," I said. "Or women."

"Oh, who gives a fuck?" Sally said.

"Where do we go from here?" I asked.

"Fern is fired," Sally said.

"Of course," I said.

"And you better have the script finished to show the investors on Monday," she said, "or our contract will be null and void, you will no longer be a part of Back to Life Studios, and all the profits from the first two movies go to me. And Hayword. Once I tell him you fucked Ryan, he won't be very sympathetic toward you. So you will have nothing."

She smashed out her cigarette on the side of her chair.

"Any questions?" she asked.

"Wow," I said, "it's as if you were waiting for this to happen."

She smiled. "I was. I knew you'd fuck it up eventually. That's who you are. Like daughter, like mother."

I got up to leave.

"I'm sorry I ever fucked you," I said. "I never knew you were such a dick."

TWELVE

I felt dazed as I drove toward home. Couldn't tell you how I got there. I wanted to call someone. But who? Mark. Mark was supposed to be my true love, but that had gone awry. I couldn't tell Hayword, not yet. I couldn't deal with him falling apart as our life was falling apart. Joanie had enough on her plate.

Clearly I needed more friends.

Sally was right about the contract. I had to perform or I was done. I had agreed to it because I couldn't imagine that I wouldn't perform. It just wasn't in my nature to miss a deadline.

I needed help.

Joanie had said magic was possible if a lightning storm was coming. "I see no sign of a lightning storm," I said, "but Nature gods, can you help me get out of this, keep my children safe, and help us live happily ever after?"

Phil drove up almost at the same moment as I drove up the drive to my bungalow.

"How'd it go with Sally?" Phil asked.

"Not good," I said.

I let Phil into the house. He looked around. "I've heard about this place for years. I figured it would be fancier."

I rolled my eyes as I shut the door. "What on earth could you have heard about this house?" Phil looked at me. "Never mind. I don't want to know."

I showed Phil to the bedroom. It didn't take him long to find the camera. This one I was able to hook right up to my computer. There we were, Hayword and I fucking our brains out. Not attractive at all. If this was what porn looked like, how did anyone ever get turned on?

I went out to my living room where Phil waited for me. We sat in silence for a bit.

"I looked around the rest of the house," he said. "I didn't find any other camera. When do you think they put the cameras in?"

I had no idea. Wait.

"Fern stopped by Friday night," I said. "She left me a note and a present. Martinelli's cider and cherry pie. I wonder if that's when they did it. She would have known I was away because we were at David's school."

It was the next day that I had started to feel stressed out, or something.

When the next day?

In the afternoon.

What had happened?

I had eaten the pie and drank the Martinelli's Fern had left.

I suddenly felt sick to my stomach.

I got up and went to the fridge, opened it, and took out the bottle of Martinelli's. Just a swallow or two remained in the bottom of it. I got a glass from the open shelves and poured a bit of the cider into it. Then I brought it to Phil. He took a sip.

"What is it?" I asked.

"It's apple cider," he said, "and champagne."

I almost fell to my knees. I staggered to the couch. Could this be true: My own daughter had spiked my cider. She had wanted me to drink again. Why?

What would happen if I became a sloppy drunk again?

Fern knew if I began drinking again I would do something embarrassing. Then she would have the photos from the camera they installed in my car and my bedroom. Or the blackmailer would have photos.

Fern was the reason everything fell apart on Sunday. She was the reason I drank on Sunday.

She did all of this to get money? Why hadn't she just asked me for money? Why hadn't she told me she was in trouble? Was it easier to ruin my life than to ask for money? Or was ruining my life the reason for it all?

My own daughter had spiked my drink.

How could she?

How could I have handed Ryan a jug of spiked OJ.

Almost handed it to him.

I had told him. At least I had told him. I didn't just give it to him to drink without him knowing.

How had Hayword and I raised such a monster?

"What am I missing?" Phil asked.

"Fern brought me this sparkling apple cider," I said. "She left it in my kitchen. It was open. I just thought she'd taken a sip before leaving it, but she had opened it so she could put alcohol in it. When I drank it on Saturday, I was tired, cranky. I didn't notice it had alcohol in it. Fern is the reason I started drinking on Sunday. She's the reason this blackmailer now has photos of me with Hayword and me with Ryan."

"Jesus," Phil said.

"Understatement," I said. I took a deep breath. "I've got to get home to David and then call Hayword and tell him."

"Is there anything else I can do for you?" Phil asked.

"Text me Johnson's office address," I said. "I might need to have a conversation with him."

"Don't go see him alone," Phil said. "He might be dangerous."

"So am I," I said.

We looked at each other. Finally he shrugged. "OK. But at least call me and tell me what you're doing."

"I will definitely try to do that," I said. "Thank you for everything. Hey, could you call Caryn at our offices? She was trying to figure out who put that list up of all the men I'd slept with. Maybe you could help her. I want it taken down. It's causing David some stress."

Phil nodded. "Will do. I think I might go see my kids tonight."

I laughed or moaned. "Make sure none of them are psychopaths."

"Fern isn't a psychopath," Phil said.

"Really?" I said. "Then what?"

"I don't have an answer to that," he said. "I'll talk to you tomorrow."

I followed him out the door. We said goodbye, and I drove up to my old house. David was inside, already home from school.

"Hello, darlin'," I said. "I thought you weren't getting home until later today." He looked distressed. "What's going on?"

"I got the mail for the Alberto Foundation," he said. "The bank statements. There are two checks written out to people I don't know. I called the bank, and they say they've got my signature on them, along with Fern's. Because there has to be two signatures, remember. The four of us, and there has to be two. But I don't know these people. They have to be organizations doing work on climate change because that's our mission. Mom, the checks are for $50,000 each."

"Oh, shit," I said. He held out the bank statement to me, and I looked at it. Yep, two checks, on the same day.

"Who were they made out to?" I asked.

He looked down at a piece of paper where he had written the names. "Sue Smith and Connie Kelly."

"Fuck," I said. Clearly made-up names.

Obviously Fern had stolen the money.

"We're a non-profit," David said. "This is against the law. I could go to jail."

"No, David, listen, you are not going to jail. I will fix this. Try to calm down. Um, get yourself a snack. I'm going to call our accountant."

I ran up to Hayword's office, sat in his chair, and then called our accountant, Marjorie Banks. We greeted each other, and then I said, "We found out that two unauthorized checks were written on the Foundation account for $50,000 each. We believe it was Fern and she forged her brother's signature. She has a drug problem. She's on her way to rehab. What can we do to make certain David isn't in trouble and that we aren't in trouble?"

"First, you need to put the $100,000 back," Marjorie said. "I can do that for you if you like. Transfer it from your savings account and put it in the Foundation's account. We need to get Fern off of everything to do with the Foundation. I'll do what I can do, but you need to talk to your lawyer, too, to see who you need to report it to."

"OK," I said. "Thanks, Marjorie."

Then I phoned Hayword. I took a deep breath. He answered.

"Hi, Brooke," Hayword said. "I've got her. She's fine. No drugs. We're in a hotel for the night."

"I've got a lot to tell you, Hayword," I said. "Fern hired the blackmailer. I don't know all the details. We'll have to ask her. She was trying to get us or Sally to pay the blackmail."

"What?"

"Yes," I said. "Phil talked to the photographer today. They also put a camera in my car and my bedroom in the hopes of being able to blackmail me. They did it Friday night."

Hayword made a noise. "What the fuck? But-but, there will be photos of us having sex. They can't blackmail us about that. We're married."

"When they put in the cameras, they left a bottle of Martinelli's apple cider and pie," I said.

"I remember you told me about that," Hayword said.

"There was alcohol in the cider," I said. "That's the reason I drank Sunday—because I had already been drunk Saturday."

"What the fuck? Why would she do that?"

"You'll have to ask her," I said. "There's more. She stole $100,000 from the Foundation. I think she may be going to jail. I called Marjorie and told her to put the money back, but I don't know if that'll make a difference."

"Fuck," Hayword said. "I think I should bring her home then, instead of rehab. We've got to figure this all out."

"Oh, Hayword," I said, "it is so fucked up. That's not even all of it." I felt like I was going to cry. "I can't tell you over the phone. Please just come home. I don't care what you do with her. Leave her at rehab. Leave her at the side of the road. I don't care."

"She's still our daughter," Hayword said.

"Who gave an alcoholic a drink," I said. "I had no fucking idea. It was apple cider. I just thought it was was cider, Hayword." I began to weep. "I had no idea. The things I did. They were awful."

"Having sex with me wasn't that awful," he said quietly.

I laughed through my tears.

"It will be OK," Hayword said. "We'll get through this."

"Sally says if I don't get the script finished, I'm done. All the profits from the first two movies will go to her and to you and I'll be out."

"Then we have to make the time and space for you to do the script," Hayword said. "If that's what you want."

"But you have no idea what I've done," I said, "since Sunday. You have no idea. You will never love me again. It will never be right. She has ruined us all."

"I'll be home tomorrow," Hayword said. "We'll fix this then. Brooke, there's nothing you could do that would make me stop loving you. Haven't you figured that out yet? It will be OK."

"I don't think it will be," I said, "but thanks for saying it. I need to go calm David down. Fern forged his signature on the checks. He's afraid he's going to jail."

"Jesus," Hayword said. "I'll talk with you tonight."

I hurried back downstairs. David was at the kitchen island, shaking. I put my arms around him.

"It's OK, sweetheart," I said. "You are not in trouble. The money is being put back even as we speak."

"Who were those people?" David said. "Who did she give all that money to?"

"My guess is that she gave it to herself," I said.

"You mean those were pseudonyms?"

"Something like that," I said. "Did you know she was using drugs?"

David shook his head. "No. Something was up. She was always mad when I talked to her."

"Really? As far as I can remember, she's always been mad." I shouldn't have said it, but I was tired of it.

"She kept talking about not having money," David said, "and how we deserved more because of how we grew up."

"Is that how you feel?" I asked. "Do you think I should pay you because you had a shitty childhood?"

David looked at me. He wasn't shaking any more. He suddenly looked like an adult. He was so handsome: a cross between me and Hayword.

"I didn't have a shitty childhood," he said. "My brother died. My mother has a chronic illness. Those are the bad things. I have parents who love me and take care of me. I live in a nice house. I always have food and shelter. That doesn't sound shitty to me."

I put my arms around him, and we embraced.

"Then why have you been acting so crappy lately?" I asked as we let each other go.

He shrugged. "Come on, Mom. You explained this to me when I was 13 years old. I've got a lot of hormones cascading through my body and my body is often ahead of my brain. It makes me fucking cranky."

"Goddamn it," I said. "You're not supposed to be swearing." I smiled.

"And I didn't like seeing that list," David said.

"But it's not true or real," I said.

"I know that now."

"I guess your electrical storm never happened," I said. "That's good news."

"Mom, do you ever look at the news? Massive thunderstorms are supposed to hit the LA area Thursday along with the lightning storm."

"I have been a little preoccupied this week," I said.

"I gotta tell you something."

Oh shit. Was he on drugs? Had he knocked someone up? Stolen something? Was he quitting school?

"Aunt Joanie called me over to look at something in her back garage."

My stomach lurched.

"She's not your aunt," I said. "I don't know why you call her that."

Yep. That's what I said. Good grief.

"So what did you find?"

"I went down there," David said, "but it smelled like something died. It was horrible. I almost threw up. I opened the side garage door and it looks like there's someone in the front seat of the Jaguar. You know, dead."

"Did you get close?"

"No," he said. "I ran like hell. Aunt Joanie told me she thought Uncle Marv was dead in the Jaguar. She called him that. I've never called him Uncle Marv. I think I've met him twice. Joanie said she didn't want to call the police unless someone was really there. She thinks he's haunting her."

"Oh Jesus H. Christ," I said. "I cannot believe she got you in the middle of this."

"Do you think she killed Marv, and she was trying to get me to take the fall for it?"

"No. She knows if she hurt you in any way I would beat her to a pulp."

David laughed.

"What?" I said.

"Come on, Mom," he said. "You're this tiny thing. You ain't gonna beat anyone up."

"You know nothing," I said. "I'm a tough old broad."

"I don't doubt that," he said. "You know, old and tough."

I slugged his arm. "Oh, aren't you funny. I'm gonna go talk to your aunt."

"Can I come?" he asked.

"Um, there might be some swearing," I said. "I won't be long."

I left the house, walked across the street and down some until I came to Joanie's driveway. I walked into the house without knocking. Joanie was sitting on the couch, as usual, sipping a drink, as usual.

"What the fuck, Joanie?" I said.

She looked surprised to see me and then terrified.

"I didn't know she was really going to overdose," Joanie said. "It was supposed to be a joke. Let's scare Brooke, you know, ha ha."

"What? What the fuck are you talking about?"

Joanie closed her mouth.

"What are you talking about?" she asked.

"Oh my gawd," I said. "So it was all a put on. Fern didn't really overdose? She asked you to come over and give her Narcan so I would think she had died?"

Joanie put her drink down. "A joke. A fucking joke. She said the two of you had been playing practical jokes on one another lately. This was just another one."

"But you called the ambulance. You really gave her the Narcan. Didn't you?"

"Because she was blue," Joanie said. "I figured that's what I should do. She was supposed to open her eyes and wink at me or something. But she was fucking dead."

"What is wrong with you, Joanie?" I said. "I found my baby boy dead. What kind of person would think it was a funny practical joke if I found my daughter dead? I mean what the holy fuck were you thinking? Didn't that seem like a screwy thought process?"

"I don't know!" Joanie said. "Fern has always been weird, and she was talking about what a stick-in-the-mud you were now, and wouldn't it be funny if you thought she overdosed. Of course now that I say it out loud it sounds terrible. But I was drunk, and my husband is out there rotting in the garage and haunting me. He's fucking haunting me. I hear all kinds of noises in the night now, Brooke."

"That's another thing," I said. "David said you asked him to go check and see if there was a dead man in the Jaguar. Don't involve my kids in your bullshit. Go down there yourself. Or call the police."

"OK, OK. I just didn't know who to call."

"So you called my son?" I looked at her. "You haven't done anything inappropriate with him, have you?"

"What?" she asked. "No. What do you mean inappropriate?"

"Have you had sex with him?" I asked. "Have you given him anything to drink? Given him drugs."

"Christ," Joanie said. "No! He's like a son to me."

"Fuck you," I said. "You have no idea what that even means. I don't want any thing more to do with you, Joanie. This is it. If you contact us again, I'll call the police and tell them you have a dead man in your garage."

"I know all your secrets," Joanie said. "The things I could tell."

I laughed. "Wow. That didn't take you long. You actually don't know any of my secrets." I turned around to leave.

"What about Marv haunting me?" she asked.

"Marv is not haunting you," I said.

"How do you know?"

"Because there are no such things as ghosts," I said. "My guess is that you're overly sensitive because you're letting your husband rot in the fucking garage. If you really think you're hearing things, maybe Marv is gaslighting you. Maybe he's got a girlfriend and the two of them are trying to drive you crazy. Get some nanny cams and put them up around the house. If someone is really doing something you'll catch them."

"That's brilliant," Joanie said. "Thank you! Are you really not my friend any more?"

"Joanie, you let me believe my daughter was dead."

"But she was dead."

"But you thought she wasn't and you thought it would be a fun prank. This is hurting my brain. I am leaving. Your problems are your own now."

"What if someone killed Marv? They could be roaming our neighborhood looking for other victims."

"Call the fucking police," I said as I went out the door.

"Christ," I said to myself as I crossed the road. Two of my best women friends gone in a day. I didn't care. Everyone needed a friend, sure, but I did not need another problem.

I hurried home. So friendless I would be.

THIRTEEN

David and I stir-fried chicken, along with broccoli and carrots we cut into matchsticks. He told me about his day in school. He smiled and laughed. I listened. We sat at the counter and ate together. I liked hearing about his friends. For a long while, Hayword and I had been worried that he didn't have any. His friends now seemed so engaged in the world. David, too. I hoped it wasn't all too much for them. I didn't hang onto that thought. I loved being with my son. It was just the two of us. I was OK with that. I didn't think about Alberto not being there, or about Fern being a drug addict. It was just me and my boy.

When we had almost finished eating, David said, "You drank on Sunday, didn't you? I'm not mad at you. I just want to know."

"I did," I said.

"Do you know why?"

I sighed. I didn't know how much I should tell him.

"The real reason is that I'm a drunk," I said, "and drunks drink."

"But you didn't for so long," he said.

I nodded. "That's true. And I didn't feel like I was about to relapse. But I wasn't truthful about my relationship with Mark. I couldn't be real and truthful with him."

"Mom," David said, "I don't like secrets."

I pressed my lips together. "Fern gifted me a bottle of sparkling cider," I said. "I drank it. Turns out, it was spiked with champagne. I didn't notice." I shrugged. "I feel really stupid. I should have known."

"That's terrible, Mom," David said. "How could she do that? I don't ever want to see her again. And to think we were so worried about her when she overdosed. I don't get it. Why would she want you to relapse?"

"I don't really know," I said. "I think she thinks she needs money and figured she could get it from me if I was drunk." He didn't need to know about the cameras or the blackmail. That information was too much for me, and I was an adult. I wasn't going to burden him with it. Not yet.

"What are you going to do?" David asked.

"Your dad and I will talk later," I said. "We'll figure out something."

"Will she go to jail for stealing from the Foundation?"

"Probably," I said.

"Good. I hope she rots there. I hope she gets some kind of STD and actually rots there."

"That's pretty specific," I said. I put my arm across his shoulders. "I am so angry with your sister. More angry than I have ever been with anyone. And I know that she's obviously got some problems."

"Do you think she's a psychopath?" David asked. "Do you think she's gonna kill us all in our sleep?"

There went his anxiety.

"I don't think she's a psychopath," I said. "Hopefully we can get her some help. Now, let's get this mess cleaned up. What do you want to do tonight?"

"Petra and Joaquin were having a game night tonight," he said. "I'd like to go for a couple of hours."

I didn't know if Petra and Joaquin were boys or girls, but I also knew that didn't seem to matter to him the way it had to me when I was his age.

"Don't you just do that on the computer?" I asked.

"Board games, Mom," he said. "Real life. In person. Like you always wanted." He grinned. I rolled my eyes.

"Do I know these kids?"

"Sure," he said, and began rattling off things he had done with them and how many times Hayword and I had met their parents.

So we cleaned up the kitchen. Then we hugged—I held him a little too long—and then he left to go play on a school night. I thought that was a good thing: It meant he wasn't worried about school.

As soon as he was gone, I headed out to Fern's apartment. Lance Johnson expected money tomorrow morning or he was publishing all of the photos, including the ones of me and Ryan and me and Hayword. I had to figure what to do about it. Couldn't kill him. I mean, come on, first, it's wrong. Second, I would get caught. Third, it would be messy. Fourth, it was not even an option. I couldn't let those photos get published, but I wasn't going to give him the money. Maybe something in Fern's apartment would explain this entire mess to me.

I still had to write the damn screenplay or lose my company. That seemed the least of it right this moment. But it was my company. Mine and Hayword's. Sally didn't deserve it. Especially with how she was acting now. What did she contribute to the entire enterprise except kissing up to people with money?

Traffic was a bitch from hell.

And not the good kind.

Soon enough I was at Fern's apartment building and then in her apartment. I had only been a couple of times. Fern liked to keep her private life private. I went up three flights of stairs, unlocked her door, and went inside. Her place was about the size of my bungalow, only narrower. She had a view of another apartment building. She said she liked it that way. It reminded her that she was in the movie business—like *Rear Window* and that Nature didn't really count for anything. I think she said stuff like that just to worry David and piss me off. It didn't piss me off. I thought it was sad.

The place smelled stale. I opened the sliding glass doors to the balcony. Heard the cacophony of traffic. But a breeze wafted in. I sighed and looked around. My stomach felt like it was in a million knots. Fern hardly had any pictures on the walls. It looked more like a hotel room than someone's home. It was so generic.

What had happened to my daughter? When she was younger she had been creative. She was always a pain in the ass. Always argued. Pushed me about everything. But she always made a place her own. We would go to a restaurant, and she would draw pictures and put them up in the booth. "This is my booth," she would say. Or if we went to a park, she would gather sticks and build a little fort, marking out her place in it. Her room in our first house was gorgeous. She picked out the rich maroon paint, made her bed like something out of the *Arabian Nights* and sometimes pretended she was Scheherazade.

Then Alberto died. The house burned down. We moved. I blinked. I couldn't remember much more about her except that she was angry with me. Everything was always my fault. After a while, I just could not stand being in the same room with her.

And vice versa.

But I had thought much of that was healed. Especially after she started working at Back to Life Studios and helping to run the Foundation. She seemed to have come into her own.

At least, she didn't seem to be blaming me for everything. Maybe that's all I noticed or cared about. Phew: I was out of the line of fire.

Only, apparently I had been mistaken about that.

I began looking through her drawers. I didn't know what I expected to find. I wanted to fix this Lance Johnson problem without her help. Without talking to her. I knew that I would have to talk to her eventually. But right now, I detested her. Right now, I wished she had died instead of Alberto.

I sucked in my breath and slammed shut the drawer I was rummaging through. No, no, no. I didn't wish her dead. That wasn't what I meant. I only meant . . . I don't know what I meant, but I didn't want her dead. Couldn't she just love me and accept me? She loved and accepted her father, and he was a flawed human being too.

I went to her bedroom. Pulled open all her drawers. Found clothes. Looked in her closet. Clothes and shoes. Where was her computer? Didn't she have bills? Paper? Did they do everything online these days?

I left her room and walked down the hallway to the second bedroom. The door was closed and locked. I shook the handle. I was about to try and kick it in—wouldn't that feel great?—when I remembered I had Fern's keys. I fished them out and tried them in the door, one by one. A small one popped open the lock and the door swung open. I had thought it was a guest room, but it looked like her office. Neat and tidy.

I sat at her desk and opened her laptop. Her emails were boring, mostly about work. Nothing to or from Jonathan or Lance Johnson. I looked in her photos. Pictures of her and Jonathan together: eating, laughing, walking on the beach. Maybe she had really liked him.

She had a bunch of folders on her desktop. One was labelled "cat." She didn't have a cat, so I opened it. It was full of about 100 photos of her and Jonathan having sex. I felt sick to my stomach. I closed it. One file was labeled insurance. I clicked on it. 50 photos. I clicked on the first photo. It was Fern naked again. Gawd. Only this time the man under her and later over her was Lance Johnson.

If she had photos of her and Johnson together as insurance why hadn't she shown them to him to get him to not publish the photos?

My head and soul hurt. I sent the file to my email, and then I printed off a few of the photos where Lance's face was very clear. I folded them and put them in my purse.

Then I went to the closet and opened it. I was so surprised that I stepped back.

"What the hell?"

Inside the closet was display shelving, and on those shelves were leather purses. About ten of them. Most of them were pastel-colored or sea colors. A few were round with flat bottoms. The rest were just like regular purses, bags, clutches with handles. I didn't know what to call them. I didn't know anything about such things except that these bags were Persephone bags made by Neptune—I guess that was what the designer called herself now. These purses cost a mint. Some were $20,000 each. Maybe more. I was looking at $200,000 worth of purses that looked like they had never been used. I picked up a light green one—sea foam green? It felt heavy. I took it over to Fern's desk, set it down, and then opened it. Inside this perfect looking bag were tiny bottles of liquor, like the ones Ryan and I had recently drained. Vodka. Brandy. Whiskey. Some wine.

I zipped the purse up again, set it back in its place, and grabbed another purse. This one was magenta-colored and it snapped open. It was stuffed with liquor, too.

It turned out all the purses were filled with small liquor bottles.

I sat in the stuffed chair she had in the room. What could this possibly mean? Had my daughter gone crazy? Why hadn't I wondered that when she secretly gave me liquor and filmed me having sex? And pretended to be dead. I still wasn't sure about that. Had she been dead or not?

I called Hayword.

"Hey," he said. "You OK?"

"No," I said. "You?"

"She's not going into rehab," Hayword said. "She wants to come home and explain it all."

I laughed. "Do you think there's another explanation besides the one where she wants to destroy my life?"

"I would say that not everything is about you," Hayword said, "except that it does appear to be all about you this time."

"I found $20,000 handbags in her closet," I said. "Ten of them. All filled with liquor bottles."

Hayword was silent for a few moments. Then he whispered, "She seems so normal."

"Are you in the room with her?" I asked.

"No," he said, "I got separate rooms."

"Good," I said. "Keep your door locked, and don't give her a key to your room. I don't trust her."

"You think she would try to hurt one of us?" Hayword asked.

"She already has," I said. "I'm just trying to lessen the damage. Talk to you tomorrow."

I rubbed my face. I was still shocked that Fern had spiked

my cider. And I was still shocked that I had helped Ryan fall off the wagon. I had pushed him off. My rage at what he had done to me all those years ago—deserting me when I was pregnant with Alberto—didn't give me the right to destroy his life.

I made a noise. I had to make it right. Or something.

I closed Fern's closet. Then I turned off all the lights in her apartment, and I left. I drove to Ryan's house. When he opened the door, he smiled wanly. Then he said, "Hello, you. Devil or demon this time?"

"Come on," I said. "Let's go to a meeting. There's one starting soon."

"Isn't there always?" He came outside and closed the door to his house, locked it. We walked together to my car.

"Maybe after we'll go for coffee," I said, "and I'll show you pictures of Alberto. He kind of looked like you."

"Really?" Ryan said. "How could you tell? He was just a baby."

"Yeah, that's right," I said. "Just like you."

Ryan laughed. And choked a little. And laughed some more. I smiled. God. How we destroy each other little by little and then all at once.

FOURTEEN

Ryan and I walked down the long stairway to the basement of the church that I had not been in since I had seen Ryan there several years earlier. When I had eviscerated him in front of an entire room of recovering alcoholics. That had not been a good night.

Now here we were again after all those years.

When we reached the large meeting room, Ryan took my hand and squeezed it, just for a moment, but long enough for Mark to see it. Yes, my Mark. What was wrong with my brain? This was also where Mark went to AA meetings. It was near his house. He knew Ryan—as Bryan. They used to play in a neighborhood basketball team together.

Ryan went down a row to grab a seat. I smiled at Mark and gave him a hug.

"Are you and Bryan friends now?" Mark asked.

"It's a long story," I said. "He drank again, so I said I'd take him to a meeting."

"I didn't know you were in touch with him," Mark said. "I thought you hated his guts."

I sighed. Fuck. I did not want to explain my life to him or anyone right now.

"Are you all right?" I asked.

He looked good. He was cleaned up. Appeared to be sober.

"I found your key yesterday morning," he said. "Is that your way of saying we're over?"

I glanced at Ryan. He was watching us. He nodded to Mark and started to get up. I waved him away. Then I took Mark's arm. We left the room, walked down the hall, and went into a smaller empty room. I sat on a wooden bench against the wall. He sat next to me but not close.

"I shouldn't have cheated," he said, "but shouldn't we have talked about it before you decided we were finished? You just left me."

"I left you a long time ago. You just didn't notice."

He frowned. "I thought we were just figuring things out. I went back to my job. You went back to the bungalow."

"Didn't that tell you anything?" I asked. "We were moving apart not together."

"You made it seem like it was nothing," he said.

"Because I'm an asshole," I said. "I can't be alone. I don't know how to say goodbye. I don't know how to be close. We were over as soon as we went to live at the beach. It just took a while. We were not living our dreams, neither one of us. You did the restaurant for me, and I thought I wanted to be at the beach. Turns out, I didn't."

"Brooke, I don't care where we are as long as we're together," he said.

I smiled. "You know that's not true. You didn't like it at the beach. You missed your house and your mother and your neighbors. You're more social than I am."

He looked at his hands. I stared at the line of his jaw. It was so beautiful.

"Do you remember the time you pulled Joanie's toe out of the faucet?" I asked.

"I didn't pull it out," he said. "You did."

I laughed. "That's right. She was trying to seduce you. I didn't blame her, of course."

Mark looked at me. "Are you flirting with me?"

"No," I said. "At least, I don't mean to. I was just remembering our beginnings. We had a lot of drunken sex. You were really a good guy."

"You were drunk," he said. "I wasn't. If I were really a good guy, I guess I would have talked you into going to a meeting back then."

"Like anyone could ever talk me into anything," I said. "Well, maybe David. My son does have some sway with me."

"Not Fern?"

I shook my head. "The truth is that I like my life with my kids." OK, with my kid. "And Hayword. I like my job or my work. I think I can do it now and stay sober. I'm not a Hollywood lifer, but I like movies. I like stories. I like being able to create happy endings somewhere, since I can't seem to do it in my own life."

"I'm OK with that," he said.

"You hated all of that," I said. "Really, I think what we liked was fucking one another, especially when I was drunk. That's about all we had in common. Plus, you are such a decent and good man. I liked your company."

"I'm sorry I slept with my ex-wife," he said.

"I'm sorry I didn't know how to say goodbye," I said, "but you do. You did the one thing you knew I couldn't . . . forgive."

"So this is it?" he said, looking around. "After everything we've been through."

I wanted to cry or scream.

"I'm not really in touch with my feelings right now," I said. "Or possibly ever. But I've got so many things going on now with Fern and the business. This feels like the end." I shrugged. "But what do I know?"

Talk about hedging my bets.

"Are you and Ryan a couple now?" he asked.

"No!" I said, a little too forcefully. "No," I said more quietly. "He told me he's had a rough time since that night when I ripped him a new one here. I feel I've got some responsibility for him."

"You don't," Mark said.

He didn't know the whole story, of course. People relapsed when they kept too many secrets, and I had a boatload of them.

"Do you want to fuck one more time?" I asked. "In the bathroom? Or here? Could lock the door. Or keep it unlocked for old time's sake."

Mark laughed. Or chuckled. It wasn't sincere.

"Maybe later," Mark said.

This time, I laughed. "Yikes. A maybe later fuck. That's cold, bro."

We both stood and put our arms around each other.

"If you ever need anything," Mark said.

"You, too," I said.

We let each other go. Mark left the room.

I sat on the bench again. I didn't know if I was relieved or sad. I put my head in my hands.

"Mac?"

I looked up. Ryan was standing next to me.

"On little cat feet?" I asked. "I didn't hear you."

"I followed you down here," he said. "In case there was trouble. Don't worry. Mark didn't see me. You all right?"

He looked so concerned. So gorgeous. He reminded me of himself all those years ago. Except different. I didn't think the old Ryan was ever concerned about anyone but himself.

He leaned down and kissed me. I wanted to push him away. Instead, I stood up and pressed myself against his body. It was a long slow lovely kiss. I pulled away and went to the door, shut it, and locked it. Ryan was looking around.

"What are you looking for?"

"A bed or a cot?"

"Fucking me up against the wall won't do it?"

"My back has been acting up," he said.

"Oh for fuck's sake," I said. "Don't tell me that."

We found yoga mats and cushions. Soon we were naked—I used my clothes as a mini-sheet so I had something between me and the yoga mats. I didn't know where they'd been.

"Condom," I said, holding out my hand.

"Come on," Ryan said.

"There's the old selfish Ryan," I said. "I don't know where your dick has been. No condom, no sex."

"My dick has been in you," he said. "Remember? I've been impotent for years."

Oh yeah.

I wanted him. He looked delicious in the semi-darkness. I also wanted to stop. Before, I could explain fucking him because I was drunk. I was sober as a mouse now. Or a judge. How would I explain this to anyone?

"I'm not getting pregnant again," I said.

"Aren't you a little old to get pregnant?" Ryan asked.

"Are you trying to get laid or punched?" I asked. "And yes, my eggs probably would be a little old now."

"I don't carry condoms around with me," he said.

I got up, still naked, and grabbed my purse. I dug around in it until I came up with a condom.

Then we got busy.

It was great. He thought I was amazing, beautiful, my cunt perfect. He was so fucking needy, and what he needed was me.

"I can't get sober without you," he said.

"I'm losing my hardon here," I said. "Less talking and more dicking."

I orgasmed. It was nice.

But it had been better when I was drunk.

I wanted to ask Ryan: What do you think? Was it better doing it drunk or sober? But I didn't. I didn't want to do anything to encourage his drinking.

Afterward, we put on our clothes and stayed on the mats. I turned on the lights and then got my phone. I found my photos of Alberto and showed them to Ryan.

"Whenever I get a new phone," I said, "I move the photos. It's not always easy. But I want to have them with me."

We looked through the pictures together. Alberto was young, of course, a baby. So he didn't look that different from one photo to another, at least not to a stranger.

"He's getting his own personality in this photo," Ryan said.

I smiled. "Yep. Seven months old." One month before he died.

"He does have my smile," Ryan said. He looked at me. "He *did* have my smile."

I nodded.

"Do you have photos of your other children?" he asked.

"Sure," I said. "Here's one where Fern is holding Alberto. And here's one of David at school last week. I have lots in-between." I scrolled through the photos. I did have lots of photos of David but very few of Fern.

"My daughter and I don't get along well," I said. "She's causing quite a lot of problems right now."

"I wish I had had a family," he said. "Fifteen years ago it seemed like a horrible idea. Now, I wish I'd done it."

"You had your chance," I said. I put my phone away.

"Really?" he said. "You would have left Hayword and lived with me, with your other two kids? You think we would have made it? Because I don't. I was obviously a selfish bastard. And neither of us had any money."

I nodded. "It would not have been a good thing. In retrospect, I see that. But at the time I was so hurt by it. When Alberto died, I felt like my grief over you leaving me had killed him. I thought I had loved you too much."

"You *thought* you loved me? What does that mean?"

"I'm feeling this concrete floor on my ass," I said. We both stood and began putting the mats and cushions away. "I think what I loved was how free I was with you. By that time, I was stiff with Hayword. I felt like he wanted me to fix everything for him, and I couldn't. So many men seem to want women to be their emotional support animals, and we're not all equipped to do that. I am an emotional kick your ass animal. With you, I could fuck your brains out and then that was it. Getting pregnant just made you another husband. I didn't want that."

I was realizing this all as I said it. The same thing had happened with Mark. Once we were settled down, he was another husband who needed me to be his emotional support person. Fuck that. I had my own problems. I laughed out loud at myself.

"What?" Ryan asked.

"I am such an asshole," I said.

Ryan held out his hand to me. "Welcome to the club," he said.

We skipped the rest of the AA meeting, and I dropped Ryan off at his house.

"You coming in?" Ryan asked as he got out of the car.

"No, David's waiting for me at home," I said, staying in the driver's seat.

"I'd love to meet him," Ryan said. He stood a few feet from the car, looking in at me. "All grown up."

"Maybe," I said, "someday. Right now I have some fires to put out."

"Don't look at me to help you put out fire," he said. "I just inflame; I don't tame." He started laughing as he said it, and I laughed, too.

"Maybe you should take up screenwriting," I said. "What a cornball."

"I actually have started writing," he said. "I'm a lot smarter than I look."

"I doubt that." I grinned. "See you later, gator." Oops. It just slipped out.

"After while, crocodile." He turned and went toward the house.

"Bye, bye, butterfly," I said to myself. As I started to drive away, the phone bleeped or farted or chimed. I put the car in park again and looked at the text. It was from Sally.

"How is that whore of a daughter?" she asked.

"Fucking bitch," I said. "You leave my daughter out of this."

"Has she fucked anyone else's husband today? And speaking of today, how is the script coming? Tick-tock. By the way, Lance Johnson contacted me. Asked if I wanted to buy photos of you fucking some guy in a car. That would be Ryan Nichols, eh? Lance wouldn't email them to me. But he is coming to the office tomorrow afternoon to show me. I bet Hayword would be interested in seeing them. After that, he would want you out of the company, too. Let me know how the script goes."

"Fuck, fuck, fuck," I said as I finished reading the text. I felt like I was going to explode. I imagined my pieces all over the car.

I called our lawyer, Mercy Price. I actually got through to her.

"I need you to go over our contract with Sally St. James," I said. "I want to get rid of her, legally, of course."

"You don't need to qualify that," Mercy said. "Well, unless you do. What's going on?"

"I'll try to make it short," I said. "Fern had sex with Sally's husband, and Sally is enraged. The third script for the *Beauty and the Zombie* film is due in a few days. I haven't started it. If I don't have it finished by Monday, Sally can say I violated the contract, and the punishment for that is I'm no longer a partner, and she and Hayword get the profits for the last two movies, the profits we had."

"I remember," Mercy said. "I advised against that."

"Yes, I know. You were right."

"Are you going to finish the script?" she asked.

"I don't know," I said. "I hope so but lots of things are going on. For one thing, Sally hinted that she is going to show some photos to Hayword, photos of me in flagrante delicto, as it were. Isn't there something in the contract about a morals clause? Isn't blackmail immoral?"

"She's going to do what?" Mercy asked. "Good grief. Are you and Hayword back together?"

"No. We're not back together. She's lashing out. And I want to use that to try and get her out of the company. She wants me out. But it's my fucking company. Mine and Hayword's. We invited her in. I want her out."

"Forward me the text," Mercy said. "I doubt that it's anything actionable. But I'll look over the contract again. Could you buy her out? Remember, any three of you can get dissolve the business as long as nothing is owed. In other words, you can't dissolve it right now because you owe the company a script. But she could say hasta la vista at any time because she isn't obligated to provide the business with anything."

"I don't think we have enough money to buy her out," I said.

"Let me do some discreet nosing around," Mercy said. "Maybe someone needs a studio head, and we could convince them to make Sally an offer. Is there anyone in town who really likes you?"

"Not in particular," I said. "Oh, you're asking me if I've fucked anyone who might do me a favor."

"You got it, sistah," she said. "I call it the Vagina Club. Whoever has been in my veejay is part of the club. I love them all and use them as contacts now and again."

"You mean you fuck people so you can use them as a contact later? That sounds nasty."

"No," Mercy said. "I don't do that. I'm just saying that if he or she has been in the vee, they are still a part of me."

I laughed. "So you're asking me to have a vagina dialogue."

Mercy groaned. "Whatever. Get back with me."

I turned the phone off and threw it in the backseat. Shit. I had forgotten to ask her about Fern embezzling from the Foundation. There was always later.

Man, this felt like one of the longest days of my life in one of the longest weeks of my life.

In reality, the shit storm clusterfuck of a week was only just getting started.

FIFTEEN

David was in bed asleep when I finally got home. I gave him a sloppy kiss on the cheek to wake him up. He laughed and waved me away.

"I love you," I said.

"You, too."

"Hey, David," I said as I sat on the edge of his bed.

"Mom, I've got school in the morning," he mumbled.

"Do you remember me saying goodnight to you when you were a kid?" I asked. "Like something we did every night. See you later, alligator. After while, crocodile. Etc."

He turned toward me but kept his eyes closed.

"No," he said. "That's from your movie *Love and Other Insanities*."

"The other night Fern asked me to say that with her," she said, "like we used to do when she was a kid. Only I never did that with her."

"You did with Alberto," he said. "Not that I remember."

He was a baby himself when Alberto was born.

"But Fern told me," he said. "She said you would do both sides. See you later, alligator and after while, crocodile. To teach it to Alberto. She said you had rituals with him but nothing like that with us. One of her many resentments."

How could I not remember that?

"Don't worry about it, Mom," David mumbled. "She'll get over it." He turned away from me. I patted his hip.

"She hasn't gotten over it yet," I said.

I went to Hayword's office and sat in it for a long time, staring at the computer, looking at websites for movie studios. I did not recognize a lot of the names. Of course, I wasn't on the party circuit.

Who did I know that might offer Sally a job?

I didn't know many suits. I was not very good at small talk, which was ridiculous. Any good socialized adult should be able to talk about nothing. In LA, it was difficult to talk about the weather. "It sure is hot, sunny, and polluted." Or "It sure is hot, sunny, windy, and polluted." Besides, talking about the weather these days just brought up images of the end of the world and how we were all pretty much fucked. Like for instance, the lightning storm which supposedly was on its way here. Just another one of those maybe things.

No. I wasn't going to go down that rabbit hole. I needed to think about who could help me get rid of Sally.

I should have been a better person over the years. Or I should have had sex with more powerful people. The only stud head I had ever fucked was Sally.

Maybe if I was nice to her now.

I pulled out my phone and texted, "Should have the script to you soon. I am so sorry about all of this with Fern. Please let me know if I can do anything to make it right."

I got an immediate reply. That was hopeful. I looked down at the text. "You can drop dead."

I set the phone down. "Well, I don't see how me dropping dead could help but thanks for the sentiment. Jesus," I said aloud to no one.

I did know two studio heads: Katherine and Oscar Bernstein of OK Studios. Maybe this was why I had dreamed about them. The Universe was giving me a heads-up. Sally had said she wished she had their catalog. They always loved Hayword and me. Maybe they could hire Sally away from Back to Life Studios as a favor to us.

I remembered Oscar had a cornball sense of humor, which was strange given he was from New York originally. When I first met him, I asked him about the name of their studio. He shrugged and said, "You know, we're not great and we're not terrible. We're OK."

Hayword had loved that. In truth, O and K were the initials of their first names.

Just then Phil phoned. When I answered it, he said, "I figured out who put the list up. It was easy as pie. Although I don't know how to make pie."

"Old joke, old man," I said.

He laughed. "Gee, thanks. It was Fern. I bet that's no surprise to you. She did not cover her tracks. I don't know why she did it."

I sighed. "I think she wants to destroy me. I don't understand. I wasn't that bad of a mother."

"Have you talked to her yet?" Phil asked.

"No, they're coming home tomorrow," I said. "That is when the shit will hit the fan. Hey, you asked me to tell you, so I'm telling you. I'm going to Lance Johnson's office tomorrow."

"To do what?"

"To talk," I said. "To talk him out of blackmail. To keep those photos out of the press."

"I asked a friend to run a background check on him," Phil said. "He's a bad dude. When he was younger, he was jailed for auto theft, check fraud, and assault."

"Anything lately?" I asked.

"No. He married, got holy. His wife has a little money that keeps them all going."

"I can handle him," I said.

"Let me come with you," Phil said.

"That sounds like a good idea," I said. "I pretended I was Fern—cuz I have her phone—and said I'd meet him at his office at 10:00. He thinks he's meeting Fern. I'll be there a few minutes early and I'll look for you."

"Sounds like a plan."

We said our good nights.

I was exhausted. I felt weird sleeping in Hayword's bed, especially right after having sex with his nemesis. Not that he would call Ryan that. What would he call him? Alberto's father. He didn't have anything against Ryan. Still he would be hurt that I had had sex with him again. Especially given . . . I had just been with him.

What was it with people and sex? I didn't really understand it. I could not remember or count how many people I had fucked. While I was married. Yet Hayword cheated on me once, and I never trusted him again.

Lately, it hadn't seemed so important.

I put my head in my hands. Too much was going on. I had fucked it all up. I couldn't fix it. Ryan and I were both drinking. Mark was drinking. Fern was whatever Fern was. My friendships with Sally and Joanie were over. Oh, fuck, I had forgotten about Joanie and her dead husband. I hoped she had called the police. If it wasn't for David being here, I would go to Ryan's house now. Why? Why? Why?

It was all Fern's fault.

I went downstairs to the kitchen. I opened the cupboard where I knew Hayword kept the wine. I pulled down a bottle of red wine. From Chateaux Who Gives a Fuck as long as there is alcohol in it. Then I looked around for the corkscrew. Couldn't find it.

"Fuck, fuck, fuck."

I breathed deeply. Breathed again. David was upstairs. My son was upstairs. I couldn't do this. Could not do this again.

I opened another cupboard. Where the chocolate was. I got a bar of 97% dark cacao. I unwrapped the bar and shoved half of it in my mouth and began to chew. I leaned against the counter and closed my eyes.

"You left a little chocolate out of your mouth."

I opened my eyes. My sleepy-looking son stood in the kitchen.

I took the chocolate bar out of my mouth and held it out to him. "You want some?"

David waved me away. "Gross! And it's all over your mouth."

I laughed, turned around, and washed my mouth in the sink. When I turned around again, David was looking at the wine bottle.

"Don't worry," I said. "I didn't drink any."

I picked it up and put it in the cupboard.

"I couldn't find the damn corkscrew," I said. "Man, sometimes I just wish I was like everyone else." I let out a little scream.

"Me, too," he said. "I mean I wish I was like everyone else.

But everyone is fucked up, Mom. They just pretend better than we do.”

I went over to him and put my arms around him. He returned the embrace. “I hope you’re not fucked up,” I said. “And quit swearing.”

“I’m not as fucked up as Fern at least,” he said.

“You are not.”

“Do you ever wonder what Alberto would be like now?” he asked.

“All the time,” I said. “I bet he’d be a lot like you, and you’d be great pals to each other.”

“Or maybe he would have been pals with Fern,” David said. “I think she really needs one.”

“You’re a good kid,” I said. “Now that I have all of this chocolate revving me up, let’s go to sleep.”

I fell asleep on Hayword’s bed. On top of the covers. I slept right through David leaving for school. He texted me his love. I went to the bungalow, took a shower, changed my clothes. Then I drove to Lance Johnson’s office which was way on the other side of town, in a place I had never been before. Fern sure knew how to pick them.

I parked. Everything depended upon these next moments. And then the moments after that.

“Let’s do this thing,” I said to no one.

I saw Phil as I got out of the car, walking toward me.

“What are you going to do?” Phil asked when he was next to me.

“You’ll see,” I said. “Don’t worry. I didn’t bring a gun.”

“I did,” Phil said.

“I wish you hadn’t told me that.”

“I’m trained,” he said. “No one is gonna get hurt.”

“Said almost everyone who hurt someone with a gun.”

We went inside the square brick office building. Johnson's office was on the first floor. We went to his huge steel door. I didn't know if I should knock or just go in. I opened the door. Inside was a tiny office with just a few chairs and another closed door. I didn't have time to think about it because Lance Johnson came walking through the back door.

"Oh, fuck," he said when he saw us. "Not you again. And the mother. I've seen your ass all over the little screen." He grinned like he wasn't afraid of anything. I wanted to punch him.

"I know about your little scheme with my daughter," I said. "I know that Sally St. James isn't going to pay you anything. I know that you have photos of me having sex. Illegally obtained, by the way. I didn't give you permission to come into my house or my car. I could have you charged with breaking and entering."

"Your daughter had a key," he said. "Besides, I can give you those photos back. Along with the memory card. Just give me the money."

"Let's see them," I said. "I want to see the photos and the memory cards for my car and house and for Fern with Jonathan."

Johnson shrugged. "As long as you have your checkbook." He turned around and headed for the back. I looked at Phil.

"I'll be coming with you," Phil said.

"No one goes back here," Johnson said.

"Mr. Case is a retired police officer," I said. "Did you know that? He is obligated to report any unlawful activities. And I would say that all of your activities regarding me and my daughter are unlawful. He's going back with you."

Johnson fussed for a bit, but Phil followed. They left the door open. I heard very little chatter. After what seemed like forever, they came back. Johnson looked pissed. Phil showed me the memory cards.

"We took the photos off his computer, too," Phil said. "And the cloud. I looked through his mail and his phone. I didn't see any more, but he probably has a stash somewhere. I've got the memory cards."

"You owe me for those," Johnson said.

"I don't owe you a thing," I said. "Well, except for these." I pulled the photos out of my bag, unfolded them, and handed them to Johnson. "I know that you're a Christian man now with a wife who is dedicated to her church, a wife who brings in most of the money. If she saw these, my guess is that your marriage would be in trouble. I wouldn't want that to happen. So I will keep copies of these, and no one else will ever know about them unless any of the photos you took of me or of Fern see the light of day. If that happens, I will personally hand these photos of you fucking my daughter over to your wife."

Johnson looked away from the photos. "I'll just tell her they're fakes. She believes any bullshit I tell her."

I nodded. "I bet she does. I can always bring Fern with me, to verify that you were fucking her."

"You would do that to your daughter?" Johnson asked.

"Given what you two were trying to do to me, I think you know the answer to that. Do we have a deal, Mr. Johnson?"

He grumbled and shifted. "I'm not getting anything out of this."

"You're not getting your life destroyed," I said. "I can't say the same thing."

"All right," Johnson said. "All right."

I snatched the photos from him. "I hope I never see you again."

I left the office. I could hear Phil behind me. We went outside into the sunshine, and I turned to Phil. He held out his hand to me, and I shook it.

"Man, I don't want to get on your bad side."

"You do not," I said. "This *was* easy as pie, my friend. I have dealt with assholes like him before. Now I need to go and deal with the asshole I gave birth to."

SIXTEEN

I did not want to say goodbye to Phil or drive back to the house where Hayword and Fern would be fairly soon. Maybe I should make them come to the bungalow, and we could have it out there. No, Fern and I had had it out at the bungalow a couple of times. No need for another round there.

I pulled off to the side of the road and looked on the contacts on my phone for Katherine and Oscar or OK Studios. Nothing. I phoned our studio. Caryn answered the phone.

"Hi, Caryn," I said. "Thanks for figuring out what was going on with that list with Phil."

"It was shocking," Caryn said. "Your own daughter. Jesus."

"Yeah, I doubt Jesus had anything to do with it."

"I heard she's fired."

"Did you hear why?" I asked.

"I know why," Caryn said. "You really should not have sex with the boss's husband."

"No, shit," I said.

"Have you finished the script?" Caryn asked, whispering.

"Not yet," I said, "but don't tell anyone."

"I'm rooting for you," she said.

"I need to ask you for a name and phone number, but please don't tell anyone I asked."

"Of course," she said. "I would do anything for you. Well, not anything. But you know what I mean."

I laughed. "This *is* Hollywood, but I think I know what you mean. Do you have the phone number for OK Studios and/or Katherine and Oscar Bernstein? Their unlisted private number."

"Hang on," she said. "Got it. I'll text it to you."

"Thanks," I said. "I'll be in touch."

As soon as I got the text, I called Katherine and Oscar. I heard Katherine's bright friendly voice say, "Hello, darlin'! I haven't heard from you in ages. How's it going?"

"Hi, Katherine," I said. "Sorry to be so long gone. Can I come see you two? I want to talk about something."

"Sure," Katherine said. "We live out a bit on a few acres. You up for that?"

"Of course," I said.

"I'll text you the address," she said. "Come to the house, not the Hex Barn. See you soon, darlin'."

The Hex Barn?

I clapped my hands together. Yes. I adored these people. Why had I cut them out of my life? To be fair, I had pretty much cut everyone out of my life from the before-Alberto-died time. But that was all in the past. Maybe now they could provide a solution to my Sally problem. Plus I could delay dealing with Fern.

I texted Hayword and asked when they would be home. He answered, "One to three hours, depending upon the traffic."

That gave me time.

I checked my other texts. David wrote, "Storm will hit this afternoon. I'm coming home early from school." I looked up. Sky was still blue.

I drove away from our village and up into the hills and beyond. I didn't think I had been out this way before. I felt myself relaxing as I drove through the green rolling hills. Maybe it would be OK, OK, OK. What would it have been like if the kids had been raised out here? Would they have been happier, healthier? Would Hayword and I have been happier, healthier? Would we still be together?

No. I was not going to do that. Too many questions with too few answers. That way led to me taking another drink.

Soon enough, I turned down a dirt road and then down a dirt driveway. Tall sycamores sheltered the road for most of the way. Just before I got to the house, the trees made way for huge rhododendron bushes and then butterfly bushes and thousands of California poppies that led me to the house. I parked alongside two other cars. To my left was a big red barn with a huge Pennsylvania Dutch hex sign of a rooster on it.

"Ah, the Hex Barn."

To my right was a path that led to what looked like a true California Ranch house, golden, one story, hugging the ground. Big old white oak trees towered over one end of the house. All kinds of flowering bushes leaned forward along the front, not blocking the many large windows. Out front on the porch under the overhanging roof and several sycamores, Katherine and Oscar sat at a wooden table and chairs. They both stood and waved when they saw me.

I hurried toward them. Katherine's hair was now long and white. She was so beautiful. Oscar was still short and stout with salt and pepper hair. They both embraced me.

"You haven't aged a bit," Katherine said. "You were always so darling."

I laughed. "And you two were and are always beautiful."

"Sit with us in the shade," Oscar said. "Have some tea." He poured iced tea into an empty glass for me.

"This place is absolutely gorgeous," I said. I breathed deeply. It was the first deep breath I had had in a long while. "Is your studio here or do you just live here?"

"We've lived here for nearly twenty years now," Katherine said. "The studio has been here about ten years in the Hex Barn. We have a couple other houses on the property that we use in our films. We live by the threes."

"The threes?" I asked.

"We told you about it," Oscar said, "when we produced *Love and Other Insanities*. We had just started it then."

I shrugged. "I've forgotten. Sorry."

Katherine said, "We give three hours a day to the land, three hours to our work, and three hours to our community. We've had a lot of privilege in our lives, we know. So we try to give back."

"We have 500 hundred acres now," Oscar said.

"Wow," I said. "The trees, the house, all the birds I hear. It's paradise." Of course, I used to think the same about the beach. I would probably be bored here, too, even though right this second, it felt like . . . home.

"We owe it all to you," Katherine said. "Without *Love and Other Insanities* we probably would have never bought this place."

"Because of the money?" I asked.

Katherine shrugged. "That and because it was such a beautiful tender movie about the value of family over work. We were looking for a house closer in for the kids, but we came here, and we fell in love. The kids loved it, too. They're all grown up now, have their own kids. How are Fern and David?"

"David is fine," I said, "but Fern has been trouble. That's why I'm here."

"First, drink your tea," Katherine said. "And then we will show you the house. Did you hear about this lightning storm coming today?"

"I have indeed," I said.

I drank the tea. They talked about their grandchildren while I listened and looked around. I felt that familiar flutter I got when I was around other people, but it began to dissipate as I sat there under the big trees.

"This place was built by a Spanish rancher," Oscar said. "I forget what year. But she was a woman. Francesca Morales."

"She had more names than that," Katherine said.

"I know, but I can never remember them," Oscar said.

Katherine said, "Me, neither. Sorry Francesca. It's cultural."

"Anyway. She raised horses. People came from all around the world to buy her horses. Her husband was a painter. They had five children. She oversaw every part of the building of this house. She wanted it always filled with family and friends."

"It has so much natural light," Katherine said. "And the courtyard is right out of a story."

"It burned to the ground in the eighties," Oscar said, "but the owners—who were her descendants—rebuilt it from the original specs. We still don't know how they did that. They used local materials just as she had. But they modernized it, thank goodness. Come. We'll show you."

They took me inside. The Great Room had a vaulted ceiling with a chandelier hanging from it. The library on one side of the Great Room had shelves up to the ceiling. The kitchen was huge, with tall cream-colored cabinets. The décor was a mixture of Mexican, Spanish, and Californian: colorful and sedate and neutral all at the same time. We walked down wide hallways and out into a courtyard that was filled with flowers, as though the courtyard was a vase and every flower in the world had been stuffed into it. It smelled like lavender mixed with roses mixed with lilacs, only not overwhelming. Above was open to the California sun.

"Oh my word!" I said. "This is amazing."

"Katherine has the greenest thumb in the world," Oscar said.

"Not a single artificial chemical used here," Katherine said. "Come, sit here." She pointed to a long wooden table in the middle of the courtyard: the only place without flowers. Carved in the center of the table were the words: *There's no place like home.* Katherine and I sat on opposite benches. Oscar disappeared for a minute and then reappeared with a plate full of sandwiches.

"Tell us everything," Oscar said as he sat down.

So I did. Surrounded by the most beautiful fragrant flower garden I had ever experienced, I told them about my drinking.

"We had heard something," Katherine said.

Then me stopping drinking. Fern and the fake robbers. Fern with a job at Back to Life Studios. And then the photos of her sleeping with Sally's husband. Fern stealing from the Foundation. Sally so angry that she was trying to get me out of Back to Life Studios.

Katherine shook her head. "You've had the troubles."

"That girl needs some help," Oscar said.

"Hayword is bringing her home," I said, "right now. We'll have it out with her tonight."

"During the lightning storm?" Katherine asked.

"I don't know," I said. "I hadn't thought about it."

"That could be bad luck," she said. "Try to do it before."

"Or after," Oscar said.

I smiled. "I heard a rumor that you might be looking for a new studio head. Would you consider Sally?"

Katherine and Oscar looked at each other.

"We are looking to retire," Katherine said. "We want to

move closer to our grandchildren. They live in your village, actually."

"You would leave this place?" I asked.

"500 acres is a lot to manage," Oscar said. "It's time. We're thinking of selling the studio, our catalog, and this place to someone who would really appreciate it."

"Would you consider selling it all to Sally St. James?"

"I don't know," Katherine said. "We didn't really click when we met. But Oscar and I will talk about it. We're not in a rush. We haven't even put out the word yet."

"Oh, thank you," I said. "That is such a relief."

"We said we'd think about it, Brooke," Katherine said, smiling.

"I know," I said, "but these last few days have been so awful that I will grasp at any straw."

"If she bought it," Oscar said, "she would have control over *Love and Other Insanities*."

I groaned. "Way to kill the mood, Oscar," I said. They laughed.

"You'd still have your stake in it," Katherine said. "That is not ours to sell."

"I've got to go," I said. "Fern and Hayword will be back soon."

"Please come back and we'll show you around the entire place," Katherine said.

"I will," I said. "Thank you."

"By the way, we've had a woman living in one of our guest cottages for the last few years," Katherine said. "Terra Lee. She got her psychology degree a couple of years ago, and she's been working as an addiction counselor and a sober companion. She does interventions. She is apparently quite good and very skilled. Unconventional. We adore her. Maybe she can help you with Fern?"

"Oh my word!" I said. "If I believed in angels, I'd say you two are my angels. I haven't seen you in so long and then this week I dreamed about you and someone else mentioned you and now I'm here and you're saving my life. OK, not literally saving my life. But I'm so excited! Yes, please give Terra Lee my contact number. We could use her help. Tell her everything. Tell her anything."

I felt giddy. Like a school girl.

We all stood. I hugged them again. Katherine looked at me. "It's going to be OK," she said.

"Or not," I said. "Alberto was supposed to be OK, but he wasn't. Now Fern. She was dead just a few days ago. I'm so angry with her. And I am absolutely terrified for her. I can't lose two children."

Katherine embraced me again. "You won't, darlin'. You won't."

They walked me out to the car. I got in and drove away, and then I burst into tears. I cried all the way down the driveway and the dirt road. By the time I was out on the main road, I was myself again: my emotions all wrapped up in a ball in my stomach.

SEVENTEEN

I turned on the radio as I headed home. Everywhere, they were talking all about the predicted electric storm.

"Climate change is about to deal us another blow," the radio announcer said. "This storm could rain down thousands of bolts of lightning every second. That's right. Every second. This storm could destroy the city, your home, your car, your future. And it's all your fault. You're listening to this as you're driving your gas-guzzling car, aren't you? Well there you go, asshole."

"What?" I started laughing. "Did he really just say that?"

Blue-black clouds were riding the southwest horizon now. Maybe this storm was going to show up after all.

Then I was back at the house. Hayword's car was in the driveway. I took a deep breath. I was about to get out of the car when my phone beeped. I picked it up and looked at it.

From Ryan. "Stay safe from the storm."

I started to text back, "I am the storm, baby." I laughed out loud. No, I wasn't going to say that. Even if it was true. Instead, I wrote, "You, too."

Then I got out of the car and went into the house.

"We're in here." Hayword's voice. In the living room. I kept walking. David was there.

Fern was sitting next to her father. She looked scared shitless.

Good.

"David, are you sure you want to be here for all of this?" I asked.

He nodded.

"So what the fuck, Fern?" I was so angry I was trembling. Fern looked at her father.

"Don't look to him," I said. "You were trying to ruin my life. You have to answer to me. You spiked my drink. You put cameras in my car and bedroom. You put a list online telling everyone this was a list of men I had slept with. You embezzled money from the Foundation and forged your brother's signature. You could both go to jail!"

I glanced over at David and shook my head almost imperceptibly.

"He won't go to jail," Fern said. "I'll tell them I did it."

"And the worst thing you did, the thing that tells me how much you hate me, is you overdosed so that I would see it. You planned it with Joanie as some kind of sick joke. Do you understand how fucking evil that is?"

Tears flowed down Fern's cheeks.

I didn't believe a single one.

"What do you have to say for yourself?" I asked.

Suddenly the room got darker. David glanced outside.

"It's here," he said.

"We better get the cars in the garages," Hayword said.

"I don't have my keys," Fern said.

I didn't tell her I had them.

"There are only three spots in the garage anyway," Hayword said.

"We'll be right back," I said.

Hayword and I went out into a day that was almost night with black clouds overhead. He got into his car and opened the garage doors. I got into my car, and then we both drove into the garage and parked next to David's car.

"What about Fern's car?" Hayword asked as the garage doors closed on the coming storm.

"Maybe she'll get lucky," I said.

"Don't you think you're being a little rough on her?"

I stared at him.

"OK," he said, putting up his hands.

"I talked to Mercy Price," I said. "She suggested that we find Sally a job too good to refuse and then maybe she'll leave Back to Life Studios on her own accord. Remember any of us can dissolve the partnership at any time for no reason at all, as long as there's nothing else in the pipe—like my script."

"We've got a whole movie about to be made," Hayword said.

I shrugged. "We'd figure something else. I talked to Katherine and Oscar Bernstein today. You were right about their place. It is amazing. They're thinking of selling it and OK Studios with the whole catalog. I bet if they offered it to Sally, she would take it. Then we would be home free. You wouldn't believe how nasty Sally is being. She's threatening all kinds of things."

"Like what?"

The lights went off in the garage. Not a blackout, I didn't think. They stayed on for a bit after the doors closed. Hayword waved his arms around, and they came back on.

"I want to talk to you later about it," I said. "Privately."

"We're pretty private right now," he said.

"Not in the middle of me chewing out Fern."

"What is it? What does Sally have on you."

I leaned against my car, and I looked into Hayword's eyes. His beautiful eyes. It was never my intention to hurt or humiliate him, yet I kept on doing it. Fuck my intentions.

"I saw Ryan Nichols," I said. "I had sex with him. In my car where there was a camera. The blackmailer has photos of that. Sally knows about it, and she threatened to tell you."

"Who you have sex with is your business," Hayword said. "It's nothing to do with me."

I nodded. "It was right after we had had sex. You and me."

"You mean this happened recently?"

"Yes, it happened this week. Monday. I was drinking. I saw him on the way to a meeting and something snapped or clicked, and I wanted to punish him."

"Is that what you were doing with me on Sunday?" he asked. "Were you punishing me by having sex with me?"

"Maybe," I said. "I don't know. It was all crazy. When I drank on Saturday and didn't know it, I think it broke me."

"Isn't that a fine excuse." He shook his head. "I don't know why I'm mad or why it hurts. You didn't promise me anything. You never have. Even when we got married you told me it wasn't what you wanted. You didn't want to be a wife or a mother. You liked the idea of us writing stories together. But Ryan Nichols. Did you really have to fuck him right after you fucked me?"

"I lost my mind. I'm sorry. I don't love him. I don't want to be with him."

"Do you want to be with me?"

"I don't know," I said.

"I didn't even know you and Mark had broken up," Hayword said.

I sighed. "Neither did he."

"I want a divorce," Hayword said.

"What? I thought there wasn't anything I could do that you wouldn't forgive? I thought you would always love me."

"I will," Hayword said. "But this isn't healthy. It's time to make a clean break of it. Same with the studio. As soon as you deliver the manuscript and fulfill your contract, I'm going ask to dissolve the partnership."

"But I love working with you," I said.

Hayword laughed. "Too little, too late, girlie. Let's go fix our daughter before this storm hits."

This was not what I expected. I thought he would be angry and hurt. I didn't think he would be matter of fact. This was the straw that broke the camel's back?

The garage turned dark again. I followed Hayword through the door and into the kitchen and then into the living room.

"Where were we?" Hayword asked.

David was staring outside. It was pitch dark, except when a lightning strike lit up the area. There was one. And then another. And another.

"I unplugged our computers," David said.

"Fern," Hayword said. "Explain yourself. We need to know what your motive was before we turn you over to the police."

I almost laughed out loud. Like Hayword would ever do that.

"Daddy," Fern said. "You can't."

"Don't call me daddy," Hayword said. "You're a grown woman. Act like it."

"I am so sorry for everything I've done," Fern said. "It's the alcohol and the drugs."

"Bullshit," I said. "You have these come to Jesus moments every few years and say you're sorry, and then you get mean and nasty all over again. What the fuck is wrong with you?"

"I don't know!" she said. "You all seem happy and content, and I am not. Mom loved Alberto so much that she left us after he died. He was that special. But we weren't special enough for her to stay with us. Emotionally."

"Give me a break," I said. "You are almost thirty years old. You should be long past your mommy issues. I made sure you had a roof over your head and clothes on your back."

"Those are things!" Fern said. "Where were you? You were drunk or fucking someone!"

"I am so sick of this fucking story," I said. "You had a great childhood. I'm sorry if you don't remember it. Then Alberto died. I drank. Our marriage fell apart. But everything else was good. Why do you focus on the few awful years?"

"I don't know!" she said. "And you've left us this fucked up world."

"Jesus," I said. "And our parents left us a fucked up world, and their parents left them a fucked up world. We've all got shit to overcome. My parents weren't perfect, but I never tried to destroy them!"

"I didn't try to destroy you," Fern said. "I thought you'd get a little drunk, do stupid things, and then you'd get sober again. Easy peasy."

I roared. "First, it isn't up to you to decide that. I did do stupid things. I slept with your father. Then I slept with Ryan Nichols who is trying to stay sober. Lance Johnson wanted to sell those photos to the tabloids. That would have ruined Ryan's life and embarrassed the hell out of us. And Sally is so angry that she wants me out of the company if I can't get the script to her. And I want a drink again more than anything in the world. You destroyed years of hard work."

"I just needed a quick way to make money," Fern said, "and no one would give me any. Sally is such a bitch."

"Do you hear yourself?" I asked. "You sound like a sociopath. You don't give a shit about any of it."

"Because you don't like me!" she shouted. "You have never

fucking liked me. That hurts. If your own mother doesn't like you, it's difficult to stay in the world."

"I have always loved you," I said. "And when you were younger, I liked you. But for the last 15 years, you've treated me like dog shit. Why would I like anyone who treated me that way?"

"Because you're my mother," she said. "You should still like me."

"I don't know who fed you that bullshit," I said. "But parents like or dislike their children just like they like and dislike people who aren't their children. Right now, I like you less than practically anyone. Anyone but Lance Johnson. Oh, by the way, I showed him the photos of the two of you together. He won't be publishing those photos of you and Sally's husband any time soon."

The room was silent. The lights flickered. But they stayed on. Thunder rolled over us and around us, again and again.

"Fern, you have a good job," Haywood said. "Why do you need so much money?"

"I don't know," she said. "Part of it is for drugs. But I've also started this business called More for More. I buy very expensive items and then I sell them for more. I take them to a party or a business meeting where there are famous people, so that I can tell people later where the items have been, and then I jack up the price because of that. People love everything that a celebrity has touched. Or looked at. Breathed on."

"Is that what those handbags are in your closet?" I asked.

"Yes, and they're all spoken for," she said. "All 20% up from retail."

"That's such bullshit," David said. "What is a celebrity? They haven't done anything. They're not better than anyone else. Why would someone pay more for something just because a so-called celebrity has been around it. It's ridiculous. That market is gonna die."

"I hope not," Fern said. "Wait. What were you doing in my closet?"

"Trying to find out why you'd died," I said, "and how I could help you."

I sat in one of the chairs. I was exhausted. I couldn't even remember everything Fern had done wrong to throw in her face.

"And of course, you are fired," I said.

"She can't fire me just because I slept with her husband," Fern said.

I looked at Hayword.

"You can be fired without cause," Hayword said, "but we had plenty of cause to fire you. You have done so many terrible things, Fern. What if your mother had driven after she'd drank your Martinelli's and gotten into an accident and killed someone?"

Fern just sighed.

The house shook with thunder. The outside was lit up from lightning.

"Don't touch any metal," Hayword said, "and don't use the faucets."

"It's pouring down rain," David said as he closed the curtains.

"I am sorry for everything that's happened," Fern said. "I won't do any of it again. I will go to rehab."

"You need to pay back the money you stole from the Foundation," David said. "That's the first thing."

"I don't have any money," Fern said, "particularly now that I'm fired."

"You have those fucking handbags," I said.

"I guess."

Grrr.

"You are a privileged entitled fucking little brat," I said. "If you don't pay back that money, we are going to have you prosecuted and put you in jail."

"OK! I will pay it back."

"By next week," I said. "You'll have to figure out your own rehab. We are not paying for it."

"But I won't have any insurance now that you've fired me," she said.

"Well, now you'll see how the rest of the world lives," I said. "Welcome to real life."

The house shook again. David was looking at his phone. "Downtown LA is on fire. And they're in blackout."

"We've got a generator," Hayword said. "If the power goes out, we'll be OK."

"Isn't that generator full of fuel?" David asked. "It it gets struck by lightning, it'll be like a bomb."

Hayword looked at me and grimaced. He hadn't thought of that—didn't know if it was true.

Just then the doorbell rang. We all looked at one another. In the middle of a once in a lifetime storm?

Hayword and I went to the door. I flung it open.

Eartha Kitten was standing on our doorstep, soaked to the bone. She smiled and held out her hand, "Terra Lee, at your service. I'm here to do one amazing thing a day for you."

EIGHTEEN

I grinned, took Eartha's hand, and pulled her out of the rain. Laughing, I hugged her.

"You're Terra Lee? Is that your real name?"

"I'll never tell," she said, "but I really did go to school and I really am an addict specialist. I was in the village when Katherine texted me about your visit. She had no idea we knew each other. So I came right up."

Hayword was watching and listening and was completely baffled.

"Eartha lives with Katherine and Oscar, on their property. She is now a trained addiction specialist, a sober companion. She's come to talk with Fern."

Eartha and Hayword hugged. Then the kids came in. It took a second, but then they ran to her and hugged her.

"Oh, David," Eartha said. "You are a young man now. Amazing. And Fern, so nice to see you. I've heard that you've tried to ruin your mother's life and you've almost succeeded. Do you want to talk about how drugs and alcohol are a good choice in your life?"

Fern's mouth fell upon. "This isn't religion, is it?" she asked.

"The religion of healthy sobriety," Eartha said, "if that's what you want. Let's go talk up in your old room. We'll be down in a while."

The three of us were left alone.

"That was a nice bit of synchronicity," Hayword said. "By the way, have you finished the script."

"I haven't even started," I said.

We went back to the living room. I sat on the couch. David picked up his laptop from the table and handed it to me.

"It's fully powered," he said.

"I need some peace and quiet," I said. "I can't do it in the middle of a lightning storm." Just then lightning flashed—could see it through the curtains—and then the electricity went out. After a little bit of time, a few lights came on in the house. The generator was working.

"I can't do it while we're figuring out whether Fern is going to jail or not."

"You've got a lot of excuses," Hayword said. "Like daughter, like mother."

"You can do it, Mom," David said. "We'll help. So the last movie ended with Aiden dead and buried. His mom Colleen visited his grave along with his girlfriend Molly. When they left, his arm came up through the grave. What's next?"

I put my fingers on the keyboard and opened an empty document. Then I typed in *Beauty and the Zombie, Part Three: Whackadoodle Times* by Brooke McMurphy.

As I continued typing, I read it out loud, "The earth breaks open and Aiden pulls himself up out of the grave. The music tells us this is a happy moment, something we have all waited for. But then the camera pans around him, and we see his face, his expression, and we know that this is a different Aiden: this is evil Aiden."

"Good!" David said. "He's alive, but he's a shit."

I looked at Hayword. He nodded. "Keep going."

"What do you think happens next?" I asked, staring at the computer.

"All the dead zombies claw their way out of the graves," David said.

I typed and read, "Aiden pulls off the swan ring his father had given him, the swan ring his mother had given his father, and throws it in the dirt. He stands on his grave looking around, and one arm after another breaks through the earth. Then one by one, the dead alien zombies pull themselves out of the ground. Their graves are all slightly downhill from Aiden. So they look up at him and put their fists in the air in solidarity.

"'The human world has ostracized us!' Aiden shouts. 'They have killed us. This is our planet now! We will show them who is in charge as we drink their blood!'

"We see a human grave-digger begin running away. Aiden shouts, 'Get him,' and the zombies run after him. We hear his screams as they descend on him. Roll credits."

I looked up. David laughed. "All right, Mom!"

"Dead alien zombies begin bursting from their graves all over the world. They are able to telepathically communicate with each other. They go on killing sprees wherever they are. Colleen goes to Aiden's grave and finds it empty and discovers the swan ring. She picks it up and puts it on her finger. She suspects Aiden is part of the murder sprees, but she doesn't know he is the leader. Molly, who is an alien-human mix, finally admits that she has been getting telepathic messages from Aiden. The newly alive dead aliens are particularly interested in getting the mixed children to be a part of their movement. Molly says she hasn't answered Aiden.

"Aiden comes on television and says that the killing will stop if the humans turn over all controls of the government to them. 'You can continue your wasteful consumption,' he says, 'and ruining your environment with fossil fuels. You can do what you want, but we will have the power, and you will do whatever we want.' Most of the people in most of the countries go along with it. They are tired of the killing. The zombie aliens use a portion of the population as their slaves, to serve them and build homes that comfort them."

The house shook again from thunder. Lightning lit up everything. David looked momentarily worried and then he said, "Shouldn't Aiden and Colleen meet?"

I nodded. I kept typing and reading aloud, "Not every reanimated alien zombie is a murderer—although most are—but several of those who aren't come to Colleen and Molly. (Remember they are both scientists.) These alien zombies allow the scientists to examine them. They learn that the reanimated alien zombies are no longer cured of the original zombie illness that brought them to Earth. In fact, the reanimation put the illness into high gear, and it is now deadly. The zombie aliens will die soon if they don't have a cure. Colleen and Molly try the cure from the last movie, but it doesn't work.

"They work night and day trying to find a cure, although they question each other. If the zombie aliens have a deadly disease, why don't they just let them die? Colleen says she can't let Aiden die, no matter how evil he is."

"Aiden could never be evil," Fern said as she walked into the room with Eartha. "He's Alberto, after all."

"He's not Alberto," I said. "We're trying to finish this treatment so I can write the script and save the business. If that happens, then you didn't ruin my life."

"We do need to talk," Eartha said.

"Not yet," Fern said. "Let her finish. So do I gather the zombie aliens are back and they're sick again and Colleen is looking for a cure?"

"Yep," David said.

Thunder shook the house and lightning flashed again.

"Maybe a little lightning à la Frankenstein's monster would do the trick," Fern said.

"Yes!" I said. I continued typing and reading out loud. "One night Molly and Colleen are talking about Frankenstein, and they both have the idea to use electricity on the zombie aliens. They try it on the volunteers, and the disease is arrested. The aliens are disease-free. Yay! Colleen asks Molly to use her ability to communicate with Aiden to let him know they have a cure for the new zombie disease.

"She does and Aiden turns up at the lab. Colleen is choked up and thrilled to see her son. Her boy is alive! What could be more wonderful?"

I stopped typing. The room was quiet again. What an amazing thing that would be, to see her son alive again. I looked up at Hayword. I could see all the pain and grief etched on his face.

I looked down at the computer again. "Colleen embraces Aiden. He lets her, but then she steps back. She explains that they've figured out a cure for the zombie disease that makes them so murderous. She's willing to use the cure on him right then and there. He would go back to being his old compassionate loving self.

"'Why would I want that?' he asks. He refuses treatment. She tells him he will die. 'We all die.' Some of the zombies do come for treatment, and they are cured. However, even after treatment, the zombie aliens begin to die again because, you know, you can't really come back to life.

"Aiden returns to Colleen and begs her to cure him of dying.

She tells him she can only cure him of his murderous rage caused by the illness. 'Without that, I have no power.' 'You'll have the power of love.' Aiden finally lets his mother cure him. He comes out of it like the old Aiden. He spends quality time with Colleen and Molly. He tells Colleen there is one zombie alien ship left. All the living zombies will leave on it as soon as it's ready and return to their home world. He announces to the world that the zombie alien takeover is done, and he asks his followers to stand done. There is still some violence, but peace begins to take over the world again. Laws are passed all over the world: The zombie aliens and zombie alien human mixes are not welcome on Earth; they all must leave. Aiden grows ill, and he dies in his mother's arms. Again."

I begin to cry as I type. "Molly leaves to help get the ship ready. She comes to visit Colleen one last time before the ship leaves. They talk of Aiden. Colleen worries about Molly's life on a home world she's never seen. Molly assures her she'll be OK. 'I left you a present in the lab,' Molly tells her as she leaves. Not long after, Colleen watches the ship take off on TV. There are shots from all over the world of people cheering. The Earth is now zombie alien free."

"Now what?" Eartha asked. "Is that the end?"

Hayword laughed. "No!"

"What did Molly leave her?" David asked.

I continued typing and reading, "Colleen remembers then that Molly said she had left something for her in the lab. Colleen goes to the lab. She sees a large white basket on the floor. She hears whimpering. 'Oh no. I hope she didn't leave me a dog.' As she gets nearer, we see a baby blanket and then a baby girl. The baby gurgles. Colleen leans over and lifts the infant into the air. She can tell from her features that she's a little bit of Molly and a little bit of Aiden. Colleen smiles. And then the baby says very clearly, 'Hello, Grandma Colleen. Momma says it's whackadoodle time, and we better be ready to run. Are you ready to run?' The camera moves out of the room and up and we see the words: The end."

"Woot! Woot!" David said as they all clapped. "That's great. I can't wait to see it."

"Good job, Mac."

"Couldn't have done it without you all," I said.

"Yeah, you could have," Hayword said.

"Give me a minute," I said. I quickly read the treatment, and then I sent it to my phone, and then I sent it to Sally—and to Damon and Paolo for good measure. "OK. Done for now."

"If we could all sit," Eartha said. The few lights on inside the house were still dim. The electricity hadn't come back on. Wind whistled around the house. I could hear distant and nearby thunder. I sat next to David. Hayword and Fern sat together. Eartha stayed standing.

"First, I'm so glad to be back here," Eartha said. "Fern has given me permission to talk freely. Fern would like to start."

"I want to apologize to my family," Fern said. "I know I'm always bullshitting and lying. You have no reason to trust me. I will try to earn your trust. I've been acting crazy. I know. Mom, I really wasn't thinking. To put alcohol in your drink to get you to act crazy is unforgivable. I was so high last week. I know that's not an excuse, but it is a reason. It's awful. This has been going on for a few months. And stealing the money. I am so sorry. I will pay it all back. I will do whatever I need to do. I'm sorry, Mom. I really didn't mean to ruin your life or try to ruin your life. I just always figure you can bounce back."

I nodded, but I was feeling very little. Except I didn't trust her. But I didn't feel as angry.

"I want to help make it right," Fern said. "However I can."

"You often apologize and then something happens and you do terrible or stupid things again," Hayword said.

Wow. I couldn't believe he was saying this. Finally.

"I think you need professional help," he said.

Fern nodded. "I do, too," she said. "I will go to rehab, and then Eartha has agreed to be my sober companion for a while. I intend to go into therapy."

"What's wrong with her?" David asked. "Why does she act this way?"

"You all experienced a trauma about fifteen years ago," Eartha said. "David got through it, probably because he was so young, and he was well taken care of through it all. Hayword and Brooke were adults. Fern was a pre-teen. She experienced her brother's death and then the house burned down and her mother spiraled into alcoholism. Trauma often causes children to kind of stop in time. Their emotional intelligence and maybe the brain itself is stuck in that time. That's what happened to Fern. In many ways, she is still a pre-teen."

Just like that, my anger melted away. I could see Fern in my mind's eye at that age, saw her wide tear-filled eyes back then. Looking at me. Wanting me to reassure her. I couldn't. I was too filled with grief. And so I left her there, stuck in that time when her baby brother stopped breathing.

"So her brain is broke?" David asked.

Fern laughed. "Yes, my brain is broke."

Hayword put his arm across Fern's shoulder. "Sorry, honey. You always seemed so tough. And you were always pushing us away, always saying you didn't need us."

"Of course," Fern said. "I was trying to convince myself I didn't need you all, I guess. I'm so tired."

I was glad Hayword could hold her, comfort her. I couldn't bring myself to go over to her.

Maybe I was just constitutionally unable to comfort another human being?

Or maybe just my children.

David leaned against me then. I put my arm across his shoulders, and he rested his head on my shoulder. Outside lightning lit up the early evening behind the curtain.

"It'll be OK, sweetheart," I whispered. "It'll be OK."

"I know," David said. "Because Fern will get well now."

I nodded. "Yes, yes, she will."

"Mom," Fern said, "do you think you can ever forgive me?"

"Um—"

NINETEEN

Just then the doorbell rang.

Thank god, because I didn't know how to answer Fern. Could I forgive her?

Rain was still pelting the windows. I glanced at Hayword, and then I got up, went to the door, and opened it. Joanie was standing on the other side of the door. She was soaking wet.

I shut the door again.

"Just the wind," I said as I came back to the living room.

The doorbell rang again.

"Goddamn it," I said. I went back and opened the door. "What?"

"My electricity is out," Joanie said. "Marv is haunting me. I keep hearing moaning."

"It's called the wind," I said.

Lightning flashed again and again.

"Please!" Joanie said.

I rolled my eyes, stepped aside, and swept my arm to let her know she could enter. Hayword, the kids, and Eartha gathered round.

"Joanie," Eartha said. "Long time."

The two women hugged. "You are soaked," Eartha said. "Let's get you a towel and dry you off."

I shrugged. Eartha was taking over just as she did the first time she came into our lives: I liked it. I did not want to deal with Joanie.

"Watch her every move!" I called as the two women went around the corner. Then I looked at my family. "Long story. OK, not that long. Marv is apparently sitting in his Jaguar in the back garage, dead. Joanie thinks he's haunting her."

David nodded. Fern laughed. "That's bizarre even for Joanie."

I thought it was too soon for Fern to be laughing.

Thunder rolled overhead again. Lightning flashed again and again. Fern moved closer to her brother.

"Is this how the world ends?" she asked.

"The world is ending all the time," I said.

Just then I heard my phone blip. I went into the living room and looked at it. Damon and Paolo both wrote on the thread that included Sally.

"The investors love the treatment," I said.

Sally wrote, too. "I like it, too. Good job."

I laughed and showed it to Hayword. "Like she means it. Oh, wait. She did a private text. 'Clever of you to show the boys. The script is still due.'"

I looked at Hayword.

"What are you waiting for?" he said. "Go write it. Use my office. A couple of the plugs work there when the generator is on."

I glanced over at my children who were now sitting on the

couch together talking quietly. I could hear Eartha and Joanie in the other room.

"No, I want to stay here. I can do it."

I began typing the script to the last *Beauty and the Zombie* movie. It felt bittersweet and perfect at the same time. The storm moved around the house like some uninvited guest doing everything it could to get inside. At some point, the five of them went into the kitchen to figure out what to eat. The fridge worked while the generator was on, but I didn't know what else. I didn't care. I closed my eyes and began writing.

They brought me salad and canned soup. Everyone chattered amiably around me. I didn't say much. I watched Fern. She seemed almost joyful. She had made promises: We would see if she kept them. I was rooting for her.

We opened the curtains at some point, turned off the lights, and watched the storm. The backyard was in light more often than dark: That was how often the lightning strikes were coming. I kept writing. I was dealing with a zombie alien invasion while sitting in our living room watching a lightning storm.

Then the doorbell rang.

"Oh my word," I said. "It's the worst storm in the century and we're getting more company than we've had in a century. I feel like I'm in a Joe Orton play."

This time Hayword answered the door. A moment later he returned to the living room with Philip Case.

This was puzzling.

"Well, hello, sailor," Joanie said.

I gave her a look as I stood. "Phil, nobody is supposed to be on the road. What are you doing here?"

"Can we go somewhere and talk?" Phil asked.

I looked at Hayword. "Let's go to my office."

Phil, Hayword, and I went upstairs to Hayword's office, closed the door, and sat around Hayword's desk.

"Did you tell her?" Phil asked.

"Tell me what?" I asked as Hayword shook his head.

"I asked Phil to do a deep dive into the Back to Life books," Hayword said.

"I know this genius forensic accountant who is very quick," Phil said. "I've hired her before."

"You could have called," I said. "It's dangerous out there."

"My son and his wife live in the village," he said. "I was checking on them, and I couldn't get a hold of either of you."

"Still," I said.

"Quit mothering him," Hayword said. "Let him talk."

"Fuck you," I said. "I wasn't mothering him. He's a friend. I was concerned."

"So you're friends now?" Hayword said. "I thought you didn't even like her."

"Ha!" I said. "I knew it."

"We've gotten to know each other better," Phil said.

"I know what that means," Hayword said.

"Fuck you," Phil said. "I wouldn't do that."

"No skin off my nose," Hayword said. "We're getting divorced."

"Could you both stop swinging your dicks around and tell me what you found," I said.

"Sally has embezzled $5,000,000 from the business in the last year," Phil said. "My guess is she has done this before because she barely covered her tracks. Most of the invoices go to On Location, a business that supposedly finds locations for movies. The business is registered to Sally McJames."

"And we haven't hired anyone to scout locations," Hayword said. "Certainly not for five million dollars."

I leaned back and laughed. "This is perfect."

"What? She stole five million dollars from us."

I nodded. "Yes. And that voids the contract. We can kick her out and take everything. She'll get nothing. We can throw her into jail."

"Embezzlement is often difficult to prove and prosecute," Phil said.

Maybe that meant Fern would be off the hook.

"You could negotiate with Sally to return the money," Phil said. "If she does that, you can tell her you won't prosecute."

"And then we split up the company and she still gets profits from the first two movies?" I said. "I don't like that."

"There are four funnel clouds!" I heard David cry from downstairs.

The three of us ran downstairs. David was looking at his pad. "Four funnel clouds in Los Angeles. They're heading this way. They are saying that everyone must stay indoors."

"They can't tell me what to do," Joanie said.

"Then go outdoors," I said. "Please."

I gazed at David's screen. The scene was like something out of a movie: downtown Los Angeles lit up by lightning and street lights that showed dark ominous tornados, like arms of a giant octopus looking for victims.

"Jesus," Phil said. "Do you have a basement?"

"No," Hayword said. "But we have a panic room. Would that protect us?"

Phil said, "I have no idea."

Eartha said, "Let's not panic."

"Hey, I was just gonna say that," I said.

"Go ahead," Eartha said.

I grinned. "No, you."

"Let's not panic," Eartha said. "Let's play some board games. We'll keep an eye on the news."

The six of them went to the kitchen table. I stayed in the living room and continued writing. I didn't care what Sally had done: I was going to follow the contract to the letter. And then I would squash her like a bug.

The storm battered the house for a long while. Then we experienced a brief lull. Suddenly I heard what sounded like squealing tires and breaking glass. I jumped up and ran toward the front door—along with everyone else in the full house. I swung the door open. Lightning flashed, and I saw a bloody man staggering toward us. It was dark again. And then lightning flashed, and the man's arms were stretched out toward us.

"Help!" he cried.

"Oh my god," I said. "It's Marv!"

I ran out into the pelting rain with Phil, Hayword, and Eartha beside me. Beyond Marv we could see a smashed car wedged up against one of our pine trees. We helped him inside and sat him at the kitchen table. Eartha got a cloth and gently wiped the blood off his forehead. Hayword got a bandage.

"I called 911," Phil said. "They can't get out here."

Where was Joanie? I looked behind me. She was cowering over by the fridge. "Is he real?" she whispered.

"Yes, he's real," I said. I put my hand on his arm. He looked a little dazed. "Should we take you to the hospital?"

"Where am I?" he asked.

"You're at Hayword's house," I said.

"Who is Hayword?"

"Christ, he's got dementia," Joanie said.

"Or amnesia."

"I am not demented," he said. "I just don't remember who I am or where I've been."

"He might have hit his head," Phil said. "We better take him to the local hospital."

"It's too dangerous," David said.

"Phil's a former cop," Hayword said. "He can take care of himself."

"I'll bring the car around," Phil said.

"I'll find a blanket for him," Eartha said.

"I'll get a drink," Joanie said.

The kids and Hayword disappeared with the rest of them, and I was alone with Marv. I rubbed his back. "It's OK," I said. "Phil will get you some help."

Marv looked at me. He winked. I squinted. Then I whispered, "Marv?"

"Yeah," he said. "I just couldn't figure out an excuse for why I'd been gone for a month. Figured amnesia could cover my ass for a while."

I laughed.

"Shhh," he said.

"She thinks you are dead in your Jaguar."

"What?" he asked.

"I went down there," I said. "Smelled like someone had died, looked like someone was in the driver's seat."

"I left my guitar there," he said. "I didn't want her touching it. She's always touching it. Probably a raccoon or something died in the garage."

"She thinks you've been haunting her."

He chuckled. "Serves her right."

"Where have you been?" I asked.

"In Mali, hunting," he said. "And other stuff. Wasn't ready to come home. She's always fucking around on me."

"You're too old to use that word," I said. "You look and sound like a dirty old man. A bloody dirty old man."

"Shhh, here they come."

Joanie patted her husband on the back. "I am so glad you're home, darling. I have been so worried. Amnesia. So Hollywood. Come on. Can you walk? Out to the car."

She helped Marv stand, and they headed out into the storm. Eartha came out with a blanket. "I'll go with them," she said.

"He's faking the amnesia," I said. "Don't you and Phil put your lives in danger for those two. They deserve each other."

"Thanks for telling me," Eartha said. She kissed my cheek. Then she called, "Fern, I will get in touch with you tomorrow. Stay sober! That goes for everyone."

Then she was gone. I leaned out the door. I could see Phil in the driver's seat. He saw me and waved. I smiled and waved, too. Then I flipped him off. He laughed. Off they drove.

David was beside me, watching. "What do you suppose that all meant? I mean in our life. Why did she think he was dead? Why did he turn up tonight of all nights? What does it mean?"

I looked at my son. "Nothing," I said. "It's just life. Most of life is absolutely meaningless."

We went back in the house and shut the door.

"That is depressing."

"It is meaningless until we give it meaning," I said. "Maybe Joanie was a toxic friend, and I needed to see it, truly. And I saw it. Truly. I am done with her."

The storm died down but did not end. I sat in the living room, writing. Fern and David said good night eventually and went to bed. David kissed me before he went upstairs. Fern kissed her father. She hesitated. I didn't encourage her, and she said goodnight and was gone. I looked up from the computer, and Hayword was gone, too.

I kept writing. Aiden came back to life. He was evil. He was cured of the disease. He was good. And then he died in his mother's arms. Again. The end.

I sent the script to Sally, Paolo, and Damon.

I felt drained. That was fast even for me.

I opened the curtains. It was almost morning. The clouds were gray. The rain was light.

I went upstairs and looked into David's room. He was sleeping. I tiptoed to his bed and kissed the top of his head. "I love you," I said.

Then I went to Fern's room. I could hear her sleep breathing. She looked so small. I went to her bed and looked down. I remembered when she was born. She had screamed like she was pissed at the world for being dragged from my womb. I had loved her so much. I wanted only good things for her. I bit my lip. Now I wanted to crawl into bed with her and tell her everything would be all right. I put my hand on her hair. "Of course I forgive you," I whispered. "I will love you always and forever." I kissed the top of her head.

I went into Hayword's room. He was sprawled all over the bed. I guess he had finally gotten used to sleeping without me. When we were together, he always left a place for me in bed. He looked younger now, as he slept. As if all the cares in the world were gone. I smiled. I felt . . . I felt . . . I felt all the love in the world wash over me as I watched him. Love for him, for the kids, for our life together. I backed out of the room and went downstairs to the living room.

I opened the sliding glass door and went outside. I walked across the grass in my bare feet. Except for a few downed branches, it looked like the house and environs had done OK. We had survived the worst lightning storm in the Earth's history—as far as we knew—unscathed. I sank to the wet ground. This was where we had spread Alberto's ashes. This was his grave.

It started to rain again, hard, and I began to sob. I had loved Alberto so much. And he died. I loved Hayword. He had disappointed me. I loved Fern, and she behaved badly. I loved David, and he was filled with anxiety. I loved them all and like Alberto, they would all die. We would all die. We would fail each other, and we would die.

I had spent the last fifteen years holding them all at arm's length. I had spent all that time holding grudges because they had failed me or worried me and because I knew it was safer to be away from them.

The truth was I loved them. I missed them. I missed Alberto.

I curled up on the wet grass and wept. The rain stopped, and I fell asleep.

Then Alberto was there. He was a young man, a handsome young man, a cross between me and Hayword and Ryan. He leaned down and held his hand out. I took it, and he gently pulled me up.

"Hello, Mom," he said.

"Hello, sweetheart," I said.

We put our arms around each other and held each other tightly. I could feel his body so warm and firm and alive.

"I miss you," I said.

"But they're all still here," he said. "You need them."

"Look, there's a rainbow," I said. "The storm must be over."

He kept his arm around my waist. "Remember, there's no place like home." He pointed to his chest and then to mine.

"Are you saying home is where the heart is?" I asked.

He nodded. I laughed. "So you would have grown up to be a cornball," I said. "Love does not fix everything. I loved you, and you still died."

"That's true," he said, "but bitterness fixes nothing. Tell everyone I said hello."

He kissed my forehead.

I opened my eyes. Hayword was kissing the top of my head. Next to him were Fern and David. "She's awake," one of them said. I smiled, and then I began to cry. And they all started crying. We hugged each other, sitting on the wet grass, and we cried.

"What are you all crying about?" I asked.

"I dunno," David said. "You started it."

Then we all laughed and fell back on the grass.

"By the way," Hayword said, "everyone got home OK. Marv is fine. And Damon and Paolo love the script."

"I don't care what they think," I said. "As long as you liked it, as long as you all liked it. The rest of them can go fuck themselves."

"I thought it was the best one yet," Hayword said.

"I liked the little girl in the end," Fern said. "I think you should call her Fern."

"You know she's a half-alien zombie," David said.

Fern shrugged. "Takes one to know one."

TWENTY

Eventually we let each other go, and we came into the house. I was soaked through. Needed a shower. I looked at my phone first. I read Damon and Paolo's texts about how fabulous the script was. "Perfection!" Sally was silent on the subject. Didn't matter. I had fulfilled my contract. There was a text message from Katherine Bernstein. She said, "We are sorry, but we can't do what you ask. Sally is not our kind of people. But you are. Call us."

"Hey, David," I called. "Don't go to school this morning."

"Why?"

"I want to take you somewhere," I said. "You and Fern and your dad. Have him call the school."

The three of them were picking up debris when I came out of the shower and got dressed. I heard Hayword say something about the lightning rod going to good use last night. Then I sat on the bed and called Katherine.

"Hello, darlin'," Katherine said. "How'd you fare last night?"

"We did fine," I said. "You?"

"A few lightning struck trees," Katherine said. "They are now works of art. We are fine. I am sorry to disappoint you about Sally."

"I'm not disappointed at all," I said. "In fact, I would have had to call and tell you some things I found out about her if you were going to offer her the job."

"We would like to sell OK Studios to you and Hayword," Katherine said. "Our entire catalog and this place."

I was stunned. Shocked. Flabbergasted.

"We could see how much you enjoyed the place," she said, "and it only seems right since your story started it. It's time for us to be with our grandchildren and put some of our money to good use. We'll give you a good and fair price, one you can afford. If you're interested."

"I don't know what to say. You've made me speechless. Don't tell anyone; they'll want to know how you did it. Let me talk to Hayword. In fact, can I bring him and the kids to your place today and show them around?"

"Of course!" Katherine said. "We have to go into the city, but come anyway. I'll leave the key under the mat."

"OK, thank you."

Then I went outside and asked Hayword if he was ready to go talk to Sally.

"Let me make a couple of phone calls first," Hayword said. "I want to keep Damon and Paolo on board to help us make the third film."

I nodded.

I helped the kids pick up.

"How are you feeling today?" I asked Fern.

"Good," she said. "Better than I have in a long while. I think I can do this."

"We'll be here for you," I said.

Hayword soon returned. "Damon and Paolo are in. They'll keep quiet. Called Caryn. Sally is at the offices."

"OK, kids," I said. "We have to stop at the office first, and then I want to take you all somewhere."

On the way in to the office, I called our lawyer Mercy and told her what was happening. I asked her to get the dissolution papers drawn up and send them to us ASAP. I wanted Sally to sign them today.

Phil was waiting outside the offices. I glanced at Hayword. "He's our muscle," Hayword said. I was nervous, but I laughed. Phil kissed me on the cheek.

"I'm security," he said. "When companies fire someone, they often have them escorted out of the building."

I nodded. "OK. Let's do this thing."

I stopped at the desk and said hello to Caryn.

"Caryn, I need you to call a locksmith and get all of the locks changed today," I said. "And get Sally off of any accounts she may have and deactivate any accounts she has, including email."

"What's going on?" Caryn asked.

"She stole five million dollars from us," I said, "so her ass is being fired."

Caryn's eyes widened, but she nodded. "I'll get it done."

Sally looked superior as hell when we came into her office. Then I said, "We know you embezzled five million dollars from the company."

She didn't deny it. "Those were legitimate expenses."

I laughed.

"I will sell all of the photos to the tabloids," she said, "if you don't let bygones be bygones."

"I don't care about the fucking photos," I said. "You called my daughter a slut. You stole from me. You threatened me. We are so over you."

Hayword said, "You violated the contract. It is against the law to embezzle and to blackmail. Our contract with you is now null and void."

"We won't go to the police or the press about this as long as you go quietly," I said. "You will relinquish all shares you have in this company. And we will owe you nothing."

"But *Part Three* will make millions."

"So?" I said. "You made no contribution to it."

"Give me a week to get things in order," she said.

"You mean to get your story straight," I said. "No. You are gone within the hour. Phil Case here will make certain of it. We'll have the papers sent to your house for you to sign today."

She didn't put up much of a fight. Maybe she was ready. Maybe she was done. Or she knew she could go to jail.

"I'm sorry it's come to this," I told her. "I thought we were friends."

"Guess you were wrong," she said. "You were always a lousy fuck anyway."

"I beg to differ," Hayword said.

I chuckled. Then I said, "Phil, she's all yours. Make sure she doesn't download anything or take anything with her, including keys to the place."

Phil stepped into the room, and we stepped out.

And Sally St. James was gone from my life.

It was a beautiful ride to the OK Studios. Fern and David talked with each other in the back seat, sometimes laughing, sometimes serious. They didn't know where we were going. I just told Hayword that Katherine and Oscar invited us out to their place. I didn't tell him anything else.

"In the middle of all this you want to go spend a day in the country?" he asked me.

"Yes."

And then we were there. Hayword parked the car, and we all got out. Fern and David ran away from the house, down a dirt road that led up over the hill, just like they would have done if they were still kids. Hayword and I stood looking around, and then we walked slowly toward the house.

"I had forgotten how beautiful it is out here," he said. "Wow."

We stood in the shade of the porch, near the table and chairs where I'd sat yesterday. Then I went to the door, retrieved the key from under the mat, and then unlocked the door.

"Wait!" Hayword said. "What are you doing?"

"Katherine told me where the key was," I said. I opened the door and motioned him inside. I closed the door, took his hand, and led him to the courtyard. We stood amongst the thousands of colorful flowers. Bees buzzed all around us.

"What's going on, Mac?" Hayword asked. He looked at the wooden table: *There's no place like home.*

"Katherine and Oscar are retiring as you know" I said. "And they want to sell the studio, this house, and all the property to us. The entire catalog. *Love and Other Insanities* would be ours. All the small beautiful movies they've made would be ours. They are the kind of movies we've always wanted to make. And now we could make more of them. I even have an idea for a sequel, twenty years later. *Love and Other Sanities.* Or maybe even a TV series."

"They are selling? Can we afford it?"

"She says we could," I said. "Hayword, thirty some years ago, we got together and envisioned a life for ourselves. We wanted to tell stories and do good. And then things went whack-adoodle. My brain got stuck on Alberto's death and my unhappiness. But I know what I want now."

Hayword looked around. "This? This is what you want? It is amazing."

I laughed. "No, well, yes, but no. I want you. I do love you. I loved our life. I want to be close to you and close to the children. But new. I want us to be our best selves together."

Hayword looked down at me. "I can't promise to be my best self."

"Quit making me laugh," I said. "You said you wanted a divorce. That's fine. I don't want to be your wifey or you be the husband. I want us to be together because we've built a life together, because we like each other, because we love each other. Home is where the heart is and my heart is with you and the kids." I took his hand.

"That is really corny," he said. "Sounds like something I would say."

"Alberto gave me the line," I said.

Hayword smiled.

"We could do the work we want to do here," I said.

He looked around. He squeezed my hand. "You had me at 'Hayword.'"

I slugged him. He leaned down and kissed me.

"What about all of your boyfriends and all the great sex you'll be missing?" he asked.

"They are all such prima donnas," I said, "and I'm good with mediocre sex."

"Hey," he said. "Man, this could be fun."

"That's the idea."

We heard the kids calling us. I phoned David and told him to come in the front door and gave him directions to the courtyard. When they saw the flowers, they both gasped.

"Oh Mom," Fern said. "I want to live here forever."

"Well, maybe not forever," I said, "but your dad and I are buying it. At least we hope so."

"You and Dad?" David said. "Are you back together? Like a couple?"

Hayword looked at me. I said, "Yes. We're all in."

"Who is going to tell Patricia?" David asked.

"You were so fond of her," I said, "so you can do it."

It was a busy couple of years. We bought OK Studios and moved into the place within two months. Katherine and Oscar bought my bungalow to be closer to their family. We rented out the house. Since Alberto's ashes were there, we didn't want to sell it. We found a nice young family who were a little strapped for cash and gave them a good deal on rent.

Back to Life Studios became a division of OK Studios, more as a bookkeeping thing then anything else. We closed the offices in Los Angeles. We hired Caryn for OK Studios, and she came to live in one of the guest houses with her wife, Cameron.

We dissolved The Alberto Foundation. We split the money between the kids and told them to do with it what they would, but that was the end of it. They had to make their own way in the world.

Fern went to rehab. (I got clean and sober, too.) She came home and lived in one of the guest houses with Eartha. It was a rough time. Fern can be vicious as hell. As her brain began to heal from years of drugs and alcohol, she became kinder and more compassionate. Damon still had a crush on her. He came around more and more. They began dating.

We put *Beauty and the Zombie Part Three* on hold for six months. Fortunately everyone was able to move their schedules around. The shoot went off perfectly.

Joanie is no longer a part of my life. Neither is Sally, obviously. I don't miss them. I miss Mark now and again. I don't see Ryan at all. I called him early on and apologized for my part in his relapse. We talk now and again, just to see how the other one is doing.

Hayword and I understand how fortunate we are. We are working on ways to give back. A portion of our profits is going to organizations that are combating climate change. We care for our land sustainably—and it's a constant learning experience.

I am happy. I feel like I've finally found home. I don't know if it will last. I am nervous to say it out loud. I enjoy my husband. Yes, we never bothered with the divorce. We work hard not to fall back into old patterns. We love the house and the land. We love OK Studios. We see Kathcrine and Oscar often.

One night a few weeks before the premiere of *Beauty and the Zombie Part Three,* Hayword, David, Fern, Damon, and I sat on the front porch looking up at the night sky after a special dinner to celebrate David graduating from high school.

Fern said, "I have an announcement."

"You're getting married?" David said.

"No!" Fern said. "Why would I participate in that patriarchal bullshit?"

"That's my girl," I said.

"Phil and Eartha are dating," she said.

"You mean you have gossip," David said.

Fern shrugged.

"Fern, I always forgot to ask you about the handbags," I said. "Why were they filled with liquor bottles?"

"It was a selling point," Fern said. "I figured it was the end of the world and everyone should stock up on booze."

I laughed. "That makes absolutely no sense."

"I agree," Fern said. "But you know what, everyone who bought a bag was so excited when they opened them up and saw the tiny liquor bottles."

"I have no idea what you all are talking about," Damon said.

"Oops," Fern said. "I may have forgotten to tell you about the handbags."

We all laughed.

"Do you think Alberto is alive somewhere?" Fern asked. "Do you think he watches us and roots for us and knows we're finally doing all right?"

"I don't know," I said. I looked at Hayword. He shrugged.

"I have no wise words on the subject," he said.

"I say if we see a falling star in the next minute or so, that means yes," David said. "Alberto is alive somewhere and he watches over us."

We all looked more intently at the sky.

Nothing.

Nothing.

Please give him this, I whispered.

Nothing.

Then a star streaked across the sky.

We all cheered.

"He's alive," David said. "Does that mean my brother is a zombie?"

"No!" Fern said. "I say if we see another star right away, it means that Alberto is happy that we're happy."

We stared.

Nothing.

Nothing.

No…

A star streaked across the sky. And then another one fell. And another. We counted ten falling stars. I made wish after wish for happiness and good health for my children.

We laughed. Cried a little bit. Were amazed.

It could have been that we went through a meteor shower. Maybe it was that time of year. I wasn't going to look. David didn't even look. In that moment, we let the mystery be.

"We love you, Alberto!" Fern called.

"We love you, Alberto!" David said.

We all stood and raised our glasses to the sky, and we cried, "We love you, Alberto!" to the night.

"Rest in peace," I added.

That is my story, and I'm sticking to it.

AFTERWORD

Beware: I tried not to reveal anything important from the novels here that would spoil your first reading of the material, but you might find some spoilers anyway. I recommend you read the books first, and then come back here.

I enjoyed writing the *Whackadoodle Times* books more than anything else I've ever written. Brooke McMurphy is so real, true, funny, and tragic. I love her outrageous truth-telling. Somedays as I wrote, I was laughing and crying almost at the same time.

Most of Brooke's disasters—besides the environmental ones—are caused by her own behavior. To be fair to her, she is also surrounded by a motley crew who make their own stunningly bad decisions that affect her life. Despite all of her flaws, Brooke is a good-hearted person trying to get through difficult days and nights while keeping her loved ones safe. Most of us can relate to this.

I will answer some of the questions I've had over the years here.

Where did the idea for *Wlhackadoodle Times* come from?

I felt helpless over climate change, and I didn't know what to do. Could I change anything by writing a novel about climate change?

I decided to try. I wanted to tell a story about a rich family whose members were completely clueless about what was happening to our planet because of climate change. I imagined them sipping champagne while forests burned around them, oblivious to their own culpability in the destruction of the world. Very quickly I realized I couldn't write a novel while thinking about trying to save the world. That felt too big! And I couldn't root for a family of idiots as I originally envisioned them; I had to find a character I sympathized with on some level.

Brooke McMurphy evolved from that desire. I saw her as a privileged entitled Hollywood scriptwriter whose life gets up-ended when a woman knocks on her door and promises to do one extraordinary thing a day if Brooke and her husband Hayword allow her to live in their garden house. I imagined it would be a story about Brooke and Eartha (the woman at the door). I wrote the first chapter with all of this in mind. I loved that first chapter. I couldn't wait to see the rest of the story unfold.

I didn't write another word on the novel for about five years. I was intimidated by that first chapter. How could I come up with one amazing thing for Eartha to do each day? That was an incredibly high bar I had set for myself and the story. But then, eventually, I realized that the story was not about Brooke and Eartha. It was a tale about one grieving woman continually falling apart and behaving outrageously while also trying to keep the rest of the members of her family safe. That's when the story came alive for me.

Brooke participates in some fairly unsavory adventures. Was that difficult to write?

No! I had a ball.

The novels are written in first person, so I was able to be in Brooke's head the entire time. I loved it. In her pain, she allows herself to say or think or do almost anything. It was freeing to be so uninhibited. I understood every stupid thing she did. I understood every feeling she had. I hoped the readers would understand, too. I don't judge Brooke: I empathize with her, and I wish her all good things. In her grief and her alcohol-addled brain (at least in the beginning), she makes one bad decision after another. Fortunately for us, her actions are also funny most of the time.

Did you do a lot of research to write these books?

Another reason I loved writing these books was because it was all contemporary, and I didn't have to do any research. I lived in the West for over thirty years, so I knew that part of California fairly well. I fudged some details for the sake of storytelling, mostly having to do with traffic. I've travelled in California and stayed in LA County many times. We were almost always stuck in heavy traffic, so it took ages to get anywhere, but I couldn't have my story stop every time Brooke left home because she was stuck in traffic.

Unfortunately, Californians deal with fire, earthquakes, and tsunamis. At the time I was writing the first two novels, I lived in Washington state, right on the border of Oregon, and we experienced earthquakes, although none were strong enough to cause damage. We dealt with wildfires nearly every summer. During the Eagle Creek fire which was across the Columbia River from where we lived, we ended up heading out of town in the middle of the night to escape the fire. Although we were never in danger from the actual flames, the smoke was devastating and life-threatening.

The lightning storm sounds like something out of science fiction. Not so much, unfortunately. In 2020, Northern California experienced a massive lightning storm with over 12,000 strikes in 72-96 hours, strikes that caused 585 new fires. Yikes!

So the disasters were real. Were the characters based on real people?

I never base my characters in my novels on people I know. Of course characteristics of people I know show up in my characters now and again. In these particular books, the relationship between Brooke and her daughter Fern was inspired, initially, by a daughter and mother I knew when the daughter was a teen. I worked with her mother at the library where I was the community librarian.

Sometimes the daughter would come into the library, and the two of them would argue. The daughter would want to do something and the mother wouldn't want her to do it. Or the other way around. Or one would say the sky was blue and the other would say it wasn't. It drove me nuts. They would stand at the checkout counter bickering with each other for what seemed like ages.

And in my view, the daughter blamed the mother for everything. For the divorce her parents were going through. For the state of the world. For the sky not being blue on a particular day. Eventually, since I was the boss, I asked the mother to please not argue with her daughter in the library. She didn't get it. She didn't understand why it would bother anyone to listen to them argue. She said that was just what mothers and daughters did. What sounded like fighting to me was not fighting to her.

In the novels the troublesome relationship between Brooke

and her daughter makes for good drama. Each time we think they are about to heal their relationship, Fern does something seemingly unforgivable. Brooke is desperate and guilty over her relationship with Fern, so she does forgive her again and again. Until Fern does the next unforgivable thing.

Where did the idea of having Brooke write the *Beauty and the Zombie* movies come from? Was it difficult incorporating that process into the novels?

Brooke thinks she's this great screenwriter who only writes scripts of meaningful stories, like *Love and Other Insanities.* She's the equivalent of a literary writer. She feels it would be beneath her dignity to write a zombie movie, but eventually she agrees to do it anyway, and it changes her life. I love that! I used to fancy myself a literary writer, but I needed to get published and make some money, so I wrote horror stories in the beginning. I was good at it. I branched out from that, but I still love writing stories with great characters actually doing something besides contemplating their belly buttons.

But back to the *Beauty and the Zombie* movies. It was a huge risk to have Brooke write the movies as part of the plot of the book. I'm a writer. I know sitting at a computer clicking away is not exciting or riveting. If it was going to be part of the novels, I had to make it interesting and exciting. As she was coming up with the plot of each script, I was coming up with the plot. I thought of the plot points as she thought of them. And I think it works really well. I wanted to know what was going to happen next, so I hoped the reader would, too.

The *Whackadoodle Times* books and the *Beauty and the Zombie* movies have similar themes. They're about grief and transformation: from the living dead into the living—or into the truly dead.

Have you thought about writing the *Beauty and the Zombie* scripts as novels?

I would love to turn the *Beauty and the Zombie* movies into books. If I ever wrote them, they would have Brooke McMurphy's byline.

What's with the covers? Why all these skinny women in ridiculously long dresses?

I wanted funny covers. The books are funny. Beautiful skinny women dressed in ridiculous dresses that no one could walk in is funny, at least to me, and representative of Hollywood's obsession with youth and the objectification of women.

Why did it take you so long to write *Whackadoodle Times Three*?

I knew for storytelling purposes what would have to happen to Brooke for a third book, and I didn't want to do it. I don't like terrible things happening to my characters. But she had not come to terms with her son's death or anything else in her life for that matter. So I had to do what I was reluctant to do. (And I'm being vague just in case you haven't finished *WT3*.) Also, I knew I had to come up with another *Beauty and the Zombie* movie, and I couldn't think of anything. In the end, it came together just as the other movies did: It came to me as I wrote them.

Did you always intend to write three *Whackadoodle Times* books?

Yes. Maybe not during those five years after I wrote the first chapter of the first book. But after that, yes.

Did you know what was going to happen to Brooke in the end?

Originally I thought she would just say fuck it in the end and go off by herself. So there's a spoiler: That's not what happened. It was clear before the end of the first book that wasn't going to happen. How would that have solved anything? She just chucks all her responsibilities and disappears? No. That wouldn't have been good for her or her family. And despite everything, she is all about her family. Still, what happens in the third book surprised the hell out of me. All of it. And yet when I think about it now, it was inevitable.

How true to life was the movie business in the books? Do you have someone on the inside who was giving you tips? If so can you send my screenplay to them?

I can't divulge my sources. I can say that the crazy things that go on in this book—while fictional—are not the craziest things that have ever happened in our beloved Hollywood. And no, I can't send your screenplay to them. I can't even send my screenplay to them.

ABOUT THE AUTHOR

Kim Antieau's novels include *The Jigsaw Woman, Her Frozen Wild, Church of the Old Mermaids, Coyote Cowgirl, The Monster's Daughter, Butch, Killing Beauty,* and many others. Learn more at www.kimantieau.com.

www.ingramcontent.com/pod-product-compliance
Lightning Source LLC
Chambersburg PA
CBHW061201190726
48288CB00001B/17